Lady Madrigal

She married by decree, loved by default, and discovered passion in the arms of a man determined to destroy her!

Elena

The woman who coveted her sister's husband vowed to steal him . . . no matter what the cost. . . .

Stefano

He knew the truth but refused to tell his hated half-brother Roderick . . . even if it meant the destruction of Madrigal, the woman he desired. . . .

Akbar Al Kemil

He kidnapped his enemy's wife, but love got in the way.

Roderick, Baron Halconbosque

He would find revenge for the death of his father . . . in the tender flesh of his enemy's daughter, Madrigal—his wife, his passion, his

SWEET NEMESIS

Books by Lynn Erickson

Sweet Nemesis
This Raging Flower

Published by POCKET BOOKS

SWEET NEMESIS

Lynn Erickson

PUBLISHED BY POCKET BOOKS NEW YORK

A POCKET BOOKS/RICHARD GALLEN *Original* publication

**POCKET BOOKS, a Simon & Schuster division of
GULF & WESTERN CORPORATION
1230 Avenue of the Americas, New York, N.Y. 10020**

ISBN: 0-671-83524-6

First Pocket Books printing March, 1980

10 9 8 7 6 5 4 3 2 1

POCKET and colophon are trademarks of Simon & Schuster.

Printed in the U.S.A.

*Dedicated with Thanks
to Miriam and Dan*

AUTHOR'S NOTE

The intrepid Visigoths, of whom Roderick speaks in the story, existed and led the Christian remnants against the Moors. The Moorish invasion of Spain in 711 A.D. put the peninsula under Moorish rule until 1492, when the last remnants of the Moors were finally dislodged from their holdings in southern Spain by the culmination of the *reconquista*.

Alfonso X, Sancho IV, his wife, Maria de Molina, and their children emerge from the history books, as do Edward I of England and his second wife, Eleanor. The Moroccan, Abu Yusuf, and his invasion of Gibraltar in the spring of 1285 are also factual.

I have tried to portray the political confusion and the lifestyle of the times as accurately as possible; Sancho IV had all the problems mentioned and undoubtedly many more. He held court wherever he happened to be, as there was no capital city of Spain. The Iberian peninsula was actually a fragmented series of kingdoms during this period, but I have used the term "Spain" to avoid confusion. (Note the great differences between Roderick's Galicia and Madrigal's Andalusia.)

Roderick, Madrigal, and their families are, of course, fictionalized figures, but their reactions are typical of the times as far as I can ascertain.

Hopefully, this book will enlighten the reader about a little-known period in Spanish history as well as provide entertainment.

Lynn Erickson

AUTHOR'S NOTE

The principal Moslems, of whom Roderick speaks in the story, existed and led the Christian remnants against the Moors; the Moorish invasion of Spain in 711 A.D. put the peninsula under Moorish rule until 1492, when the last remnants of the Moors were finally defeated from their holdings in southern Spain by the colmination of the reconquest.

Alfonso X, Sancho I, his wife, Sancho's brother, and all children appear in the history books, as do Edward I of England and his second wife, Eleanor. The Mira Vila, Abu Yusuf, and his invasion of Algeciras in the spring of 1278 are also factual.

I have tried to portray the political conditions and the strife of the times as accurately as possible. Since Navarre had all its problems mortgaged and under constant money stress, I've held upon whatever transpired to be, as there was no King [or?] of Spain. The Iberian peninsula was still a fragmented series of kingdoms during this period that I have used the term "Spanish" to avoid confusion. Note the great differences between Roderick of Galicia and his people's attitudes.

Medieval feudalism and their families are, of course, a hundred percent, but their reactions are typical of the times as far as I can discover.

Hopefully, this book will enlighten the reader about a little-known period of Spanish history as well as provide private entertainment.

I. von Zuckschwerdt

Chapter 1

Even before the smithy had lit his morning fires or the roosters had crowed their predawn hunger, the faint noise of two boarhounds fighting over a deer shank could be heard echoing through the great hall at Castilla-verde. The soft meadows surrounding the moat and battlements were bathed in summer dew and proved the castle's name to be apt; the deep pine forest below was alive with numerous scurrying creatures that provided the fief with its ample food supplies.

Lord Jaime Castilla-verde, the Earl of Tarbella, had always been immensely grateful that his ancestors had had the foresight to build Castilla-verde in southern Spain. Located in Andalusia, or al-Andalus, as the Moors had called the fertile land warmed by the Mediterranean trade winds when their armies had invaded and conquered it, his holdings produced sufficient wild game and crops to feed his family and serfs year-round. And now that summer had at last arrived, the earl looked forward to a prosperous yield.

In the frail hours of this June morn in 1285 the earl slept peacefully in the opposite wing of the castle from his daughters. They, too, were still slumbering—except for Madrigal. She had already lit a meager fire and was brushing her waist-length black hair and plaiting it into one thick straight braid to hang tidily down her slim back. She smiled to herself and donned a thin blue linen mantle, her fine aquiline features reflecting the dim glow of the fire. Madrigal felt the promise of warmth in the cool morning air and looked forward to a solitary ride through the forest.

1

This would not be the first time she had slipped unnoticed from the confines of the castle; indeed, the green-eyed beauty had frequently escaped undetected. She knew well that a maid of eighteen should be chaperoned at all times, but her acts of disobedience only fueled her thrill of adventure. Of the earl's four daughters, she alone felt the need to sow the wild oats of youth before a binding marriage and the bearing of babes aged her prematurely. She thought fleetingly of her oldest sister, Rosa, whom she loved dearly but did not see too often, since Rosa had married several years ago and lived some distance away.

Covering her hair with the hood of her cloak, she glanced about the large chamber for her woven herb basket, her mind imagining the deer, rabbits, and myriad of tiny creatures romping through the woodland in the pink light of dawn.

She collected her basket and, on tiptoe, peeked out the chaliced window to make certain that the drawbridge had been lowered for the village maids to enter. Seeing that it was already down, she hurried toward the door, an impish smile tilting a corner of her pretty mouth.

"Dios mío!" she gasped suddenly. Maria, her personal lady's maid, was silently entering her chamber. A pout tugged at Madrigal's rosy lips while disappointment played over her chiseled features.

"Milady, you must not venture out alone today of all days. 'Tis the feast of San Juan, and it would not be seemly for you to anger your father." The old woman's voice was querulous; her eyes were narrowed in disapproval of the young girl's behavior.

"Hush, old one! Your prattle would wake the dead. Calm yourself, and I shall return ere Papa has even risen for mass."

Madrigal was not about to be delayed by a tongue-lashing from Maria and strode purposefully toward the door. However, she felt guilty that she had caused tears to well up in her faithful servant's eyes, and she paused to add apologetically, "I am sorry to worry you, sweet Maria. If you will sleep here by the fire, no one will be the wiser, and I shall fetch you some fresh herbs for the stiffness in your bones."

The elderly servant turned her back on Madrigal to hide her frustration. The young girl had always done exactly as she pleased, and to argue with her was, at best, a futile waste of time. Madrigal's precious mother had died bearing Teresa when Madrigal was only six; inexplicably, the earl had always doted on Madrigal, allowing his most beautiful daughter to go without proper discipline. If the truth be known, thought Maria, Madrigal often let her impetuous heart rule her sharp mind, resulting in behavior that was unbefitting a lady of her highborn station.

"Pray go safely," Maria whispered as Madrigal closed the heavy door behind her.

Although the long, cool hall was still cloaked in darkness, Madrigal easily found her way across the damp granite stones and soon stood before her sister Elena's door. Elena had been so low in spirits of late that Madrigal fleetingly thought of inviting her to join in the morning adventure, but she realized the girl would only scoff at her plan. Elena had a way of taking a kind gesture to mean pity.

Poor, coldhearted Elena, thought Madrigal as she removed her hand from the wrought-iron door handle. Even as a child, Elena had hidden the left side of her face from view. Madrigal had often prayed to the Virgin and asked why she herself had not been birth-scarred instead of her lovely sister. The mark was

3

only the size of a hen's egg, but Elena envisioned her whole body hideously disfigured by a damning act of God.

The bakers in the kitchens were not surprised to see Madrigal enter their private domain, for the lord's daughter had done so before, and if Lady Madrigal wished to behave like a commoner, it was most assuredly not their concern.

"Oh! The breads are so tempting!" she exclaimed while hurriedly snatching a succulent bun from the cooling rack.

Ignoring the raised eyebrow of one of the bakers, she strode out the opened door into the bailey, where she tightened her mantle about her head, and continued into the stable yard. There she roused a sleeping lad from his warm bed of hay and ordered the confused boy to saddle her favorite palfrey. The fresh smells of hay and well-oiled leather mixed with manure assailed her nostrils delightfully. She had often thought that her favorite odor was that of an armor-clad gallant returning from battle—leather and metal, pitch and brave sweat—the smell of maleness.

A small voice startled her out of her musings. "Madrigal, I thought 'twas you I saw from my window!" Juan de Vegas was approaching with his customary graceful elegance, his dark head held erect.

"Oh, Juan! It would seem I have awakened the whole of Tarbella this morn," she said ruefully.

"No, *preciosa*. Only me. Might I not be allowed to escort you? Please, Madrigal, you know your father's orders about venturing alone outside the castle walls!"

She disliked it when Juan, her betrothed—or anyone else, for that matter—pleaded with her, but he was so kind and considerate that she hated to hurt his feelings. Juan, slight of build, attractive, and barely taller than

4

she, was her lifelong companion, friend, and yes, brother, too. She looked into his large brown eyes and saw his concern for her safety. She almost despised herself for causing him worry, but she was determined to have her morning alone in the forest.

"Juan, in barely a fortnight we shall be wed. I wish so to steal a moment to myself this day. Please don't fret, for when I return, you may have a kiss," she whispered low so that the stableboy could not overhear. "Perhaps two kisses, after the feast tonight!"

"'Tis plain and true bribery! But I accept the promise and shall hold you to your word, Madrigal." His face was lit up with pleasure, his voice melodic.

Madrigal had once before allowed Juan a kiss and found it an agreeable experience which had bordered on affability. Of course, she had witnessed the copulating dogs in the hall—pigs and cows, too—but never had she envisioned her own self engaged in the marriage act. Elena had often spoken bravely of the sexual union and felt certain it would be pleasurable, but Madrigal was not as convinced as her sister. In any case, she thought to herself, surely a kiss is harmless between friends like us.

"Hasta luego," she whispered over her shoulder as she led her horse out into the bailey.

Passing the men-at-arms was an easy matter, for Madrigal was well known and well loved at Castilla-verde. Soon she had mounted her horse and was racing across the lush meadows, free of the encumbering moat and high battlements. She drank in the summer dew and tossed back her cloak, allowing her braid to escape its confines. The deep blue silk ribbon she had tied in her hair caught the first rays of sun filtering through the morning mist. The green seclusion of the deep forest below drew her onward, and the wet earth gave way to the horse's hooves. Deer and sheep alike seemed not to fear her presence and grazed lazily among the lower foliage; birds sang a welcome morning song.

She raised her emerald-green eyes skyward to catch sight of a soaring falcon stalking a pond goose, the sun reflecting off its long wings. She reveled in the bird's freedom and longed to join its oneness and perfection within the scheme of its universe.

Soon she and Juan would stand before Padre Sebastiano and speak the everlasting marriage vows; soon she would know of men and bear Juan many heirs. She wondered if her freedoms would be totally lost, or if Juan would allow her to retain some measure of individuality.

The falcon drifted slowly lower, then lower still, until it hovered in the air above the goose—then instantly, purposefully, it struck downward. Diving at an incredible speed, with claws sharp and ready, the attacker swooped at the unwary prey and struck powerfully. The serenity of the woods was shattered by the gurgling cry of the goose and the victory screech of the hawk.

Madrigal shuddered inwardly at the sight, but this was nature and the way of God; had not she herself gone on the hunt? Wherein lay the difference?

She watched until the hawk and its victim were well out of sight, then she turned to see a fallen log which promised to grow healing fungus on its dark, hidden side. The undergrowth was wild and brambly, so she tethered her horse to a pine and ventured through the thicket. The molds and forest herbs, prepared as only she knew how, produced a variety of medicines, fragrant scents, body oils, and often, flavorings for food. Like her mother before her, Madrigal understood the wise use of the bountiful herbs provided by the summer woodland.

On into the deep forest she roamed, until the height

of the sun told her it was time to return to the castle. She hastened back to her waiting palfrey and began to remount.

Suddenly, with her foot hopelessly locked in the stirrup, the undergrowth crackled, causing her horse to bolt and throw her against a rock. When she opened her eyes a few moments later, her head was aching unbearably. She put a hand to her brow and felt a sticky gash; her fingers came away stained with red. Her horse was nowhere in sight.

Trying to regain her senses, she began to ease herself up into a sitting position. It was then that she caught a movement out of the corner of her eye. The bushes in a copse of nearby pines seemed to be parting. Her full attention was swiftly riveted onto the rough undergrowth. Then the brush parted, and two small beady eyes glared horrifyingly into her own.

Her breath snatched in her throat and her forehead dampened with cold perspiration. To stare into the face of a giant boar, whether one was armed or not, meant certain death.

The massive hairy beast pawed at the earth with its hoof; it snorted low, static grunts while its deadly teeth showed in its slavering jowls. Madrigal stiffened in terror, trembling in the endless seconds before the creature would begin its feral attack. She dug her heels into the ground and imperceptibly inched back against a rock. Her blue ribbon fell to the ground, loosening her carefully plaited braid; her cloak slipped from her shoulders, revealing her cream-colored linen gown. The grisly monster took a step forward, then another.

Madrigal closed her eyes; there was nowhere to run, no safe place to hide; moreover, she was too paralyzed with fear to move a muscle. She began to see visions of her father's face when her corpse was discovered, if indeed the boar left anything of her at all.

A tear slipped down her pale cheek as the beast moved triumphantly closer, foot by foot, to its victim; its foul, hot rasping breath could be heard clearly in the still air.

Madrigal put the back of her hand to her mouth and whispered against her skin, "*Madre de Dios* . . . I pray you to forgive my sins . . ." The boar's coarse hair bristled at her audible words; it snorted loudly, and saliva trickled from its mouth.

She fluttered her eyelids, unable to relinquish a last look at life; her lashes were wet with tears, her green eyes wide in an agony of terror.

Suddenly the creature flicked its small ears and turned its grotesque head heavily. The shadowy figure of a knight mounted on a great war charger emerged suddenly from the depths of the forest. The sun glistened on his drawn sword and raised shield, blinding her eyes for a moment and making his surprising appearance seem ethereal.

The knight slowly moved his mount closer to the boar. The raven-black horse did not seem to fear the beast and flared its nostrils in challenge and anticipation; the rider sat tall and confidently in his saddle, taunting the boar by his presence to abandon its quarry.

Madrigal bit the back of her hand to halt a scream of terror, for she saw that the animal was bent on having its victim and seemed not to accept the knight's challenge. It tore at the earth in fury and turned its full attention back to Madrigal.

The rider, sensing the creature's indecision, drew up his blade with a loud, throaty war cry. The boar spun around, its short back legs raising the dust, and roared a thundering approval of the knight's challenge. It charged.

Madrigal screamed as the boar narrowly missed the great horse, which reared up on its hind legs and then came down. The knight slashed low with his sword and

8

nearly severed the boar's neck in a deadly accurate sweep.

The incident had happened so quickly that Madrigal could not believe her eyes. One moment she had been in the direst peril; the next, saved by a strange knight appearing from within the dark depth of her forest.

Taking her eyes from the bloodied boar, she stared at the mysterious man who was dismounting to view his slain prize. He appeared to be highborn, a baron perhaps, and was clothed in battle attire: a hauberk and helmet, a tunic of light wool under his chain mail, and high leather boots with spurs. His size was large for an Andalusian, but his frame was in perfect proportion, easily carrying his height. His shield bore an unfamiliar crest of gray and purple in which was centered a fierce black hawk that grasped a small creature in its claws.

The knight, once finished with the boar, came to Madrigal in long strides. When he stood above her, hands on his hips, he was at once struck by her dark beauty and wide emerald eyes. She was still trembling, and her innocence and fear compelled him to an unaccustomed softness. He reached down to smooth her long, flowing hair from her bloodied brow. As she backed away instinctively from his touch, the knight straightened his stance but did not withdraw his steady gaze.

"You need not fear me, little swallow—it was but chance that brought me this way, and thanks to the Blessed Virgin that it did. I am no ogre." His voice was deep and reassuring. As he spoke he removed his helmet and revealed a mass of cropped, unruly hair that was golden where the sun caught its curls.

Then Madrigal saw his face, and her breath caught in her throat, so that her intended words of thanks came out incoherently, much to her surprise.

"I—I cannot thank you enough—" She faltered again, gazing at his amber-flecked eyes and hawklike

9

features. He was an awesome-looking man, handsome, yes, but frighteningly so, with a hard mouth and harshly structured features.

Holding her green eyes with his own tawny ones, he said, " 'Tis unseemly for even a village maid to roam about so freely! Is there not someone you meet here?"

He thought her a common serf! But she feared to let him think otherwise. "No, great knight. I meet no one. Now I must go." She tried to rise, but her legs shook and she was dizzy from her fall.

His arm came around her easily and steadied her, and he lifted her chin till her eyes met his. Madrigal felt quite afraid but strangely breathless, while still willing him to release her.

"Fairest maid, allow me to see you safely home, for I would know of your whereabouts." He chuckled at her reaction. "And will seek you out this eve." His tone, for all its laughter, was serious.

"I thought you a gallant knight, but 'tis an oaf I see you are, who detains a lady when she would be gone!" She twisted against his iron grip.

"An oaf, say you?" His handsome head tilted back in mirth at the brave words of the trembling wench, and he would have liked to tarry with her longer, but the press of urgent matters to attend to forced him to release her with regret.

She eyed him warily while gathering her fallen mantle and scattered herbs. Her jade eyes were wide as she began to back slowly away from his hard stare.

The knight stood motionless, watching her careful retreat into the forest. "Flee, my bird, but do not forget that we have unfinished business!" His laughter resounded in the still air as he turned to collect the dead boar. Then he noticed her blue silk ribbon lying near the rock where she had fallen. He strode over, picked up the feminine keepsake, and tucked it into his tunic, a smile playing on his hard mouth.

Madrigal trusted that her palfrey had long since returned to the castle, and knowing that her father had probably already ordered a search for her, she hastened through the tall pines and finally emerged into the lush meadows below Castilla-verde. The battlements loomed reassuringly above her and she heaved an enormous sigh of relief, while breathlessly vowing to the Holy Virgin that she would never again venture out alone and would henceforth obey her father in every way.

Chapter 2

Lord Roderick Halconbosque, the Baron of Compostela, having safely tucked away Madrigal's ribbon, turned to whistle for his manservant, Renaldo. He still chuckled silently to himself because the green-eyed wench had seemed to fear *him* as much as she had the deadly boar.

Renaldo appeared from the brush in which he had hidden himself. Although always nearby, Renaldo was skittish by nature and usually uncommunicative with other humans, save his master. The pathetically thin vassal had inherited his leanness from a long line of spindly ancestors who, for the most part, resembled a pack of ferrets. But it was not his cadaverous appearance that made Renaldo uneasy among his fellow men. It was, instead, the fact that he had only one eye.

Some years past, the Moors had deemed it necessary to gouge out one of his eyes before releasing him after a bloody siege. At the time, he had considered himself fortunate to have retained the other eye, not to mention his tongue and limbs. Others had not fared as well. The Moors' custom was to release a few hostages to tell of their prowess in battle. The freed prisoners were, however, methodically mutilated as a warning to their fellow Spaniards that the same fate awaited them. And so it was that Renaldo now preferred to keep out of sight allowing only Roderick to be close to him.

Renaldo grinned down at the slain corpse of the boar, then assisted his master in tossing the bloody mass of hair and meat across his own saddle. His long, slender nose twitched with delight at the trophy-sized beast the baron had so bravely faced.

"Lord, 'tis a giant beast you have cut today! King Sancho will feast well tonight, methinks."

"*Sí*, Renaldo, we shall all stave off hunger this eve and warm our aching bodies by the hearth—but not if we tarry here overlong!"

They mounted their horses and headed through the woodland toward Castilla-verde, their final destination.

Roderick had passed near the fief many times before with King Sancho, but his sovereign had always been rushed, and they had never quartered on the land. That the earl had been a staunch partisan of Sancho's father, Alfonso X, could make such a stopover uncomfortable. But this time Roderick had been able to persuade the king to travel the short distance to Tarbella on the pretext of commandeering new soldiers for the Gibraltar campaign. If King Sancho suspected that Roderick had ulterior motives for the side trip, he had not said so. If the truth be known, thought Roderick, he himself did not know what he could gain by facing the dastardly earl as a grown man. He did not harbor the idea of murdering the blackguard, but he was bent on wreaking a vengeance of indeterminate nature.

Two decades of haunting nightmares had occupied him with visions of disembodied limbs and his father's face, first loving and full of life, then disfigured and pained, calling out for revenge from the cold grave. As if it were yesterday, he saw the high plains of central Spain baking under a pitiless sun. The stench of blood, the odors of fear and death, the bodies heaped on the battlefield, assailed his nine-year-old senses. He and his half brother, Stefano, nearly ten years his senior, stood watching their father being tossed to the ground by a pair of guards. An ungodly scream rose in the air, and the figure of Castilla-verde, the hated, insane Earl of Tarbella, charged forward. Drawing his jeweled scimitar, he hacked mercilessly at Roderick's father until the baron's head and limbs rolled free of his body. This murderous act of treachery was a result of the perpetual wars among the Christian princes, and his father had fallen into the hands of the ignoble earl. Roderick's eyes were full of pain and hatred. The green and black coat of arms of Castilla-verde was etched forever in the depths of his young soul.

Roderick shuddered and cleared his mind of that fateful day. Now he thought only of the moment he would face Castilla-verde, the moment of truth so long awaited.

He wondered if the earl had sons, and how many. Did they stay at Castilla-verde? Or had they fought for King Sancho on the hill of Gibraltar? Perhaps he even knew one of them and had battled side by side with him against the Moors. Would the blackguard earl remember him? Surely not; he had been but a boy.

When the two men finally broke free of the forest, they entered the sun-drenched lea below the castle through which Madrigal had run only a short time before. The hot sun reflected off the high grass, already causing the air to rise in shimmering waves of heat. The glistening green blades of grass reminded Roderick of emerald-colored eyes and shining long hair. He remembered the touch of her round shoulders in his grip; the promise of firm breasts beneath her linen gown; her budding woman's body, soft and yielding.

Roderick's life had been totally free of feminine ties, save for those of his mother, Lady Gwendolyn, a gentle and retiring Englishwoman. There had been little time for the comforting aspects of life. When he took a wench to bed, he left her easily in the morning. He thought again of the lovely dark woman in the forest and knew that Renaldo could be sent throughout the fiefdom to fetch her to him.

Roderick, in his twenty-nine years, had never lain with a virgin. Untouched women were known to make heavy demands on their first lover, and he had neither the time nor the patience for unwanted bonds. He assumed that the green-eyed vixen was far from virginal; she appeared to be around eighteen, and one so beautiful could not remain untouched for so many years. Why, she had probably been in the forest for a tryst with some clumsy lover! Ah, yes, he silently mused, that little one has known many men, and when I tire of her nagging, I shall send her away with ease and a single gold *tarín*.

"Lord Roderick, isn't that Castilla-verde?" Renaldo broke into his pleasant train of thought by indicating the stone battlements rising loftily above them.

"*Sí*, Renaldo. Unfurl my banner and that of our king. Make our colors known."

"Do you think we might partake of some wine before returning to escort the king?" Renaldo's voice held a note of hope.

"Yes, my thirsty friend, if there is enough time in the hours of daylight left, we shall indeed warm our bellies. But make certain first that the boar is taken to the kitchens."

"It will be done, my lord." Renaldo would now be more than happy to unload the smelly carcass from his saddle.

The baron of Compostela put on his helmet, then

signaled Renaldo. They spurred their tired mounts and galloped across the narrow drawbridge, entering the bailey with a flourish bespeaking the status of lieges of the king.

Chapter 3

Confusion and pandemonium reigned throughout the castle when a king's knight was seen riding up to the fortress.

The earl had been arguing with Elena over her sister's misconduct earlier that morning. Elena, one year older than Madrigal, could never understand her father's total devotion to the sister who so resembled her, they could pass for twins. The manner in which he always took Madrigal's side caused her to fall into long depressions, broken by occasional outbursts of wrath.

"Elena! Are you not grateful for your sister's safe return? Did you not see the blood on her brow? Where is your compassion, *hija?*"

"*Claro,* Father, but don't you think sweet Madrigal would be best off locked in her room? *Siempre* you see only her beauty, never her thoughtless sins against her family." Elena's voice shook with jealous frustration.

"Speak not to me of sins, Elena, for Padre Sebastiano has already been sent for and will hear your sister's confession—"

His words were cut short by Teresa, his youngest daughter, who fairly flew down the grand steps into the central hall to announce the arrival of a "glorious knight, clad all in armor bespeaking great wealth!"

Elena's face softened. "A knight, say you? Father, the child must be dreaming." But she hurried to the huge oak doors and threw them open, to find that Teresa had indeed been accurate.

Immediately the earl summoned his men-at-arms to

the hall and demanded that they welcome the stranger. The trumpets heralded from atop the battlements, setting the hounds to baying and bringing the servants and vassals running to the bailey.

As Roderick rode up to the impenetrable doors, where the earl and two of his daughters had gathered, he found a grand welcome indeed. Even Renaldo was impressed with the turnout, but wished his leather skullcap covered his hideous deformity from the stares of the local wenches.

Roderick dismounted with an ease belying his stature and ascended the eight stone steps. At last he was facing his archenemy, the Earl of Tarbella. The superhuman effort he made to control his emotions surprised even himself. He looked long and hard at the earl, a muscle tightening in his jaw, until the awkward silence was broken by the host, who thought this knight was the fiercest-appearing man he had ever had the misfortune to meet.

"Sir knight, I am the Earl of Tarbella, Jaime Castilla-verde, *a su disposición.* My humble dwelling is at your disposal." The earl showed no recognition of Roderick, nor did he appear to notice the hawk crested on the baron's shield.

"Lord Jaime," Roderick replied with a deeply exaggerated bow. "I ride ahead of our noble King Sancho, who shall billet here with his wounded, returning from the battle at Gibraltar. I, sir, am his servant and vassal, Roderick Halconbosque." Still no recognition of the family name, thought the knight. "Baron of Compostela." His voice was gruff and cold, and Castilla-verde shuddered at the thought of such intruders.

Roderick removed his helmet and stared rudely at the earl, but the nobleman merely turned to indicate his daughters, who stood impatiently behind him, waiting for an introduction.

It was then that Roderick first saw Elena and his angry tension was replaced by surprise. *Dios mío!* he thought. She looks like the swallow—but no, even though her face is half hidden by her wimple, she cannot be the same wench—still, those slanted green eyes . . .

"May I present two of my daughters, of which I claim four." The earl chuckled nervously. "Lady Elena and Lady Teresa."

Roderick stepped closer to Teresa and took her small white hand in his own rough one, kissing it gently. He turned to Elena, narrowing his eyes as he studied her face. "Lady Elena." And he repeated his gesture to Teresa, kissing her hand. Could these hard green eyes, filled with open desire, be the same eyes that earlier had been filled with terror? Could this beautiful face, which spoke of bleakness and chill, be the same face he had hoped to touch?

"King Sancho rides here, you say, sir knight?" Elena flashed him a bold look. "And will you be long with us? I pray your stay will be comfortable."

Roderick looked from Elena to Renaldo; his vassal also recognized the young woman but was as confused as his master.

The tall knight and his companion were then ushered into the great hall and, once comfortably seated, were offered a flagon of rich red wine. Roderick could not take his eyes from Elena; great was his wonderment, until it occurred to him that the green-eyed wench in the forest was probably an illegitimate offspring of the despicable earl, bearing an uncanny resemblance to Lady Elena. He took special note that the young woman hid her face self-consciously, almost in the shy fashion of Arab women. Yet she was a rare beauty, which any fool could plainly discern.

"The wine is cordial and the chair comfortable, but I must make haste now back to our king, ere he takes

17

notice of my long absence." Although his words were spoken for the earl, Roderick had directed them to Elena, who took great pleasure in his attentions. He finally turned to the earl. "Renaldo will fetch a boar that I offer for the evening feast. The beast nearly ate heartily of a village maid this morn—"

His words were cut off by a gasp from Elena, then by a bid for silence from her father, who showed an unusual display of authority.

It was Teresa who added to Roderick's bewilderment. "*Sí!* We all know well of the boar—"

"*Silencio!* Women's prattle shall see me to an early grave, I fear." The earl had hoped that Madrigal's folly would remain the family's secret, but plainly this was the same knight who had earlier rescued his daughter. How was he to explain her shameful behavior in front of the king? Perhaps Madrigal should be locked up—but what if the king planned to stay for weeks? Although he could see the knight's bafflement, the earl was unable to decide what he should do.

Roderick felt the tension in the air and wondered at the look on the earl's face. He drank down the remainder of his wine, and rising, headed through the hall toward the bailey, where his horse was being fed and watered.

Renaldo hurried out after him, ordering an idle serf along the way to fetch the boar from his mount.

Elena followed Roderick to his horse; she fought back the urge to touch his broad, muscular back. Before mounting his horse, he turned and gave her a charming smile which made his features as handsome as any she had ever seen. "I trust we shall meet again this evening, Lady Elena." Her heart leaped at his clear meaning, and she watched him ride out with a cold smile on her sensual lips.

The king's two faithful forerunners crossed the

drawbridge, and while doing so, came close to knocking Padre Sebastiano into the moat some twenty feet below.

Roderick hailed the padre with an apology, but his words were lost on the aged father, who was mumbling aloud, for all to hear, something about "the immortal soul of a wayward lass."

While heading down through the lower meadows, Roderick wondered if he should have led his king here to Tarbella, for these Andalusians seemed a strange lot indeed. But as they entered the forest once again, the sharpest image in his mind was that of the earl's face—older now, yes, but definitely a face from the past, a loathsome face, remembered from a long-ago battlefield.

Chapter 4

When Padre Sebastiano had finally left, Madrigal was weeping and shaken. The well-meaning disciple of God had spent nearly two hours chastising the young girl for her evil sins against womanhood, state, and, above all, the Church.

She was seated on the edge of her bed when her father entered her chamber.

"*Niña mia,* dry your tears and straighten your dress. 'Tis your own folly that has brought you pain this day—where is thy courage?" The earl's voice was gentle and soothing, but still her tears flowed.

"Oh, Papa! I must confess to you that . . . well . . . the knight—Teresa told me, and I saw him from my window!" Her voice was weak and barely audible, but she knew she had to tell her father to save him later embarrassment. "Papa . . . he was the same knight, and plainly he saw my face! He thought me a village wench and . . ."

"*Sí, sí,* I know. But I have a sound idea. You will attend to his armor and bathing when he returns—"

"But, Papa! Elena has always cared for your guests. I cannot!"

"You will obey me! And 'tis time to see to your duties, for soon you will wed Juan and must know how to bathe a man." He softened his tone. "When the baron is rested and clean, you will explain your folly and beg his understanding."

"But he—he was rude to me, Papa! I cannot face him again. How could you possibly understand! Oh, please, let me see out this feast night alone in my chamber."

The earl was displeased that Halconbosque had insulted his favorite daughter, but still, explanations had to be made for Madrigal's unseemly behavior.

"'Twas only that he thought you a village maid and has been months in battle. Never mind, Madrigal, 'tis soon enough for you to know the ways of men. You must not shirk our custom regarding male visitors. The women of the household have a responsibility to them, and bathing them is a sign of hospitality."

"Papa, please—Elena is taken with him, Teresa told me. Cannot she bathe him?" Madrigal looked beseechingly at her father and he nearly gave in, but this time he was determined to see her obey. It wasn't often that the king visited Castilla-verde!

"No. Elena shall see to the needs of the king. He does us great honor with his coming and must be made comfortable by the eldest and most practiced. Now, rest yourself awhile, for 'tis a grand feast tonight and your day has already been overly full."

Jaime Castilla-verde left the trembling girl, a look of satisfaction crossing his features. For once she would succumb to *his* will. However, his decision to force his innocent daughter to tend the knight did not make him feel very secure, for Roderick appeared to be lusty in body and spirit. The earl breathed a silent prayer that the man would behave in a manner befitting an honorable guest.

Madrigal was awakened by Maria's gentle nudging and quiet voice. "The king has arrived! A noble day indeed! You must dress now and seek the baron, for already Elena is with our king."

She rubbed the sleep from her eyes and noticed the light in her room was already dim with evening. Maria had dutifully laid out a rich purple silk gown with a gold embroidered hem. It was her finest gown, befitting even a queen. She would not wear a wimple this night, for a young woman could dress her hair neatly and wear it wound around her head in braids, even though this fashion was scorned by Elena.

While Maria fussed over her toilette, Madrigal tried not to think of the ordeal to come. She closed her mind to Halconbosque's face and tall form while chatting idly with her maid.

"Are there many soldiers of the king?"

"*Sí*, hundreds, my lady. They rest around fires in the meadows and even in our bailey. There are three great knights in the castle itself, besides our king. It is said that your father is worried they will tarry too long and eat everything down to the last grain of rice!"

"'Tis not your business, Maria. Did Papa order enough serfs to tend their needs?"

"Oh, yes, the great hall is filled with at least twenty extra servants for the meal. It will be grand indeed, I think."

"Maria . . . I swore today that I would obey Papa in every way, but I do not think that I can wait upon this

21

knight. I . . . you see, Juan and I have never . . ." Madrigal found she could not even speak of such things to her servant.

"*Sí*, I know you to be innocent. Still, my lady, your mother herself did these chores without complaint—"

"But, Maria, she was married!"

"Not at first. 'Tis a fact that your sweet mother first met the earl in the guest chamber at her own castle." Maria smiled at the surprised look on the girl's face. She finished wrapping the thick black braids around Madrigal's ears and stepped back to view her handiwork.

The lady was beautiful! Even the gash on her brow was barely noticeable now, and the color of her gown enhanced her creamy complexion.

Madrigal stood, allowing Maria to tighten the silk ribbons around her hips. "I must go now, *verdad?* I do wish my hands did not shake so." She straighened her shoulders and looked around her chamber. Odd that I feel my world somehow tumbling around my feet, she thought.

Roderick Halconbosque's quarters were located in the same wing that the earl occupied. His bath waters were heating over a glowing fire in the hearth. A large tankard of wine had been carefully placed on a plain cypress table next to an oversized wooden chair covered only by an intricate tapestry.

It was in this not-too-comfortable chair that Roderick sat wearily, drinking his wine, wishing only to sleep and avoid Elena's promised attentions. When he had arrived back at the castle, bringing with him King Sancho and some two-hundred-odd soldiers, he had immediately been confronted by Elena. She had personally insisted on guiding him about the ancient castle and grounds, but seemed more interested in coyly lowering her lovely dark lashes at him than in paying heed to the tour. He had thought how beautiful she could be if only her face and manner were not so hard, so bitter. The face that should have been soft was, instead, brittle-looking—not unlike a lovely face in the repose of death.

Roderick sipped slowly on his wine, his right leg thrown carelessly over the arm of the chair. His eyes finally closed, freeing his mind of thought . . .

Madrigal tapped lightly on his door. He did not answer. Perhaps, she thought, I tarried so long with Juan in the corridor that the baron has gone down to the great hall already. Well, it is Juan's fault if I came too late! Her betrothed had been sulky and hurt because she was to attend Roderick, and she had needed to assure him that a highborn baron meant nothing to her or to her father. Praying that the knight would be absent from his quarters, she tapped lightly again, then turned to leave.

"*Sí . . . Sí,* enter." The voice was gruff and annoyed, but plainly he was there after all.

Madrigal took a deep, calming breath, then turned the handle and entered.

Roderick did not look at her straight on, but his quick glance assured him that the lovely dark-haired girl was Lady Elena. But why did she linger at the threshold?

Madrigal glanced about the chamber, noting his hauberk and helmet already tossed in a heap for his manservant to polish. The gray tunic he wore was grimy, and his boots were dusty from hard riding. His tawny hair was flattened from long hours beneath a helmet; his mouth was turned downward in a bored scowl.

She knew he would be surprised to see her instead of Elena, but she hadn't reckoned on his reaction when he finally took a close look at her as she approached the firelight. His eyes narrowed on seeing the gash on her forehead, and he slammed the huge mug on the table and bolted to his feet.

"You! What trick is this?" Confusion played in his amber eyes.

"I am Lady Madrigal," she said weakly, "sister to Elena . . . We are almost like twins, you see . . ."

"I see . . . 'tis no ruse, then. But why was I not told of your existence?" His voice softened, but only slightly.

"Papa thought it best if I explained personally about my—my journey this morn, and since you did not seem puzzled about Elena—that is, since you didn't mention anything—well, he thought it wise to say nothing himself."

He laughed then, surprising her with his sudden change of heart. Perhaps her shame could be kept secret from the king after all. Papa will be pleased, she told herself.

Roderick strode over to where she was standing. He looked down into her face and lightly traced a finger over the cut on her brow. Madrigal felt oddly shaken by his gesture but then remembered the real reason for her presence.

"The water boils over the hearth, Lady Madrigal—should you not carry out your duties?" His tone was tinged with sarcasm.

"Sí, Barón . . ." She fled from his mocking smile and was so unnerved that she grabbed for a scalding pot without using the cloth holders, letting out a sharp cry when she burned her fingers.

Roderick was at her side immediately, taking her small hand and soothing her.

"Do you always have such difficulty?"

"No . . . 'tis just that I have never . . . that is, only with sisters. You see . . . Elena sees to the needs of our honored guests, but Father insisted, and now I find I cannot . . ." Madrigal was on the verge of tears, for

24

she had never felt so helpless. Her normal brave composure was crumbling like the ancient walls around her.

"Absurd! You *can* and you *will*. 'Tis unbelievable that first you roam about the forest unescorted and then you dare to tell an honored guest you will not serve him! I am in dire need of a bath! What manner of woman are you to deny me?" His harsh words belied his tone, which was amused rather than angered.

Roderick pulled his tunic over his head and tossed it to her. He then sat on the bed and motioned her to remove his boots. Madrigal stiffened her resolve and went toward him, throwing the tunic carelessly to the stone floor. Her forgotten blue ribbon floated out of the shirt and landed beside it.

"My ribbon! You thought to bring it back—" But she cut her words off, knowing he could not have known her identity, much less her home.

"'Twas lost, and I mean to keep it."

She was embarrassed by his explanation and felt her face flush hotly, but said no more. When his boots had at last been removed, she again went to the fire; this time, however, she adeptly carried the heavy pots of water to the fine marble tub and completed the job of filling his bath. She did not turn around, but instead, waited nervously for him to finish undressing by himself. She prayed silently that she would not be asked to assist him further, and closed her eyes against the sound of his arrogant laughter.

She remained in this position until she heard him lower himself into the hot tub with a huge sigh of pleasure. Then she turned to collect his soiled clothing.

"Fetch me my wine, Lady Madrigal."

She obediently brought him the flagon but kept her eyes averted, nearly spilling the liquid into his naked lap.

"Now, kindly scrub the battle filth from my back."
His hawklike features were no longer amused; his tone
was weary but commanding.

Madrigal said nothing, for she was trapped. She
picked up the bar of scented soap, kept especially for
guests, and looked down at his huge frame. His wide
shoulders were muscular and tanned, his sinewy arm
flexed while drinking his wine; she found herself awed
by the obvious power of the man. His arms and legs
were lightly furred with hair, and she was thankful that
she could not see the rest of him.

"Your hair needs soaping, Baron. Shall I wash it?"
she asked.

"*Sì*, and it needs shearing. Fetch my blade, and pray
take care to trim only my hair and not my neck!"

She removed the knife from his leather belt and
slowly, with great care, began to crop his mass of
light-streaked curls—leaving his hair shorter, but still
thick and unruly. Then she soaped his hair and back,
fascinated by the variety of old wounds covering his
body.

"You sport many scars, Baron. 'Tis a map of battles.
Can you remember where each came from?" She tried
to sound casual as she tentatively prodded a few of
them.

"Not really. One soon forgets such trifles . . . I have
been thinking just now of your sister. She hides her
beauty, does she not?"

"Yes, she has always done so. 'Tis only a small
birthmark, but Elena does not think it so tiny." She
surprised herself by wondering how interested Lord
Roderick was in Elena.

"A sister so cool, and marked as well. A pity, I
should think." His voice was pensive.

Madrigal tossed the soap in the water and nervously
stalked the chamber. "Elena is beautiful . . . and kind,

26

too. She is much brighter than I," she declared defensively.

"Nor does she support such a temper, I wager. Now, finish scrubbing me, woman," he commanded.

She was still annoyed at his insult to her sister. The conceited oaf thinks himself too worldly for Elena, she fumed inwardly. We shall see, for my sister knows much of how to please a man.

Moving back toward him, she began to soap his chest, her eyes averted from his mocking gaze. Then she poured freshly heated water over his head and torso and thought her job done.

He sensed her naiveté and allowed her to edge away while he unashamedly scrubbed his private parts. A smile caught his lips as he realized he had grown large in her presence, and he idly wondered if she had noticed.

"May I leave now, my lord?"

He glanced over at her. Her body was tense, her green eyes wide and questioning, and he almost rose from the bath to embrace her. But she was, after all, not a serving wench, but the daughter of an earl. He checked his urges and rose instead to towel himself, affording her a glimpse of his aroused manhood.

Madrigal had never seen a naked man before, and his sudden climb from the tub left her gaping, open-mouthed. She finally realized that she was staring unabashedly at his groin and that he was grinning at her.

Roderick wrapped the linen cloth around himself and went to the bedside, gathering the fresh tunic left there by Renaldo.

"Have you never seen a naked man, Madrigal? Where has your father kept you?" he asked while dressing himself openly in front of her.

"Of course I have seen a . . . a man before—many

times, sir," she lied. "And I cannot imagine why that should concern you in any way!"

He answered her with an amused look that clearly told of his disbelief. "Can you not, my little swallow?"

Madrigal tossed her head defiantly. The presumption of this man! "May I go now that you have displayed yourself, Baron?" Her tone was scathing.

Before he could stop himself, he had reached out for her and crushed her to him. His lips sought hers eagerly, wildly, and then he remembered where he was, and he released her abruptly.

"Yes, you may go now. But know that I am not yet done with you, little swallow!"

Madrigal regarded him with eyes flashing green fire. She was breathless from his kiss and enraged at his flagrant behavior. "I am quite done with *you,* sir! Make no mistake about that, for soon I shall be wed to a man who merits my attentions!"

She stomped out of the chamber, leaving the baron standing there alone, narrow-eyedly considering the revelation of her upcoming marriage.

It was then that the first seed of a plan of vengeance came to him; it sprouted, tiny and uncertain, but grew steadily stronger in his mind. His cold look of a moment ago slowly changed to one of determined assurance.

Chapter 5

Madrigal had left the knight's chamber in a rush, striding quickly along the corridor, her face hot with rage and hurt pride. How dare the arrogant fool talk to her like that! A picture of his nude, well-muscled body as it rose dripping from the water, covered with delicate

28

tawny fuzz, appeared unbidden before her eyes, and she felt again the pressure of his manhood against her gown. She winced as though struck, and quickened her pace down the hall.

Suddenly she stumbled on a loose stone. She looked up, startled, to find that the candle in every wall sconce was out and the hallway was darker than usual. How careless! she thought. I must mention it to José. A ray of light fell across the floor in front of her feet, and she saw that a door had come ajar. The portal belonged to a seldom-used chamber in which the window had been broken since last year, and her father did not have any extra *tarínes* to replace it with the precious glass from Sevilla. The candles must have been snuffed out by a breeze, Madrigal surmised. But why was the door open? José must be getting too old to care for the ancient, drafty castle.

Well, at least she wasn't injured. Madrigal made a mental note to talk to her father about José. Things were falling to pieces around them. *Verdad,* they had plenty of food and their own strong red wine, but gold was very scarce what with the new king struggling to fend off Moorish attacks while attempting to gain the noblemen's support against his deposed father, Alfonso. Madrigal's lips turned up in a smile. Why did she insist on thinking of King Sancho as the "new" king? Only because of her father, she supposed, continuing down the corridor. Jaime Castilla-verde had been one of old King Alfonso's supporters and always referred to young Sancho as the "new" king, even though he had had that title for seven years, although unofficially. Her brow furrowed; she hoped that Sancho was not too aware of her father's leanings, as this could put him in dire peril. King Sancho could easily take the family lands away, depriving the Castilla-verdes of their entire existence. It had been done before, she knew, three hundred years ago, when the Moors had overrun their fiefdom. Her ancestors had been deprived of their holdings for a century, doomed to be landless wanderers and soldiers, until the lands had been wrested from the decadent Moors and returned to their rightful owners. It had been a terrible time for the Castillaverdes, and they were only now recovering from the devastation to their former strength and wealth.

Madrigal turned down a well-lit corridor into a newer wing and stopped at a narrow window slit to look down into a small, out-of-the-way courtyard. On the ground were the broken vestiges of a pool and a fountain, a few scattered blue mosaic tiles, a cracked piece of statuary, left as a mute reminder of the former inhabitants of the castle. All other signs of their previous ownership had been sorted out and destroyed by the avenging Christians, embarked on their holy crusade, their *reconquista*. She crossed herself, praying to the Virgin that her family would never undergo such treatment again, and promised herself to be especially polite to King Sancho tonight at the feast.

Madrigal straightened and smoothed her raven-black hair. She would go to Juan and ask him to escort her to the meal tonight; then that fearful bully, Lord Roderick, would see she had no need of *his* attentions! Perhaps Elena would take his mind off her; Elena would relish that.

The familiar door of Juan's room appeared on her right. The chamber was always kept ready, for Juan often rode over and stayed the night, and her father always welcomed him as the son he had never had. Juan had been there for two days now, ostensibly to aid in the preparations for the feast, but really, she thought, to be near her.

Madrigal was about to knock on the heavy oak door but noticed it was already open a crack. She pushed on it lightly. It swung open smoothly while she called her fiancé's name in a low tone. A strange muffled sound, a sob or a moan, drifted toward her. Was Juan ill? Madrigal tensed to rush into the chamber, to call out for help, but her words froze on her lips. The slight form of Juan, her beloved, her betrothed, was astride a young Moorish servant. Juan was pumping his loins rhythmically into the boy. Madrigal recoiled against the doorframe and clutched her stomach in horror; she had seen enough animals doing precisely the same thing to know the act for what it was. For a moment her numbed body refused to move, and her eyes continued to take in the scene, recording it indelibly on her brain. Juan's back was to her; he did not realize she was there. Every black, curling hair on his buttocks stood out in stark clarity to her unwilling stare; the way his dark head bent to nestle in the boy's neck burned itself into her consciousness. At last her paralysis faded and she stepped backward quietly, now hoping he would not see her or ever know that she had witnessed such a foul, unnatural deed. She held herself in check as long as she could, then burst into a run down the halls, gasping and sobbing.

Thankfully reaching the sanctuary of her chamber, dim with flickering shadows from the single candle, Madrigal slammed the heavy door and threw herself on the bed. Juan! Her friend, her husband-to-be, demeaning himself in such a disgusting manner! Madrigal understood little of such things, but she had heard whispers in the kitchens and stables, and she knew such things were forbidden by both man's law and God's law. How could she marry a man who indulged in such a sin, who even seemed to *enjoy* it? She could tell no one of her discovery, no one! Not even gentle Padre Sebastiano. The shame of it made her face turn hot. She could never marry Juan now; his very touch would shrivel her skin! But how could she break their betrothal? She had been Juan's bride-to-be for most of her life, and all her plans and hopes were centered on living at Montenegro, Juan's castle, only a few miles to the east. Was her life to be destroyed, changed, broken into fragments?

Her body shook with sobs; the day had been too much for her. She could not attend the dinner festivities in the great hall. She knew they should be starting by now and that her father would be wondering where she was, but the thought of joining the boisterous crowd below made her shrink further into the heavy green velvet bed hangings.

Finally her sobs quieted and her mind began to function normally once again. She got up and splashed cold water on her face from the pewter ewer. The cloudy mirror showed a red, swollen visage; if anyone came looking for her, which surely would happen at any moment, she had to appear calm. No one would ever know why she was so upset. Her very honor depended on it.

Chapter 6

The revelry in the great hall had not yet reached its peak. The guests had not had enough time to drink themselves into a stupor and were still attacking the massive piles of food Jaime Castilla-verde had provided. Crisp roasted fowl, bowls of early fruit, great crusty loaves of bread, and loins of the wild boar disappeared quickly. The guests were also treated to mounds of fluffy saffron rice dotted with pimentos, vegetables, and shellfish; innumerable small pots of rich flan; and delicacies such as sautéed prawns and stuffed squid. The servants bustled about, filling and refilling flagons with the rich, velvety wine made on the grounds.

A trestle table had been set up crosswise at the head of the great hall, raised above the two long wing tables that stretched along the sides of the hall. King Sancho IV, called Sancho the Brave, a slight man of medium height and quite fair because of his German ancestry, sat in the place of honor at the center of the raised table. Jaime Castilla-verde was on his right and Roderick Halconbosque on his left. Elena and Teresa flanked this trio, but one chair was empty. Three lesser knights sat on either side of them, eating mightily of the first good food they had had after weeks of battle. Roderick was pensively sipping his wine from a hammered silver flagon, a bemused expression on his face. Lord Jaime appeared nervous, picking absentmindedly at a haunch of venison on his plate. The king had eaten heartily, then pushed his heavy, carved chair back and half reclined in it, holding his flagon on his stomach and occasionally directing a word at Elena, Roderick, or the earl. The dark circles under his eyes were the only testament to the months of heavy fighting and his worries over the unstable state of Spain.

Elena had been placed next to her father, which had piqued her, as she could not talk intimately to Roderick. The empty chair next to him spoke eloquently of Madrigal's absence.

Roderick leaned slightly forward to address the earl. "I do hope, sir, that I did nothing to upset your daughter this eve. I wonder at her absence from this merry feast in honor of the king."

"It is intolerable, Lord Roderick. I cannot understand what is keeping her. She is a headstrong girl, but to display this kind of rudeness to our sovereign . . . I cannot imagine . . ." Castilla-verde's face settled further into its lines of worry. His hand plucked ineffectually at a morsel of meat on his plate. "I shall send another servant up to fetch her. Mayhap this time she will join us. You—Consuela! *Por favor,* go up to Lady Madrigal again and relay the king's wishes to her that she descend to the great hall immediately."

"*Sí,* Lord Jaime," said the plump serving girl, and ran quickly to the stairs and disappeared.

Several minutes passed while the earl fidgeted, Roderick smiled, and King Sancho tried pointedly not to notice the tension suspended in the air.

Then Lord Jaime emitted a sigh of relief. Madrigal was descending the main staircase, looking pale but composed as she approached the table. He noticed that all eyes were turned appreciatively toward his beautiful daughter's entrance.

She curtsied to King Sancho and kissed his great signet ring without raising her eyes.

"Please excuse me, your Highness, I was not feeling too well, but I have . . . ah . . . recovered now. I hope you are enjoying your meal."

"So this is the fabled Lady Madrigal. She certainly lives up to the glowing reports that have reached my ears. Please, milady, be seated and partake of this glorious feast," the king entreated generously.

Madrigal shot a glance at the lower table and saw Juan, delegated to the lesser ranks, scowling at her as she seated herself next to Roderick. Her heart contracted, but she managed a faint smile in Juan's direction.

"Well, Lady Madrigal, at last we are honored with your presence. I hope and pray that helping me to bathe did not truly make you ill!" Roderick smiled wickedly as he poured wine into her flagon.

"No, sir knight, my . . . indisposition most certainly was not *your* doing. Have no fear on that score," she said between clenched teeth.

She was relieved when Roderick became involved in a conversation with King Sancho and her father about

34

the present political situation. She tried to eat but could force only a few morsels past the lump in her throat. She finally gave up and merely sipped her wine, avoiding Juan de Vegas's eyes.

"I realize, Lord Jaime," King Sancho was saying, "that my company and I are a burden on you, and we shall be gone shortly, but I am forced to recruit some of your serfs for my army. Abu Yusuf and his men are still trying to capture Jerez and control Gibraltar and the strait. If they are successful and overrun the countryside—well, you can see why I ask *you* for reinforcements. You are directly in their path."

"Of course, my liege, I understand, and I am willing to help in any way I can, but this is a poor fief and I have few serfs . . . I shall make arrangements on the morrow and provide you with as many hands as possible. I hope that will suffice, King Sancho, as I have no gold, no sons, not even a knight to send with you."

"I would certainly appreciate even a dozen men from the fief, the more so, Lord Jaime, since I know your true feelings lean more toward my father than to myself." Sancho smiled condescendingly at the alarmed earl. "But never fear, milord. I believe fairness and justice earn more allies than a heavy hand, and I hope to win you and all the lords of Spain to my side one day."

Jaime muttered something at this point, but Sancho silenced him with a hand.

"Ah, do not apologize, Lord Jaime. We all know my father, Alfonso, to have been a truly great king, but alas, he emptied the coffers of Spain in his artistic endeavors to be crowned as Holy Roman emperor. It was an unforgivable weakness in a king, sadly enough for the people of Spain. He threw our country into an uproar with his latest ridiculous attempt to disinherit me, and now the Moors have attacked to take advantage of our plight. And to think he was called Alfonso the Wise. A misnomer in some ways, I greatly fear."

Jaime knew he was on dangerous ground here and tactfully changed the subject. "How fare your wife, Lady Maria de Molina, and your children?" But again he found himself on tenuous ground.

"Ah, Maria still frets that the children are dubbed illegitimate since the pope excommunicated me, but I am sure that problem will be settled long before my oldest inherits the throne. So many problems, you see, Lord Jaime. Often I am sorry I felt the call to sovereignty, but someone besides my poor dead brother's son had to rule Spain. These are difficult times, sir. But let us change the subject, *amigos,* to a happier one."

As the conversation continued desultorily and the wine was quaffed steadily, Madrigal grew more exhausted. She stifled a yawn with her hand while her father's favorite brindled hound fought over a bone under her feet, snarling and growling. Could it have been only that morning that the boar had attacked her, and that she had first seen Roderick? She glanced at him sideways from under her lashes; his profile was bold, silhouetted against the candles. His hair was roughly tousled, as though he had just run a hand through it. She was glad that any mistakes she might have made while barbering him were masked in the golden curls.

Roderick's eyes met hers at that moment, and he smiled lazily, insolently, at her. She wrenched her eyes away and looked down at her hands. A hot flush spread from her neck to her face. Just then a particularly loud barking erupted under the table, and Madrigal jumped inadvertently. Roderick laughed, drank off his flagon of wine, and turned to the king, showing Madrigal his broad back.

The feast continued interminably for Madrigal; she felt she would surely fall asleep on the table, as many of the guests had already done. The luckier ones had chosen to curl up on benches along the walls or to make their unsteady way to the stables. Elena was in her element, vibrant, delighting in the male attention she was receiving. She was already half draped over the knight seated next to her. He appeared to be quite pleased with her amiability but kept gazing at Madrigal with a puzzled expression, as if he could not believe that there were two so alike. Teresa had long since retired to her bed, worn out by the long day of excitement.

King Sancho was still relatively sober and was obviously accustomed to sitting through long dinners, but Lord Jaime appeared to be a bit muddled; he laughed often and his words were slightly slurred. Roderick was quietly pensive. He seemed to be brooding, his chin sunk onto his chest. He did not appear to be drunk, but he had imbibed a great amount of wine during the evening. He knew he would have to leave for battle shortly, and his old wounds ached at the thought of long hours in the saddle, the hot mesh armor irritating his neck and arms.

In spite of his bodily exhaustion and the wine, his mind was alert and sharp. He had tried to ignore the girl sitting next to him, so near that her faint fragrance reached his nostrils from time to time. The knowledge of her closeness left him tense, while her father's presence, which should have been disturbing, left him untouched. A strange situation, thought Roderick. Here I sit within an arm's reach of the dastardly earl, and all I can do is ogle his daughter! And she is obviously the dearest one to him.

Roderick's earlier embryonic scheme came to mind again. He had conceived of it in a moment of lust, but perhaps it had other merits. To have that nubile body in his arms whenever he pleased, to command that proud spirit—above all, to wreak a slow, delicious vengeance upon Castilla-verde while actually enjoying himself! How the earl would suffer in vain the torments bestowed on his favorite daughter! Roderick examined the plan from every angle. The fiancé was a problem, but a royal order could not be countermanded by anyone. The young whelp would just have to find himself another wench.

For years now, Sancho had bidden Roderick to settle down; he needed Halconbosque's sons as squires to his own, and he wanted more loyal families behind him, large families. Roderick's single state had often caused him to lecture his knight on the merits of married life. Roderick had always agreed but replied that he had never found the woman who would please him. Well, now he had found her. Ah, the ironies of fate, he thought, the blackhearted earl's daughter to wife! In a few years he would toss her back to her father, her spirit broken, her will destroyed. As the earl himself would be broken and destroyed.

He waited for a lull in the conversation between Sancho and Lord Jaime, then leaned to his right to catch his sovereign's ear.

"Sire, I wish you to be the first to know the good tidings," he said softly. "I have at last chosen a wife, as you have so often advised me. I think you will be pleased with my choice."

"*Verdad,* Roderick, this comes as a great surprise to me! Who is this most fortunate of women?"

"Lady Madrigal, my liege."

"Lady Madrigal! A beautiful creature, *claro,* but you have known her so short a time. Are you certain of this choice?"

"Sire, I have never been more certain of anything in my life. It shall be Lady Madrigal, or none at all."

"Roderick, my friend, I know you to be a deter- mined man, and if you have chosen her, I am sure she is right for you. And so it shall be! Have you spoken to her father?"

"No, sire. Actually . . . I was hoping you would speak in my behalf. I have no experience in such matters. I . . . ah . . . find myself quite out of my element."

"Roderick," laughed Sancho, "you have at last come up against something that baffles you, I see. You find it easier to fight battles, I vow."

"Well, waging war is an area in which I have had a great deal of experience, but this . . . this matter of marriage . . . I confess it confounds me."

The king rose and banged his flagon on the table to gain the attention of the company. When the din of merrymaking subsided, he began to speak.

"Lord Jaime Castilla-verde, I have wonderful news. My old friend and loyal knight, the Baron of Com- postela, Roderick Halconbosque, most respectfully wishes the hand of your daughter, Lady Madrigal, in marriage and has asked that I arrange this matter with you." Sancho paused to allow the fortunate father to accept gratefully on behalf of his daughter. A marriage bond to the king's handsome, virile, and rich friend would be an unbelievable stroke of luck for the obviously genteel but poverty-stricken Castilla-verde family. But the earl looked shocked, his mouth hanging open in surprise.

"King Sancho . . . I . . . we . . . do not deserve such an honor. I do not wish to insult such illustrious guests, but my daughter Madrigal is already betrothed to a neighbor, Sir Juan de Vegas. However, my daughter Elena is unattached, and I would be more than happy to bestow her hand upon Lord Roderick . . ." Jaime's quavering voice faded under the combined stares of the king and Roderick.

Elena had straightened instantly upon hearing the king's words, her red lips glistening from the continuous flick of her small tongue over them. Madrigal had not moved; she sat erect in her chair, but her face was as pallid as the moon by day, her eyes large and brilliant in the pale oval.

King Sancho turned to Roderick and fixed narrowed eyes upon his tall friend. What a damned difficult situation this could turn into! he thought irritably. He wondered if Roderick had known of Lady Madrigal's betrothal, but assuming Roderick had anticipated the sensitive political problem that might arise, he thought not. He saw that his knight's mind was made up; there would be no other woman for him. Sancho quickly decided that the father would have to be brought around and the girl convinced that her present fiancé was not worth angering the king over. The poor de Vegas would have to find himself another wife, for surely his well-being was not as important to the land as that of Roderick Halconbosque.

Sancho nodded in the girl's direction with a smile. "Lady Madrigal will, I am sure, be most pleased to accept my blessings on her forthcoming marriage to Lord Roderick." He then turned his royal gaze upon the trembling Castilla-verde. "And you, Lord Jaime, will rejoice to unite your ancient and honorable family with one as illustrious as that of Halconbosque. As compensation for the breaking of his betrothal, the gentleman in question will receive one hundred pieces of gold from the royal treasury."

"Yes, of course, King Sancho," the earl sputtered. "We are honored to betroth Madrigal and Roderick." He threw a glance at Madrigal, begging her with his eyes to forgive him. One did not argue against a direct order of the king! Strangely enough, although Madrigal sat stiff and pale in her chair, she said nothing. She just stared straight ahead, her lovely red lips compressed tightly together.

A figure rose from the lower table. It was Juan de Vegas, his face dark, his voice strident against the background noises as he addressed the king.

"Sire, with all due respect to your royal person, I must protest this arbitrary breaking of my betrothal to Lady Madrigal! She and I have been promised since we were mere children. We love each other!" He looked beseechingly at Madrigal, wishing her to reinforce his words. She said nothing but noticeably avoided his eye.

"I can understand your anger, lad," the king said, "but there are some things one must give up for the benefit of all concerned. This is one such case. There are many other women in the world, and you are still young . . ."

"There is no other woman like Madrigal, sire! And if I cannot have her, you can be certain I will not find happiness in any other woman's embrace!" Juan's voice broke; he whirled from the great hall, slamming the huge door behind him. The sound echoed in the suddenly quiet chamber for a moment, then was drowned out by the snarling of a dog.

Madrigal had shrunk into her chair at Juan's last remarks; she knew him so well that she understood the shock and misery he was undergoing. But, *por Dios,* to have her promise to him broken by the king himself! It was truly a relief. Poor Juan, he would suffer, but he would forget her; it was better all around. Perhaps he was on his way to indulge his vile habits with the servant boy again.

Then the reality of her situation suddenly struck home—betrothed to that arrogant bore! But surely the deed was not yet done and he would return with the king to battle the Moors. Perhaps he would die of a wound or a disease, as so many did, God forgive the thought, or would lose interest in her. There were so many things that could happen between now and the fact of marriage to him. At least her current problem was neatly solved.

The king bestowed another smile on Madrigal. "Lady Madrigal, I am sorry to have your betrothal to Lord Roderick spoiled by an angry suitor, but I can understand why any man would be distressed to be deprived of your company for life. I wish to give you my blessings and my hopes for a happy future with my friend Roderick, and for many strong sons to help us against the Moors." He took her cold hand in his and kissed it lightly.

Madrigal murmured something polite in answer but did not dare raise her eyes to the king's. She was afraid he would see in them the confusion that consumed her mind and the open contempt she felt for Lord Roderick.

Lord Jaime was surprised to see his fiery daughter so docile, but he was also relieved that she was behaving so well. He sent a silent prayer heavenward for her continued compliancy, and then began worrying about the dowry he would have to present to her future husband. The terms of the marriage contract plagued him. So many questions whirled around his fuddled brain that he gave up seeking answers and emptied his flagon with every toast to the newly betrothed couple.

The king was nearly ready to mount up and ride south to continue his war against Abu Yusuf's army. Because of his imminent departure, the castle had been in an uproar since before dawn, with the cooks preparing a huge breakfast for him and his knights. The horses were snorting impatiently before the huge front doors, waiting to be mounted. The squires held the bridles of the mighty war chargers in readiness for their masters. A ragtag crew of a dozen or so serfs from the environs of Castilla-verde were nervously bidding farewell to their mothers or sweethearts. They would be issued weapons and armor when they arrived at Jerez and would soon be fighting the Moors. An astute foot soldier could gain much by being in the right place at the right time on the battlefield—plunder, a higher rank bestowed by a grateful knight—anything was possible in war.

King Sancho emerged from the great hall, wiping the last traces of breakfast from his mouth with the back of his hand. He spoke to Lord Jaime for a time. Teresa, Elena, and Madrigal had been told to be present for the leave-taking, and they stood respectfully by their father as he listened to the king. Roderick joined the group at the top of the steps as Sancho descended to his waiting men.

"Lord Jaime," Roderick began, "we shall wed this autumn, when the campaign is over. Have the banns posted and draw up the marriage contract. I have given Padre Sebastiano full instructions. Be sure to guard my betrothed with great care, sir, as I wish no further incidents such as the one under which I met her, *entiende?*"

Jaime paled at Roderick's stern tone of voice. How was he to control his headstrong daughter any more effectively now than he had in the past?

"You have my word, Lord Roderick. No harm shall befall her."

"Bueno." Curtly dismissing the earl, Roderick turned to Madrigal and drew her firmly aside.

"Madrigal, my little swallow, I see you are looking as lovely as usual this fine morn. And to have risen from your bed at such an early hour to wish your betrothed Godspeed. 'Tis surely out of a love unknown before in the heart of a woman. Is that not so?" His tone was sarcastic. He lifted a lock of glossy black hair and let it slide off his finger.

Madrigal jerked her head back and glared up at him. "It is not on *your* account that I am here, believe that, sir!" The words hissed out vehemently.

"Nevertheless, my lovely, you are here. And why is it that you have neatly avoided me for the last two days? Do you not enjoy my presence?"

Madrigal made an exasperated sound and tried to shake him off, but he held her arm in a viselike grip and forced her to look at him. His golden-brown eyes were angry, menacing.

"You *will* listen to what I have to say, my wife-to-be. Your father has instructions and knows what to do, but I shall warn you, too. There will be no more trips alone into the forest, or anywhere else, for that matter. You will abide by the rules of propriety. I want no whispers or gossip about my fiancée. You will obey me!"

Madrigal yanked her arm out of his grasp and swung around to face her father, who had nervously been watching this interchange. Elena was glowering, barely able to contain her displeasure at not having been chosen by Roderick. When he finally approached her and kissed her hand in farewell, sparks flew from her green eyes. To Teresa he gave a chaste kiss on the forehead, and she smiled at him shyly.

Roderick descended the steps and mounted his black charger, swinging his leg easily over the horse's back. The king gave the signal to advance, and the Castillaverdes watched the company disappear down the path leading into the forest, a cloud of dust remaining in its wake.

Suddenly a figure on horseback galloped past the castle from the east and followed the king's retinue. Madrigal recognized the colors of Juan de Vegas when she saw his squire racing after him. With a gasp of dismay, she realized that Juan was joining the king's army, most probably because of her and their broken marriage plans. Slim, fastidious Juan, who could not bear dirty clothes, poorly prepared food, or even a dead cat on the road. How would he survive the rigors of the battlefield? He would surely be killed, and it would be her fault.

The future seemed bleak to Madrigal at that moment. Tears welled up in her eyes at the thought of poor Juan dashing gallantly off to war. Perhaps the tears were also for herself, doomed to marry a man she feared and hated. Madrigal wiped her eyes roughly and straightened her spine. She was not married yet, and she had the whole summer to rectify her predicament. She would certainly have her own way, despite Roderick Halconbosque, despite the king himself. She had always prevailed before, and she would do so again.

Chapter 7

For some weeks now, Madrigal had been sleeping well past her normal rising hour, but this particular morning a cool breeze coming through her chaliced window caused her to stir and grope for her discarded coverlet. As she tossed about her bed seeking warmth, she slowly became aware of the chill in the air. Her eyes opened with a start and she sat up, reminded instantly of the oncoming autumn. Then she sighed in relief, knowing that her marriage was still several weeks in the future; she realized it was only late August and that the cooler weather was but a fluke of nature.

What has come over me? she wondered nervously while trying to nestle back down under her coverlet. Each day that passes now sees my freedom slipping away. As she lay musing on the past few weeks, Madrigal felt both sad and apprehensive because her summer had sped by so rapidly. In her mind's eye she tried to conjure up Halconbosque's face, but she could discern only a vague image of a tall, fierce-looking knight, mounted on a great steed. The vision reminded her once again that if she had not roamed about the forest alone that June morning, and if she had not met that deadly boar, and if . . . Her mind screamed back at her to cease fretting over the inevitable future that lay in store for her. Yet another part of her mind said, You are not yet wed, the vows have not been spoken . . .

When Maria finally entered her chamber, Madrigal knew for certain that the hour was late. "Maria," she sighed, "if only I could hold on to the summer forever. I hate to feel the first chill of autumn."

"*Sí*, milady, I know. But spending your days abed will not keep the hours from passing," the maid replied, scurrying about the chamber to perform her tasks.

Madrigal sat up and tossed her raven hair back while stretching languidly. "Maria, Papa says I must go and live in Galicia, but I think I shall remain here. After all, Halconbosque is forever fighting by his king's side, and why should I be alone at—"

"Milady! 'Tis not my place to speak, but do not dwell on the impossible. Know that we shall surely travel to Galicia and remain there, for your husband-to-be is no simpering fool to allow his wife such freedom."

"What do you know of him, old one? Why, the wedding has not yet taken place—he might be wounded, or even dead, for all I give a whit!" The instant the words were spoken, Madrigal wished she had held her sharp tongue, for such thoughts were unchristian and to voice them aloud was sinful.

Maria crossed herself and looked long and hard at her ladyship. With her brows knitted together, she approached Madrigal and placed a wrinkled hand on her arm. " 'Tis the king's will that you marry the baron and bear him heirs. Any sensible woman would give all she has to be wedded to such a noble and wealthy man. Madrigal," she continued more slowly, "a few words of advice from an old woman who loves you. The choice is not yours to make, but your father's and your king's, and you will find happiness if you can accept the man as he is and give up some of your willful ways."

Madrigal weighed the servant's words, but still her mind rebelled. As she donned a green linen tunic she replied, "Most assuredly you speak the truth, Maria, but I cannot pretend to care for him when in my heart I feel afraid."

Maria began to braid Madrigal's hair. She knew the girl had assessed the situation correctly, for although the baron was endowed with exceptional good looks, there was much to fear in his demeanor. She tried to speak reassuringly. "We shall come to call his home ours, and while he is at war, you will have his babes to raise and cherish. And handsome babes they will be indeed!"

Maria's words did not bring comfort to Madrigal; instead, she felt shaken by the mere idea of engaging in the marriage act.

"Oh, Maria, let us not talk of it. He won't return for weeks yet, and I will think of something," she said while viewing her reflection in the wavy wall mirror. Her jade eyes looked steadily back at her, but inwardly she did not feel so confident.

Once finished with her toilette, Madrigal left the bedchamber and went to seek out one of her sisters for company during the morning meal. As she descended the stairs into the great hall, she was reminded of the numerous times she had raced through the kitchens and out to the stable. To be free again! To ride alone through the forest without care! But then she remembered Halconbosque's parting words: "There will be no more trips alone into the forest . . . You will obey me!"

"The oafish knave," she murmured aloud, "thinks to frighten me into submission—"

"Good morning, Madrigal," said Teresa as she bounded up to her older sister's side. "The rolls are all cold now. Why do you stay abed so long?"

"I don't know, Teresa. But I am here now and shall spend the morning teaching you a new stitch for your tapestry." She seated herself and began to nibble halfheartedly on a hard bun with cheese.

"Elena upset me this morning and then left with Papa to see a sick calf in the lower meadow," Teresa remarked while toying with a bunch of fresh grapes, much to Madrigal's annoyance.

"Stop fiddling!" Madrigal said sharply, then quickly soothed her innocent sister. "Pay me no mind, Teresa. Now, what did Elena say to make you unhappy?"

"She told me that Roderick didn't like you in the least, and that you will be miserable and he will beat you . . . maybe even put you in his dungeon with the rats for the way you speak to him!"

"Nonsense! We are to be married, aren't we? He must like me." Her words were meant only to calm Teresa. Why did Elena always create havoc where there was none? Dungeons indeed! She shuddered slightly and wondered again why Roderick had chosen her to be his wife. She could think of no sound reason at all.

"But will he beat you?"

"I'd run him through first with my knife!" Madrigal laughed confidently, then rose and delighted Teresa with a flourish of an imaginary dagger.

"You wouldn't! He's much, much bigger and stronger than you, Madrigal! I know you are jesting!"

Madrigal sat down again and regarded her sister seriously. "You like him, don't you?"

"Oh, *sí*, Madrigal! He is so gallant. And you are the loveliest woman in all the land. I wish I could come and live in Galicia, too."

Madrigal thought to herself that she had many reasons for not wanting to marry Roderick and leave her home, her little sister ranking high among them.

The quiet of the moment was suddenly broken by the rapid entrance of her father, Elena close behind him. He did not stop to give his hounds their customary pat but strode immediately to where Madrigal and Teresa were sitting.

"I fear we have received bad tidings this morn, Madrigal." Lord Jaime cleared his throat nervously and took her hand in his. "A messenger came from Montenegro and told us that Juan has been carried back to his home with a wound."

Madrigal slowly came to her feet. "Is he . . . will he be all right, Papa?" Her lower lip was trembling, and suddenly she felt sick to her stomach.

"*Sí, sí,* little one. The serf assured me 'twas only a small wound and he would recover."

"Papa, you would not just tell me that? Oh, I must go quickly to him! Have the horses saddled and tell Maria to fetch my herbs," she called over her shoulder to an attending servant. She did not wait for her father's approval but raced toward the steps leading aloft to fetch her cloak. Once inside her room, she felt guilt wash over her for having thought so little about Juan de Vegas of late.

She was gathering her cloak and turning to leave when Elena entered her chamber and closed the door.

"Elena . . . please, not now. I must go to Juan."

"How very kind of you, Madrigal," Elena said slowly and evenly, her green eyes narrowed, "to think of Juan, when surely your mind is on your betrothed. I wonder what Roderick would think of your visit to Montenegro?"

"Elena, you have a twisted mind! The baron would, of course, understand my concern for an old friend. Now, let me by and cease this inane prattle."

"Naturally, sweet sister—and I wouldn't dream of telling your betrothed," she whispered, allowing Madrigal to open the door.

Madrigal fled down the long corridor toward the stairs, but not before she heard Elena call after her, "Undoubtedly you are correct. The baron will understand completely."

If only Elena would show some measure of compassion, she thought while nearly flying down the steps and out the door. The two mounts were saddled and Maria was waiting with the herbs. Madrigal's father stopped her with a quiet reminder.

"Remember, Madrigal, ride straight to Montenegro, and if necessary, spend the eve there and return on the morrow." Then he added, "Perhaps a guard should accompany you after all."

"Papa, we shall take the road. Do not fret." She kissed him on the cheek and hurriedly mounted her palfrey before he could detain them further.

After Juan had volunteered his services to King Sancho, Madrigal had neither seen nor heard from him. In fact, the evening of the feast had brought so many shocks that she had had no time to speak with Juan, much less give him solace. But now she recalled how repulsed she had felt when she had witnessed his shame earlier that day. Thank heavens he had not seen her!

She had put the episode from her mind until the evening, a few weeks after Juan's departure, when she and her father had a talk. Now she remembered their discussion with utter clarity.

He had said, "Madrigal, although it has been expected that you and Juan would wed, things are not always as simple in our lives. I trust you spoke with him before he left? I fear the lad was most disappointed and the baron was most discourteous."

"Papa, Juan and I were not afforded a moment. How did you expect him to feel after King Sancho shattered our plans?"

"*Niña,* you know how I was persuaded by the king. I could offer our liege no less. Halconbosque is from one of the most noble families of our land, and 'tis a great honor he bestows upon Castilla-verde. His manner will soften once he has married."

Then she had changed the subject suddenly, the question nearly bursting from her. "Papa, do some men prefer . . . that is, do they like men better than women?"

"But of course, *hija.* Many men would rather spend their time in the comradeship of fellow males. They enjoy the ribald banter, the drinking—"

"No, Papa, I did not mean *that* way. I only wondered if a man would not sometimes prefer . . . prefer another—"

Somewhat shocked by her meaning, but not unaccustomed to Madrigal's blunt and bold observations, he had interrupted her. "*Sí, sí.* 'Tis not a genteel subject, Madrigal, but yes, sometimes after months in battle a man longs for, well, for affection from another. In truth, the ungodly Moors engage themselves in sodomy quite often, I fear." Then he had wondered at her interest. "What puts such notions in your pretty head, Madrigal? You cannot be speaking of Halconbosque!"

"No. 'Twas only that I overheard the stableboys jesting about such things." She had lied easily, not wanting to mention Juan's name.

As she and Maria rode toward Juan's home, she recalled her amusement at her father's wonder that she might have thought Halconbosque preferred men over women, and a smile touched her lips as she envisioned the furious reaction of her betrothed had he overheard their conversation.

Chapter 8

Montenegro sat nestled on the outskirts of the forest before them, and Madrigal thought of how relieved she had felt after that talk with her father. She had come to realize that Juan de Vegas was still her friend and that she could not hold his preference for men against him.

A serf from Montenegro approached them, and Madrigal, along with a weary Maria, entered the manor and was led swiftly to Juan's mother, Lucia, weeping softly at his bedside. Madrigal did not speak at first, but gazed painfully at Juan's pale form. He had grown even thinner, and the circles under his eyes somehow made him appear older than his years. She longed to reach out and touch him but feared that he might awaken.

His mother finally acknowledged Madrigal's timid greeting and managed to reply, "Lady Madrigal, bless the good Lord that you have come. His arm surely festers, and I fear . . ."

"There, now, Lady Lucia. I have brought my herbs and I shall stay with Juan until he has healed. I promise," Madrigal whispered.

"My, how lovely you have grown, Madrigal. 'Tis many months since I have moved beyond these walls . . . How is your father?" She relapsed into sobbing quietly once again. Madrigal removed her cloak and turned back the bedcovers so that she could assess the damage done to Juan's arm. He stirred restively as she undressed the ugly slash and bade Maria to make up a

poultice of herbs. She felt his brow, which was mercifully cool to the touch, then applied the salve to his
upper arm and rebandaged it, thinking that perhaps her
services were not needed here, since he had apparently
received medicinal attention on the battlefield.

Having done all she could for the moment, she
re-covered his sleeping form and approached Lady
Lucia, somewhat more concerned for the elderly
woman's health than for Juan.

"Milady, please let me see you to your chamber. You
can do nothing here but upset yourself further, and I
shall stay with Juan." The frail woman seemed not to
hear, so Madrigal eased her to her feet while whispering that her son was in no danger and only in need of a
good rest.

"Maria, see the lady to her rooms and remain with
her. I shall have food sent there shortly."

Madrigal ordered trays of food to be brought to
herself and to the older women, then sat by Juan's side
the remainder of the day. She retired that evening to a
guest chamber, after leaving a trusted servant with Juan
and sending word to her father of her intended stay.

The following morning saw Juan propped up in his
bed and making idle conversation with Lucia and
Madrigal. His mother was so relieved, she was able to
respond almost with gaiety to Juan's recount of his
prowess in battle. As the day wore on pleasantly,
Madrigal decided to spend another night at Montenegro so that she might talk privately with Juan when he
was more fully recovered.

At dusk she strode out alone through the ruins that
had once been fortified walls built by Juan's ancestors
to protect Montenegro from the Moors. The western
sun cast long, sleek shadows among the fallen stones
and reddened the soft earth beneath her feet. While she
roamed aimlessly through the pine-scented grounds,
she thought long on this war-torn land, and of the death

of Juan's father under the unholy lances of the Moors. So much death . . . centuries of occupation that would not be forgotten for ages to come. Praise God that it was over . . .

The last rays of slanted light weakened, and Madrigal returned to Juan's chamber to check his dressing and bid him good night. He watched her approach and knew an aching sadness for his loss. She was so desirable, not only because of her matchless beauty but also because of her wild, free heart and unaffected compassion. She would have made the perfect wife, the adored mother. But never would a man tame her.

"You are still awake, Juan." She thought for a moment, then asked, "Can you find it in your heart to forgive me? We've not had a chance to talk since the night of the feast, and . . ."

"'Twas not your doing, Madrigal. This I know, for I've had a long time to think on it. Now I wish only for your friendship and your happiness." His brown eyes searched her face and found a sorrow there. He wondered for a fleeting moment if she felt the loss as greatly as he did; it would do no harm now to try to give her comfort. "In these past weeks I have been thrown in the company of Halconbosque, so much so that I have gained a respect—"

"Juan! Please, I do not wish to speak of him. I care not what manner of man he is." She felt shaken and undone by his mention of the baron.

"*Cállate, mia preciosa.* Allow me my dignity for just this once. There is no man who can match his skill and devotion to battle—'tis as if he has a devil riding at his back, or mayhap I should say an angel at his side. A braver man there is not, and when day is done he sees personally to the wounded and slain, whether they be knight or lowliest slaves. It is not an easy thing for me to say, but truly Madrigal, the man has many redeeming qualities that will please you greatly."

"It would seem that the Baron of Compostela has won all hearts save mine," she murmured while rising. "Come, now, it is time you sleep. *Hasta mañana.*" Her normal composure was sorely shaken and she hurried from his chamber.

The next day dawned bright and warm, but before the noon hour great black clouds were rolling across the horizon, threatening to spill their burden in torrents of rain. The night before, Madrigal had slept peacefully, feeling that Juan had forgiven her. She had planned to travel back to Castilla-verde today, but now she was uncertain whether to stay another night or attempt to return before the storm broke. While she was passing the time, she decided to visit Juan once again.

They were engaged in a heated debate over the use of the longbow in the hunt when a commotion emanating from the hall below startled them. Silence followed, and then they heard the distinct echo of a determined footfall growing louder as it approached Juan's door.

Juan eased himself into a sitting position. Madrigal, dismayed, slowly backed away from the sound.

"What in the name of God is going on!" Juan demanded. "Where are those useless guards when they are needed?"

Suddenly the footsteps stopped and they both stared apprehensively at the doorway. Endless seconds later the door burst open, nearly splintering from its hinges and causing the candle in the wall sconce to be extinguished. The hall was dimly lit, and all they could perceive was the figure of a tall, armor-clad knight, still wearing his helmet.

Madrigal, horrified and suddenly weak-kneed, let out a short gasp.

The stranger surveyed the chamber somberly as he removed his helmet. Madrigal was certain he was the devil himself, until the room became brightened by a quick bolt of lightning, followed immediately by a loud clap of thunder. Instantly she recognized the intruder: Roderick Halconbosque.

"Gather your cloak, woman—you're leaving," he said tightly, a murderous scowl on his face.

Madrigal's heart beat wildly from the shock of seeing him and from the furious tone in his voice; she remained frozen to the spot. When he saw she would not come on her own, he crossed the room in a long stride and grasped her by the shoulders.

"Do you dare defy me even now, wench!" he bellowed, shaking her roughly.

It was then that Juan found his voice. "Unhand the lady, Baron! She has done nothing to deserve your wrath!"

Roderick kept his eyes on Madrigal but directed his words to the injured lad. "You fought with valor and courage on the battlefield, boy, but do not test my patience in matters that are not your concern." However, he released his grip from Madrigal, allowing her to slump limply against the hard stone wall.

"I won't tell you again, Madrigal. Collect your belongings." He indicated the door to her.

At that moment she felt her strength return like the stinging snap of a whip. Her voice was low with unrepressed outrage. "How dare you enter another man's home like a fiendish brute! Be gone from my sight, you ungodly—"

Before she could finish her diatribe, Roderick had grabbed her again, and this time he slung her over his shoulder and strode out of the chamber, leaving Juan open-mouthed and completely helpless.

The force of being crushed against his hauberk left Madrigal breathless and immobile for a time. Then she was out in the teeming rain and tossed across the front of his hard leather saddle. Her hair had come unbraided and fell in total disarray; her linen gown clung to her shivering body. She felt completely humiliated.

Roderick ignored her angry protests and attempted to mount while keeping a firm hand on her rump to still her. In desperation, Madrigal shot her foot out and caught him unawares, causing him to stumble backward.

"By all that's holy, woman!" he exclaimed in utter amazement.

She quickly slid off the opposite side of his horse and grasped the handle of his sword, which was sheathed in his saddle. The great steed skittered backward, leaving Roderick and Madrigal facing each other, neither willing to give ground.

His gold-flecked eyes challenged hers, and he stated flatly, "You either sheath my sword or use it."

"I should run you through for your brutal treatment of me, you cowardly knave! You are rude and beastly beyond description! I despise you!"

Roderick studied her pensively for a moment; he saw the brave front she presented, but tears of frustration brimmed in her eyes, and her whole body was trembling from chill and fear. All in all, she was intoxicating to view, standing there dripping wet. The dangerous look on his face began to ease as he appraised her figure and her beauty.

"Come, now, Madrigal, perhaps I was a little too hasty in my actions. Put down the sword before you harm yourself." His face relaxed further into a lazy half smile, which she eyed warily.

"Do *myself* harm! Ha!" she spat in reply.

He saw that she would not give in, and to save the situation he quickly lunged for her arm, trying to deflect the sword from her. His catlike movement was her undoing, for she had not seen it coming and was shocked to find herself crushed against him, with the sword flung far from her reach.

"You blackguard!" she hissed, feeling his arms tighten about her.

"Lady Madrigal, I yield to your temper." He spoke with unaccustomed amusement in his voice.

He had come to punish her for her indiscretion with de Vegas, and now found himself soothing her instead. The lady was quite obviously spoiled, and her behavior was a disgrace. He could find no sensible way to deal with her.

"Let us return to Castilla-verde and more peaceably discuss your improper behavior."

"I need not explain my actions to *you, Baron!* I came here to tend my friend's wound—and that does not concern you." Still she struggled against him.

"Mayhap I have wrongly judged you, little swallow. My leaving the battlefield may have been impulsive, but knights often take brief respites. In any case, I . . . I sought to see how you fared in my absence. Then Elena told me of your whereabouts and—"

"Elena! I should have guessed! And what, pray tell, did my sister inform you?" Madrigal looked up into his face and saw the error in his thinking.

"That you had flown to be with your lover . . ."

"My lover! No, *Baron,* Juan de Vegas and I grew up together and are merely the closest of friends."

"I would not hold the past against you. But if you speak a lie, Madrigal, I shall soon know the state of your virtue."

She bit her lip in frustration and decided not to grace him with a reply. Let the arrogant fool stew, she thought wickedly.

Avoiding the subject altogether, she said, "I shall catch my death out here. Allow me to fetch Maria and my cloak, and we shall find our way home." He finally released his tight grip and took her back inside.

When the women were readied and their mounts saddled, Madrigal descended the stairs and was surprised to see Halconbosque still waiting for her. "I thought you had gone on ahead."

He looked at her still-damp form, and a dark frown covered his handsome face. "It would seem that you shun my warning and would travel again unprotected, milady. I suggest you put aside your independent ways and pay more heed to your own safety." His tone left little for her to say in defense.

"Sí, Barón," she replied meekly—too meekly, he thought.

Madrigal, with her maid, rode ahead of him, and he found he could not take his eyes from her. He knew that if the lady were less comely, he would have struck her on the spot for her open defiance; he vowed he would no longer be overcome by her charms and would take action to see that she obeyed him.

When they reached Castilla-verde and entered the bailey, Roderick assisted the rain-soaked women in dismounting and then turned to Madrigal. "I would speak with you privately after the evening meal. Now, go dry your garments." His tone, although weary, was gruff and dictatorial.

"We shall speak *now,* Baron," she replied acidly. *"You* sought *me* out! How soon you forget! I would have none of you save for the command of your king. But I am no dim-witted slave to become a meek possession of yours. In truth, you would be wise to look elsewhere for a bride!" She flashed him a scathing look and fled into the castle, but not before she had seen an angry snarl twist his lips.

Lord Jaime Castilla-verde watched the scene from the portal and thought it best not to speak with his daughter just then. He did, however, stop Halcon-bosque.

"Baron, my daughter is overly headstrong but will soon come around to more gentle ways. She will surely mature with marriage and motherhood."

"Old man," Roderick replied disrespectfully, "the banns have been posted long enough. Make your daughter ready, for we shall wed within the week."

Lord Jaime would not have said anything more to the brute, but he greatly feared for his daughter's safety once she married him. "I shall not tolerate mistreatment of Madrigal, Baron. If you cannot find kindness toward her in your heart, then there should be no marriage."

Roderick laughed cruelly. "Lord Jaime, before I seek my rest, remember these two things. First, we shall indeed be wed. And second, I shall use or, if it be the case, *abuse* your daughter in any way that pleases me. There is nothing you can do to alter her destiny." Roderick turned on his heel, leaving Jaime Castilla-verde alone to ponder the note of unadulterated venom in the younger man's voice.

The earl felt an immense burden placed on his shoulders; his serene world of a few months ago had been inexplicably changed with the sudden appearance of Halconbosque. The knight seemed bent on causing pain to his family—no, not to his whole family, he mused, but just to his favorite child.

Then Lord Jaime began to wonder why Halcon-bosque had selected Madrigal for a bride, even though her sister Elena was available. What possible reason could the man have for wanting to marry a woman for whom he openly displayed his distaste? Great was Castilla-verde's confusion, and the more he pressed his mind for an answer, the more elusive the answer became.

If Lord Jaime found his emotional well-being disrupted, then Roderick found his doubly so. As he reclined on the bed in the guest chamber, Roderick could attain no peace of mind, nor would sleep come easily to him. There was no pleasure in treating Madrigal with kindness or, surprisingly, in causing her distress. Even speaking to her father of abusing her had left a bitter taste in his mouth. But he was determined to strike at the old man where it would hurt the most, and the anguish he proposed to inflict could come only through Lord Jaime's daughter—his precious Madrigal.

Fatigue finally overcame Roderick and he dozed fitfully. Soon he was far from Castilla-verde, groping blindly through a dense fog, and beneath his boots a hand crept upward in the miasma and barred his escape. His father's face appeared in the distant mist through which the sun was breaking, his unearthly voice beckoning his son to come to him. Roderick tossed and turned on the bed but could not find his way out of the bog. The disembodied hand attached itself to his leg and pulled him slowly, inevitably, down beneath the murky vapors.

When he finally woke, Roderick's entire body was soaked with sweat, and he felt an enormous oppression. He flung his legs over the side of the bed and bellowed harshly to Renaldo, who was sleeping nearby. "By God, man! There you sleep idly while I'm in need of a bath to wash this filth off me! Fetch me a serving wench!" He hollered after the retreating Renaldo, "And be certain she has a civil tongue in her head!"

Chapter 9

Madrigal had declared a private war; there was no other word for it, Maria thought. Ever since Roderick's return, the lady had been intolerable. She had scarcely taken a morsel of food, and her already slim form had grown more lean and angular. She had even refused to heed her sister Rosa's calming words of advice. Rosa and her hsuband, Enrique de la Jara, had arrived two days ago and were now engrossed in the wedding preparations.

The elderly servant looked around the girl's bedchamber and sighed over the scattered pieces of precious china broken earlier that morning when Madrigal had had another tantrum. She turned her attention back to her mistress, who was still stalking the room in a fit of rage.

"And I don't give a whit for all the *gran barón's* gold—why, he's just an arrogant oaf! I despise him!" Madrigal cried while wringing her hands in front of her. "I won't marry him! He can go to the devil!" She plumped herself before her mirror and pulled her silver brush through her long tresses.

"You must obey the command of the king, and 'tis best you accept it, milady," Maria scolded, taking the brush from Madrigal before she could damage her lovely hair.

"I should have refused the night of the feast of San Juan, but I was so tired, and there were graver matters of concern that plagued me." She had spoken absentmindedly. "I could bow to the wishes of King Sancho more willingly but for the baron's shameful behavior at Montenegro, and with all the servants watching!" Her brilliant green eyes narrowed in memory of the rough treatment she had received at Roderick's hand. "If he had but apologized, or come to me this past week . . ." Her whisper sounded more like a sob to Maria.

"Teresa has found him an apt companion. In truth, milady, all save you find his company pleasant," Maria chided. Madrigal eyed her suspiciously in the mirror but remained silent while she continued. "You have only to leave your chamber and seek him out, child. Elena has been burdening him with tales of your tantrums. And she has even told him you look like a skeleton!"

"*Bueno!* Mayhap he will look elsewhere for his pleasures," Madrigal snapped.

"Milady! 'Tis no subject for amusement. A lusty man

62

would not find comfort long in the arms of a bony woman. And no matter what you may see now as truth, once married, you will suffer greatly if your husband has a wandering eye." Maria stopped brushing Madrigal's hair to answer a timid knock at the door.

Selina, one of the castle's serfs, came hesitantly into the room with an armful of white silk and lace. Madrigal at once recognized her mother's wedding gown and winced.

"Is it not grand!" Teresa exclaimed, bursting into the chamber on Selina's heels.

" 'Tis only a sore reminder of tomorrow's event, my sister. I see not veils and lace, but chains instead," Madrigal replied in a moment of bleak sadness.

"Lord Roderick has declared it proper for even a queen," the twelve-year-old replied, undaunted by her sister's imagery.

"Have I no privacy at all? Does he seek to choose the very clothes on my back? Lord above! The man's gall has no limits!" Madrigal jumped up and began to pace the cool stone flagging. "Well, I won't wear it. My mother would not wish me to don her wedding gown with a heavy heart—"

She was interrupted by the appearance of Elena, who pensively took in her sister's latest display of obstinancy while unconsciously stroking the birth scar on her cheek.

Elena dropped her hand, squared her shoulders, and walked to Madrigal's bed, seating herself gracefully. "A heavy heart, say you? Sweet sister Madrigal, are you so blind you do not know when you are well off? Come, now, try on the gown, or Roderick may deem it necessary to call off this farce."

"You bring a glimmer of hope, Elena. Mayhap if I simply refuse to be fitted, he'll return to Gibraltar and leave us to our normal habits!"

"No, milady," Maria chided, "your sister seeks to

brew trouble, I fear." The old woman had never held her tongue when Elena was about, for she saw evil in her very soul.

"Out! Out, all of you! I would speak to Madrigal alone for once," Elena shrieked, suddenly losing her icy control.

Teresa, along with Maria and Selina, grudgingly left them alone in the chamber. A dark cloud of despair settled over the young girl as she ran down the stairs and out into the bailey. She realized that most conversations were over her head, and therefore she ignored them, but the look in Elena's eyes was clear: Elena would like nothing better than to see the wedding plans fall to ruin.

Hearing the familiar ping of the smithy's tools, Teresa hoped that Roderick would be in the stable overseeing the tradesman as he wielded his heavy hammer and forged the necessary ironworks for the fief. The smell of horseflesh and burning iron reached her nostrils, and through the open shop front she saw Roderick assisting the smithy while they shod his great war charger.

"Baron! Baron!" she called out breathlessly.

"There, now, my little one. What is so urgent?" he asked while gently stroking his steed's nuzzle to quiet him.

"It's Madrigal—well, really Elena! You see, Madrigal won't try on the beautiful gown, and then Elena threw us all out—and she's in one of her black moods!" The young girl lifted her face beseechingly to Roderick.

"Slowly, little one . . . there, now, that's better," he said when Teresa had calmed herself. "It appears to me that Lady Madrigal has had enough time to accustom herself to her duties. Mayhap I've been too lenient with her."

"Come, Roderick, I'll take you to her chamber. She will listen to you. I just know she will." Teresa's face lit up with the prospect of Roderick's talking to Madrigal. After all, she thought, once Madrigal knows him as I do, she'll adore him, too.

Roderick relinquished the care of his mount to the blacksmith but would have preferred to remain in the shop, where he felt very much in his element. The hot odor of steel, the touch of fine leather, the crackle of hay under his feet, these things he knew and loved; he felt a comforting sense of familiarity around them. But a woman's realm and the soft, intoxicating aroma of her perfume always left him ill at ease. Still, he knew the time had come to seek out his betrothed and speak his mind to her.

The pair left the shop and walked purposefully across the wide bailey to the castle proper. Teresa's face was relaxed as she scampered before him; Roderick, on the other hand, had a scowl covering his hawklike features. By God, she'll learn to obey, he seethed inwardly. I've given the wench full rein to work out her restlessness, but this is too much. The wedding is on the morrow and she best be prepared! Then he recalled her plea of illness this past week and his wrath heightened further. Yet it was he who had begun the argument with his hasty accusations at Montenegro, and in truth, he did not know how to deal with her. Teresa had been carrying tales to him all week of her sister's behavior: the temper tantrums, the unladylike language, the unnecessary starvation. Now he reasoned that to allow her to continue her stubborn ways would be a grave error on his part; it was his moral duty to quell her rebellious nature once and for all.

They finally approached Madrigal's room, and without so much as a knock, Roderick walked straight in and interrupted the sisters' conversation.

"Oh!" Madrigal's eyes opened wide in surprise.

"Is that all you can say, my dear?" he replied while politely ushering Elena and Teresa out. He reclosed the heavy iron-hinged door firmly and turned back to confront his betrothed. He stood quietly, raking her body boldly with his gold-flecked eyes. She was thinner. Her lovely aquiline features seemed more prominent, and he thought her perhaps even more beautiful now. The sweet female fragrance of lilac reached his consciousness. He could not help noting that her small waist was bound by a sash over a thin blue linen gown that did little to hide her firm, round breasts. He felt a tightening in his groin that he strove to ignore, for his purpose in her bedchamber was most definitely of a different nature.

To Madrigal he appeared fearsome indeed, in spite of his good looks. Why must he break into my domain and then brazenly denude me with his eyes? she flared. I truly loathe him. A pox on him! She had nearly said that aloud.

Instead, she asked, "And to what purpose do I owe this visit, Baron?"

"I've tolerated your ill-bred behavior long enough, Lady Madrigal." His voice was firm and low-pitched. "And now I understand you refuse to be fitted for your wedding garment. I thought perhaps if I were to oversee the fitting of the gown . . ."

"Oh! You would not dare!" she gasped.

"Think you not?" He went to the door, and opening it, called loudly for Maria to come at once. Madrigal inched slowly backward until the granite wall arrested her retreat and she was standing in a shaft of warm light under the chaliced window. She felt at a loss; should she submit to this latest outrage, or should she claw his eyes out?

Maria appeared timidly at the portal, and Madrigal finally managed to say, "I'll try on the gown, Roderick, but only if you leave here at once!"

"No, my little swallow. I've submitted to *your* will long enough. On with the dress!" The angry lines in his face deepened; he thought she looked like a sleek tigress, ready to pounce.

Madrigal remained poised in the amber light, gaping open-mouthed at him. He crossed the space between them and roughly tore the sash from her waist. She felt frozen and trapped, then realized he truly meant to tear the clothing from her. Suddenly she brought up her small fists and began to pummel his chest with all the hatred that had been lodged within her.

Rather than feeling infuriated, Roderick was amused by her latest temper display. Nonetheless, he took hold of her wrists and held her firmly at bay, grinning openly now at her futile efforts and thoroughly enjoying the physical power he possessed over her.

"You find this amusing?" she stormed, her eyes tear-clouded.

"Actually . . . yes. Extremely so, my dear."

"Let go of me, you brute, you ox!"

He answered her insults by tossing his head back and chuckling loudly while slowly dragging her writhing body toward the bed, where he gave her a harmless shove and left her sprawled indignantly, wishing she had a sword at hand.

Seeing the genuine fear and loathing in her green eyes, he thought better of stripping her and teaching her a well-earned lesson. No, he rationalized, I shall wait until tomorrow's eve to have her totally submissive, and then she'll come to heel.

"I won't . . . I cannot undress before your stare! Please, I'll put on the gown—but don't shame me thusly!" She had misunderstood the look of hard determination etched on his furrowed brow.

"Lady Madrigal," he said slowly, "I'll not shame my wife-to-be, but do not try my patience again. I expect to find you grateful and demure at our wedding tomorrow, or, by God, woman, you will find me a formidable opponent!"

He marched to the door. She could feel her breath release itself slowly while she righted herself on the bed. Before he closed the door behind him, he added, "And consider yourself fortunate, milady—for watching a scrawny wench unclothe herself is not my idea of an afternoon's pleasure!"

Until that moment Madrigal had never imagined how deeply another's words could wound her very soul. The unfamiliar ache in the pit of her stomach left her shaken and bitter. With slow determination, she rose and faced the trembling servant; she wiped the tears from her cheeks and began to pull the blue gown over her head.

Oh, yes, she thought self-righteously, I'll walk to the altar meekly and even gratefully, but my turn to wound your pride is nigh, Lord Roderick Halconbosque.

As Maria nervously fitted the gown to her slim form, Madrigal became more and more convinced that the plan Elena had proposed only minutes before would work; by tomorrow night all of Madrigal's worries would be past, and Elena would have the man she so convincingly claimed to desire.

Chapter 10

Madrigal was quite taken aback when, on the day of her wedding, she finally emerged from her chamber and viewed the elaborate preparations that her family had made. She cringed at the obvious cost of the affair and said as much to her father, but he put her fears to rest when he explained that the expense was Roderick's.

It was midafternoon and already the minstrels were wandering about the great hall, snatching pieces of cheese and liver patés while backs were turned. The dogs strained against their chains, nervously yawning and stretching; servants rushed to and fro, toting silver trays of succulent meats and fruits and heavy wooden casks of wine. Great vases of fresh colorful flowers were placed near the door through which Madrigal and Roderick would reenter the castle following the brief ceremony in the bailey chapel. Behind a large oak table on which the mugs and casks of wine were placed, she spied Renaldo stealing a pinch of well-rounded bottom from a giggling servant girl.

Madrigal mentally noted that the air was full of sweet aromas and mirth; she had seldom seen such happiness at Castilla-verde. She was immensely glad that even the servants would eat well this eve, for such was the age-old custom of medieval Spain. The serfs had often gone hungry in lean years and the great hall had seemed quiet and oppressive. But now, with fresh rushes on the floors, newly beaten hangings on the walls, and polished silver and copper jugs, bowls, vases, and plates arranged tidily for the guests, Madrigal was suddenly proud of her ancestors and noble bearings.

Even Elena seemed invigorated and spoke kindly to the bustling serfs, who took her directions cheerfully. Both she and Rosa had an inborn flair for arranging the feast setting with grace and charm.

Madrigal smiled to herself, for if all went well this eve, both she and Elena would realize their most profound wishes. She felt herself being swept up in the gaiety of the preparations and began to issue helpful orders to the servants.

She was sneaking a warm piece of honey cake when Roderick and Teresa came up behind her.

"I'm relieved to see your appetite has returned, milady," he said sincerely.

"Baron, 'tis bad luck for you to see me before the wedding!" Apprehension played in her voice.

"Bah! Such superstitions mean little to me, Madrigal. One forges one's own fate. I place little stock in old women's fairy tales."

His voice was reassuring and he placed a hand on her arm, sending an odd tingling sensation down her spine. She moved slightly away and noted the relaxed charm in his face this day. She actually found him quite handsome when he allowed himself to be, but then she remembered how easily his features could twist into a dark, brooding scowl.

Madrigal saw that his hair had recently been sheared, and although it was unruly, the cut was nearly perfect. She spoke in haste. "And who, may I inquire, cropped your hair?"

He laughed "Only a fair, buxom serving lass, milady. And as you were indisposed, she also bathed me!" His golden-moted eyes danced with pleasure when he saw her reaction. He had managed to spark a flame of jealousy in his bride-to-be, even if she did not recognize the emotion herself.

"I suppose you think to bait me, milord. Well, this day I shall not rise to the hook," she parried. "Was it not just yesterday you bade me to be demure and grateful? Now, if I might take my leave, sir, I must dress for the affair."

The neighboring guests and distant relatives filled the small chapel with brilliance, their fine attire elegant in the column of multicolored, fading light pouring through the gilded, stained-glass window above the altar.

Padre Sebastiano, Roderick, and Madrigal's brother-in-law, Enrique stood sedately watching her entrance on the arm of Jaime Castilla-verde. The golden light turned her gown and lace-trimmed silk wimple the color of autumn wheat, enhancing her fine, clear skin beneath the folds of lace and sparkling jewels. Her heavy tresses were ambered beneath the opaque wimple; she looked outwardly composed and serene.

Madrigal's eyes found Roderick in the mass of color-clad bodies. He was attired in a fine surcoat of rich green silk trimmed with gold braid around the neck, his crisp white undertunic showing the long, fitted sleeves. In the red velvet cloak that completed his dress, he bespoke his position and wealth, appearing strikingly handsome and self-assured.

Kneeling before the padre, Madrigal could feel her small, cold hand clasped firmly in Roderick's warm one; the high-pitched Latin words flowed in and out of her consciousness, leaving her wondering if any bride had ever really heard them. Then it was over. The cherished vows had been spoken before God, binding man and woman together for a lifetime. Roderick and Madrigal stood and faced each other; finally, inevitably, their lips came together.

Although they stood properly apart, Madrigal felt a hot surge of blood pound in her temples when his lips covered hers searchingly. This was most assuredly not like the chaste kisses she and Juan had traded; Roderick's mouth was confident and strong, and her will to resist him fled rapidly. She felt his hands tighten possessively on her shoulders, and when his lips finally left hers, she saw a look of growing desire in his narrowed gaze that made her senses throb.

Perhaps she had mistakenly judged his aptitude for sensuality, she was suddenly shocked to realize. But she had entered into an agreement with Elena, and she meant to stick by her decision in spite of her fleeting wish to taste his mouth once again.

Only a few more hours to endure, she mused as they led the entourage across the bailey and into the great hall, where she was flooded with well-wishes and assaulted by strange, eager lips.

"You realize, my dear, 'tis a difficult task to stand by

idly, watching so many men have their pleasure with you. I feel robbed!" Roderick jested, tracing with a finger the ruby necklace at her slim throat.

"Milord, you overly flatter me, I vow. Should you not be making merry and dancing with the spinsters?" she asked cheerfully, taking note of how perfectly his lips curved.

"I suppose 'tis my duty," he whispered into her ear, "but I await only the moment when I make you my wife. Can we not put aside our stormy past now?" A smile tugged at one corner of his mouth.

"I suppose we must, milord—" She was interrupted by Elena, who claimed a dance with the groom.

Madrigal ate little and drank too much of the wine that was offered during the host of cheers and toasts. She danced until her satin-enclosed feet ached, and finally she removed the silk wimple, allowing her hair to tumble freely down her back in a raven mass. Roderick took note of her slightly intoxicated state but thought it best for her own enjoyment of their first union.

At last Madrigal was allowed to seek the privacy of the wedding chamber. As she entered the prepared room, leaving behind the fading but lewd cheers from the guests, she suddenly felt drained and exhausted and somewhat dizzy. She took a deep breath and looked into the reproachful eyes of Maria, who had come earlier to the chamber, not with the young girl's toilette articles, but with a small leather pouch containing a day gown and a cloak.

" 'Tis a dark and unholy deed you do, my child. I beg you to reconsider." Her face look haggard and saddened.

"Hush! Help me off with the wedding gown—I've little time to spare."

"And do you suppose the baron will allow you to escape him so easily?"

For a moment Madrigal thought to tell her faithful servant the whole plan, but she decided against it, for, in truth, the bargain made with Elena had been conceived in a moment of desperation. But still, she could not back out now; it would mean . . . She stole a timid glance toward the ominous, darkly shadowed bed.

She finished donning a light green linen gown and wrapped the dark, hooded cape around her. Where was Elena? Her heart leaped at the question.

"Hurry, Maria. Gather my belongings and stow them away, then meet me at the stable."

Once alone in the chamber, she began to fear that Roderick would come before Elena had arrived. She could never face him now. Her anxiety, however, proved unfounded when the door opened soundlessly and Elena glided in, a ruthless smile on her lips, her body covered provocatively in Madrigal's own loose dressing gown.

"Go, Madrigal—hasten," she urged while snuffing out the candles in the leather wall sconces, leaving only the dim firelight to cast deep shadows across the room.

Chapter 11

Roderick stood a small distance from the bedside. He gazed at the lovely girl's naked back and doubted that she really slept. He then proceeded to finish undressing and approached the bed, his heart thudding in anticipation of the long-awaited joining.

She looked soft and warm, her figure deliciously curved in the faint red glow of the fire. He knew a hot, pounding ache in his groin.

"Madrigal . . . come to me willingly and I promise

there will be little pain and much pleasure," he urged her softly, gently rubbing her neck and shoulders. Unexpectedly, she turned to him, keeping half her face hidden in the shadows. Her arms went around his neck possessively and she sought his mouth hungrily. Roderick gathered her surprisingly supple body into a tight embrace, pressing her deep into the covers on the goose-down mattress. She arched her back against his heavy weight and sought his manhood with her bared thigh. He stiffened as confusion overcame his lustful desire, and he turned her face toward him with a steady, slow gesture.

Not certain that his voice was his own, he said, "Madrigal . . . is this real, or am I dreaming?"

" 'Tis no dream. I long for you so," she moaned in a strange, low sob.

What had been only faint suspicion moments before became an agonizing reality. The shock of the truth hit him like a lance in the chest, more painful, more violent than any remembered wound. He sat bolt upright, naked, and drew her yielding body into the flickering light.

"Bitch!" he hissed through clenched teeth, the cruel snarl on his lips rippling an icy shiver along her limbs.

"God, Roderick! Please!" Elena begged hoarsely. "It was Madrigal's idea—she loathes you, do you not see?" She tried frantically to pull him to her again, but Roderick was sickened and repulsed.

"Get out of here, Elena—before I choke you!"

"It's this scar . . . is it not? This accursed scar!" she nearly shrieked, pulling her hair back and turning her head so that the blemish glowed redly in the firelight.

He looked at her for a moment, then answered her, measuring his words carefully. " 'Tis not your face that bears the blemish, Elena . . . 'tis your heart."

Cold, bitter rage replaced her heated longing. She

stood haughtily before him, her firm breasts rising and falling rapidly with emotion. "One day, Baron, you'll come willingly to me. You'll tire of her hatred and shrinking flesh and you'll long for a warm body." She dragged the loose gown around her and tried to leave with some degree of dignity.

He rose and went to her, covering himself with the linen bed sheet. "Not so quickly, Elena. Where is she?"

Elena knew fear then. She glared into his tortured face and unwillingly replied, "At the house of Maria's sister, Julia." She slammed the door behind her.

Roderick stood for a long moment staring at the door. It was not really Elena whom he blamed, it was Madrigal. He grumbled something unintelligible to the empty air and searched his mind quickly, suddenly remembering that Teresa had pointed out the small mud-brick house on one of their rides together. He only hoped he could recognize Julia's house in the moonlit night.

He donned his mail and boots hurriedly and rushed to saddle his mount, not caring whom he flung aside in his urgent haste.

Roderick clenched his fists at his sides and stared down at Madrigal's sleeping form while the two old women moaned helplessly in a corner. She had apparently fallen asleep immediately, for she was still wrapped warmly in a hooded cloak. By God, where is her moral sense of duty! he fumed. She actually dares to look like a small, innocent child sleeping peacefully!

"I'll be damned if the little wench will escape me this easily," he muttered in annoyance, tinged with fury.

His emotional state was unstable at best. Hatred mixed with desire; then another emotion, unnamed, tugged at his consciousness. For a brief instant he longed to cradle her in his arms, to ask why she feared and loathed him so deeply. But Lord! she had wronged him. His body tensed involuntarily; his features were chiseled marble.

"Madrigal! Madrigal, wake up!" he commanded, shaking her roughly.

She stirred slightly. Then her eyes flew open to see his wrathful stare. "How . . . how did you come here? I . . . I don't . . ."

"Elena kindly told me of your whereabouts." He reached down to grab hold of her, but she curled up and cowered in a corner of the narrow bed. He straightened again and saw the undeniable terror on her face.

"Do you fear me so much?"

"Sí . . . I do. I am not ready for marriage—I was forced into it by you!" she wailed, tears streaming down her cheeks.

"It is unfortunate that you feel this way, Madrigal. Yet I recall you were prepared to wed Juan de Vegas." He was growing angrier by the second. "And by all that's holy woman, I can offer you far more! Lord, the boy is hardly grown." From the look of horror in her wide eyes he knew she did not understand the advantages of being married to an experienced man. In exasperation, he said, "Our marriage is a fact. There are no more corners to hide in, Madrigal. I've waited long enough, and this very eve we shall consummate the vows, like it or not!"

She fell to sobbing, and in between her gasps, she moaned, "Please . . . I am not given to begging . . ."

"And I thought you brave! Come with me peacefully or I shall drag you out." He extended his hand for her to take, but she ignored the gesture. His glower darkened; no woman had dared defy him before, and she was his wife!

76

"So be it, my bride! If you will not come willingly to our bed, then I must force you." Then, as an afterthought, "Mayhap you fear I shall find you already deflowered. Is that it?"

Why must he always think the worst of me? she seethed. Well, I'll not answer the insult. "Go to the devil!"

He grabbed her arms and swung her struggling body over his well-muscled shoulder, ignoring the open-mouthed stares of Maria and Julia. He carried her out to his horse and slung her over the saddle, his rough hand on her buttocks to keep her still.

Madrigal was so dizzy and weak by the time they reached Castilla-verde that she retched violently when Roderick nearly dragged her across the bailey.

In answer to her illness, he stated, "If you had not drunk so much wine, milady, you would not now be vomiting!" But he allowed her to finish, handing her his handkerchief to wipe her lips.

Jaime Castilla-verde, cowering as he viewed the scene from the entranceway, hesitantly approached them. "I must insist that you unhand my child—"

"If you interfere here, old man, she will suffer far worse. Now, get out of my way!" Roderick lifted the girl up and carried her into the castle proper. Madrigal hid her face on his chest until they reached the wedding chamber and he tossed her unceremoniously onto the bed.

"Undress!" he ordered threateningly.

There was nowhere else to run, no one to turn to for help. She knew her fate was sealed when she looked into his hard, determined face. She could fight, scratch, and kick, but the end result would be the same. So she capitulated, vowing to be brave and to endure in silence the inevitable degradation. She came slowly to her knees, and keeping her tear-brimmed eyes averted from his intent stare, she took her clothes off, hugging the day gown to her nude body in embarrassment and shame.

"Stand up!" he demanded, impatiently awaiting the first glimpse of her promising body.

She did so. He reached forward and slowly took the gown from her shaking hands. She stood innocently naked before him, brave tears streaking her flushed cheeks.

"A bit too thin, my dear, but you'll do," he stated matter-of-factly. Yet he knew differently as his eyes traveled over her shrinking flesh, lingering on her long, slender limbs, her exquisitely rounded and ripe breasts, her creamy skin. She had a perfectly formed body.

"Must you shame me this way?" She wished there were some way to cover herself, but her hands could keep little from his intense scrutiny.

"'Tis no shame in it. We are man and wife." And then came the unanswered question that had tortured him these past weeks. "Are you untouched? Tell me now, Madrigal." His face had become an unreadable mask again; he braced himself for her answer.

"*Sí,*" she whispered, then saw his face relax into a lazy, arrogant smile.

He began to undress but kept his eyes on her, not wishing to miss her reaction. "Look at me, wife."

She allowed herself a quick glance, and upon seeing him standing erect before her, she felt like fleeing. He was a large man, unlike the slighter, darker Andalusians. Light brown hair furred his chest, arms, and legs. His broad shoulders tapered down to a narrow waist and hips, and his long legs were well shaped, yet lean. She dared another glance at him, only this time she stared in wonderment at the aura of power encompassing him.

"Does my nakedness embarrass you, milady?"

"Well . . . yes," she admitted.

He closed the short distance between them. "In time you will come to feel at ease." His voice was filled with infuriating self-assurance. He took her face in his hands, and slowly, gently, his mouth found hers. Roderick was careful to take his time with her. He let his lips linger on her neck and in the hollow of her shoulder, sending tingling sensations to her very core. Then he pulled her body closer, until she could feel his manhood, large and hard, pressed into her stomach. She tensed then, shuddering as if from the moist night air, and frantically fought the sudden weakness in her knees.

Roderick held his impatience in check and merely stroked her back and her long black hair. After a time she relaxed a little, letting weariness overcome her momentarily. But in the back of her mind she knew the worst was yet to come: the culmination of all her hopes and fears and fantasies.

When he ached to hold her, he swept her into his arms and placed her lengthwise on the bed. Her flesh burned from his touch and she stared up at him, confused emotions evident in her jade eyes.

"Relax, my swallow, and I promise there will be little discomfort." He left her briefly and returned with the customary earthen jar of oils, which he placed near at hand. She felt doubly chilled and naked in his absence.

"Roderick . . . I am not certain I can go through with . . . with this."

"Hush, sweet. Let me do all the worrying." He knelt down beside her and kissed the nape of her neck until she emitted a small moan of pleasure. He let his lips search lower still, arousing the upper flesh of her breasts. When she finally seemed quieted, he gently cupped a firm breast into his hand and traced a circle around her nipple with his tongue, playing with the rose tip until it hardened, then moving his mouth to the other breast.

She felt like squirming under his planned assault; her legs stiffened with an unknown anxiety, then relaxed. His mouth seemed to scorch her wherever it touched, and she found herself murmuring unintelligible words.

"Let go, Madrigal . . . do whatever feels right." His breath fell molten on her skin. She brought her arms timidly around his neck and kissed his muscled shoulder lightly while his hand traveled down over her hip and nudged her legs apart, caressing her flesh slowly. His fingers—gently, expertly, found her soft mound and began to stroke her sensitive peak with infinite care.

"Oh, Lord," she whispered when her insides leaped from his circular touch. He could not help but be entranced with her innocent charm, compared with the many women he had known. There had been village wenches and noble courtesans, all eager, all fully experienced in the art of carnal pleasure. But never had he been so anxious to taste of a woman as he was now, as he had been ever since he had first laid eyes on her.

She felt his mouth on her bosom again, more urgently now, while his hands continued to fondle her burning flesh. She brought her knees up, shuddering, then straightened her legs. Her breath came unevenly and she moaned uncontrollably.

Roderick took great care not to frighten her; he hoped that if he did not press her, she would reach a pleasurable height. Finally he heard her groan incoherently, and her body shook for an instant while she clasped him tightly to her. She felt completely at ease and wondered what there had been to fear. In truth, she admitted, his intimate caresses had been fulfilling.

Then she realized he was still hard and demanding against her, and she grew afraid when she saw him apply the oil to himself. Roderick, however, was aware of her mounting tension. He coaxed her with words of reassurance while his hand searched for her tiny opening. When he found it, his finger gently plied the inner flesh, trying to make his entry easier.

"Try to relax again, my sweet, and after a moment you will feel no pain," he said, placing his organ at the lip of her small opening and realizing the way would be difficult indeed.

She was terrified by his mention of pain and by how he was poised above her, like a preying hawk. Panicking anew, she squirmed and twisted until he could no longer find the path.

"Roderick . . . I'm frightened!" she cried while struggling frantically against him.

"Madrigal, I am only human. I cannot wait forever." In truth, he could no longer contain his desire to possess her. He pinned her forcefully under him, saying, "I do not want to harm you." He urged her legs apart with his knees, and finding the entrance once more, pried her open with his fingers, then worked his manhood upward until he had gained entry. He gazed into her terrified eyes and thrust once, then twice, fearing she would break. Yet she did not, and her body finally yielded the passage fully to him. It gave him no pleasure to hear her cry aloud, and he stilled his movements until she only whimpered.

"It's over, my little swallow. Nothing but pleasure from now on, I swear."

She felt him move again, in a natural, even motion that filled her belly, then emptied it. The pain had eased and was giving way to the rapturous ache she had experienced earlier.

He groaned against her neck. "I've waited a lifetime for you, my sweet . . ." and he jerked and shuddered and held her tight. He had never imagined a woman could affect him so; she was thin, too thin in fact, and she was contrary in nature. Yet somehow the wench had managed to crawl under his skin when he had least expected it. He wondered if her virginal state had not moved him to unaccustomed passion.

While Madrigal lay contentedly under Roderick, blushing slightly over what had just passed between them, she suddenly remembered her and Elena's plot to trick Roderick into taking Elena in her stead. She even remembered praying that Padre Sebastiano would be persuaded to change the name on the marriage papers. How utterly absurd it all seemed now! Yet how could she explain it to Roderick? There were no words; mayhap she should simply apologize. "I am truly sorry about Elena, Roderick. I . . . I did not know. I behaved in a foolish way."

"Never mind that now." He eased himself away from her and then said quietly, "You'll need a towel, Madrigal." The concern in his voice bespoke his innocence in dealing with a virgin. "Lie still." Going to the pewter washbasin, he retrieved a large linen cloth and tenderly removed the red stain from her thighs.

Madrigal was both embarrassed and touched by his attitude. Her whole world was displaced and shaken, yet she found the man lying next to her a different person now. Perhaps, after all, she mused, I shall endure his caresses. She allowed him to draw her against him in a gentle embrace; she fell asleep easily, her heart light with the joy of newfound womanhood.

Sleep did not come to Roderick; his mind whirled with unknown emotions. He allowed images from his worst nightmare to haunt his tortured brain. He had married the girl for one reason only, to cause her pain and anguish and then to send her back to her father, who would see his most treasured possession destroyed by his own bloody deeds of twenty years past. And there had been the deceit with Elena. Madrigal lay peacefully next to him now, but she had been unwilling to do her duty and he had had to force her to return with him from Julia's. Undoubtedly he would always have to force her. But wasn't that the plan? To give her a marriage of misery and abuse?

The darkness into which he stared gave way to deep gray; then a dim white light streaked unimpeded into the chamber, dispelling the shadows as it amassed strength. Quietly uncurling his young wife from his embrace, Roderick slipped from the bed and washed the sleepiness from his eyes. He dressed for battle and packed his belongings so that Renaldo would not have to disturb Madrigal. He hoped she would not awaken before he left for Gibraltar; his mood was ugly and he thought it best to depart before she rose. Something akin to regret washed over him, for he had vowed to pursue his plan of vengeance. Still, after what they had shared, he knew it would be difficult.

Perhaps it wasn't fair to her, he thought while descending the stairs, but such was fate. She had to suffer. Her father would pay a dear price for a long-ago act of bestiality.

Roderick found a serving wench to prepare breakfast, and then he and Renaldo sat down to eat the fare. Roderick's mind kept recalling his total enjoyment of his bride, her reluctant yielding to his caresses and her unbidden cries of pleasure. But he fought the memories and swore to dispel her charms from his brain. His guard had slipped this one time, and he promised himself that from now on, he alone would enjoy their union. She would receive no further tenderness from him.

Suddenly there was a scream from above, in the direction of the wedding chamber. His arm made an involuntary movement toward his sword, causing him to spill his flagon. Cursing under his breath, he flew up the stairs and down the dimly lit corridor, sword in hand. There, with the door flung open, stood Madrigal, hastily dressed and looking as if she had seen the devil himself. When she brought up a trembling hand and pointed toward the door, Roderick understood what had caused her fear. Affixed to the hard wood with a silver paring knife was the dead body of a toad. He turned his attention back to Madrigal and sheathed his sword.

" 'Tis only a wedding-night jest—done in poor taste, I'd say." He drew her, still trembling, into his arms.

" 'Tis no jest! 'Tis a sign of evil that the witches use to warn a victim!" she cried.

"Believe in witches' tales if you must, Madrigal. They are but ridiculous superstitions dreamed up to frighten naughty children. These castle walls, my sword, the birth of a foal—they are real. Not ignorant superstition."

"But, Roderick, you are wrong!"

"Enough!" he ordered while leading her down the hall toward the stairs. Damn, but women could be foolish! He had thought the Moors had attacked, from the way she had shrieked!

When they reached the main door, Madrigal suddenly realized he had obviously planned to depart without a word of farewell.

"Roderick . . . why did you not awaken me? I thought . . ."

"*Silencio,* woman! You may as well get used to it, my dear, for I come and go as I choose, and I am not accustomed to answering to anyone." His voice was deep and arrogant, so like the man she had grown to despise. Still the tears welled in her eyes in spite of herself.

"What of last night?" She had spoken before she realized that Renaldo was standing nearby. Roderick drew her aside while motioning his vassal to ready the mounts. Then he held her by the arms and bent to kiss her. He had only meant to give her a patronizing brush with his lips, but he found himself crushing her against his armor in a fierce embrace.

He pushed himself away with a strange look in his golden eyes. "No more riding unescorted. And try to improve your manners, my sweet. I'll return as soon as I have leave from our king." He descended the stone steps and mounted his great black steed, then whirled off into the waxen morning mist.

Madrigal ran down the steps and to the drawbridge, to see him disappear from view. She thought he had turned once to look back, but it had probably been a trick of the eye. "So this is to be my fate," she said aloud to the uncompromising void that threatened to engulf her.

Chapter 12

To be free of the drafty castle after days of rain! thought Madrigal. The sun had finally emerged from its blanket of clouds and the world was resplendent. The crops in the fields were bursting, ready for harvest. Orange blossoms from the orchards planted by the Moors saturated the air with their heady fragrance.

Madrigal was so happy to be outside and on horseback, she hardly noticed the armed guards her father had insisted accompany her. Maria also accompanied her, bearing the discomfort of the long ride with patient sufferance.

"Maria, pray do not groan so! It is not much farther to Rosa's. The coast lies over the next rise, and soon we shall see the tower!" Madrigal was excited; she sounded like the innocent young lass she had been a few short weeks before. She could almost believe she was still an unattached girl on a pleasurable solo jaunt, instead of a respectable married woman waiting for her husband to return from war.

The small party finally topped the last line of low hills and was struck by the fresh tang of salt air, cool and refreshing. La Torre lay just ahead, near the ancient ruins of a Phoenician tower for which it was named. Madrigal's oldest sister, Rosa, and her husband, Enrique, lived on this pleasant fief along the Mediterranean and had asked Madrigal to visit them before leaving for Galicia. Madrigal had finally convinced her father to let her go, as she desperately needed to be free for a time. He had seen her off with misgivings, fearing Roderick's wrath if anything should befall the baron's young wife.

The travelers from Castilla-verde found a gracious welcome at La Torre. Madrigal had always been close to her calm and dignified oldest sister and was especially fond of Rosita, her only niece, a charming, dark-haired cherub of three. Rosita threw herself on Madrigal with glad cries, thrilled to see her favorite aunt, and the party disappeared, chatting happily, inside the spacious castle.

While Maria prepared Madrigal's bath in the guest chamber, the sisters reclined on the large, draperied bed and gossiped unendingly. "And what think you of married life now, Madrigal?" Rosa asked shyly.

Madrigal hesitated, then realized she had no ready answer to the question. "I fear my husband is a hard man, but I have been with him so little that I truly cannot say. I am not entirely resigned to leaving my home forever, that is certain, Rosa. How will Papa get on without me? You know how flighty Teresa is, and Elena . . . well, if one of her black moods falls upon her, she is useless to anyone. I am really worried!"

"I know, little sister, but they will manage quite well, you will see. Enrique has promised to travel in that direction often and told me he will keep watch on Castilla-verde."

"Kind, thoughtful Enrique—you are lucky to have such a man, Rosa. Roderick is so cruel at times, and yet he can also be tender. Faith, I do not understand the man at all, nor do I understand why he was so determined to have me to wife. In truth, Elena was lusting for him from the first moment she saw him ride up, but he never paid her much mind."

"Elena!" Rose scoffed. "She would do just that. It serves her well. Mayhap this husband of yours is more perceptive than you think!"

"Rosa, it is unkind to speak so of Elena. You have never liked her, I know, but she does not deserve your scorn."

"*Sí, sí*, Madrigal. I am wicked to think so badly of her and I shall confess tomorrow morning. The padre will have a suitable punishment for me, I am certain, but nevertheless, it is the truth. Now, tell me, how long can you remain at La Torre? I have so many things planned for us to do. You will be as lighthearted as a lark in a few days!"

"Father said I may stay a week. He is so terrified of Roderick that he wants me home a full month before my husband is to return." She giggled. "Poor Papa, he is afraid he will be blamed for one of my 'escapades,' as he calls them."

"*Bueno*, we have time, then, *hermanita*. Oh, here is your bath. I must go down to the kitchens and make certain that lazy cook is preparing dinner. You will see when you have your own household to care for—it is a chore!"

The days passed lazily, delightfully. Madrigal relaxed, played with Rosita in the late-summer sunshine, and took long walks on the nearby beach. She loved the long rolling of the waves on the pebbled shore, the call of the sea birds, the cleansing sharpness of the salt air. She strolled in the orange groves with Rosita and crushed a shiny green leaf in her hand to smell its sweet perfume. The little girl led her to the kitchen gardens, and, like two mischievous children, they picked succulent vegetables and ate them while the juice ran down their chins. It was an idyllic time for Madrigal; her body filled out and the dark shadows under her eyes disappeared. She put the future from her and gloried in the delights of the present.

Rosa was busy supervising the servants in the great hall, where they were sweeping out the old rushes and replacing them with newly cut ones, when her *mayordomo* approached to announce the arrival of a visitor, a strange knight and his vassal.

"Devil take it!" muttered Rosa. "Here I am covered with dust, and the hall is in a turmoil!" She straightened her work dress and hurried to the entrance doors.

Roderick Halconbosque swept her a low bow. *"Buenos días,* Lady Rosa. It is good to see you again. I hope I do not disturb you unduly, but I have come to escort my wife back to Castilla-verde. Your father told me she visits you."

"Oh, *claro,* Lord Roderick, you are most welcome to La Torre. Madrigal is taking a walk on the beach . . . mayhap I could send a servant to fetch her for you." Rosa thought frantically. This handsome knight's hard expression belied his calm tone. Was he angry at her father, at Madrigal, or at Rosa herself? And Madrigal had thought to be home a month before his return! What had gone askew in their plans? *"Por favor,* enter and have a cup of wine while you await her."

"Muchas gracias, milady, but with your leave I shall fetch her myself. I have need to stretch my legs after the long ride."

"Certainly, Baron. The beach is but a short distance,

just down that path." She pointed to a sandy track winding through the grassy dunes.

"If you could provide refreshment for my man, Renaldo, and have our horses cared for, I would be most grateful, Lady Rosa. I shall return shortly with my wife."

As Rosa led Renaldo into the dusty hall he shot worried glances over his shoulder at Roderick. He disliked his master to be out of his sight for long. Roderick gestured to him in exasperation and turned to follow the path to the beach. He was hot, gritty, tired, and thoroughly annoyed at having been forced to travel the extra miles to La Torre to find his wife. That girl never seemed to be there when he sought her! But he could not be too cross with her this time, as he had returned early, and Lord Jaime had assured him that Madrigal had been accompanied by armed guards. Roderick hardly knew himself where the irresistible impulse to see Madrigal again had come from. He had planned to put her from his mind and battle the Moors with his usual single-mindedness. But he could not escape his thoughts of her; they haunted him constantly. Images of her naked body filled his dreams, waking and sleeping: soft, yet strong and supple, her white skin glowing in the candlelight, her round, firm breasts rising and falling with each breath.

And so, hating himself, he had made his excuses to the king, who had teased him for being an ardent young husband, unable to bear separation from his bride.

He rounded the last sand hill and saw her walking along the water's edge, her shoes dangling from one hand and her yellow linen skirt looped up around her knees. He stopped for a moment to observe her in this peaceful setting; she seemed to belong here, to fit into the natural background so easily.

He moved across the sand toward her while gulls

wheeled and shrieked overhead and the sea breeze caressed his parched face. She was walking away from him and had not seen his approach. Her feet splashed in the bolder waves that washed up to shore. He called her name, but she obviously did not hear him above the roar of the surf. Then her step faltered, and she stopped as though sensing something behind her. She stood for a moment, then slowly turned to face him. Her eyes widened in an expression he could not describe: bewilderment, apprehension, a sudden flash of gladness. Her face was very still.

Roderick thought to try lightness this time. "Well, my errant wife, I have searched you out once more. I am afraid this is becoming a habit with me." He thought he heard her release her breath in relief.

She smiled uncertainly, her lips curving up tantalizingly at the corners. "Why have you come, Roderick? My father must have told you I would be back shortly. You had no need to ride so far."

"I do not trust your father in the matter of your welfare, little swallow, so I came to escort you home myself. Let us return to the castle—Renaldo is waiting."

"Oh, let him wait! Who is Renaldo, your master or your servant? I came down here to view the sunset over the water. Walk with me, and you will see one of God's glories in this world!"

Her infectious spirit tugged at him; he found he could not deny her wishes. His heart contracted with apprehension—was he on his way to becoming a henpecked husband? But his feet followed her slim figure, his eyes taking in the provocative movement of her hips, her shapely legs and delicate ankles. The sight of her was like water to a thirsty man. He lengthened his stride to walk at her side, and they strolled silently along the beach for a time. Much to his surprise, he found himself taking her hand, almost shyly, but she only turned her head and smiled at him. The ethereal afternoon light was giving way to pink dusk; the sun was beginning to splash colorful streaks across the deep blue sky.

They came to a huge piece of driftwood, silvery and venerable in its steadfastness, and sat down on it to watch the golden orb sink below the watery horizon. Peace filled Roderick, a peace he had not felt for many years; he remembered feeling like this when he was a small child, before his father had been killed. His large, rough hand covered Madrigal's small one, and she turned her face up to his to search his eyes. Then he had no choice but to bend his head and touch her lips with his. Unaccountably, the kiss became long and searching; she made no attempt to move away but returned his ardor. His other hand came up of its own accord and stroked her satiny cheek, her flowing hair.

They broke apart briefly; then he reached a hand behind her neck and pulled her gently to him. They both felt the same slow, building passion, a passion that had all the time in the world to fulfill itself. They slid down to the soft sand, locked in each other's arms. His hands explored her face, her breasts, her slim hips. He traced the outline of her lips with one finger, then kissed them leisurely.

Madrigal's breath quickened and she closed her eyes, the hot flush of desire filling her belly and surprising her with its intensity. She felt no surprise, however, when he undid the clasp of her belt and slid her gown off. The cool air caressed her bare skin sensuously, the still-warm sand silkily. Roderick quickly removed his tunic, hose, and boots and lowered himself over her smooth form. He felt the whole length of her under his body; she seemed so small and delicate, so precious. She sighed and opened her eyes. "Yes," she whispered, "take me . . . now."

He entered her slowly, almost painlessly, and she

gave a low cry of relief, arching her hips to meet him. He rose on his arms and loomed over her in the growing darkness, almost withdrawing his instrument of fulfillment, then entering her, then withdrawing, until she felt she would scream from the intensity of her feelings. Her breath came in quick gasps and she writhed under his thrusts, her body reaching frantically for something beyond, something vital, something absolutely inevitable.

And then she knew what it was, for her body took over and blossomed, opening itself to the ultimate sensation, shuddering, exalting. As she reached the pinnacle, he also achieved the climax of his passions and spilled his seed deep within her. They returned to their surroundings slowly, as if from a long journey, to find themselves entwined on the cooling sand. They looked at each other and reveled in the closeness of their bodies.

Roderick smiled, a slow, warm curving of his mouth, then nuzzled her neck and spoke softly into her ear. "Now, my sweet, *now* you know what it is to be a woman . . . and to be *my* wife."

Chapter 13

Since leaving Salamanca, the party had journeyed across an immense flat plain bounded by low ochre mountains. Madrigal had enjoyed the brief trek through the scholarly town, for the fame of the University of Salamanca was widespread, even though it had been founded little more than fifty years ago.

The countryside had been monotonous outside Andalusia: brown plateaus, brown hills, brown plains. She was depressed by the unendingly sere landscape, relieved only by the towns they passed or the occasional winding rivers that cut painful scars in the earth's surface. It was entirely different from the lush green forests and hills of her home, its mood as spare and somber as Andalusia was warm and gay.

They had taken the less-traveled northwestern route, Roderick had explained, because it was shorter, and so they had missed the ancient towns of Córdoba and Toledo and the more colorful scenery of the north-central route. The boredom of days on the road was hard to bear; the heat and dust were constant irritations. Nor did Roderick help her mood; he was withdrawn and silent, avoiding her noticeably, except for the few times when he had entertained her with brief descriptions of his home and his family. He had an English mother named Gwendolyn, of whom he spoke fondly, and a half brother named Stefano, of whom he spoke little, saying only that he was "a good sort, but a touch ungodly."

Madrigal had timidly asked him once about his father, curious as to why he had never mentioned the man. He had given her a curt reply—"My father is dead"—then harshly spurred his horse and disappeared for the rest of that day.

After their meeting at La Torre and their return to Castilla-verde, she had begun to think her husband was a kind, tender man. But then he had had to leave her at Castilla-verde until King Sancho released him once more; and since he had come back from Jerez, his behavior had been cold and distant. And now they would be together for a long while, for the King did not require his services until late October, when the treaty with the Moor Abu Yusuf would be signed at Burgos. Until then, Roderick's time was his own.

He and Madrigal had left immediately for Galicia, a

long journey north through Spain. There were fifty men-at-arms accompanying them for reasons of safety, as well as a pack of train mules carrying Madrigal's belongings and many new items he had bought for her in Sevilla, much against her will: rich silks for more suitable gowns, linens, a few pretty trinkets she had admired.

Now Madrigal could not understand what had transformed Roderick back into the cold, hard stranger he had formerly been. What have I done? she wondered desperately. Have I displeased him? Am I cold and lacking? Mayhap he prefers Elena after all. She searched her memory but found no answer.

At night they slept either in a tent or in an inn if one was available. Often Roderick arrived to share their bed after Madrigal was asleep, or when she had just lain down for her night's rest. He would strip off his clothes, stretch out with his back to her, and quickly doze off. Twice he had taken her selfishly and carelessly, then rolled away and fallen asleep. After these incidents, Madrigal felt so ashamed and humiliated that she had sobbed into her pillow. It was becoming increasingly difficult to maintain her brave front. Even Maria had noticed that something was amiss. "What ails you, child?" she had asked more than once. But Madrigal had been too crushed to reply.

They made their slow way north, buying supplies in villages where Roderick's heavy purse of gold caused the merchants' eyes to bulge greedily. Thankfully, they met with no armed bandits or Moorish raiding parties, although they heard the peasants speak of such attackers in the more southerly areas.

After more than a fortnight, they at last entered the greener, more hilly countryside of Galicia. Roderick became animated, although his attitude toward Madrigal did not change. He was unceasingly cold and withdrawn, almost rude to her in front of the others. She rarely saw him now, as he was usually off hunting or scouting ahead. She spent her time talking to Maria, or to a few soldiers who seemed friendly toward her. The men were unfailingly polite but dared not show too much interest in their lord's new wife, for they feared his dangerous temper. They agreed among themselves that Madrigal was a plucky young thing; she never complained and stood up marvelously under the obvious inattention of her husband.

One afternoon the party crossed a huddle of hills, accidentally scattering a herd of grazing sheep and angering the barefoot shepherd to whom they belonged. He shouted something obviously rude, in a dialect that was foreign to Madrigal. Roderick threw back his head and laughed, then replied in the same dialect and tossed a coin to the peasant. He whirled his huge black charger around and galloped back to his entourage. Surprisingly, he pulled up beside Madrigal and began talking animatedly to her. She was so stunned by his sudden attention she remained speechless.

"That old character brings to mind the toughness of my people," Roderick chuckled. "None of your Moorish corruption in these hills; the people here are strong and independent. 'Tis a pity you do not understand the dialect—you would have appreciated his suggestion!" He laughed again, looking young and engaging.

"My ancestors led armies down from these hills to fight the Moors over five hundred years ago," he continued. "The last vestiges of the great Visigothic kingdom of Hispania emerged from destruction to claim our land from the ungodly heathens. And to think five hundred years later, I am still fighting Moors in the south because *your* countrymen are too weak and tainted to destroy the infidels!"

Madrigal was afraid to reply. Perhaps it was better when he ignored her, she thought. He sounded so impassioned.

"And did you know that my father's line can be traced back to a Visigothic prince of the Roman Empire?"

"I assure you, Lord Roderick, that my family can also trace its ancestry back as far as—"

He cut her off as if she had not spoken. "My mother is from England, Cornwall to be exact, and is from the hardy race of the Gaelic there. What a strange coincidence that my parents were each descended from a branch of the Gauls, related tribes, mayhap."

Madrigal was not quite sure who the Gaelic or the Gauls were, nor had she ever met anyone from a country outside Spain, except the Moors, of course, whom she considered somewhat less than human. Roderick's words and manner confused her anew, and she began once again to worry about meeting her new mother-in-law, Lady Gwendolyn. Madrigal pictured her as a hulking savage, wearing animal furs and sporting long blonde braids. She could conjure up no other image of an "Englishwoman," no matter how hard she tried; she only hoped the lady spoke Spanish.

Roderick now rode silently by her side, watching her face. She was so occupied in thought that she did not notice his intent gaze. Her lovely visage was serious, the thin dark brows drawn together in a slight frown. He wondered what transpired in her head these days, and felt a twinge of pity rise in him. Every time he was near her, his gentler feelings came to the fore against his will, and so he was avoiding her as much as possible to keep from falling into that tender trap. He excused himself hastily, cantering away to the front of the line to talk with the captain of the guard, with whom, on the whole, he felt more comfortable.

That evening they rested in a small village on a hillside. Madrigal and Roderick took a room at the local inn; scant, dirty, and flea-infested though it was, it at least offered a bed. Madrigal used her own sheets and blankets to avoid touching the dirty bedclothes already there. Roderick stayed below, drinking wine with the innkeeper and the captain of the guard. She could hear hearty laughter and the murmur of voices as she drifted off to sleep.

She was awakened sometime later by the sound of Roderick's voice. At first she thought it was morning and he was waking her for breakfast, but then she realized it was still dark and his voice was oddly strained. He began to thrash around in bed, breathing in quick gasps, muttering disconnected words. Soon she recognized the word "father," repeated several times.

"No!" his voice rasped. "Your head! Oh, my God!" His next words were incoherent. Then his teeth grated, making an unearthly noise. "I shall avenge you . . ." He flailed about, frightening Madrigal with the intensity of his nightmare. She reached over timidly to touch his arm and awaken him. She felt his skin; it was cold and clammy. Gathering her courage, she shook him by the shoulder, calling his name softly. He gave a violent start, then relaxed, mercifully awake and gulping deep breaths of air.

"You were having a nightmare, Roderick," she ventured weakly. "I thought it best to wake you, as you seemed so . . ." She did not want to say the word "terrified," so she left the thought unspoken.

" 'Tis nothing," he finally said. "It is a dream I often have. Pay it no heed. Now, go back to sleep. I shall not disturb you again. We have a long day of travel tomorrow and shall arrive the next day at Halcon-bosque. Get your rest." He turned his broad, bare back to her and spoke not another word.

Two mornings later he cantered up to her to point out the distant, gray stone towers of his home, then rode off in a cloud of dust. Madrigal felt her heart quicken in apprehension. What lay in store for her at Halconbosque, the falcon's aerie?

Chapter 14

With all the strength she could muster, Madrigal tried to stifle the tears threatening to spill from her eyes. How can he simply stand there with his mother, *my* mother-in-law, and not even introduce me or glance in my direction? she wailed mutely.

A misery-laden hatred toward him flooded her as she still sat sidesaddle, waiting for him to help her dismount. Her clothes were the worse for wear; dirt smudged her right cheek and her hair was dusty and tangled under the faded blue cloak. She had pleaded with him to allow her a moment to wash and change by the river Ulla's banks, but he had curtly refused.

She looked again at the *mayordomo*, a storklike, pale blond Englishman who, she later learned, had come here when Gwendolyn had married. She turned her attention back to Roderick's mother. Her beige gown was of the finest quality of silk, her headdress trimmed in gold filigree. She was bedecked as if for the entrance of a king, certainly not wearing the everyday attire that was customary at Castilla-verde. Madrigal winced when she thought of her own gowns in comparison to Lady Gwendolyn's.

Roderick held his mother in an affectionate embrace, laughing and jesting easily with Patrick, the steward. The three of them standing there, so effortlessly refined, so arrogant, so fair, further reminded Madrigal of her own inadequacy. She sniffed weakly, wondering if they would simply enter the castle and leave her sitting there. How *could* he shame her this way?

"Mother, I have a surprise for you," he said finally. "I realize she looks a bit haggard right now—but here, let me introduce you."

He came down the stone steps, looking infuriatingly boyish, and assisted Madrigal from her horse. The open hatred in her green eyes startled him, but he gave her a patronizing grin. " 'Tis quite safe, milady. Mother may appear severe, but she is truly a lamb underneath." Then it occurred to him that Madrigal was furious with him for leaving her so long in the courtyard. A wife must be treated with care, he thought with irritation.

"I cannot thank you enough for making me feel so at home!" she hissed, heavy sarcasm dripping from her voice. When they ascended the steps, her feet felt as if they were fashioned of lead; her brow was perspiring.

"Mother, this is my *wife*." He looked down at Madrigal. "Lady Madrigal Castilla-verde . . . daughter of the Earl of Tarbella."

Madrigal curtsied deeply.

"Roderick, she is charming, and I am pleased you have taken a young wife." Lady Gwendolyn turned to Madrigal. "Rise, my dear. I am certain you are weary and would like to refresh yourself."

She told Patrick to have a serving girl show Madrigal to Roderick's wing and make her comfortable there. Her manner was unfailingly polite. She was a handsome woman with a tall, slender frame, unreadable classic features, and Roderick's topaz eyes. A woman with but one son, who, when she meets his wife, says two words and then dismisses her as if she were a lowly baker's daughter! Madrigal fumed inwardly. What manner of heartless family have I married into?

99

"Lady Madrigal," his mother called after her, "when you have rested sufficiently, I shall see you privately in my rooms."

Arrogance! The family was diseased with ruthless arrogance, Madrigal decided as she was led up the huge stairs and down a long, dim corridor to Roderick's chamber. By the time she reached his rooms, and there seemed to be many, she realized the extent of the Halconbosque wealth. Everywhere she looked there were fine icons, gold-threaded tapestries, urns of silver and pewter, stained-glass windows, and heavy, hand-crafted furniture of impeccable and elegant design.

While she doffed her dusty attire and sank into the most luxurious bath of her life, Roderick chatted idly with his mother in her sewing chamber, a flagon of wine in his hand. "I'm afraid I've told my wife little of our family, Mother. Our marriage was a hasty affair."

"So it would seem, my errant son," she said. She was not given to poking her nose in where it was not wanted. In this respect, Lady Gwendolyn was English to the core.

"Have you nothing more to say? Come, now, Mother, I know that shrewd brain of yours." He grinned at her with affection.

"I have many questions, yes, but I am sure you will explain in your own time and way. Is that not so?" Her golden eyes narrowed at him; she wondered if, this time, he had gone too far. What reason could he have for marrying a girl he hardly knew? Yet the girl was a rare beauty indeed, and it was easy to see why Roderick had taken her to bride—but did he love her?

Taking up her needle once more, Lady Gwendolyn renewed her sewing. "She is a lovely girl. It was thoughtless of you to leave her in the bailey so long. I would never have allowed the insult, but I thought she was a war prize. Were you not my son, I would think

100

your upbringing had taken place in the stables! Where have your manners gone?"

" 'Twas you who said I have no genteel ways, milady. Do you so soon forget? . . . But wait until you see her rested and bathed! I fear your jealousy!" Roderick stretched his long legs comfortably in front of him.

"Your brother returns this eve from his duties, so go now and wash yourself, for we shall welcome your bride with a feast and merriment this night."

"Oh, yes, I forgot. The lady's family . . . her family had little gold for fine dresses and I hoped your seamstress could—"

"Naturally," she interrupted him, "she shall have the finest sewn gowns. She must look the part of a baron's wife."

"I may as well give you fair warning," he added as he tossed down the remaining wine and rose to leave. "She sports a proud temper and may throw the gowns in our faces. I had a difficult time persuading her to let me purchase the silks and linens." He laughed deeply, closing the door behind him.

Roderick made his way to his old chambers and found Madrigal dressed in her best day gown, the one he remembered from the morning of their wedding. He was pleased with her effort to impress his mother. As he watched the well-rounded serving lass finish braiding Madrigal's glistening hair, he felt a surge of desire, but also something else: a sudden longing to degrade her, to see her grovel at his feet with pleas of mercy on her proud lips. Why the devil did she affect him that way? he wondered bitterly. He knew the answer. It was her damn pride—the way she held her head and the quick flash of fury in her eyes when tears should flow instead. It was also because she was the hated earl's favorite daughter.

"Well, are you going to sit there staring at me, or are

you going to tell me where to find *her Highness* for my hour of approval!" Madrigal hissed at him, still angered by his earlier behavior and extremely nervous in her mother-in-law's domain.

"How dare you take out your vile temper on my mother!" he roared. "If you continue to defile her good name, I will shut you up permanently in the dungeons below! Is that quite clear?" He drew his brows together menacingly.

"Oh, yes! But, of course, I should have known!" she cried. " 'Tis perfectly fine to treat *me* like a leper, but when it comes to *your mother*—God, how I wish to be back at Castilla-verde!" Tears streamed unchecked down her cheeks as she envisioned herself rotting away in the ice-cold dungeons.

Why the devil did she have to cry now? His ire of a moment ago vanished and he tried to embrace her.

"Don't touch me!" she shrieked, shoving him away with a burst of energy, and turned to the mirror to pat her tears dry. Roderick laughed in amazement at the inner fire she possessed.

"I am . . . sorry for abusing your mother's good name. Truly I am, for 'tis you alone who angers me, husband! Now, let me be, and I shall find my way to her." Madrigal glanced at the dark serving girl, who stood in a corner suppressing a giggle, and added acidly, "I am certain this wench can see to your private needs!"

Her head held high, Madrigal swept out of the room and down the long corridors to the great hall, from which Patrick directed her to Lady Gwendolyn's wing. At first she thought to knock lightly, but her self-esteem insisted she confront the older woman more boldly, with a show of pride and dignity. Since Roderick had deemed her of high-enough birth to be his wife, his mother would have to accept her in that vein. She squared her shoulders and knocked confidently.

A deep-voiced reply came from within. Madrigal entered and approached the elegant woman with a firm step. She had the impression of warmth in the lady's private domain, yet she was certain that was simply wishful thinking. She curtsied.

" 'Tis kind of you to receive me, Lady Gwendolyn."

"Please be seated, my dear." Roderick's mother indicated the comfortable chair in which he had sat only a short time before. "A cup of wine after such a long journey?"

"Please," replied Madrigal, suddenly feeling in need of fortification.

Lady Gwendolyn poured. "I often indulge myself in a taste before the meal hour, although that will be our secret, *n'est-ce pas?*"

"*Sí.*" Madrigal was fascinated by her easy use of a foreign language and wondered just how vast her experience was in the world at large.

"I apologize for my son's ill manners this afternoon. He has always been rude, in spite of numerous whippings." Lady Gwendolyn went on for some time about Roderick's childhood, and Madrigal found herself relaxing against her will. "My son tells me I shall be jealous of your beauty, and I can see now that he is correct." The serene woman smiled warmly.

"You flatter me overly much, Lady Gwendolyn." But Madrigal was secretly delighted and amazed that Roderick found her beautiful, for he had never mentioned her looks to her. Usually he made her feel childish and awkward.

"*Por favor,* Madrigal, call me Mother now. I insist, for I have waited many a year to have a daughter, as I have only sons left."

"Sons?"

"Ah, I see Roderick has told you nothing of our family. 'Tis no secret. Lord Guillermo, my late husband, brought Stefano to me when he was but a lad and his mother had died. He is my son, for he is the son of my husband." She spoke with an open heart that touched Madrigal deeply. Such women were true Christians, and were few indeed.

"Yes, I do see now, Lady—*madre*. I—I would like to have a mother again, for mine has been gone a long while, and only my faithful Maria was there to raise me." Madrigal went on to tell about her three sisters and how her father had managed to see to their needs since the death of his wife.

Lady Gwendolyn smiled and nodded. "I feel we shall be *amigas*. I can tell these things. Now, my child, I must rest before the meal, and 'tis best you see to your husband." Then she added, "He tells me that if my seamstress were to stitch you a few gowns, I would find them thrown in my face. Is this so?" The lines around her golden eyes crinkled in amusement.

"I am . . . embarrassed that he would tell you such things. But you may as well know that I have a shameful temper and must confess often."

"My daughter, a word of wisdom. My beloved husband once confessed to me that a fiery woman would forever kindle the loins of her husband."

Madrigal gazed at the graceful lady who sat tall and erect in her chair, the waning amber light resting softly on her chiseled profile. "I would be proud to have your seamstress prepare a few gowns for me. *Gracias, madre.*"

Retracing her path down the long halls, she marveled that she could have so badly misjudged Roderick's mother. There was a reserved arrogance in the woman, true, but her self-assurance had put Madrigal completely at ease, whereas in Roderick the same arrogance emerged as unrefined severity.

Dressed in her finest green silk gown with a chartreuse wimple highlighting her jade eyes, Madrigal descended the granite stairs with Roderick. He was bathed and refreshed, his mood relaxed and jovial, his features handsome. After Madrigal had gone to his mother, he had dismissed the pretty serving girl and seen to his own needs. He grinned openly now, remembering his last visit home when he had whiled away the nights with the very same wench; her hands had been skillful and her body yielding. She had begged him for more, time and time again, until the day's first light. Yes, he decided, he would find another post for her immediately; it would not do to have her drop a vicious word in Madrigal's ear.

"I cannot imagine why you go off warring so often, Roderick. You seem quite happy here at Halconbosque," Madrigal said while taking his proffered arm to enter the great hall.

"True enough, my swallow. But 'tis a poor subject with me, and I do not wish to spoil my good mood." His face clouded momentarily.

"Of course, my husband. Before we join the family, I would like to apologize for the comment I made about your mother. She is a grand lady indeed, Roderick—a joy to converse with."

He searched her eyes. His mother could not have mentioned the vile association that the name Tarbella had for him, he reasoned, since Stefano and he had kept the truth from her; she knew only that her husband had died in battle.

He nodded. "*Sí,* my mother is a ray of sun, warming all who know her. I am glad you have seen this."

Before she could wonder at his odd stare of a moment ago, she felt her body being swung lightly around and strong hands clasping hers. "*Verdad!* A jewel—no, an emerald, I'll wager. Ye gods, Roderick! What a prize!"

"Lady Madrigal," Roderick said, "may I introduce my half brother, Stefano?"

She felt a hot flush on her cheeks as this handsome stranger perused her with his dark, compelling eyes. How different from Roderick he appeared. He was shorter than his brother but well proportioned, nevertheless, with black, wavy hair marvelously silvered at the tips. His features were a softer version of Roderick's, made exciting by his sensual lips. Whereas Roderick often reminded her of a soaring falcon, Stefano brought to mind a sleek cat calmly watching its prey but ready to pounce.

Roderick took careful note of the look in Stefano's eyes and did not mistake the color in Madrigal's cheeks.

"No words of welcome for your brother?" He sought Stefano's attention; his mood turned inexplicably ugly.

"But of course, little brother," Stefano replied while they exchanged knowing glances. "Come. Let us tilt the mug together and talk of your prowess in battle."

Roderick heard the old, familiar note of rivalry in his bastard brother's voice. Yet he knew there was no help for it; facts were facts, unfortunate for Stefano though they might be. Surely his brother had come to grips with reality by now. Mayhap in some distant age a man might be born out of wedlock and share in the family name, but that was not the custom in this century.

They reached the cask of wine, and drawing off a hearty load, tipped their pewter mugs and guzzled the homespun grape with gusto and cheer, each still trying to outdo the other.

The ladies watched the childish display with mixed emotions; Madrigal saw only the sport, while her mother-in-law saw a long-standing love-hate relationship. The men downed another mug and then another, until their speech was slurred.

At last Stefano drew Madrigal into the revelry and eyed her with approval. "Surely no gem so rare has sprung from this accursed land. Come now, Madrigal, what fairy land do you come from?"

She giggled at his flattery, nearly choking on a sip of wine. "No such place, I fear. Only a small fief in the south. My father is Jaime Castilla-verde, the Earl of Tarbella."

"Who?" he sputtered, his smile fading abruptly.

"You heard her correctly, Stefano." Roderick's face sobered; his look was scathing.

"But this is inconceivable! Surely not the black-hearted earl—"

"Enough, Stefano! The lady knows nothing of such things!"

While Madrigal stood there unable to understand Stefano's bewilderment, he eyed her narrowly, finally comprehending the dark and sinister act his brother had committed. It was Lady Gwendolyn who saved the failing situation by insisting they partake of the succulent food prepared in Madrigal's honor. The meal would have been a total loss except for her smooth, flowing conversation, which kept an argument between the brothers from erupting in full fury.

Madrigal ate in silence; her brain whirled from the confusing thoughts that threatened to send her flying from the hall. One thing was clear, however. Her husband harbored some secret reason for his peculiar behavior—secret only to her, she mused. And now the talk appeared to tiptoe delicately around the subject of her home. Perhaps they think me beneath them! she raged inwardly.

By the finish of the long meal, she was utterly exhausted and wished only to sleep. She glanced at Roderick. "May I take my leave? I am so tired, I fear I shall have to be carried to bed."

Stefano did not wait for his brother's reply. "Mayhap my brother would allow me to carry you for him!" He laughed coarsely at Roderick's scowl, his words slurred with drink.

Lady Gwendolyn rose. "I think this day has seen quite enough excitement. Let us all retire." She took Madrigal's hand and led her to the stairs. "Tomorrow we must begin to train you in your duties. You are mistress of the castle now, and there is much to see to daily, I fear."

"*Sí, madre.* My husband also spoke of your skill with horses, and I hope you will feel up to a ride."

"Marvelous. We shall ride together on the morrow." Lady Gwendolyn looked genuinely pleased with Madrigal's suggestion.

Roderick broke into their conversation. "I shall, of course, accompany you."

"You were not invited along, my son," his mother said, leaving him taken aback, as always, by her strong will.

A deep smile crossed his face. "Here, now! I have spent weeks training my wife to be demure, and already you seek to reinforce her damnable independent ways!"

By the time he and Madrigal reached his chambers, he was in an amiable mood. They undressed in silence, both exhausted from the hard ride and the day's tensions. Roderick snuffed out the wall sconces and tossed himself onto the huge bed with a satisfied sigh.

"Roderick," she whispered, "I think your family is delightful. I'm . . . well, to tell the truth, I am relieved." He smiled at her, the moonglow lighting his eyes. "Your half brother is quite charming and dashing, is he not?" Immediately, she could have bitten her tongue, for she should have remembered how easily a simple, innocent word could darken his mood.

"I know my brother all too well, wife. He is an unmarried man of questionable ethics where women are concerned. I would be greatly displeased if gossip should reach my ears where *you* are concerned." His tone was harsh, insulting.

"You think that little of me?"

"Let us say that half the bailey children are of dubious parentage—and leave it at that." He turned his back on her and began to snore loudly.

She lay there thinking of the events of the past summer; of her father and sisters and that long-ago morning in the forest when she had first seen the Baron of Compostela.

Before she fell asleep, she thought of the blue silk ribbon she had lost that morning, and she wondered if he still kept it.

Chapter 15

Roderick had been absent for several days, attending to his widespread fief. Madrigal felt more at ease with him gone than she dared to admit even to herself. Lady Gwendolyn spent a great deal of time with her, ushering her throughout the immense castle and pointing out all the large and small tasks which needed attention: the cleaning and sweeping to be overseen, the foodstuffs to be collected and stored, the laundering of linens, the polishing of silver, brass, and copper. So many more chores than at Castilla-verde, Madrigal thought; half the day was taken up simply by walking along the stone corridors. She hadn't realized how lazy the army of serfs could be if not supervised properly. No wonder Lady Gwendolyn was more than happy to have a new mistress at Halconbosque to share the heavy burden! She only hoped that Patrick would not be a problem; he was so devoted to the Englishwoman and so cold to *her*.

Madrigal busied herself within the bailey confines but wondered how long Roderick planned to be away, for Stefano was becoming somewhat of a nuisance. Not that she wasn't flattered by his attentions, but his excessive charms, in contrast with her husband's lack of courtly manners, made her uncomfortable.

Stefano indulged himself frequently in both wine and the fairer sex, rarely lending a hand to the administrative affairs of Halconbosque. Madrigal understood the tremendous burden placed on Lady Gwendolyn in Roderick's absence, but she realized that, thankfully, some areas of the fief needed practically no supervision at all, owing to the competence of certain bailiffs.

One glorious October day she and Lady Gwendolyn decided to ride out from the castle to enjoy the colorful autumn foliage. They had not gone far when Lady Gwendolyn began to feel somewhat breathless, so Madrigal escorted her back to Halconbosque. Then, assured that the older woman was comfortable, she rode out alone, knowing full well that Roderick would be furious if he found out.

As was her wont, she was drawn deeper and deeper into the natural surroundings, unconcerned for her safety. The fragrant, crisp yellow foliage, the crunch of autumn leaves under the horse's hooves, the brilliance of the sun on half-barren branches, held her captivated. She tethered her mount to an inviting oak and stretched out lazily under its boughs, basking in the dappled sunlight.

She must have slept, for the shadows had deepened when she was roused by a crackling sound close by. She sat bolt upright, looking cautiously from side to side. Then she caught a glimpse of a young man shouldering a deer shank through the trees. From his poor attire and wary attitude, she realized at once that he was a poacher.

110

"Stop at once, I say!" she called to him, swinging hurriedly atop her mount and ducking through the undergrowth.

The man did as he was bade, emitting a pitiful sigh when he let the weighty carcass fall to the ground. He stood there, eyes hooded, shoulders bent, and watched her dismount.

"Your name, serf!" she commanded.

"Roberto, milady," he replied obediently.

Her eyes flashed with fury at the obvious outrage. "What fief do you come from, Roberto?"

"Halconbosque." His voice quivered.

"Are you so daft as to risk your life for a taste of the baron's meat?" she asked increduously.

He looked beseechingly into her green eyes. "No, milady, 'twas not for me! My little ones are starving and my wife is about to birth!"

She thought he was going to weep and guessed him to be a bad liar, knowing that Roderick cared well for his serfs and vassals.

" 'Tis a lie, Roberto. Lord Roderick looks out for all his people," she said sternly.

"Come with me . . . you'll see for yourself!" His tears flowed freely then.

Lord, she mused, he's either a grand actor or sincerely in dire straits.

" 'Tis probably a grave error, but I shall indeed come and view your hungry family," she allowed, remounting and indicating that he should lead the way.

When they arrived at his rough-hewn hut, he said, "You shall see now, milady, that I speak truthfully."

Madrigal followed him into the dimly lit single room he called home. The smell of sickness assailed her nostrils and nearly gagged her. Two small children huddled terrified, in a corner while their young mother lay on a filthy straw mattress, moaning weakly.

111

"Dear God above," Madrigal muttered, seeing the wretched agony of the small family. How could anyone endure such poverty? She steeled herself and went over to the woman, now writhing convulsively on the straw.

"How long has she been thus?" she asked Roberto.

"A day, milady." He added, "The other whelps came quick, but this one is stubborn."

"Roberto, run as fast as you can to Halconbosque. Seek out Lady Gwendolyn and tell her I have sent you to fetch the midwife. Hurry!"

After Roberto had left to do her bidding, Madrigal swept the floor around the swollen-bellied young woman, replaced the lice-ridden mattress with her own clean woolen cloak, and mopped the girl's forehead when she screamed in agony. As for the small children, Madrigal wished she had told Roberto to bring food from the castle, but the mother's welfare came first, she reflected.

And then the full weight of this family's predicament fell on her. Roderick, their lord and master, who but a few short days ago had bragged to her about the fine condition of his fief, was responsible. "Ha!" she choked, her stomach churning with shame.

Each time the woman's pains came, Madrigal grew more convinced that the poor thing would surely die. She knelt down with the stricken children and prayed, more ardently than she ever had before.

An indeterminate length of time passed; dusk turned to darkness, before she heard a horse pounding along the path. She rose and raced to the door, hoping it was help from the castle.

When the large horse skidded to a halt in front of her, she immediately recognized Roderick as its rider, even in the poor light. What was he doing here? she wondered, wrapping her arms around her against the chill air.

112

He dismounted quickly and helped down a middle-aged woman who sat behind him. The midwife went inside at once.

"Where's Roberto?" Madrigal demanded, barely able to contain her disgust.

"By God, woman! Is that all you can say?" Roderick jerked her around by the arm, pinning her against the rough cottage wall.

"You—you unholy monster!" she gritted through clenched teeth, her hair falling loosely over her face and shoulders.

He brought up his arm to silence her with a blow, but the hatred pouring out of her eyes froze his hand in midair. Then he took her face in his rough hands and arched her neck back so far that she thought he truly meant to kill her. Madrigal struggled uselessly against his iron grip, loathing him more with each passing second.

"I hate you! You are a despicable devil!" she hissed.

He grabbed her hair and glared into her flashing eyes. "This time your wandering shall not go unnoticed. You shall taste the bite of my whip on your flesh and know that I am to be obeyed!" He tightened his grasp on her hair, causing her to wince in pain.

Suddenly she ceased her efforts to fight him off, and taking hold of her linen dress, she tore the delicate material until her shoulders were bared in the moonlight.

"Whip me now, you unholy dog! For on the morrow I'll be gone!" she cried hysterically.

"Damn you," he cursed under his breath while releasing her hair and pulling her to him, an anguished look on his face.

They stood locked together for a long moment, until he murmured with great difficulty, "Why? Why can't you obey me? I was called here in the black of

113

night—after hours of searching for you—can't you fathom my anger?" He tilted her chin up.

" 'Twas no fault of mine! You lied to me. How can you expect corpses to till your fields and harvest your crops? What manner of beast are you?" Tears of frustration hung on her dark lashes; her lips trembled.

"Corpses? What do you mean?"

"See for yourself. Then deny me the truth."

He took his cape and wrapped her in its folds, and they entered the hut. Roderick glanced around the small room, slowly absorbing the miserable scene of poverty. He had witnessed the depths of horror in his many years on the battlefield, but these inexcusable living conditions caused him to experience a helpless feeling of disgust.

Madrigal's stare was fixed on a small bundle of cloth lying next to the deathly ill woman. The midwife shook her head at Madrigal, indicating the still-born infant contained therein.

"And the mother?" Madrigal's fists were clenched.

" 'Tis in God's hands, milady," the midwife said, crossing herself. "I'll not leave her side this night."

Roberto burst in at that moment and rushed to his wife.

"There will be food and clothing brought to you by morning." Roderick's voice was heavy and strained. He said no more and led Madrigal outside, lifting her easily onto her horse and mounting his own behind her. They rode for some time in silence.

Finally she turned to him. "What manner of man are you, my husband?"

He looked straight ahead. The sky was streaked with starlight; the woods offered him their black depths. Some moments later he said hoarsely, "These people of the land . . . they are Halconbosque . . . they are my children."

The thick emotion in his voice echoed through the night and then died. Silence hung sadly in the air, broken only by the faint stirring of the branches and the tired beat of the horses' gaits. Madrigal wondered once again to what sort of man she was wedded.

Chapter 16

Lazy shafts of early-afternoon sunlight stretched across the cool chamber when Madrigal finally opened her eyes. Her body still felt weary, but her mind was alert, remembering the night before. Maria sat across from her, skillfully tatting a lace while eying her mistress.

Madrigal rose, still dressed in her torn gown and Roderick's cape. She yawned deeply, then sat back down on the bed. "Maria, there's something I must tell you. But 'tis to be our secret, at least for now."

"Sí, Madrigal."

"In truth, I suspect I am with child—nearly two months, I think." She waited for Maria's reaction.

The servant left her chair and came to her mistress. "I can remember when your mother spoke the same words—it seems but yesterday! 'Tis a blessing, for the babe shall bind your marriage!"

"No! I'm telling only you about the child, for we must leave this place at once. I cannot bear the sight of my husband!"

"But why? Surely . . ." Maria's face was wrinkled with age and dismay.

"Why? For he is cruel beyond measure—'tis all you need know!"

Madrigal dressed herself in a lemon-colored gown and paced the room nervously. She did not know how to escape the castle but felt that, no matter what, she had to find a way.

"Has this something to do with the argument between your husband and his brother?" Maria asked thoughtfully.

"What argument?"

"Milady knows I am too old for gossiping, but the serving wenches in the kitchens had much to chatter about today!" She waited for Madrigal's permission to continue.

"Well?"

"It would seem that the baron went straight to the hall this morn and found Stefano there. They quarreled fiercely for some time over the state of the lands, until Lady Gwendolyn intervened before blood was drawn."

"Maria, please make your point," Madrigal said impatiently.

But Madrigal was not to hear the tale's end, for at that moment Roderick entered the chamber and rudely dismissed Maria. He looked exhausted. His hair was unruly and his leather jerkin dusty, his face appearing old beyond his twenty-nine years. Above his right brow an ugly bruise was visible, confirming Maria's story.

Madrigal wisely kept her mouth closed.

"Have a bath prepared for me. Then return, for I don't wish a cackling wench to bathe me this day." He began to undress, tossing his undertunic and jerkin carelessly on the stone floor.

She went out to have warm water fetched; she felt cowardly for not telling him immediately of her intended departure.

When the deep tub was filled and Roderick sank into its depths, he called, "Come and wash my back, for I would talk to you now."

She went over to him as ordered, still fearing his black mood, and silently soaped his broad, muscular back. He relaxed under the gentle pressure of her touch. "I am shamed in my own wife's eyes," he said with no little difficulty, "for I left my fief in good order and returned to find my people starving. I alone am to blame."

Madrigal continued to bathe him in silence, thinking about his argument with Stefano and his open disgust with himself. Yes, he had said *he* was to blame, but, after all, the fief had been left in Stefano's charge. Mayhap the blame was not Roderick's.

"I see," she said pensively. " 'Twas Stefano's fault, then . . ."

"No. I placed too much trust in him, for he has nothing to gain here at Halconbosque and has no reason to care for the lands. 'Tis a sad truth that I failed to see until too late."

"But the least he could have done was to have the people fed!"

"Ideally so. But in recent years his interests have lain elsewhere. Drink and women have claimed his good reason."

She handed him a linen towel and watched him stretch out naked on the bed. As always, she was awed by the powerful look of him. There was much to sort out in her mind now, and she felt guilty for not seeing the true explanation for the condition of the fief.

"There's much to do in the next weeks . . ." He stifled a yawn. "So much to be done . . ." His eyes closed, and sleep overtook him.

Madrigal spent the late afternoon in the company of Lady Gwendolyn, then returned to her own rooms with a sudden desire to change her gown for the evening meal. She dressed elegantly in a soft blue silk garment, spending a lengthy time on her hair, which she braided and wound around her head, framing her face delicately.

Upon completing her elaborate toilette, she went to awaken Roderick. He heard her entrance and watched her light the wall sconces, her curves silhouetted by the candle glow behind her. He felt a tightening in his groin as she approached the bedside.

"Roderick," she whispered.

"Milady," he replied, startling her, then playfully pulling her onto the bed.

"Oh! You'll spoil my toilette!" she giggled, feeling a rush of pleasure course through her belly.

He brought her lips to his, cradling her head. He teased her with nibbling kisses, his tongue searching hers, then crushed her to him and took her mouth with heated passion. When at last he withdrew his lips, he rested his head in her fragrant hair, holding her tight. She returned his embrace while letting her hands explore the hard muscles on his naked back, then lay peacefully still in his arms, idly wondering why he did not pursue the game.

"Mayhap they await our presence for the meal, Roderick."

"*Sí, sí,*" he groaned, allowing her to rise and straighten her attire.

Watching Roderick pull on his tunic and jerkin, she thought it best to warn him about Stefano's condition. "Your brother is in an ugly mood tonight, I fear, for while you slept he drank overly much."

"I am not surprised. But pay him no heed, Madrigal. I'll handle my elder brother. Now let's be off, for I am starved this night."

The dinner went smoothly, considering Stefano's intoxicated state; they talked matter-of-factly about the oncoming winter and the necessary improvements to be begun the following spring. Unlike Castilla-verde, Madrigal discovered, this castle and its lands were kept in a constant state of change because of the keen interest of their master. No wonder Roderick was shocked to find a shortage of food among his people during his latest absence. As the conversation continued between Lady Gwendolyn and Roderick, Madrigal listened with great interest to the vast administrative details of the actual running of the fief. Roderick seemed confident that the serfs would see a change in their lifestyle before the week was out; he took the temporary backsliding of their fortune in his stride, now that he had come to grips with it. She began to take great pride in the way her husband handled his affairs, and toward the end of the meal she had formulated a vague idea in her mind, which she voiced aloud.

"Roderick, would it be possible to introduce some of the methods used here to Castilla-verde? If only the lands could be restored to their former grandeur, I feel my father—"

"Roderick? Assist your father?" Stefano banged his flagon on the table. "You make jest, of course, milady!"

Roderick had known that it would be only a matter of time before Stefano told Madrigal the truth about her father. He also knew that his bringing her to Halconbosque was not working out as he had planned. Certainly he felt a great desire to possess her, for what man would not? And if Stefano did not keep his mouth shut, she would have further cause to hate him.

"Stefano! I would have a word with you alone," he said, rising and leading the way into a private chamber off the hall, leaving Madrigal completely bewildered at the abrupt end to the conversation.

Roderick did his best to control the rage that swept through him. "Stefano, where my wife and I are concerned, I'll not tolerate interference!"

"Come, now, little brother, do you expect me to

believe your marriage is a coincidence? I would only like to know what dark plans you harbor for your wife." His words were slurred.

"You go too far, Stefano! What I plan to do with my wife is *my* business alone. I am lord and master here!" Roderick was furious that Stefano dared to question his motives.

Stefano's mind raced back to the brutal slaying of their father. He thought hard for several moments, then recalled that the Earl of Tarbella who had hacked their father to pieces had been Jorge Castilla-verde, not Jaime, the earl's brother. He saw the face of the small lad who had stood so proudly alongside him, too young to have remembered the given name of Halconbosque's murderer. He had nearly forgotten it himself, since the issue had never come up before. For a brief, fleeting moment Stefano thought to tell Roderick of his mistaken identification.

"Do you really know who our father's slayer was?" he asked.

Roderick's eyes widened at the stupidity of the question. He was both taken aback and enraged, barely able to answer him.

"I have not forgotten. My memory serves me well—but does yours?"

Stefano knew then, without a doubt, that Roderick thought his wife the daughter of the treacherous earl. At that moment he decided to let him believe what he wanted to believe; his long-felt jealousy of Roderick spurred him into wanting to enjoy a certain ruthless power over his younger brother.

Roderick spoke as if to himself. "For twenty long years I have lived in a nightmare. I have fought my enemies with a rage that engulfs my being, yet still I can see our father's face as if it were but a moment ago. And you ask me if I remember. Yes, brother, I do

120

remember." His voice came out ragged, touching Stefano deeply in spite of his decision.

After a short time, Stefano said, "Think what you will, Roderick. Destroy yourself if you must, but I won't stand idly by, watching you abuse Madrigal." Then he added, "You don't deserve her."

Roderick leaned back against the wall and crossed his arms to keep from breaking his brother's neck. "And I suppose you think *you* do?"

"Yes, why not? I can give her love and comfort—"

"And a name? My *bastard* brother!"

Stefano struck Roderick across the cheek, a forceful blow that brought blood to his lip.

Roderick did not move or uncross his arms. He spoke through clenched teeth. "That's twice in a day's time you have struck me, Stefano. I would advise you to think hard on doing that again, for the next time will see you to an early grave."

Stefano did not for a minute doubt Roderick's ability to keep his word. He also knew he had baited his brother and kindled a spark of jealousy in him, the knowledge of which surprised Stefano.

"So be it, Roderick. I do not wish to quarrel with you over the girl or her father. 'Tis your affair and not worth forfeiting my life over." He turned to leave, then added with deep sincerity, "I meant what I said, though. Do not harm Madrigal."

Roderick was not angry for long about the argument; they had fought before. Nevertheless, he wondered just how much Stefano cared for his wife. And had she given him reason to hope? He dismissed the idea temporarily and pondered on Stefano's prospects for the future. The man would have to be given some responsibilities at Halconbosque, for he was surely suffering from drink and lassitude.

When Madrigal saw the caked blood on Roderick's

chin, she started to rise and go to him. A look of distaste for Stefano crossed her face, but he seemed not to care, for he had seated himself across the hall and was busily engaged in pinching a young, full-bosomed serving wench. Lady Gwendolyn arrested Madrigal with a hand, knowing that Roderick woud scoff at the fuss.

"Be seated, my son," she ordered. "'Tis not my wont to interfere, but I have lost three sons and two daughters before they could walk. I say nary a word when you go to battle, nor when you travel about this danger-ridden land. But here, at Halconbosque, I will *not* tolerate these quarrels, for often they end in bloodshed."

"*Sí, madre.* I shall respect your wishes, as I have always done." He smiled at her with ease, charming his mother but never fooling her.

Madrigal felt that Lady Gwendolyn had expressed her own feelings exactly. She was amazed by the truth, for so often in the past she had secretly told herself that he could be killed and she wouldn't care a whit, but now, hearing his mother's words, she felt strangely apprehensive for Roderick.

Roderick and Madrigal took their leave. The day had been unsettling, and they both were physically and mentally exhausted. When they reached their chambers, Madrigal went straight to the towel stand and returned with a cloth to wipe his cut. His reaction was unexpected. He took the cloth rather roughly from her, and holding it to his cheek, moved to his favorite chair and stared mutely out the chaliced window into the silent night.

Madrigal went to her rest that night alone. When she turned on her side, she could almost feel his topaz eyes boring into her back.

He had indeed altered his position and was staring at her prone form. He stretched out his long, sinewy legs and folded his arms, his eyes never leaving her. She looked small and slight under the coverlet, he mused, feeling the familiar tightening in his groin. When she was with him, he found it hard to be angered for long with anything she said or did, but he was certain that in a short time the thrall of her body would fade; then, mayhap, he would send her back to her father. First, however, he would break her damnable spirit and bring her to her knees.

He closed his eyes, envisioning the look on Castilla-verde's face when he saw his beautiful, plucky daughter looking old and haggard beyond her years. Perhaps, Roderick thought, he would leave a few permanent marks on her body as a fixed reminder of his loathing for the name Castilla-verde.

He cursed under his breath, wondering what spell had been placed on him to cause this hellish ache in his groin whenever she was near.

Chapter 17

Roderick's mood had greatly improved: Madrigal saw this in the way he smiled, in his enjoyment of his meals, in his more relaxed demeanor with his family. He had been enormously busy for days now, ever since the incident with Roberto; thankfully, his wife had survived. The men-at-arms were hunting game for the serfs; the grain in the storehouses was measured out fairly so that all families would have bread for the winter. Tanned hides and rough woolen cloth were apportioned in accordance with the number of people in each family. Madrigal was amazed at her husband's limitless energy, at his ease in handling problems. Here was another side of this enigmatic man that she had never seen—the lord of the manor, in charge of every detail of the complicated world that was his fiefdom, and responsible for every life therein.

Stefano kept very much in the background but met them for meals in the great hall, where he put on a bold front to Roderick, who was coldly polite to him.

Lady Gwendolyn was obviously unhappy with the tension between them, and later admitted this to her daughter-in-law as the two women were sewing gold braid and tiny seed pearls on Madrigal's new burnt orange gown. She dropped her work in her lap and sighed.

"My hands are becoming stiff with age. It is hard to grow old alone, but mostly I fear for my two boys. When I die . . ."

"*Madre!* How can you speak of dying? Why, you are yet strong and healthy and full of life. Do not tempt fate by saying such things."

"Oh, Madrigal, my passing will not be tomorrow, but one of these years it will come. I am afraid only for my boys, that they will destroy each other as did Cain and Abel. Roderick is so hotheaded and Stefano so bitter. They quarrel dreadfully, they always have, but yet I know they love each other. It worries me."

"You must rest your mind. They are grown men and will surely come to some solution. We shall pray for guidance, and mayhap, with *two* women here to show them the gentler ways—who knows?"

Lady Gwendolyn laughed. "Yes, perhaps you are right, my child, but in any case, your presence is a great comfort to me."

Madrigal looked at the lovely woman in gratitude; she felt she had at last found the mother she had lacked all her life.

They sewed in silence for a time, but presently Madrigal began to giggle.

"What is it, child?" her mother-in-law asked.

"Something has just struck me as comical. Here I sit, stitching so carefully on this beautiful gown, and when it is finished, I doubt that I will even fit into it anymore!" Her voice warbled with laughter.

"What are you saying, Madrigal? Do I understand you correctly? Are you . . .?"

"Yes," Madrigal answered, looking down at her lap. "I do believe so. I have missed my time twice now."

"Why, 'tis grand news! Have you told my son?"

"No." Her voice held a note of alarm. "Please do not tell him. I shall do it in my own good time."

"Certainly, Madrigal. I would never deprive you of the pleasure of telling your husband you are to bear him a child. I shall keep my own counsel."

That evening the meal was served in an atmosphere of generally high spirits. Stefano had been set to the task of directing the hunters and had applied himself energetically. He looked tan from his expeditions and was in a good mood, regaling the others with a tale of a great boar he had outwitted that very day. Madrigal shuddered, remembering the fetid odor of the boar she had faced that long-ago morning. She looked across at Roderick, unable to believe that so much time had passed and now she was wed to her rescuer and about to bear him a child. She was so deep in thought that she heard only the end of Roderick's sentence.

". . . and so, *madre,* I think I will be able to visit Santiago de Compostela soon to take care of some business there. I must see David ben Avrahim—he will have the yearly tithes for me."

Madrigal snapped to attention instantly. "Oh, Roderick, are you going to Santiago? It has always been a dream of mine to pray in the church of Santiago. May I accompany you?"

Lady Gwendolyn looked doubtful. "Mayhap you should not, child. " 'Tis a rough road . . ."

"Nonsense, Mother, she is as tough as a cat. If she wishes, she can accompany me. She may well enjoy the sights of the city." Roderick's words surprised Madrigal; she had steeled herself for a battle of wills. This was too easy!

"We shall be sorry to lose your charming company while you are gone, Lady Madrigal. These old stone walls will be as lonely and cold as they were before you came." Stefano reached over to touch her hand, all the while looking at her soulfully.

Madrigal withdrew her hand as unobtrusively as possible as she heard Roderick's words, low and angry. "Never fear, Stefano, you have Carlota to amuse you—that is, until her belly swells too much to allow you between her thighs!"

Stefano merely chortled and turned back to his silver goblet, to empty it and fill it once again.

So, thought Madrigal, it is to be a truce between us, an armed truce to be sure, but mayhap better than open warfare. Roderick had not seemed to desire her lately in a physical sense, but this did not bother her very much, since she had been very tired and bilious in the mornings, no doubt because of her pregnancy. Otherwise, she could tell that Roderick was pleased she got along with Lady Gwendolyn and took some of the burden of managing the castle from her aging shoulders. He was a strange one, though, one moment smiling and warm, then suddenly changing to cold antipathy, as if he had forgotten for a moment to keep up his wall of hostility.

That night in their chambers, however, she looked so young, so happy, that he could not resist giving her a brief kiss on her cheek. Somehow his lips met hers instead. Had she turned her head on purpose? His wonder was wiped away by the feel of her soft, warm mouth, and he lost himself in a long, hungry, searching kiss. He felt her arms slide around his neck and hold him, but surprise was gone, replaced by a raging desire to explore every inch of her body; it had been so long since he had allowed himself to be vulnerable to her delights.

"Oh, Roderick," she breathed, clinging to his tall form. He kissed her again, deeply, then picked her up easily and carried her to the bed. Almost savagely, he pulled off her belt and loosened her dress, sliding it down her body and casting it aside. He knelt next to her on the bed, then lowered his head to kiss her belly, then each breast, then her throat, until she moaned and writhed with pleasure. He undressed impatiently, tossing his clothing atop hers. She lay quietly on the bed, her round breasts rising and falling rapidly. He lowered himself and she rose to meet him, thrusting with her hips in the age-old rhythm of love. They moved together urgently, molded into one by passion, and she felt his hot seed spill into her an instant before her body took over, soaring on the surge of a mighty wave.

Afterward they lay entwined, breathless, and damp with sweat. She turned her head to nestle into his neck and smiled to herself, a secretive, fulfilled woman's smile. As she drifted off to sleep she heard him whisper, "My swallow," and felt him gently kiss the top of her head.

But the bliss of the night faded into a gray and threatening morning. Roderick was infuriatingly reserved, avoiding her whenever possible, but polite when they were thrown together. She was spun into confusion again. What manner of man *was* he, to make sweet love to her one moment and ignore her the next? She grew weary of her constant agonizing over the situation, and thought that if it persisted, she would be forced to do more than merely present a bold front to him.

But this problem and the proposed trip to Santiago

de Compostela had to be put aside for another time. That afternoon the impending storm brought, not rain, but an unexpected guest to Halconbosque—none other than Elena!

Chapter 18

If Madrigal was surprised to find Elena at Halconbosque, Roderick was no less so. But then he recalled that she had pleaded with King Sancho to allow her to seek out introductions to some of the noblemen at court. And since the Gibraltar campaign was now at rest, King Sancho had traveled north to hold court, so Elena's presence on Roderick's doorstep was not without reason.

Madrigal, having quelled her initial shock at seeing her sister, became unduly concerned for her father's welfare at Castilla-verde. Seated at one end of the massive dining-hall table, she expressed her trepidation. "Elena, I'm pleased to see you here, of course, but what of Papa?"

"Father is fine, I assure you. Did you think I would stay forever in that Godforsaken land?" She sipped from a heavy flagon of wine, handed to her by the ever-present Patrick.

"No. I know how ardently you dislike the remoteness of Castilla-verde. I only worry over Papa, 'tis all."

Roderick sauntered over to Elena, leaning his thigh against the wooden table, and chatted idly about the recent court gossip.

Lady Gwendolyn expressed the usual words of amazement at the likeness of the two sisters, but Madrigal hardly heard her, for she was wondering about the apparent good rapport between her husband

and Elena. She did not know that Elena had spent hours smoothing Roderick's ruffled feathers before he and Madrigal had departed for Halconbosque. Nor did she know that he had accepted Elena's effusive apology for her behavior on the wedding night, albeit with reservations.

He had never mentioned that night, Madrigal realized suddenly, picturing Roderick and Elena alone in the wedding chamber at Castilla-verde. For the first time it occurred to her that perhaps he and Elena had taken their pleasure before he had retrieved her from Julia's. The idea was not at all unreasonable. In fact, she thought, seething inwardly, I shall come right out and ask the arrogant knave for the truth!

The heavy oak doors swung open, and Stefano entered the hall with a grand flourish.

"He looks absolutely dashing," Madrigal exclaimed aloud, causing heads to turn in his direction. Stefano indeed appeared the picture of health, having ceased his heavy drinking several days ago.

"Ye gods, what's this?" he gasped when his eyes rested on Elena.

The introductions were made while Stefano perched himself on the other side of Elena, leaving her cheerful and breathless from the attentions of two extremely virile men.

Madrigal suddenly rose, and heading toward the stairs, said, "If you'll excuse me, I have a raging headache and shall seek my rest."

In the privacy of her chamber, she dismissed Maria curtly and began to pace up and down, awaiting her husband's arrival. She stopped in front of the mirror more than once to view her figure, pulling at her rose linen dress and expressing dismay at her slightly rounded belly.

She grew bored and anxious, finally sitting down to stitch. Soon after Roderick came in. He had drunk his fair share of wine, for he looked carefree and wore an infuriating smirk on his face.

"I trust your headache has gone, milady," he commented while seating himself across from her, his long, muscular leg swung casually over the arm of the chair.

"For what it matters, yes." Her green eyes flashed sparks at him while she absentmindedly brushed a stray hair from her brow.

He watched her face pensively as she stabbed savagely at her tapestry. How unlike Elena, he thought, somewhat pleased with her obvious display of jealousy. Madrigal's innocence was so apparent.

She threw down her sewing and went to the window, her back turned to his gaze.

"Stefano's quite taken with Elena. Does that please you?" he asked casually.

"Elena's place is with our father, not traipsing about Spain," she remarked acidly.

"What is this great love for your father? At least Elena sees him for what he is." His face darkened momentarily.

She whirled around, her features twisted with anguish. "But of course! You and Elena hold yourselves above him because he's not as clever or worldly as you! I won't have you speak of him this way! Do you hear?"

He jerked himself out of the chair and crossed the room, grabbing her none too gently by the shoulders. "I'll speak any way I wish, milady! If you but held your husband in half the esteem you seem to hold your father—"

"Unhand me! I love my father, he's kind and gentle—something *you* wouldn't know about!" She shoved him away, her fury threatening to overwhelm her. "Leave me be! I cannot abide your nearness! Go seek out Elena!" Her voice was almost a shriek.

"So 'tis that. You're not jealous, are you, my sweet?

Did you know that Elena told me I would seek her out one day when I tired of your coldness? You'd like that—'twould be reason enough to spurn me!" His face was dark and unreadable, sending a chill up her spine.

"Yes," she murmured. "It wouldn't be the first time, would it?"

"What are you saying?" His golden gaze narrowed.

She squared her shoulders and glared at him. "You bedded her—on our wedding night—and I was daft enough to let you take my virginity on the same soiled linen where you and she—"

He struck her then, for the first time. Her head reeled sideways from the stinging slap, but she managed to hiss, "Does milord feel better now?"

"Damn you, Madrigal!" He grabbed her again, causing her to bring her hands up to her face in defense. "It was *you*, woman, who sent her to my bed!"

"I hate you, Roderick!" she cried before he could deny the lie about Elena and himself.

"Hate me if you will"—his voice was suddenly hoarse—"but you'll lie under me or, by God, I'll make your life a misery!" His hand tore the front of her gown while she fought him desperately. He stripped her totally, bruising her flesh when she sought to protect herself. She flailed him and swore at him when he carried her, naked and terrified, to the bed, tossing her roughly onto the quilts. He stood over her, a strange look of determination on his face as he undressed.

"This is rape—you've no right!"

"Exactly, milady," he replied viciously as he snatched her arms over her head and lowered his powerful body onto hers.

He neither kissed her nor touched her anywhere with his hands. He merely ravaged her. She wept, both from pain and from humiliation, her flesh shrinking from his wine-laden breath.

And then it was over, quickly. He rose and viewed

the scene, a bitter taste of bile rising to his mouth when he saw her shivering on the bed, her flesh bruised, and red splotches rising on her delicate skin. A sweeping feeling of shame and satisfaction coursed through him.

She lay there mutely for some moments before pulling the coverlet over her trembling body; then she spoke. "You are well versed in the art of rape. I trust it comes from years of ravishing and pillaging the towns—"

"*Dios!* Stop it, Madrigal! Do you think I enjoyed it?" His heart lurched in his chest. Did she think him that inhuman? "I only meant to teach you a lesson, not to hurt you," he attempted to explain.

"Well, you failed! Utterly! You're not to touch me again—*ever!* For I will kill myself! I swear I will!" she cried pathetically.

He sat down on the bed and groped for her hand. "Come, now, I'm not such a brute. Please stop shaking, and let's join the others for the meal. You'll feel much better."

How can he be so insanely arrogant? she thought wildly. I speak of killing myself and he thinks only of the evening meal! "I'll not be joining the festivities!" she hissed at him.

"You will accompany me, Madrigal." His voice was stern now. "Just remember that you're my wife and I'll see you obedient, or else . . ."

"Or else you'll beat me until I am? Now I really know what a monster I've wed! All right, husband," she said, swinging herself from the bed under his hard stare, "I'll join you ever so meekly!" Her words dripped with heavy sarcasm, and she vowed never to forgive him for his brutal attack.

On their way down the long corridors she was surprised that her appearance was as serene and tidy as it was. She had donned a flowing violet silk gown and pulled her hair loosely around her face, covering the

132

ugly red mark on her cheek quite nicely. She remembered Roderick's touch when he had helped her finish the task of hiding the bruise. Her eyes had refused to meet his, but still he had let his fingers linger on her face for an unnecessary moment.

She walked ahead of him a few steps, her figure visible in the alternating light and darkness of the candlelit halls. He winced on noticing that she seemed to move somewhat stiffly, probably from the soreness caused by his attack, he thought. And yet, he admitted to himself, he had derived a perverse sort of pleasure in exerting his strength and power over her. How had she managed to bring out his worst aspects and make him commit, and actually enjoy, an act as unchivalrous as rape?

For the meal, Madrigal sat with Stefano on her left and Lady Gwendolyn at the head of the table. Stefano was in his element this evening, chatting away all through the feast with charm and wit. Madrigal found herself swept into the cheerful banter and began to relax, allowing Stefano to flirt outrageously with her. She was certain he acted this way only to attract the attention of Elena, who was deep in conversation with Roderick and Lady Gwendolyn. Well, it will do me good to feel needed and pretty in someone's eyes, she mused, and returned his compliments gaily while she sipped more wine than was her habit.

Roderick did not fail to notice her behavior. He seethed behind a mask of friendly interest in Elena's idle prattle. And each time Stefano leaned close to his wife's scented hair, Roderick almost choked on his food.

Finally, when Roderick would have retired for the night, as had Lady Gwendolyn, Madrigal held back, allowing Stefano to refill her empty flagon and totally ignoring her husband's plea.

Roderick leaned toward her and spoke softly into her

ear, but with a deadly serious tone. "If you think to punish me, my wife, it will not work. Now, make your apologies and leave Stefano and Elena to drink the night away." He straightened, waiting for her to rise and obey his wishes. But she turned her back to him, dismissing his words completely.

Roderick clenched his jaw and strode furiously toward the door. He'd be damned if the little witch was going to goad him into another quarrel!

"Roderick . . . Roderick! Don't leave yet!" Elena cried, approaching him. "We've hardly had a chance to see one another. Come, stay for a while." She smiled coyly up into his eyes.

He allowed himself to rejoin the trio, deciding to finish off the wine cask alone if necessary, so that by the time they finally staggered up to bed, his head ached abominably and his mouth was dry and tasted of acid.

Madrigal followed him silently down the halls. When they reached their chamber door, however, she continued to the next room, used for sewing, and containing a none-too-comfortable couch on which to rest. Roderick stood with his hand on the door latch, viewing her latest act of defiance with a certain exhausted sadness. When she closed the sewing-room door, leaving him alone in the hall, he finally entered his own chamber and began to undress, telling himself to allow her this one evening of open disobedience. After all, he rationalized, he had abused her cruelly, and perhaps she was justified. But before he had closed his eyes, her image came unbidden to his mind: her soft flesh and long, slender limbs; her hips swaying when she walked before him; and her eyes, especially those emerald-green eyes.

"I'm utterly bewitched," he muttered aloud, rising and hastily donning his tunic.

When he entered her room and stood over her, he almost wished he had remained alone, but she just lay there staring up at him, veiled confusion in her eyes.

He stooped down and gathered her into his arms, carrying her effortlessly back into his own chamber. She spoke neither a word of protest nor of approval.

Having deposited her gently into the comforting quilts, he said, "This is where you belong," then added, "Like it or not."

She rolled over, showing him her back while thoughts raced through her agonized mind. If only he could give me some indication of affection—anything at all! she cried to herself. She knew that the apparent need which had brought him to her a moment ago was merely an act of possessiveness. " 'Tis the most you're capable of," she whispered into the silence, but she received no answer. Roderick had already fallen asleep.

Chapter 19

Since Elena's arrival, Madrigal's normal routine was thrown into turmoil. Elena regarded each new day as if it were a holiday. In fact, Madrigal had seldom seen her sister so gay and carefree.

Elena ogled every passing knight or high vassal and took great delight in the attentions of Stefano, even though she found his words of undying devotion rather boring. Madrigal watched her sister carefully whenever Roderick was about, for he had not given her an answer as to whether he had slept with Elena on the wedding night. To Madrigal, no answer at all was an admission of guilt.

Her relationship with Roderick had deteriorated to a sad parody of a marriage, she realized, but she was grateful for the reprieve from him. She had often confessed her darkest shame to the priest at

Halconbosque: her involuntary response to her husband's caresses. And when Roderick ceased to demand use of her body, she no longer felt guilty in the eyes of God, or so she told herself.

Maria or Lady Gwendolyn would often beg her to tell Roderick about the baby, but in this matter, too, Madrigal was obdurate. She began to hope that he would go off on some campaign when her time of confinement drew near.

A week after Elena's arrival, Roderick began making arrangements for the annual hunt and subsequent feast, to which the neighboring lords and their ladies were invited. The castle was in an uproar over the preparations, and on the day of the hunt Madrigal was so exhausted that she doubted she could ride out.

Lady Gwendolyn and Patrick had, thankfully, assisted her in selecting the appropriate rooms for each guest and in checking the storage cellars for the various foods and wines that would comprise the fare. There were plenty of surplus meats in case the hunt was unsuccessful.

Madrigal remained in the great hall the entire morning, greeting the twenty lords and their wives. By the time they were ready to proceed with the hunt, she approached Roderick wearily.

"Would it be rude if I stayed here to make certain everything is ready for the feast?"

Although he thought she looked a bit pale, he considered her excuse for remaining at Halconbosque a weak plea to avoid his company. "Yes," he said curtly. "Now go and dress properly, for we shall not come upon the game until the chill of evening, and that silk gown you are wearing will surely not keep you warm."

"But I'm hot all the time! I can't bear to don those prickly wools!" Indeed, since her pregnancy, Madrigal had been extremely sensitive to heat.

"This, milady, is not Castilla-verde! You are in the

north now, and trust me, the evening air will see your death. Now, be gone before I lose all patience!"

After she had left, he wished his tone had not been so harsh, but whenever he was near her of late, his mood turned inexplicably ugly. In truth, he thought, the only thing he liked about her was watching her, and even that pastime had come to make him feel strangely dejected.

The party left the castle confines shortly after noon, an entourage of serfs following with ample supplies of food and wine for the long day ahead. At first Madrigal tried to keep up with Roderick's grueling pace, but finally she dropped back to ride with Stefano and Elena and then took a different path, eventually becoming separated from the main party altogether. She decided to turn the event into a private ride, defying Roderick's wishes once more, and to go back to the castle shortly.

She rode alone for some time, eventually coming to the crest of a gently sloping hill from which she saw the hunting party in the distance. Already they appeared to be having some success, for their horses were rapidly stirring up dust. She was about to turn her horse and head back when she glimpsed an odd movement in the bushes far below. As she sat fixed in the saddle, trying to pinpoint the activity, she saw a flash of bright blue and wondered if a member of the hunt had encountered some difficulty.

Madrigal eased her mount partway down the brambly slope, then tethered it and went the rest of the way on foot. The sight confronting her made her stop short in amazement, for rolling in the grass before her, their clothes discarded in the brush, were two naked bodies. A hot flush of shame rose to Madrigal's face, but she remained frozen to the spot in fascination and disgust; the pair was none other than her sister and Stefano!

She did not know how long she remained there, wide-eyed and horrified, but finally she began to back away silently and slowly, praying they wouldn't discover her. Then she turned and began a headlong sprint to her horse, running straight into Roderick. Her mouth hung open and her hair was flying wildly.

He grabbed her by the shoulders. "What in the name of God are you up to now?" His tone, although harsh, was mildly relieved.

"Nothing . . . I . . . my horse . . . please, Roderick, let go of me!"

"Not until you tell me what's amiss. Come, now, milady, I'm not such a cur," he teased, wondering at the terror in her eyes.

"Nothing, I say! Nothing at all!" She attempted to pull herself away, but he started to coax her in the direction from which she had run.

"If you won't tell me, then I shall see for myself what frightened you so."

"No, Roderick! *Please,*" she begged, making him all the more curious.

Madrigal was convinced he would be livid, for a married woman who committed an indiscretion was shamed enough in his eyes, but an unmarried lady, especially a guest of Halconbosque, was quite another matter.

When they finally reached the unwary couple, she blanched at the thought of what Roderick would do to her sister. But his first reaction upon taking in the situation was to thrust Madrigal behind him. His eyes traveled over the scene before him, momentarily fixing upon Elena's white, rounded buttocks being pounded into the unyielding earth, her legs entwined around Stefano's back, a guttural sound coming from her hidden face.

Stefano, however, was not as engrossed in carnal pleasure as Elena, for he noticed the intruders first, his body tensing visibly as he met Roderick's hard stare. He pulled himself quickly away from Elena's squirming body, leaving her sprawled helplessly under Roderick's detached perusal.

Madrigal remained behind her husband, covering her eyes in embarrassment for her sister. She pictured Roderick whipping Elena until her flesh was raw and bleeding.

Elena, finally aware of their presence, sought to cover herself with her discarded cape. She was red-faced, shocked, and humiliated, but oddly enough, she strove first to cover the birthmark on her face and not her naked flesh.

Still not a word had been exchanged, and finally Madrigal peeked around her husband's back to assure herself that Elena and Stefano were really there. Thankfully, they had dressed themselves and were decent now, so she allowed herself to stand by Roderick's side. Daring a glance at his face, she was surprised at what she saw, for he was not blackly enraged. Instead, he was smiling singularly at the couple. Madrigal was at a loss to understand his queer behavior and still expected him to fly into a tirade at any moment.

It was Stefano who broke the awkward silence. "Alas, my brother, we've been discovered. No lectures, *por favor.*"

How can Roderick take this so lightly? Madrigal thought frantically.

Finally Roderick spoke, his tone unbelievably humorous. "I would only hope that you keep Mother from finding out." Then, to Elena, "Lady Elena, you take a great risk for a woman unwed . . . for a sprouted seed, once taken root, may well keep you full-bellied."

"I have my ways, *Baron,*" Elena muttered sullenly.

Madrigal could hardly believe her ears. He was not angry at all! Not even shocked! Well, if he was not, certainly she was horrified. "Roderick may find this amusing, but I do not! 'Tis base and disgusting!"

"Oh, sweet, innocent Madrigal!" Elena replied in a honeyed tone. "You cannot be as naive as you pretend. No one here is shocked, dear sister, but you."

Stefano, to his credit, was somewhat embarrassed by Madrigal's presence. He straightened his shoulders and looked at Elena. "Perhaps Madrigal is right to be shocked. After all, her eyes are not used to viewing . . . to seeing a man and a woman . . . never mind," he faltered. "But I wish to be an honorable man, Elena, and with these two as witnesses, I ask for your hand in marriage. What say you?"

Elena was not often taken aback, but this proposal of marriage left her speechless for a long moment.

"I honestly . . . Stefano . . . 'tis unnecessary for you to marry me just because of Madrigal. I'm truly flattered, but . . ."

"You do not have to answer me now, Elena. Only tell me I may hope."

"Of course," Elena answered quickly—too quickly, Roderick thought. She went on, laughing now. "We should take Madrigal to court, where all the noble ladies jump from bed to bed—and often with their spouses' approval!" She smirked at Madrigal's reaction of horror.

"That's enough, Elena," Roderick said tightly. "My wife knows nothing of such behavior."

Elena's eyes flashed wickedly at him. Her words dripped with venom. "Why, you sound jealous, Roderick. Is that possible?"

"Oh!" Madrigal gasped before he could reply. What could make Elena say such outrageous lies? "Roderick sounded no such way! He only wanted to protect me!"

"Did he?" Elena mocked. "Or does he wish *your* behavior to be more womanly?" She swung her hips seductively as she walked over to her horse and remounted. "Come, Stefano."

Stefano followed her with a shrug of his shoulders; he

would never understand women. Roderick, on the other hand, felt otherwise when he looked into Madrigal's eyes. He attempted to take her in his arms, but she pushed him away, viciously.

"Surely you can't believe I am jealous of Stefano and Elena?" His tone was incredulous.

"Why not?" she cried. "What man who has lain with a woman would not be jealous in such a case?"

"*Dios!* Madrigal, I won't stand here ignoring our guests and quibbling with you. I won't even qualify that question with an answer." He took her arm and tried to lead her away.

"Don't! If you were the last man on earth, I wouldn't let you touch me!" She pulled her cloak tightly around her.

"For you, my swallow, I *am* the last man on earth, and the first!" He followed her, laughing heartily as she tossed her head to indicate her indignation over his last statement.

After he had rejoined the hunt, Roderick came back to the castle with the trophy boar of the day, much to Madrigal's disgust, for he behaved at the feast that night as if nothing had happened to dispel the day's pleasure.

By the meal's end, nearly all the guests were either drunk and snoring loudly or slightly less swelled with wine and gossiping among themselves. Madrigal, seeing that the feast would continue until dawn's first light, decided to retire before she was drawn into another sorry conversation with some drunken, foul-breathed lord. She managed to sneak away while Roderick and Stefano were laughing at a lewd joke offered by one of the guests. Once undressed, she splashed some cool water on her face and sought the heavenly comfort of her bed, pulling the covers down and stretching lazily. Suddenly her eyes fell on a foreign object in the bed, barely visible in the dim light. She leaned over to examine it, then jumped back, her hand clutching her mouth and cold fear sweeping up her spine.

In the middle of the bed lay a coiled snake, its patterned skin furthering her terror. After an unending moment, she gathered her wits about her and edged her way around the granite wall to the fireplace, where she grabbed hold of the cast-iron poker, then cautiously approached the bed.

When she was close enough to strike the snake, it occurred to her the reptile might already be dead. To make certain, she stirred the quilts with the poker. The serpent made no apparent movement. But it could be sluggish from the cold air, she thought, so she brought the weapon over her head and struck the snake full on the head. Again and again.

Then she put on her gown and left the chamber, stumbling in her haste to reach the great hall. At the top of the stairs, she glanced down and saw something that filled her with more emotion than she had experienced moments before in her room. Stefano had passed out at the table, and Roderick, his feet propped up on a chair, sat with Elena on his lap, a bright smile lighting her face. At that moment Roderick and Elena looked as young and suited to each other as any couple Madrigal had ever seen. A jealous rage engulfed her, causing tears of frustration to brim in her eyes and blur the scene below her.

Roderick looked up slowly, as if he sensed her presence, and met Madrigal's eyes. He said something to Elena, who rose from his lap. Madrigal's heart pounded in her chest; her knees were weak.

Roderick thought she was about to faint. Damn Elena anyway! he raged inwardly. She was always draping herself around him whenever Madrigal was absent, whispering endearments in his ear. He wouldn't have paid attention to her even now, except that her latest vows of love were so outrageous as to make him laugh aloud. And now Madrigal had real reason to doubt his faithfulness!

Elena, feeling no embarrassment whatsoever, passed Madrigal on the top step without a word. However, her lips twisted up at the corners into a wicked half smile. Still Roderick sat there, seeming determined not to move, so Madrigal forced her legs into motion and went down to him.

"I thought you had retired," he said, then realized he had only worsened the situation.

"So it would seem, milord." Her voice quaked.

"Let's talk before this goes too far."

She sat down against her will, for there was little else she could do at the moment.

"What you witnessed now was Elena at her best. 'Tis time you know, my wife." He turned her head so that she faced him. "She often comes to me when you're elsewhere—look at me!" he demanded. "Do you hear what I'm saying?"

"*Sí,* but I don't believe you. I'm not stupid, Roderick. If it were true, you would cast her away."

"Mayhap . . . I admit guilt for enjoying the flattery, but your sister does you wrong nevertheless."

"I cannot, will not, believe Elena is really that cruel!"

He hesitated for an instant, then said, "Use your wits, Madrigal. She may not be cruel, but you plainly saw her leanings in the field today. There are women born to a certain need, a craving . . . Never mind. Just believe that I speak the truth."

"I don't know, Roderick. I'm often confused by your glib explanations. I'll think about it."

Then she told him about the snake, catching him in the middle of a long drink of wine, which he choked on, then spit the remainder out. She hadn't expected him to

143

display such bewilderment, for he rose suddenly, then raced ahead of her, up the stairs and down toward their chambers.

Once in the room, he said, "Thank God the thing was dead, or . . ."

"But it wasn't, I don't think . . ."

"What? Who would do such an evil thing?" His face was dark with rage, making her glad that she faced him only in the bedroom and not in battle.

She tried to calm him. "The creature must have climbed the vines and only sought warmth under the covers, 'tis all."

"I doubt that! Remember the toad on our wedding-chamber door?"

"*Now* who is superstitious? 'Twas probably as you said that morning, a jest in poor taste." She touched his arm reassuringly.

He suddenly pulled her roughly to him, as if he meant to crush her. He murmured in her hair, "I won't leave this week, then, Madrigal."

"What? Leave when?"

"I was sure I told you. King Sancho signs the treaty with Abu Yusuf in Burgos at the end of this month. I am to witness the event, but I won't go."

She allowed him to continue his embrace; inexplicably, she experienced a feeling of desolation. Still, she managed to urge him to wait upon his king for the unprecedented event, knowing he must go. Finally he relented, marveling that she was so calm.

Roderick checked and rechecked the chamber, making certain that the glass-paned window was closed tightly. When he was assured that the room was safe, he swept his wife into his arms and placed her carefully on the bed, surprising her with his gentle touch. Since a few guests still remained in the great hall, it was his duty to see them through the long feast, and he left Madrigal alone in the room.

Once he had quietly closed the door behind him, her reaction was one of relief, for it had seemed that he might want to bed her. She shuddered at the notion, knowing that her flesh still burned unaccountably where he had touched her, even though Elena's flesh had also been recently touched and burned by those same strong hands.

Chapter 20

The light of dawn slanted through the shutters of the room and fell across Madrigal's face. She stirred and woke, shivering in the morning chill. She snuggled closer to Roderick's warm body under the coverlet, then remembered he was to leave for Burgos that very morning. The fact of his departure gave her a sense of both relief and regret, neither one able to banish the other. He would be gone several weeks; by the time he returned, she would surely be showing the babe. She should tell him now, before he left. Her heart contracted at the thought of his reaction, but the deed would have to be done.

Roderick rolled over toward her and threw an arm across her stomach. His face was close to hers and was still relaxed in sleep, so she regarded him at her leisure, trying to decipher his character. As if he read her mind, he opened his eyes and met hers; he yawned.

"Well, sweet, I'm off this morn. Have you a token of your affection for me? Something I can remember you by?"

"Oh, Roderick, what do you think I am? I won't—"

He silenced her words with a kiss. Her exasperation faded; unwillingly she began to feel the familiar ache of pleasure build in her belly. She determined to remain passive and unresponsive; she would not be a wanton woman like her sister! But her breath came quickly as Roderick began to stroke her body in all the places he knew so well now: her velvety back, her firm breasts, her rounded hips, the secret softness between her thighs. Her eyes closed in ecstasy as he brought her senses to an unbearable height of passion.

Suddenly he stopped touching her. Madrigal's eyes flew open and saw his crinkled with laughter.

"So, my beauty, you try to pretend that none of this pleasures you. Shall I leave you now?"

She felt a flash of fury. How dare he play with her, then leave her panting like a bitch in heat and *laugh* at her? She rolled over onto her stomach and drew the blankets up over her head. But his hand gently drew the covers back and his warm breath touched her neck.

"I'm sorry, *preciosa,* truly. I merely jested. The union must not always be so solemn, you know, but you are not ready for that. Maybe someday . . . Come, let me make up for my ill-considered words."

He pulled her to him and kissed the soft, hollow place where her neck joined her shoulder. She grew less rigid in his embrace, and after a time her rage changed to passion, just as strong in its intensity, but infinitely more pleasurable. When he finally entered her, she could hardly control the compelling urges that held her in their power. Her body moved of its own accord, whirling beyond sensation. She heard her cry of release as if from afar, then was plummeted back to her bed, her husband's hard, muscular form resting atop her, nearly pressing the breath out of her body.

Roderick rolled off her and propped himself up on an elbow, idly playing with her disheveled hair. He spoke his thoughts aloud almost before be had realized it. "How can one so fair be the daughter of such a bloodthirsty blackguard?"

She snapped to attention, hardly believing her ears.

"*My* father? My father is the kindest man on earth! How can you speak of him so? You don't even know him!"

He had turned his back to her, and it seemed that her angry words merely bounced off its broad expanse, infuriating her even more. His voice cut across the space between them; it was cold, low, dead-sounding.

"Your father never told you, of course. Why should he? You weren't even born yet. Your father murdered—yes, *murdered*—my father in cold blood." He rushed on, heedless now. "He beheaded him and then hacked him to pieces in front of my eyes . . . and I was but a child of nine. Now you know, and I leave it to you to judge the man, as I have had to judge him these twenty years."

He turned to her then, almost afraid to see how she would react to his long-cherished secret. What he saw confirmed his worst fears and made him suddenly wish he had not spoken so hastily.

She sat on her knees, white-faced, horrified, a spectrum of emotions coursing across her features. And then he saw a deep, comprehending anguish fill her eyes with hate and despair.

Her love-bruised lips quivered as she said, "And you . . . married . . . me, the purpose of which I see now . . . oh, yes, my husband . . ." She let her head fall onto her chest and sobbed uncontrollably.

Roderick observed her pain with mixed emotions; pity tugged at him for a moment, but then he hardened his heart. He knew it had to be; it had been fated for two decades, and neither of them could escape the evil deeds of the past. Madrigal had stopped sobbing, but tears still overflowed as she lifted her head to face him proudly.

"I care not how you came by your damnable information or what you saw! I *know* that my father is innocent of your detestable lies and never, do you hear, *never*, did such a thing in his life! I refuse to believe what you say. May the holy saints protect you, for your words are lies and our marriage is a lie. You are an evil and sinful man. I can no longer live with you as your wife. You have tortured me enough, and I will tolerate no more!"

Madrigal ran quickly to a chair, and grabbing the cloak thrown across it, wrapped it around her naked form, then fled the room.

Roderick sat on the edge of the rumpled bed, feeling as if he had fought a bloody battle and emerged wounded and sick. He put his head in his hands and tried to think. She is upset, he told himself, but she will calm down in time and come to accept that I am her husband in spite of everything. I shall let her recover for awhile—she won't want to see me. Her pride will hold her back, but she will come around. Perhaps Mother will talk to her . . .

Madrigal's heart was bursting with pain as she ran down the hallway. His words had explained so many unanswered questions. And now she knew the truth: he hated her, her father, her whole family. He had married her only to achieve a disgusting scheme of revenge. She knew she had to escape from this cold, heartless prison, it was an absolute necessity now. She felt the walls close in on her, suffocating her; her breath snatched in her throat and she was blinded by her tears. She reached the top of the stairs leading down to the great hall and began to descend rapidly to escape before Roderick could follow her, but her foot caught in the hem of the voluminous cloak and she lost her balance. Her arms flailed as she tried to regain her footing; the folds of cloth impeded her and she fell heavily down the hard stone staircase, coming to rest, unconscious, at the foot of the stairs.

Lady Gwendolyn heard a noise as she entered the great hall after an early visit to the kitchens, and assumed the dogs had gotten loose again. Sighing with vexation, she moved quickly across the stone floor to see what mischief they had done. Instead, she found Madrigal lying by the stairs, unconscious, dressed only in her cloak. Lady Gwendolyn prayed she was not too badly hurt, and quickly called a servant to bring a damp cloth, then to fetch Roderick, while she arranged Madrigal's limp form into a more comfortable position, resting the girl's head on her lap. The terrified servant brought her the cloth and dashed up the stairs to seek out Roderick.

Lady Gwendolyn stroked the girl's forehead with the cool cloth and pushed the long hair back from her pale face. There was a blue bruise on her forehead, but her breathing seemed normal. The poor child, thought her mother-in-law; what a terrible thing to happen! How could Madrigal have been so careless to fall down the stairs? She was encouraged to see her eyelids flutter, then open. Madrigal's eyes were unfocused, but gradually she became aware of her surroundings.

"There, there, relax, Madrigal. You will be all right. You just had a nasty fall and hit your head. Roderick will be down in a moment and he can carry you upstairs—"

Her words were cut off by a low, agonized cry from Madrigal. "No! Not him, never! Don't let him touch me!" She became so distraught that she tried to rise, only to sink back, dizzy and sick. Lady Gwendolyn did not know what to do; obviously, she thought, they have had a quarrel, and perhaps Roderick should be kept out of it, as the mere mention of his name seems to incense poor Madrigal.

Madrigal cried out again, but this time in pain. She doubled over and moaned, feeling a deep, tormenting knife thrust into her womb. "Oh, the baby! Something is wrong—oh, God, my baby!" she cried in anguish.

Lady Gwendolyn tried to remain calm, knowing her

149

own assurance would help the young girl immeasurably. "Madrigal, these things often pass and all is well. You must be calm and strong for the baby's sake." She looked up then to see Roderick descending the stairs, two at a time.

He knelt by Madrigal's side and whispered, "Little swallow, are you hurt? . . . Oh, my God . . ."

Madrigal did not answer him. Tears welled from under her closed eyelids, and she turned her face away.

"She must be moved to her bed, Roderick. I do not think she has any broken bones, but she may be about to miscarry, I fear." His mother spoke quietly to him, not wanting to alarm Madrigal further.

"*What?*" he exploded, filled with disbelief and confusion. "Miscarry? Was she with child, then? She told *you* and not *me?* I cannot believe it!"

"Roderick, 'tis plain there is some trouble between you. I do not wish to pry, as you know well, but *something* drove this innocent child nearly to kill herself and her baby, *your* child!" Her expression was stern. "I can only pray that whatever brought her to this will not burden your conscience. *Bastante!* Carry her upstairs and we shall see what can be done."

Roderick lifted Madrigal easily, eliciting a moan of pain from her, but she was too weak to resist his touch and could only whisper "no" over and over as he carried her up to bed. Lady Gwendolyn made her comfortable and sent for Maria to watch over her, then quietly left the room. She was surprised to find Roderick downstairs at the large table, drinking lavishly from a tankard of wine; normally he never drank so early.

"Mother, I'm not leaving. It would be cruel . . . although the king expects me." His face looked haggard.

"You will go to Burgos," she declared. "You only upset her. You can do no good by staying. Fulfill your duties to the king. I shall send word with Stefano if I feel you should return. We shall take care of her, and I'm sure she will recover. She is young and strong. The baby, though, I do not know . . . We must pray for the baby's life."

"*Dios sacro* . . . " Roderick whispered, his head in his hands, tousling his dark gold hair unknowingly. His mother could not resist putting a slim hand on his tawny mane; she had not seen her son in such torment since his father had been killed in battle.

Roderick straightened up, gathering his wits about him, and called loudly for Renaldo to ready his horse. His face was grim, but he went about his preparations and quickly took his leave with Renaldo.

During the week that followed, the household at Halconbosque was hushed and sad, for the young mistress remained ill. She did not lose the child then, but suffered from intermittent cramps all week. Lady Gwendolyn feared more for her mind than for her physical health as Madrigal was distant, detached from reality. She lived in her own world of misery and pain, and no one could reach her there, not even faithful Maria. At the end of the week she began to hemorrhage, and then Lady Gwendolyn feared for her life. She sent Stefano to Burgos to fetch Roderick in case the worst happened, but she knew it would take almost a week to get there and another to return. That evening Madrigal lost her baby.

Elena was surprisingly tender with her sister, reading to her or embroidering near her bed to keep her company. She felt the pains as though they were her own, and they frightened her terribly. But nevertheless, she was a great help to Lady Gwendolyn.

Several days after the miscarriage, Madrigal felt much improved in health but was still pale and weak. Her mind, however, was recovered, as if the shock of losing the baby had somehow restored her pride and fire. She knew what had to be done and never hesitated in implementing her plan.

"Elena," she said that morning, "I must leave this place, for I cannot in good conscience stay with that husband of mine who hates me, and I him!" She nearly spit the words.

"What will you do? He will return soon, and you are much too ill—"

"I am *not* too ill! I shall leave and you will help me. I need a wagon, that is all. Lady Gwendolyn will help me, I know. I want to go home!"

Elena fetched Lady Gwendolyn and the two women tried to dissuade Madrigal, but she was vehemently set upon returning home and would not listen. Lady Gwendolyn finally relented, fearing the girl would indeed lose her reason if she were forced to stay. Elena herself was not against going, as that would solve the problem of Stefano, whom she had absolutely no intention of marrying. And perhaps separating Madrigal and Roderick would make him more apt to look in *her* direction, she mused.

Roderick's mother arranged for the wagon, a rough affair at best, as well as a dozen guards to accompany them on the long journey. Since making the decision to leave, Madrigal seemed to improve rapidly, even walking around her chamber to pack her things. She deliberately left all the gowns that Roderick had provided for her, and took her old garments and a new, heavy winter cloak.

The party left at dawn the next day. A cold mist covered the land and the tree branches were black and bare, forbidding in the dim light. Lady Gwendolyn feared for the girl's health and safety on the long trip, but her arguments had long before been exhausted, and she could do nothing to dissuade her daughter-in-law.

Madrigal knew she would miss Lady Gwendolyn, who had become a mother to her, but she could not stay at Halconbosque for her sake alone. She had to flee the claustrophobic walls that were filled with dead hopes and broken promises. She hugged Lady Gwendolyn tightly and shed many painful tears; then the small group moved down the road toward the south. Madrigal sat stiffly, vowing not to look back at Halconbosque.

A few days later brought Roderick, Stefano, and Renaldo galloping through the heavy gates in great haste. They were exhausted and dust-covered, their mounts lathered and on their last legs. Roderick threw himself down off his horse and burst into the castle. The great hall was quiet and deserted. He covered the floor in long strides and raced up the stairs to the room in which he had left Madrigal on that fateful day. The door was open, the room empty. He spun on his heel, his heart thudding, and bellowed. Was no one about the place?

Lady Gwendolyn appeared in the doorway, an unfinished piece of tapestry in her slender hands.

"Where is Madrigal? Is she . . .?" he panted, still winded from his dash up the stairs.

"No, my son," said his mother hastily, knowing full well what he feared. "Madrigal is quite well, I believe, although she lost the baby." She could see his large frame relax its tension and slump tiredly. "But she has gone—she has returned to her father . . ."

"And you did not try to keep her here?" His words cut sharply across her own.

"Of course I did, Roderick. But you must know Madrigal when she is determined. There was no holding her."

"Why did she leave, sick as she was?"

"Ah, that, I fear, you would know better than I. She did not say, but she acted as if the very devil pursued her."

153

He said nothing, knowing all too well what had driven Madrigal from Halconbosque. He could feel his fury rise, but he grudgingly admired his wife's courage.

Lady Gwendolyn smiled compassionately at him. "I understand, my son. I shall miss her, too." And then, to comfort him, "It will not be the first marriage in which husband and wife lived separately."

He looked hard into his mother's eyes. "Have no fear on that score, *madre*. You will not miss her company long, for there will be no separation in *my* marriage!"

Chapter 21

The familiar battlements of Castilla-verde reached skyward in the distance as three riders made their approach through the lower meadows below the castle. The armor-clad men showed distinct signs of exhaustion and hard travel; their great steeds were lathered and blowing hard into the crisp air.

Many a time Roderick had rehearsed what he would say to Madrigal when he arrived. His intended speech took on a number of forms ranging in content. One moment he thought to take her away with him whether or not she protested; the next moment he rehearsed words describing his passion and his need of her, and his sorrow over the loss of their child. He had even considered calling her cowardly and stupid for foolishly running away from him while his back was turned.

By the time they entered the bailey, Roderick had no planned speech ready at all and had begun to doubt the sanity of his being there. Regardless of how he felt or what words he would say, he knew she would shun him, for it was more than obvious she hated him now and wanted nothing to do with him. By God's will, he almost raged aloud, she's my wife and belongs only to me. I'll not tolerate this separation!

They dismounted and went boldly into the hall, unimpeded. There seemed to be no one about, for even their approach had gone unnoticed. This was odd indeed, even at Castilla-verde.

Some moments later Teresa came to the head of the stairs, and seeing Roderick, she raced down and threw her arms around his waist, sobbing miserably. His heart always contracted at the sight of this child, for she gave him her open and unabashed love.

"Come, come, now, Teresa—have you missed me so much?" He picked her up and held her tenderly while kissing her forehead. Still she wept.

Stefano, never having been to Castilla-verde, took in the dilapidated condition of the many-centuried fortress and marveled at its ancient structure. He wondered, also, where the father and Elena were and why no men-at-arms were visible.

"It's so awful . . . you've come too late . . ." the little girl cried.

"What are you saying, Teresa?" Roderick's voice showed definite signs of weariness and a tinge of impatience.

"Elena says she's dead! But Papa thinks—"

"Who, Teresa? Who's dead?" His heart pounded heavily in his chest.

"Madrigal!"

While Roderick clutched a chair behind him for support, Elena appeared in the doorway, shocked to see the men there.

Stefano ran up to her and grabbed her shoulders. "I cannot believe it! What is that child saying?"

Elena's eyes were red-rimmed. "That Madrigal . . . is most probably dead . . . or worse." Her voice was subdued.

Long moments later, her reply crept into Roderick's stunned consciousness. When he spoke, his tone was agonized and distant. "What do you mean . . . or worse? Is she dead or not?" The question seemed to be torn from his dry throat.

Elena went to him and took his hand in hers. " 'Tis a long story, Roderick." She proceeded to tell him what had happened on their journey home. They had been ambushed, and no one had seen Madrigal since before the attack, at least no one still living to tell of her fate. The only information they had was that her wagon had been at the rear of the column and that the ambush had definitely been the work of the Moors. It seemed that the front of the column, where Elena and Maria had been riding, had escaped unharmed. She ended by saying, "It does not really matter if she lives or not. Can you imagine the torture they have put her through? She's undoubtedly been raped at least—"

"Shut your vile mouth, Elena!" He shoved her from him, a look of numbed pain on his face.

"Well, 'tis true! No honorable woman would wish to stay alive after that! I told Father as much, but he's still out there somewhere, hoping!" She raised her voice shrilly.

Stefano went to her side. "All hope is not lost, Elena. Often a captor may keep his charge safe for ransom."

Roderick lifted his face; he had not had time to think of that, and Stefano's words were like a dim flicker of light at the end of a tunnel.

"Elena, did either you or Maria see or hear anything at all?" he asked.

"I told you, no!"

"Then fetch Maria—I must talk to her!" But Elena just stood there, unable to comprehend Roderick's desperate attitude.

It was Teresa who had the presence of mind to bring Maria to him. He questioned her for some time before accepting the fact that neither woman knew a thing.

Stefano persuaded his younger brother to seek a few hours' rest so that he might think more clearly. Roderick relented after much haggling and sought out his former quarters. He felt he could not bear to sleep in the bed that had seen the loss of Madrigal's virginity and her awakening into womanhood.

Some hours later he awoke in a cold sweat, having dreamed fitfully and restlessly. The old nightmare of his father returned, but this time his father's disembodied hand became Madrigal's, and her voice cried chillingly to him from the mist. Before he rose from the bed, Madrigal's image came again to his mind with great clarity. He saw her in every imaginable way: naked and writhing under a faceless man's brutal assault; her lovely, shy smile when amused and at ease; her dark frown after he had purposefully taunted her. Roderick left the room that afternoon trying to quell the thoughts that threatened to drive him insane. He had learned in battle to concentrate on the immediate task and never to seek a glimpse into the uncertain future.

When he reached the hall, he saw that Jaime Castilla-verde had returned with his men-at-arms and the few guards from Halconbosque who were still alive.

Approaching the earl hopefully, he asked, "Any word?"

The nobleman fell exhausted into a chair and looked up into Roderick's hard stare. "Yes, there is news. Whether or not 'tis good or bad I cannot say." He went on slowly. "We have found one of your men-at-arms, a man named Diego. He lay wounded in a house near the place of the attack. Before he died, he told me that Madrigal was taken alive by the men of Akbar al-Kemil."

"Akbar!" Roderick also eased himself into a seat, then pounded the table with his fist. "My old enemy! By all that's holy, this may be good news!"

"I fail to see how this ungodly Moor, this Akbar, can bring hope to your heart!" The earl was aghast at Roderick's reaction.

"Why?" Roderick replied. "Because he's an honorable man. We've met in battle many a time, and if Madrigal is in his hands, she will be treated with due respect."

Castilla-verde's face lit up and his breath came quickly. "I pray . . . I pray this is true."

Elena placed a hand on her father's shoulder. "Father, 'tis possible that Akbar himself was not there. Surely his men would have abused Madrigal . . . "

Castilla-verde swung around, and in a voice unlike his usual one, he thundered, "We can always hope, daughter!"

The next morning Roderick and Renaldo left Stefano at Castilla-verde and rode out to seek a clue to Akbar's whereabouts. Although it was a difficult task, Roderick knew that a few gold coins placed in the right palm might eventually prove well spent. The Moors who lived in Gibraltar were not wholly Arabic or Spanish in their inclinations, and their loyalties could often be swayed by the mere mention of money.

After the two men had ridden out that morning, spirits were high at Castilla-verde. Roderick had a way of taking a bad situation in hand, leaving those around him with a sense of confidence and hope. In this respect, Lord Jaime had awe for the man's qualities.

Even when Roderick and Renaldo returned several days later with no news, Roderick managed to put them immediately at ease by his assurance that it was only a matter of time before his offer of gold in exchange for information would find a taker.

And so they waited. They waited and made plans for

the time when they would hear word of Akbar, or perhaps receive a ransom note. It was decided that Roderick would go by himself to Akbar's camp, for he stood a better chance alone than accompanied by an army. Roderick knew his enemy.

Stefano agreed to return to Halconbosque shortly, for the fief could not be left alone so long. Roderick trusted that, this time, Stefano would attend to his duties, but he said nothing, hoping his half brother had learned his lesson. Stefano delayed his departure as long as he could in the hope that he might win Elena's hand; she had still said neither yes nor no to his proposal of marriage.

Roderick spent his time in the company of Teresa, who had promised not to mention Madrigal while they waited. He avoided Jaime Castilla-verde, for he still believed the man, despite his gentle appearance, was at the root of all his troubles.

One chill afternoon, while discussing a new sheath for his sword with the fief's tanner, Roderick heard a commotion in the bailey. He rushed out, thinking it might be news of his wife. There stood a frightened young Moorish girl of about eighteen; two awesome-looking men-at-arms were holding her needlessly between them, as if she were an assassin. Needlessly, Roderick thought, for she appeared harmless.

"I seek the baron . . . please, is he here?" she pleaded.

Roderick took the girl in his charge, ushering her into the hall and offering her liquid refreshment. True to her religion, she refused any wine but accepted some cool cider gratefully. Then Roderick waited patiently for her tale of woe, knowing she would talk around the issue with flourishes, like the swirling arabesques in Arabic script. He did not mind the amount of gold she would surely request, but he wished she would begin her tale. This one is smart, he told himself, for she seemed to survey both her surroundings and Roderick thoroughly before revealing her purpose, probably judging to the copper how much she could ask for.

Finally she told Roderick where Madrigal had been taken. He was completely nonplused, for no mention of money was made. He was not surprised, however, to learn that his wife was in Morocco, at the home of Akbar al-Kemil. Roderick had deemed it possible for his old enemy to have returned home. The first image that came to his mind was Madrigal's shock when she found her captor to possess four wives.

He looked at the girl keenly, causing her to drop her gaze. "You have helped me greatly. Now I shall return the favor. What is your pleasure? If it is in my power, it will be yours."

She smiled, then, at his knowledge of the Arab custom of a favor for a favor. "My father's boat can take you across the strait, but, alas, his only boat has a large hole in its side, and my father is a poor man. Without his boat, we all go hungry."

So that was it! The girl's father knew the whereabouts of Madrigal and would take Roderick there, but only if his "large hole" were repaired, or, Roderick mused, a new boat were provided.

As it happened, a new boat would have to be purchased, for the "hole" turned out to be the entire port side of the craft, which lay crippled in a remote bay. Arrangements were made for Roderick and the girl to travel at dawn to the coastal town of Tarifa, where the father already had his eye on the right boat.

The family went to bed that night with the first real ray of hope in weeks. The drafty corridors of the castle were unusually quiet at an early hour, for all within the ancient walls slept the heavy sleep of exhaustion, all except Elena, who stole silently down the halls to Stefano's chamber. She did not return to her own room until dawn, when Stefano joined Roderick in the great hall, for the older brother was heading back that morning to Halconbosque with Renaldo and the few remaining guards.

They ate a hasty breakfast while the horses were readied. Roderick had taken on an extra mount for the Moorish girl, Zena, so as to travel quickly. When they finished eating, they went out to the bailey. Stefano stood next to his own steed, wondering where Elena was and recalling her wild lovemaking. She had still not given him an answer to his proposal but had promised to decide before spring.

Suddenly she appeared at the door, then came down the stone steps and walked straight toward Roderick. She had dressed in her finest silk gown, her hair arranged cleverly to cover the blemish. "Roderick, I would like to wish you luck, although I fear your *wife*"—she spit the word out—"has been raped so many times she'll be useless—"

"That will do!" Roderick warned, a scowl covering his face.

Elena's tone heightened. "Please, Roderick! Reconsider! I'm here now, and I . . . I am yours."

Stefano was approaching her to say his farewells when he overheard her declaration. He crossed the distance separating them and spun her around roughly. "What is this, Elena—some joke? You want *him*? And straight from my bed?"

Flinging her hair back from where it had become loose, she hissed, "Yes, I love him! Did you think I would marry a . . . a bastard? A *penniless* bastard?" She laughed wildly in Stefano's shocked face.

Roderick stood back, for he saw the sparks in his brother's eyes as Elena, still laughing, tried to free herself from Stefano's hold. Then ruthlessly, inevitably, Stefano struck her, not merely a slap, but a blow from the full force of his hand. Elena sprawled on the ground, lying on her side, blood trickling from her lips, an ugly purple welt rising on her cheek. She remained conscious and, unbelievably, said nothing to Stefano but looked straight at Roderick, a strange smile on her lips.

She murmured through the blood in her mouth, "Roderick . . . you see! Madrigal would not suffer so for the love of you, would she? Would she?"

"No, Elena, in truth she would not." His voice was compassionate, for he had never before suspected the extent of Elena's illness. And when he mounted his steed and headed out alongside the grim Stefano, he whispered honestly to himself, "In truth, she would not."

Dust rose mercilessly from the pounding hooves in the bailey; then the disturbance ebbed, the sound reduced to a faint echo. The dust settled back upon the horses' wake and powdered the figure in the pretty silk gown who was weeping pitifully.

Chapter 22

The doctor's hands were cool and gentle as he examined Madrigal; nevertheless, she was very tense, for she had never been touched in this way, not even by Roderick. Because she had been bleeding constantly for weeks, Akbar had insisted on having his physician examine her, assuring her that the learned man was an expert who always cared for the women of the household. The doctor would not be permitted to see her face to face, but would examine her through a curtain with holes in it to accommodate his hands. It was routine, Akbar had repeated more than once, and had to be done before she wasted away from her distressing illness.

She tried to detach her mind from the physician's exploring hands and thought back on how she had come to be in this horrible predicament. Of course, it was her own fault for having decided to return home, and she had the most intense guilt feelings when she thought of what might have happened to Elena, Maria, and her guards, all on her account. She knew for certain that three guards had been killed, for she had witnessed their death with her own eyes, but as for the rest, she had no idea what was their fate; she had not seen them at all during the attack.

The attack . . . it still remained a nightmare in her mind. She had been tossing fitfully, trying to find sleep in the wagon. She had known they were close to Castilla-verde, perhaps half a day's journey at their snail's pace. Her health had suffered from the long journey; she realized now that it had been foolish for her to undertake such a trip. But anything was better than remaining at Halconbosque with a husband who despised her.

She had been so weak that she had hardly moved from her pallet even when they had stopped for the night. She had bled intermittently, watching her strength and health drain slowly and inevitably away. In her weakness she had thought she was imagining things: noises, shouts, the unearthly screams of a wounded horse. She had dragged herself up, clinging to the low side of the cart. The scene that had met her eyes was one of carnage; a band of Moors had attacked the small group of guards around her. She had prayed that the rest of the men along with Elena and Maria, had somehow escaped the attack, for they had been riding ahead of her slow wagon. Madrigal had seen three of Halconbosque's loyal guards slain quickly and two more surrounded and disarmed. It had seemed to happen in slow motion; the battle cries of the Moors, the rearing horses, the blood and flashing swords had been episodes in a hallucination. Madrigal had sunk back weakly, a black miasma encroaching on the edges of her vision.

She had probably passed out for a few seconds, for she had opened her eyes to a circle of strange faces looking down at her. Their pointed helmets had looked so foreign, so fierce. The faces under the helmets had had black beards, black mustaches, and dark eyes. She had closed her eyes again to dispel the vision, but a voice had broken into her dream.

"Are you injured?" One of the disembodied faces that floated before her had spoken in a pleasant, slightly accented voice full of concern.

"No." She had heard her own voice sounding weak; her lips had not wanted to form the words. "I do not think I am injured . . . but . . . who are you?"

"I am Akbar al-Kemil. There has been unnecessary loss of life here today. My men are warriors, returning home, and not ambassadors of the new treaty, I fear." His face had grown thoughtful for a moment. "And now we shall have to do something with you." He had turned to his men and spoken rapidly in Arabic. They had answered him, but it had sounded garbled to her ears, their voices rising and falling strangely.

"Please, sir, please . . . my home is not far from here, at Castilla-verde. If you would but return me there . . ."

Akbar had laughed then. "I hardly think we would venture near your home, especially after this . . ." He had motioned to the grotesquely twisted bodies on the ground. "No. We will have to take you with us; it is my only choice."

Madrigal had felt so dizzy and sick and weak, she had not had the strength to fight back.

Akbar had shouted orders and his men had quickly disposed of the dead bodies. She remembered having wondered vaguely what had happened to the captive guards of Halconbosque . . . had she dreamed they had been dragged from her sight, their horrible screams filling the air? Had anyone been left alive?

She recalled that the small cart carrying her had been hurried, not toward Castilla-verde, but farther south, toward the coast and their waiting boats. She did not remember much of that trip, as she had dozed or lain in a stupor most of the time. Once on board a small sailing craft, she had been somewhat revived by the cool sea breeze and had almost lost her terror with the gentle rocking of Akbar's boat. As they had headed toward Tangier, Madrigal had felt a certain amount of satisfaction in leaving behind her disappointments, her broken marriage. But then she had thought of her father and his dreadful fear when he found out she was no longer safely with her husband. And Maria, Elena—what had become of them?

They had made port in the evening and Akbar had quickly arranged for a litter to carry Madrigal to his home, a few miles outside Tangier. Her impression of the city had been fleeting: lights, exotic odors, guttural Arabic shouts, curious stares. Then she had been helped onto the curtained litter and whisked away. She vaguely remembered having been lifted off and taken to a soft bed in a scented room; then all had mercifully gone dark.

She had been awakened by a strange sound, the chanted cry of the muezzin calling the faithful to prayer. Although its meaning was unknown to her, she was soothed by the foreign words that filled the morning air.

She had looked about, enthralled by her luxurious surroundings. She had been in a large, airy, light room, the same room she was in now. The bottom section of the walls was tiled in bright designs, and the top part was covered with tapestries and rich silk hangings. The many windows were covered on the outside with delicate iron grillwork. Colorful silk cushions lay on the carpeted floor, and the bed in which she had slept was on a raised platform and uncurtained, unlike beds in Spain. A brazier sat in the corner of the room but was not lit in the present warm weather. A bowl of fresh fruit had been placed on a carved wooden table near her bed, but she had had no appetite.

A few moments later the door had opened, and a slight figure swathed in veils had entered the room and approached Madrigal.

"My name is Pitra. My Lord Akbar has provided me to care for you and to translate, as I speak your language. The master wishes for his private physician to see you, milady, and kindly requests that you tell me of your malady." The voice emerging from the veil was almost childlike.

"Pitra, I'm so weak and confused . . . what will become of me? Where am I?"

"Milady, I cannot answer all your questions. Lord Akbar will answer them. But you are near Tangier, in the home of our glorious Lord Akbar al-Kemil, Adha al-Allahu. But now, please tell me of your illness."

Madrigal had spoken of her miscarriage and her long journey from the north, although she had not provided any details. Pitra had left her then, returning shortly with delicious mint tea and hot, fragrant flat bread. Then she had proceeded to bathe Madrigal from an enameled basin filled with scented warm water. She had combed out her long black hair, which had been quite a chore, for Madrigal's hair had not been properly seen to for days. When she had finished, she had brought Madrigal a pale green silk robe.

Pitra had then left, explaining to Madrigal that she was ready to receive Lord Akbar, who had been waiting with much patience for the toilette to be finished. Although Madrigal had felt weak, her anger had risen again. I will find the strength to confront this Akbar! she had promised herself.

She had dozed again in spite of her anxiety, for she had awakened to the light touch of a hand on her shoulder. The vaguely familiar face she had remembered from the attack had looked quite different. Akbar was now clean and perfumed, carefully groomed, and dressed in immaculate, tight blue pants and a shirt beneath a brilliant white, loose-sleeved robe.

Madrigal had straightened up with a gasp, embarrassed at having fallen asleep at such an inopportune moment. The Moor had smiled at her confusion, showing perfect white teeth above his neatly trimmed black beard.

"My wilted blossom, do not distress yourself. You are very ill. Pitra has explained your . . . ah . . . condition to me and my doctor, Izak, a most skilled man, I assure you. Now, do you feel strong enough to answer a few questions?" He had spoken perfect courtly Spanish, but with a light accent. His dark eyes had seemed kind and understanding, his touch cool and restful. Madrigal had found herself relaxing but still fought to maintain her strength and dignity.

"Lord Akbar, I demand to know when you plan to return me to my father. And what fate befell my sister and trusted servant? How dare you attack an innocent party of women!"

He had laughed, taking her hand. "Too many questions, my little flower. First I would know the name of your family, and then how in the wisdom of the Prophet you came to be traveling on that road. And in your condition! I must admit, my curiosity bests me!"

Madrigal had withdrawn her hand quickly and tried

to sit up straighter in the bed, to face this man with pride. He had noticed her struggle and put his hands on her arms to push her down into the pillows.

"My name is Madrigal Castilla-verde," she had said proudly. "My father is Jaime, Earl of Tarbella, and I was traveling from the north to . . . visit him." She had certainly had no desire to explain the circumstances any further.

"But you are married, Lady Madrigal, as I see by the ring on your finger. Where is your husband, and how could he let a precious gem such as you be gone from him for even a moment?"

"My husband is still in Galicia." Her face had grown taut, and her fingers had played nervously with the gold band.

"Galicia, ah, that is very far . . . and who is your husband?"

Madrigal had looked down at her hands. "He is Roderick Halconbosque, Baron of Compostela." She had looked at him then, her wide green eyes filled with pain.

What a treasure, he had thought. Halconbosque, his old enemy! So this was *his* woman . . . His face had remained impassive, but he had wondered at the anguish in her eyes.

Finally he had said, "Yes . . . Halconbosque. The colors of your guard did look familiar. Your Lord Roderick and I have met often." Madrigal had looked surprised at his words. "I mean that we have faced each other in the field of battle, and he is a formidable foe, the *barón*."

"Yes, Lord Akbar, so I have heard."

He had been shocked at the open bitterness in her voice.

"Lady Madrigal, I have not yet decided what to do with you. It is a ticklish situation, but for the time being

168

you will join my household and will remain here until you are well. Then you will join my wives in the harem."

"Your *wives?* And how many do you have, pray tell?" Madrigal's voice had been weakly outraged; her face had grown as white as his robe.

"I have only four," Akbar had replied modestly, "and one is my elder brother's widow. The Koran expressly orders a man to take his brother's widow."

"Only four!" She had laughed faintly.

"Madrigal, my own father had forty-two wives and one hundred and fifty children before he died. It is our custom."

"Yes, I see . . . and am I to join them? What will they think of that?"

"What they think is of no consequence. They are mere women and will do what they are bidden." Akbar had stated this so matter-of-factly that she had not been able to argue.

"And now," he had continued briskly, "I have brought my physician to see you. He waits outside to examine you—"

"Examine me!" Madrigal had tried to rise but had been gently pushed back. "I shall let no dirty, ignorant charlatan examine me! I'd rather die!"

"You will die, too, if he does not treat you. My doctor is a very experienced and learned man who studied for years at the University of Cairo. Do not dare to insult him by comparing him with your dirty bunglers!" His tone had been sharp and had left her open-mouthed, but he had gone on to explain what his physician, Izak, would do. He had then brought him in and introduced him to her. The doctor was a thin, ascetic-looking man whose clothes were elegant and dignified. He had been gentle with her and had asked innumerable questions, many of which had shocked and embarrassed her. Then he had set up a curtain and proceeded to examine her.

Madrigal was thankful now that he could not see her face, for it was hot with shame and mortification. At last his inspection was over, and he went to the basin in a corner of the room to wash his hands. Madrigal waited patiently for his opinion. This man was obviously not in the same class as midwives or the butchers in Spain who called themselves doctors. Perhaps he could really help her, she thought, her spirits rising.

Izak approached and sat in the chair next to her bed. He was silent for a time, drying his long, supple fingers with a small towel. Madrigal could not bear to look at his hands.

"Milady," he began, speaking excellent Spanish, "you have a fairly common condition, caused by your miscarriage and aggravated by the long journey you undertook . . ." He cleared his throat. "I can assure you that your present malady can be cured . . . but I must tell you that you are unlikely to conceive again. There are some problems . . ." He cleared his throat again. "I shall not go into the details . . . but you will be well again shortly, and I shall give Pitra the directions for the treatment."

"What do you mean? I shall never be able to bear a child? Surely that cannot be! If you can cure me . . ." Madrigal was trying to stay calm, but a feeling of despair threatened to overwhelm her. His words could not be true! She would not accept them!

"My dear child, you will be well and perfectly normal, but you will probably, and I repeat, *probably*, not be able to conceive again. Frankly, I am surprised you are not in worse condition, but a few weeks will see you healthy again." Izak was kind and his words were meant to comfort her, but the thought of a lifetime of barrenness, with never a baby to hold or a toddler to chase, nor a grown child to lighten her old age, was like death to Madrigal.

She lay back on the luxurious pillows, feeling nothing except a void, a vast dark, bare place where hope had once lived. She stared, unfocused, into the distance and saw only an empty future stretching desolately before her.

Chapter 23

Adha al-Allahu did not in any way resemble the castles of Madrigal's experience. Although it lay across the small body of water from her own home, the huge edifice was altogether unconventional, its high, spacious, sun-bleached rooms seeming to invite a cool breeze from every angle. Deep, wild spectrums of color assaulted the eye everywhere and even bathed the halls, which were remarkably sunny and cheerful. There was nothing in disrepair, not even a loose stone or a torn silk hanging. Copper, brass, and silver ornaments were placed and hung throughout the rooms.

The slaves who waited on her smallest whim were of every nationality, coming from places of which she had never even heard. They dressed in cool linens or fine silks and had a fragrant scent about them that proved their cleanliness to their master.

Madrigal stood pondering these things while looking out of an arched window, open to the northeast. She could see the Mediterranean lapping at the white sand and the green vegetation dotting the shore. What on earth had made her picture an arid expanse of desert stretching as far as the eye could see? And beyond that, she remembered, were hot, steaming jungles, inhabited by men with ink-colored skin and deadly spears, and by giant, fierce animals with gleaming tusks. She idly wondered if these, too, were misconceptions of this immense continent. How pitiful her education now seemed.

Since she was fully recovered, she would have to move into the harem, the thought of which frightened her no small amount. The veiled women whom she had glimpsed looked mysterious and exotic, as did the huge, oily-skinned black men who had been castrated before being allowed to guard Akbar's wives. The eunuchs were awesome creatures, scantily clothed, but often wearing brilliant white turbans that contrasted sharply with their ebony skin. Madrigal shuddered to think that she, too, would soon be guarded by them. The fact that they had been castrated did not ease her discomfort. Thus far she had no complaints about her treatment; she had been pampered, fed, and clothed extravagantly, and felt and looked better than she had in weeks.

Madrigal absentmindedly watched a small fishing vessel tack its way through the currents toward Tangier. She squinted her lovely green eyes at the horizon, idly wondering if what she saw was Spain, but then decided it was only a cloud bank settling over the passive sea.

Akbar approached her silently, observing her profile when she thought she was alone. "You look toward Spain. It is a waste of time." He reached over and toyed with her loosened veil. She recoiled at his touch. "Ah, still you fear Akbar! That is foolish. I am merely a bookish man forced to fight for his emir."

She tried to regain her control of a moment ago. It would not do to have him see her terror. "I am told I shall be moved into the harem this day. Once again, I

172

beg you to return me to my father. He is rich," she lied, "and would pay a handsome sum . . ."

"You think Akbar a fool?" he laughed. "The lands of Castilla-verde are poor! Only when the Moors occupied them were they worth any value."

"Yes . . . I see. I had forgotten how well traveled you are in *my* country!" She straightened her back and glared defiantly into his intent gaze.

"Please, you must remember that I seek no more wealth. What pittance your father could place in my palm is no more than a grain of sand to me."

She knew that Akbar spoke the truth, for he was reputed to be the most powerful and wealthy man in all Morocco. No, she mused, I'll not be able to bribe him with money, but what else have I?

As if he read her thoughts, he stated, "I would be a fool, a thousand times over, to let one so beautiful slip through my fingers. Come, let us take refreshment together." He led her through the archway into the courtyard. Rainbow-colored pillows had been placed in the shade of a palm, and a silver goblet of mixed juices was offered to her. Madrigal thirsted for a flagon of rich red wine, but Moslems never drank, she remembered; it was against their religion.

She regarded him from under the fringe of her dark lashes while sipping slowly at the cool drink. He was tall for a Moor, though not nearly as tall as Roderick, and his close-cropped black beard was sprinkled with silver. His skin was deep olive, his limbs finely shaped and well muscled. Although Akbar appeared strong, her husband was more powerfully built, she thought suddenly, then wished that Roderick's image would cease to haunt her imagination.

Akbar sat watching her silently, too. He had seldom seen one so lovely and pure, and although he had been afforded a few glimpses of her perfect body when she

173

had been ill, he still longed to see her fully unclothed. He watched her color heighten as he eyed her hungrily; he admired the creamy skin that betrayed her nervousness, for Moorish women were too dark-complected to reveal their true feelings with a blush.

Akbar clapped his hands. Immediately three slaves appeared. One cleared away the goblets while another checked Akbar's striped pillows; the third set a hookah pipe by his side. After Akbar had explained to Madrigal the simple workings of the pipe, he sat back and enjoyed the intoxicating hashish. He did not, however, offer it to her, for the status of women did not permit such a gesture.

By the time the late-afternoon shadows had crept across the courtyard, she was quite tired. Akbar remained motionless, his eyes closed. At first she thought he slept, but then she saw his hand brush away a fly from his brow, so she assumed he had simply chosen to ignore her. Finally, when a slave came for her, Akbar reluctantly opened his eyes. "You will go to the women's quarters now."

She fidgeted with her veil, refastening it at the side. "When am I allowed out, Akbar? I must know!"

He grinned widely. "My poor little rosebud, it is not a prison. How provincial you women from the north are! Go, now . . . I shall call for you from time to time."

That was it. She was dismissed from the outside world and cast into a maleless domain where no one even spoke her tongue! Her heart sank in misery, but she rose and followed the eunuch meekly. And to make matters worse, she suddenly remembered, surely his four wives would detest her, making her very existence even more wretched.

When they reached the entrance to the harem, however, she was heartened to find Pitra there. The young Sicilian girl took Madrigal in hand, chattering away in Spanish. Madrigal recalled that Pitra had said that Akbar had traded her for one of his own slaves in order to keep Madrigal company and to translate her wishes. Now she felt more at ease with the servant girl there to greet her.

The first impression she had of her surroundings was one of wealth and color, sunshine and laughter. There were children playing around the fountain that was the focal point of the large, octagonal, tiled courtyard. Eight graceful archways led to the sleeping quarters and baths. On the right side of the fountain was a long, low, hammered brass table on which sat an immense crystal bowl of ripe pomegranates, which the children could taste at will. She guessed there were at least ten youngsters, behaving in a disreputable fashion that would not be tolerated in Spain. And yet no one seemed to mind their cheerful noise. Madrigal learned later that there were times for play, for learning the scripts, for napping. It appeared that the young were the center of the harem, especially the male children. The women did not seem to mind Madrigal's presence; in fact, they took no notice of her at all. If it had not been for Pitra, she would not have known where to put her belongings or to lie down to rest.

As she stood uncertainly in the portal, veiled servants began carrying in steaming platters of food. "You will eat now," said Pitra.

"Yes, of course." Madrigal yawned and stretched her arms tiredly; she could hardly believe the sun had not yet set. Even though her health had been fully restored, she often felt rather sleepy in the evenings. It would not do to insult these women, however, so she followed Pitra to the brass table where the others were already seated.

The women of Akbar's harem had ignored Madrigal

when she had first appeared on their threshold, but now they were watchful and subdued. The eldest wife, perhaps twenty-eight or so, seemed to lead the group; if she took fruit or vegetables, the others did so, and when she spoke they were quiet and attentive. Madrigal knew at once that she would have to befriend the eldest if she wished to survive among these women.

Pitra told her that the eldest wife was named Yasmin and had been married to Akbar's dead brother. Madrigal looked Yasmin over, finding her more dark and lovely than the others. And as Pitra remained poised above Madrigal, fanning her with a palm leaf, she informed her mistress about the other wives. Raiisa was Akbar's favorite, Pitra explained, because "she was very good under the man," and Madrigal took note of Raiisa's air of seductiveness and her perfect curves. A bitch in heat, thought Madrigal wickedly. The two other girls were very young and shy, posing no real threat. Yasmin, on the other hand, was certain to make her life miserable; she glared rudely and contemptuously at her, goading the others into doing the same. Madrigal wondered if the Arab woman might be persuaded to help her escape. It was a thought, but too soon, she realized.

Madrigal was still unnerved when the serving women returned to prepare the evening baths. She gasped in shock when Pitra told her she must bathe also. But in the end, in front of the children, wives, and servants, she sank naked into the huge, oil-scented pool. When they pointed openly at her body, chattering rapidly, she desperately wished she could disappear.

As a last bulwark to her failing confidence, she asked Pitra to tell them she was a married woman, and when their eyes revealed their interest in this new knowledge, she had Pitra tell them about her recent miscarriage. Unbelievably, their reaction was what she had hoped for. Suddenly they were next to her, speaking in Arabic to Pitra, who could barely keep up with the translations.

"I also lost a child," said Raiisa sympathetically.

One of the younger wives asked, "Where are you from? Will you be ransomed?"

Only Yasmin held back slightly, then finally ventured to inquire, "This husband of yours . . . how many wives has he?"

Madrigal thought for a moment, then wisely replied, "Only myself. You see, we love each other very much."

Hearing that outrageous fib, Yasmin relaxed, and she, too, looked more kindly on the young Spanish captive.

The next morning was filled with female gossip as they watched the youngsters embark on their lessons with a tutor, a eunuch. Madrigal had some difficulty learning all their names, but by the noon meal she was able to address each child with an Arabic greeting. She even learned to face east for the frequent and lyrical prayers.

Unlike Spanish children, who were frightened into submission by fearful stories of hellfire, these youngsters possessed a natural sense of duty and confidence at a very early age and were afforded much individual freedom. She thought that she would raise her own children this way, but then remembered the doctor's words. A feeling of doom settled over her, and she wandered off to a private corner of the harem.

Akbar's oldest son, an eight-year-old named Jemil, approached her. He spoke to her directly, amazing her with his fluent Spanish. "You are saddened. I would like to understand this."

"You speak Spanish?" She still could not believe her ears.

177

"*St.* My father insisted that I learn, for someday I also shall cross the sea." He thrust his chest out proudly, almost making her wince at the thought of this Moorish child invading her country. How many more of them were there? she wondered.

Then she answered his question, her head held high. "I am unhappy that Akbar holds me a prisoner. I wish to go home."

He thought for a moment, his oval black eyes never leaving her face. "I see . . . but isn't our life better here? My father says it is."

"Well, it is not my desire to stay. My homeland means much to me."

The boy appeared surprised. "But you are only a woman! What *you* want is of no matter."

She was taken aback by his attitude; her eyes flashed. "In *my* country a woman is allowed many freedoms in life!"

Jemil turned and walked away, contemplating this strange revelation.

Later that afternoon Raiisa was summoned to Akbar, and it was more than obvious for what purpose he needed her. As she left the harem, she looked the role of seductress, having darkened her eyelids with kohl and bedecked herself with gold and jewels. Madrigal noticed that the other wives did not appear jealous or envious, even when Raiisa returned with eyes limpid from the aftermath of lovemaking. Madrigal shivered in the warm evening breeze, suddenly realizing that Akbar might call on her one day to perform the same act for him. Then what would she do? What if, when she denied him, he had her beaten? Or worse. Perhaps he would have her killed!

By the time the meal was served, she had talked herself into a state of terror. The more she attempted to quell her panic, the more she found she could not. Her brow was damp from perspiration and her mouth was dry. Then a sudden, inadvertent longing to escape engulfed her. She realized that the notion was not unsound if she could but keep her wits about her and reach Tangier. She knew so little about such things; her familiarity with the world of intrigue was limited to Roderick's battle stories and the fairy tales on which she had been reared.

As she sat cross-legged on a silk pillow, ostensibly partaking of the fruits and meats, her mind worked feverishly. If she could get to Tangier, she might find sanctuary in the Catholic church Pitra had told her about. Mayhap the priest could obtain a boat to carry her back to Spain.

She turned to Pitra, who stood awaiting Madrigal's pleasure, and asked, "How far is Tangier?"

As the question appeared completely innocent, Pitra replied, "Not far. A morning's walk or an hour's fast ride."

"Someday I might persuade Akbar to allow me a visit there," she fibbed easily.

"Oh, milady! I should not think so—'tis no place for a woman of your stature!" The Sicilian girl could not imagine why anyone would want to leave the comforts of Adha al-Allahu for the squalor of the city. It never occurred to her that the beautiful young foreigner might have another reason for wishing the information.

The women retired for the night after the children had been fed and bedded down; Madrigal thought the tots would never fall asleep. She waited impatiently, feigning slumber in her own alcove until all was silent, and still she made no movement. Finally, certain that her flight would not awaken them, she silently crept by the archways and sought the entrance door to the harem. Thankfully, the guard was absent from his post and stood several yards down the corridor with his back turned to her. There was no time to waste; he might return at any instant. She took a deep breath and fled in the opposite direction.

The guards at the gate were not so easy to fool; they kept their posts for what seemed an eternity, and finally, when she thought all hope for escape was lost, she formed a plan. She looked frantically around her for a small object. Spying a pile of pebbles in the inner courtyard, she stole over to them and retrieved a small handful. Then she hid herself in the shrubbery next to the iron gateway and tossed first one stone, then another, until the guards heard the faint disturbance and rushed inside, past her hiding place. Quickly, but on cat's feet, she flew through the gate, undetected, and did not stop her breathless run until she was near exhaustion. Still, she managed to keep up a steady pace on the tree-lined edge of the road leading to Tangier. By the first streaks of thin light, she was winding her uncertain way through the narrow, empty streets of the city.

Her heart pounded heavily and her breath was labored, but her mind was alert and excited by the realization that she was almost free. Only a few minutes more, she prayed hopefully, and she would find the church.

A light rain began to fall, misting her vision and drenching her scanty dress and veil. She could feel her perspiration mixing with the moisture, causing her to shake from the chill wetness. Tears began to stream down her cheeks as she raced futilely from street to street, unable to locate a church of any description.

Then the sound of a horse's hooves, ringing harshly on the ancient stones underneath them, could be heard echoing in the streets. Closer and closer they thudded toward her, until her terror was complete and she stood backed against a crumbled wall, eyes wide in fear.

Rounding a corner, then emerging like a wraith from the dismal mist, came an ebony Arabian, viciously spurred on by its rider. Breath snatched at Madrigal's throat, and her heart threatened to burst as she fixed her gaze on the steed's flaring nostrils and frenzied, white-ringed eyes.

The horse pranced heatedly before her now, reined in tightly, causing her to press herself further into the wall. Before she knew what had happened, the rider had caught her arm and hoisted her up, the great horse rearing excitedly. Then, with his forearm crushing her breasts, the horseman let out a deep, triumphant cry of conquest and urged the lathered Arabian forward.

Chapter 24

Madrigal's return to the harem had been accomplished so easily that she wondered if Akbar's wives even suspected she had been gone; perhaps they thought she had been summoned to their lord during the night. She shuddered, fearing he would indeed summon her shortly and punish her in some fiendish way known only to the ungodly. She lived under this cloud of uncertainty for several days, growing more and more anxious as time passed without a word from Akbar.

Life in the harem was quite comfortable, much more so than at Castilla-verde, for Akbar's home was run smoothly and graciously. The physical aspects far outweighed those at Madrigal's home or even at Halconbosque. She spoke with the four women in her few words of gutter Arabic, picked up from the Moors living near Castilla-verde, or let Pitra translate for her when her thoughts grew more complicated. The wives included her in their prattle and their fuss over the children, in the daily gossip about the costly clothes and jewels, and grew very curious as to Madrigal's world. They found it hard to believe that Spanish women could walk out of their homes, alone and unveiled.

"But don't the men attack you when they look upon your face?" Raiisa asked.

"No," Madrigal laughed, "at least not usually. They are accustomed to it. Women are everywhere, in the marketplace, at festivities—"

"Ooh!" Raiisa cried. "I could not bear all those filthy men looking at me!" She shivered deliciously.

That morning the dreaded summons came. One of Akbar's huge eunuchs bowed heavily, showing his many folds of flesh, and told Madrigal that Lord Akbar wished to see her at once in his private book room. The enormous slave led the way, waddling through innumerable corridors until he came to a carved, inlaid wooden door. He pushed it open, waved her in, and was gone, leaving her on the threshold of a wondrous sight.

The large room before her contained shelf after shelf of books, bound in colored leather and intricately hand-tooled in gold leaf. All bore the swirling Arabic script. Ancient ivory scrolls filled one long shelf, protected by a glass panel. The library resembled a storehouse of irreplaceable jewels.

Then she saw Akbar seated cross-legged on a soft cushion in front of a low, elegant desk of shining ebony wood. His dark head was bent over a piece of parchment and he moved a plume across the page, dipping it intermittently into a gold inkwell. He did not look up, and she was at a loss to know what to do. She had expected imprisonment, a beating, a scolding at the very least. But this man was busy writing and did not even seem to notice her!

She stood quietly for several minutes, afraid to move. Then he put down his plume and looked up. She was further unnerved when an errant ray of sun, slanting through the window, lit his face as he spoke.

"You will dine with me this eve, Lady Madrigal. Wear your best finery—I wish to be surrounded by beauty." He was silent for a moment, watching her intently. She could not help but squirm under his acute regard.

"I have written a poem to you; your beauty has inspired me," he went on. "I even wrote it in Spanish, which is a bit difficult for me, but I have persevered." His sculpted lips split in a smile, showing his white, even teeth in the golden light. "Would you like to hear it?" He answered his own question. "Of course you would. How foolish of me to ask . . ." He read from the parchment, glancing at her from time to time:

"Drown in her sea-green eyes
　　I shall!
Dive and dive again for
　　love.
Swim in her beauty as in
　　a lake;
Cool, yet hot as the lightning spark from above.

She trembles like a bird
　　afraid,
But within beats a heart
　　as strong
As any man's desires for
　　his love
When he travels from home too long."

He sat back and assessed her reaction. "It is fair to say I have some trouble with your language. It will not bend to my will like my own does."

183

"I . . . I am sure it is very fine, milord," Madrigal said, still reeling from shock. "I have little experience with poetry, or with those who write it."

"No, certainly not. I keep forgetting what a primitive country you live in. Your men do not have the leisure for poetry, but they should try it sometime—it disciplines the intellect."

Madrigal tightened her lips at his obvious insult. It would not do to anger him, however; hasty words had caused her enough problems in the past.

"My Lord Akbar," she finally ventured, "I humbly beg you to release me and return me to my father."

"Ha! The lioness humbles herself! I like her better spitting and clawing, with a gleam in her eye."

"Please . . . I must know the fate of my sister . . ." Madrigal's throat constricted and tears pricked her eyes.

"Enough! Do not attempt to ply me with your female wiles! I have no intention of returning you . . . yet. Why, you are one of my spoils of war! I have earned you!"

"War! You make war on defenseless women and call it honor! You are nothing but a coward, a bully! You men are all alike, thinking you own us!" She stamped her foot in helpless fury and turned her back on him.

Akbar rose and walked toward her. "The spitfire returns! I am sorry to have angered you, my beauty. However, no harm befell your sister at the hands of my men. We know that most of your party escaped safely." He laid a hand on her shoulder and saw relief flood her features. "Come, let us speak of other things. I do not wish to argue. Sit here by me." He led her to a low divan near the large, sunny window. "Have I told you the story of Adha al-Allahu?" His tone was mild.

Madrigal was immensely relieved at his words. He was not angry at her outburst; he had not even mentioned her escape attempt. What kind of man was he? She shook her head in answer to his question.

"In your language that means 'sacrifice to Allah.' My great-grandfather named it thus when he came from Egypt to make his home here. He was a government official and had been sent by the emir to bring enlightenment to these people and to oversee our invasion into al-Andalus." Akbar let his hand come to rest on her thigh, lightly brushing the thin material of her gown. He continued his narrative. "His family was originally from Alexandria, the pearl of all cities, and he hated to leave, for his heart remained in his homeland. But duty called and he came to Morocco and built this home. Here he raised his children and spent his life collecting these books from as far away as Babylonia and Persia. And so it was named, a sacrifice to Allah, for indeed the man had given up much."

Madrigal tried to ease her leg away from his touch; he smiled at her effort and allowed her more room on the divan. She relaxed, then listened in fascination to the rest of Akbar's tale.

"My great-grandfather accomplished one thing in his life, though. He made his *hajj*, the journey to Mecca, but alas, he was nearly eighty years old then and desperately ill. Nothing could stop him when his mind was made up, so, in spite of his illness, he ordered a special litter built and brought twenty black slaves to carry it two thousand miles to Mecca! What courage! He worshiped at the tomb of the prophet and died on the way home. That was of no importance, for his pilgrimage had been made, and he now abides in a garden where all is beauty and women are forever made virgins again after each night of pleasure." He smiled broadly at his words and watched Madrigal to see if she understood his allusion, but she was looking down at her hands and blushing.

"Come, now, my treasure, do you not feel better? Was that not a marvelous tale? And every word of it is the truth, I swear upon the hump of the camel that bore Mohammed."

She finally glanced at him from under her long black lashes, an irrepressible smile curving her rosy lips. "You tell a good tale, Akbar. I thank you."

He extended a slim brown finger and traced the curve of her lips. "My heart swells to see you smile, Madrigal. Your beauty is great whether you are angry or sad, but it is even more glorious in the sunshine of your happiness. Mayhap I shall be able to make you smile more often."

Madrigal drew back from his touch; a frown clouded her features. "You can make me smile by returning me to my home, and by nothing else!"

His curving black brows came together. "Be gone, woman! You are beginning to try my patience!"

Madrigal whirled and fled from the beautiful library, her lips pressed together in angry defiance.

When Madrigal entered Akbar's elaborately decorated main chamber that evening in response to his orders, she trembled with apprehension. Why had he insisted that *she* dine with him? Hadn't she made it plain that she wanted only to go home? This would be her first evening alone with him, she was certain he would mention her futile escape attempt and demand payment for his hospitality. Madrigal almost turned and fled, but his eyes had met hers and she forced herself to approach him.

The room she had entered was enormous. Several lofty arches led to other alcoves but gave the effect of one huge, open area, tiled in radiant colors. Exquisite filigree work was everywhere; a fountain splashed in the center. Several veiled slaves stood behind Akbar, who was comfortably seated on crimson silk cushions.

He wore a deep violet robe and an intricately woven blue turban. In all, he was a compelling man, ensconced in Oriental splendor as he was. The last streaks of a brilliant red sun slanted across his face and made his eyes appear amber.

Her breath caught suddenly because the light cast a devilish aura across his visage. He indicated the pastel Persian carpet beneath his cushions. "Be seated, milady. May I be permitted to comment on your excellent choice of yellow tonight?"

She seated herself a proper distance away. "*Gracias,* milord. But I fear that my health is somewhat poor this eve. May I be allowed to sup with milord at a later date?" What an accomplished little liar she was becoming! The thought brought an unbidden look of shame to her eyes.

"Ah! But I must summon the physician at once!"

"That will not be necessary," she said quickly.

"Very well, it shall be as you say." He clapped his hands for the liquid refreshments. She fidgeted with her veil, her eyes downcast, unable to bear Akbar's infuriatingly smug smile. "Lady Madrigal, a small favor to your host," he said, rising and then kneeling next to her. She felt incredibly hot and shaken, but certainly he would not maul her in front of the servants!

"Hair such as yours, the color of the raven's wing, should not be bound away from sight." He reached around the back of her head and unfastened the veil; his eyes never left hers as he adeptly untied the carefully arranged bun. While the heavy, silken tresses fell slowly between his fingers, she felt an odd, tingling sensation spread through her belly. Lord! What was happening to her stern resolve to avoid this man's attentions? What sort of wanton had her husband turned her into, that a strange man's touch could affect her at all?

Akbar sensed her unease and thought that perhaps

he was proceeding too rapidly with her seduction. He backed off and returned to his cushions, then summoned the slaves to bring in the meal.

They made polite, everyday conversation during most of the fare, until Akbar remarked, "I did not know my enemy Halconbosque was a married man. How was he so fortunate to have found you?"

She grew edgy and squirmed on her pillows. "We met only last spring, Lord Akbar. There is little to tell."

"Not yet wed a year! But why would he allow you to travel alone . . . and so far? I fear I am confounded!" He selected a ripe plum and sucked on it sensually, his dark eyes fixed on her face.

"Really, Akbar, I have no wish to be rude, but I prefer not to discuss my marriage."

His deep, throaty laughter surprised her. "Now I see! Or do I? You were fleeing him, is this not so?" He reflected for a moment, then said, "What a proud fool he is to let a woman such as you—"

"Please!" she cried. "My past is forgotten, buried. I will not discuss it!" She had risen and walked to an alcove, staring hopelessly out toward the sea.

He came up behind her and gently leaned her back against him. She resisted for a moment, then gave in, her unwanted tears spilling onto her cheeks. His lips brushed her fragrant hair and his fingers tightened ever so slightly on her shoulders. " 'Tis best to lighten the heart through the gift of words, lest that fragile organ burst from pain too long withheld."

"That is a beautiful thought, Akbar," she murmured. "If only I could."

He turned her around to face him, his lips resting on her brow for an instant. "You must tell me, and I swear on the Prophet's beard that only I shall know your secret."

It would be a relief to talk to someone, she thought. Perhaps this stranger would be best.

Once back on the cushions, she wiped her eyes with her fingers and straightened her back. "In my country, I would have confessed to a priest. Mayhap your ears are better, for my shame is great."

He gazed silently into her brimming, emerald-green eyes as she slowly began to tell him of her first meeting with Roderick. "He looked so awesome—frightening, I suppose—mounted on his huge horse with the sun glistening on his sword and shield." She went on to describe how the king had commanded their marriage and how she had feared Halconbosque. She spared Akbar nothing, relating somewhat red-faced, her involuntary response to her husband and his subsequent rejection of her; her dislike of his black moods and his threats to mistreat her.

"And did he beat you?" Akbar asked.

"No," she replied, but then went on to speak of her discontent when she had become pregnant and of her sister's visit to Halconbosque, including Elena's obvious and blatant lust for Roderick.

He broke in once again. "Madrigal, this sounds to me much like a normal marriage in your country."

"Normal!" she cried in disbelief.

"You misunderstand," he protested. "Halconbosque is an arrogant and proud warrior whose valor on the field of battle is great, this I know well." He laughed. "But in the world of women . . . well, I fear he has much to learn. The man sounds smitten by his love for you, Madrigal, probably his first true love, and he needs time to adjust to his own feelings." Akbar took her hand carefully.

"If only that were so, but alas, he has sorely used me, for in truth, he took me only as a tool of revenge against my father. A sick, insane plot—"

189

"Wait! I have become lost," the Moor interrupted her.

"He thinks my father is the man who cruelly murdered his own father when he was a boy!" She cringed, remembering Roderick's brutal accusations.

"Is this possible?" Akbar lifted a dark brow.

She sighed deeply. "As God is witness to my words, I swear my father is incapable of harming another human being."

"Didn't you tell your husband of his error?"

"*Sí, sí*, I did, but he turned from me and would not listen. He matters little for he wed me only to avenge himself upon my father. There is no love, only tortured hatred for me. I miscarried, in truth, fleeing from Roderick's wrath."

"Will he have you back?" Akbar's tone was full of concern.

"Never. We despise each other. My leaving was a blessing for us both. 'Tis God's will." She allowed him to clasp her hand more tightly, searching his dark eyes for understanding.

Akbar was silent. His mind retraced the many times he had faced Halconbosque in battle. He recalled when Halconbosque had spared the life of a young Moorish guard, sending the boy back to camp with a message for Akbar himself. The boy had recounted the story, concluding, "And when the baron spared my life, he bade me seek you out and ask if you must use children to do your battle." Now Akbar smiled to himself, remembering his reaction to the message; at first he had been angry, but then he had seen compassion in the words. No, Akbar mused, Madrigal's impression of her husband was somehow twisted, for though he was undeniably dangerous, he was not cruel. In fact, the Moor held Halconbosque in high esteem.

Finally Akbar spoke. "For reasons of my own, I fear you have misjudged your husband and have probably sinned greatly against him by your flight." Then his tone softened. "How could I possibly believe, seeing your unearthly beauty before my eyes, that he is content without you? No, milady, at this very moment he is searching for you."

"Believe what you will, but rest assured that he bids me good riddance, and I bid him the same."

Akbar motioned toward the shadows across the room, and two very sensual-looking girls appeared before them, clad in loose, transparent garments. Then a wailing, rhythmic sound commenced from an unknown source, the likes of which Madrigal had never heard before. She thought it was composed of tiny bells and high-pitched drums. The women rotated their hips to the beat of the music, their arms whirling above their heads, then snaking down to their sides. Their scanty attire fully revealed their lithe bodies, and Madrigal found she could not tear her eyes from the spectacle.

Akbar, however, had his keen black eyes on Madrigal. He smiled at her reaction; his loins began to ache in anticipation. He wondered briefly if her response would be willing or somewhat restrained; he hoped she would come to him easily, for rape was not his fancy.

The girls finished their seductive dance and, giggling, left the chamber. The music continued in the background, but no one was visible, not even a serving slave. Madrigal turned to face Akbar, a dreamy look in her eyes, her body relaxed now. She felt no fear of him when he began to caress her silky hair and kiss her slim neck.

He murmured in her ear, "Ah, my jeweled treasure, you drive me to madness . . . Come, lie back."

As she did so she wondered at his gentleness, his complete, unselfish concern for her. She knew suddenly that she wanted this dark, virile Moor to possess her, for her heart ached with a need to be loved and pampered. Here was a man capable of giving himself honestly and warmly, without using harsh words or an iron grip to force her into submission.

"Akbar, please . . ." she whispered.

He propped himself up on an elbow, his hand stroking her breast through the thin material of her gown. "Are there ghosts between us?"

"I do not understand," she replied.

"You shall have me if, in truth, your eyes can close and see only *my* face." His voice, although husky, was strangely demanding.

"But I am here with you . . . and Roderick is far away. I hate him!" Why did he have to bring up the bitter subject of her husband?

"Mayhap." He thought a moment. "But can you honestly say your body does not ache for *him?*"

"No! You are wrong!" She felt her nerves tense and she sat up. "Why, you're as arrogant as he! He is like that—he'll take me only if he can dominate my thoughts—my very soul!" She rose abruptly and glared down at him. "He beds me only when he wants to prove his total possession of me!"

Akbar measured his words slowly, deliberately. "And so shall I."

Chapter 25

By the following afternoon Madrigal had accepted in her mind the full impact of Akbar's obvious intentions toward her. He was really no different from Roderick, she believed, for he had also wanted complete possession of her—and that she would never give to any man!

At least Juan de Vegas had been willing to accept her on her own terms, she recalled, allowing her to retain a measure of freedom. But Akbar had nearly wooed her with soft words of love, and all the while he had been unwilling to bed her as a person with feelings of her own. In fact, she had spent the entire morning trying to convince herself that she had narrowly escaped infidelity through her own lack of good sense. She would not be so easily seduced again, she vowed silently. Both Akbar and Roderick could go straight to the devil for all she cared!

The women of the harem had been coolly polite to her since her meal with Akbar the previous evening. But she was determined not to let their behavior daunt her. She went about the business of eating and bathing alone, avoiding conversation even with Pitra. In the late afternoon, to escape her whirling thoughts, she sought permission to walk on the beach with a eunuch in attendance. Akbar granted her this small concession, and she left the confines of the harem.

The beach was nearly deserted; only two of Akbar's sons were frolicking in the surf, with a swimming master looking on. She avoided their company and walked westward toward the setting sun. It was still light, but chilly, so she wrapped her cloak around her to fend off the sea breezes.

She began to marvel at Akbar's foresight in having his sons trained in the art of swimming; one day it might become necessary for them to do so in all conditions, she thought, feeling the nip in the air. It was unfortunate that her own kinfolk knew so little about the sport.

She walked for some distance, her bare feet sinking into the sun-warmed sand. Several times she stopped to examine an interesting shell or pebble. The waves were cool and gentle this day, teasing at her toes. She looked over her shoulder to note that the eunuch hung back respectfully some hundred yards, and, satisfied, she breathed in the salt air and strolled on. Suddenly the image of Roderick on the beach at La Torre rose in her mind. His unusual tenderness that day had made her so happy. She sighed and tried to put him from her thoughts.

While bending to view a small, beached fish, she thought she heard a gull screeching overhead and glanced skyward, but there was none. Frail, long-legged birds scurried ahead of her, running to and fro with the motion of the waves, and she smiled at their constant movements. She walked on for several more yards and heard the shriek again; still no gull was in sight. Yet something was amiss. Even the frail birds seemed to sense it, and they ceased their movements. She cast her eyes seaward, hearing the same cry of a moment ago, and then she spotted the creature. It was certainly not a bird, but appeared to be a large, floundering fish. No, she thought suddenly, not a fish, but a body! Was it an animal?

She raced up the coast until she stood directly opposite the body. The wind carried the scream to her ears again, and she realized it was a plea for help—a human cry!

The current looked smooth enough, but why was the person clawing helplessly at the ripples? In a split second of recognition she heard her own name echo across the expanse of water. "God in Heaven!" she cried aloud, for it was Akbar's son Jemil out there.

A moment of indecision, then she threw off her cloak and entered the water. Almost immediately she felt a strong current surround her and thought it to be a riptide. Panic set in at once; still, it was too late to retreat, so she tried to ease her fear and let the waters swirl her north and west. The distance separating her from Jemil lessened by the second, and she marveled that she was still afloat.

Madrigal had swum but once in her life, when her brother-in-law had urged her onto a sailing raft five years ago. The raft had overturned and she had made her way, alone, back to shore. But this was different; the tide was strong and cold, unwilling to release its grasp on her. Like the boy, she also struggled to keep afloat.

Because Madrigal did not fight the current as strongly as Jemil, she managed to reach him before he lost consciousness. She grabbed at his sodden shirt, frantically maneuvering to keep them both above water. Trying to support his body and hers seemed impossible. She panicked. The boy flailed helplessly at her, and finally she struck him on the chin, rendering him unconscious but much easier to handle.

It had been only a few minutes since she had entered the water, but her strength was nearly gone from the unaccustomed exertion. Just as all hope for survival appeared lost, she felt a strong eddy whirl them about and spit them, miraculously, into calm waters. The riptide disappeared, and the normal swells began to carry them toward the beach. She tightened her grasp around the boy's chest and prayed as a large wave picked them up and tossed them onto the shore, nearly drowning them both in its final crash.

Madrigal scrambled to her feet, and with much choking and spitting, managed to drag Jemil toward the dry sand. There she collapsed next to his inert form, wretchedly vomiting the salt water and falling into a daze.

Later she vaguely recalled strong black arms carrying her, and then blessed warmth driving away the chill. Much later she awakened to the soft coaxing of distant voices and a stomach gnawing with hunger.

It was morning; the bright glow of her quarters assured her that she had indeed slept a full night. Jemil sat at her bedside, a huge smile lighting his young face.

"Allah be praised," he said.

She smiled back at him. "I cannot tell you of my relief at seeing you sitting here, Jemil. I thought you dead for certain!" She reached over and placed a hand on his shoulder.

"And we thought *you* dead!"

"What happened? How did we get here?"

"The swimming master sought help when I was found missing, and he and your guard spotted us floundering toward shore. By the time my father arrived, you were very close to death, but I had awakened"—his eyes grew very round—"and I thought you drowned for sure!"

Madrigal did an odd thing then. She laughed, and when her peals of mirth continued, the boy laughed, too. They giggled until she thought her sides would split. Whether it was from relief or from the plain and simple joy to see the light of day, she neither knew nor cared. All that mattered now was to be alive.

"What an adventure!" she gasped.

The harem wives stood cheerfully at the door, laughing nervously along with Madrigal and Jemil. Yasmin, the boy's mother, was so happy that words failed her altogether, and she ran to Madrigal and knelt at her bedside, grasping her hand and kissing it.

After some time had passed, Madrigal managed to dress more properly and eat a hearty meal. Jemil stayed by her side all the while. Pitra finally appeared to inform Madrigal of Akbar's wish to meet with her in the courtyard, this time, of course, at *her* leisure. She finished the enormous fare, and with Jemil tagging along, went to her audience with Akbar.

"Please take a seat, Madrigal," he offered. "I can find no words in your language to express my gratitude."

She smiled. "Words of thanks are unnecessary, Akbar. I merely did what anyone would have done under the same circumstances."

He ignored her explanation and turned to Jemil,

indicating he should speak. Jemil cleared his throat. "In my insignificant life I have but one purpose now, and that is to protect you from harm, Lady Madrigal." The boy squared his shoulders. "One day I shall save your life, and, in Allah's wisdom, my debt will be paid."

Madrigal's mouth was open. She hardly expected such a promise and could think of no way to reply. At last she found her voice. "Jemil, 'tis not a custom in my country to be so beholden to one whose life you have saved. In truth, I shall not accept your pledge, for the burden is overly heavy on one so young."

Akbar silenced her with a flourish of his hand. "The debt is a debt of honor, and my son is proud to bear the burden."

"But, Akbar," she protested, "someday I shall return to my home. Your son cannot possibly be with me then!"

"It is Allah's way to mete out justice. And so it shall be. Though mountains and seas shall come between, *He*, in His infinite wisdom, will see the debt paid."

She could only respond, "If you say so . . . I mean, who am I to know the scheme of things?" She laughed then and relaxed a little, knowing she could not dissuade them from their purpose.

"My son has asked me to consider returning you to your home." She gasped audibly. "And I have considered this."

"Oh, Akbar, if only I could!" she cried.

He smiled at her and she fell silent, afraid to put her feelings into words. "In the spring," he continued, "I shall see you safely home. I, too, owe you a debt for saving the life of my son."

She took a deep breath and sank back into the cushions. Finally she murmured, "Thank you." Although spring seemed a long time away, she was

197

immensely grateful to him and said no more. Akbar was a man of his word, and she knew he would keep his promise no matter what ensued.

The next two days passed quickly as Madrigal found warmth and friendship within the confines of the harem. She enjoyed the female chatter that Pitra translated for her. Jemil constantly stayed by her side and flattered her with his words of undying devotion. He even went so far as to declare his love. "Ten years' difference in age is not so much, is it?" he asked.

She smiled at him. "Very little indeed."

"Then if your husband should . . . well, if some evil were to befall him . . . you would be free, yes?" He kept his eyes downcast.

" 'Tis a dreadful thought, but yes, if I were widowed I would be free."

The boy squirmed in embarrassment. "You are the most beautiful woman in the world, except for my mother, of course. I could provide well for you."

She fought to stifle the laugh that threatened to burst from her. It was quite evident that Jemil had grown to worship her, and she felt a certain pride in his declaration. She placed her hand tenderly against his soft cheek. "I am greatly honored that you deem me worthy of your protection. I shall always cherish the thought, Jemil."

"But if someday I take you for a wife, you must remain in the harem with my other wives!" he declared.

"*Sí*," she giggled, her attempt to appear humble failing miserably.

Madrigal thought of the oncoming winter, which she would spend at Adha al-Allahu. It would be long, yes, but she was growing fond of these people, even if they were Moors. She planned to spend the time learning their tongue, and perhaps she would be allowed to study astrology with Jemil's tutor. There was much to learn here, the prospect of which excited her quick mind. And now that she knew Elena and Maria were most likely safe and well at Castilla-verde, she felt secure, almost at peace, in her surroundings. The only remaining problem, she mused, might stem from Akbar, although he, too, could be handled if she used her wits. The fact of her barren condition she had put at the back of her mind, for there was no man she wished to bed, nor one to whom she wished to bear a child.

Chapter 26

The south side of the central courtyard was warm in the morning sun, protected from the sea breezes. Akbar took tea there with Madrigal each morning, unless he was tending the affairs of his large holdings. It was a relaxed, informal time; a servant would bring them strong mint tea and tiny, delicious honey or sesame seed cakes, then leave them to their conversation. Often Jemil would appear for a few moments, but his angry tutor would quickly escort him back to his studies.

It was December now, and Madrigal was describing the Christmas celebrations at Castilla-verde. Akbar delighted in her presence, her lilting voice, her sparkling contentment. He regretted his perhaps too-hasty promise to return her to her father. It was humiliating for any man to be so taken by a mere woman; likely it was a blessing that she would be gone in the spring. Akbar held himself tightly in check, never allowing his desire for her to emerge. The temporary inconvenience would be well worth it when she finally succumbed to him. He wanted her whole and complete, acquiescent, totally possessed by him, and he knew she was not yet ready for that. But his patience would be rewarded;

kindness and gentleness would win her in the end, whereas force and passion would not.

She already thought him a kind protector, a man of honor and learning. It was but a small step to physical desire, and Akbar had great faith in his attractions of power and persuasion.

"Akbar, you did not even hear me," Madrigal was saying, slightly annoyed at his inattention.

"*Perdóneme,* my rose, I was lost in contemplation of your beauty."

She blushed at his words, causing him to smile. "I was saying that I wish I could visit a priest. I have not said confession in so long. It would ease my heart, truly, to take communion."

"You have nothing to confess, my dear, unfortunately for us both," he said dryly. "But if you wish, I shall send for the priest from Tangier."

"Thank you, that would be very kind!"

"Do not thank me, Madrigal. It is nothing. I wish I could do much more for you." He allowed his gaze to follow the lines of her slim body under the silken robe. "Do you like the bracelet I sent you? I see that you wear it." He lifted her hand to admire the delicately worked, gold filigree band set with emeralds and diamonds. It was worth a king's ransom.

"It is *beautiful*," breathed Madrigal. "But so valuable! I honor you by wearing it here, but I shall not take it when I leave."

"It is a gift," Akbar growled, frowning. "It is *our* custom to accept a gift gracefully. To return it would be a grave insult."

"I must ask your pardon, then, for I am still not entirely familiar with your customs. I shall keep it and treasure it all my life, Akbar. You are too generous."

"Generous, ha! I have a dozen or so like it for the dancing girls if they please me. You cannot even imagine the extent of my generosity if you—"

His words were interrupted by a eunuch who bowed and apologized profusely for interrupting his master's ease, but a messenger from Tangier was at the gate and insisted he had vital information for Lord Akbar al-Kemil. The eunuch's lip curled in disgust as he spoke, showing his great contempt for this visitor and all his lowly ancestors.

"Send him in. Mayhap the fellow really has a message of some importance, although he most probably wants a few coins." As Madrigal rose to leave, Akbar pressed her down into her chair. "No, stay. It will only take a few moments, my pearl."

The eunuch ushered in a vile-looking, filthy creature, with open sores oozing wetly. Amazingly, Akbar seemed not to notice or to care about possible infection, but greeted him familiarly.

"So it is you, Musa. And what news do you bring this day that is so vital?"

Good heavens, Madrigal thought, Akbar knows him by name! The man straightened up and threw off his ragged hood. She was astonished to see that he was young and rather attractive despite his filth, and that he smiled, showing white, even teeth. He spoke eloquently in Arabic. She listened carefully, hoping to follow the conversation, but she caught only an isolated word here and there. As she sat watching the two men, she began to wonder if Musa were not one of Akbar's spies—she had never seen a real spy before!

Akbar listened seriously, his brows drawn together in a slight frown, his fingers drumming on the arm of his chair. Madrigal's ear suddenly caught a familiar sound in Musa's narrative; then she heard it again. He had mentioned Roderick Halconbosque! She strained to understand even a word of the story, her fingers clenched in her lap and nervously twisting her gold ring.

Finally Musa stopped speaking, and Akbar gave him

some rapid orders. The young man returned to his cowering posture and scuttled out, his rags flapping around his lean shanks. Akbar turned to Madrigal and saw her tense expression.

"You understood?" he asked gently.

"No, no, I heard only the name—my husband's name. Tell me, please, what did the man say?"

"It seems that I was correct. Your husband has no intention of letting you go so easily. He is in Tangier now, and has been seeking a boat to take him to Adha al-Allahu. The man has risen in my estimation . . ."

"*Madre de Dios,*" Madrigal whispered. "What am I to do?" Her eyes were wide with terror, her face white and pinched. "You must hide me, or tell him I am gone! Something!"

"We shall see what can be done . . . mayhap he will tire and give up the chase."

"You do not know Roderick. When he is determined, nothing stands in his way—nothing! He is a devil! He will kill me!"

"Now, now, my dear, do not panic. This husband of yours could not be such a monster as you say. I would not let him harm you in any case. Now, return to the women's quarters, and I shall await Halconbosque's pleasure. Calm yourself."

Roderick sat impassively in the small craft, his arms folded to contain his impatience. He was not at all certain he could trust the shifty-eyed boatman he had hired at an outrageous price, but the man had sworn on Allah's honor that he would deliver him to Adha al-Allahu—what an outlandish name for a man's home! They sailed around a jutting headland and a white, crescent-shaped beach came into view. Above the beach, on a rise, stood a white edifice, a low, sprawling shape on the brush-dotted hill.

Roderick heard the boatman say something in garbled Spanish, and he thought he caught the words "Akbar al-Kemil" and "Adha al-Allahu." So this *was* Akbar's retreat. What a puny place it seemed: no walls, no moats, no drawbridge, not even one tower. The fool! Surely anyone with a small army could fire the place and destroy all those within. Roderick suddenly wished he had brought his men with him—they would have made short work of this abode!

The boat nudged bottom a few yards from shore. Roderick thanked the boatman politely and waded in to shore. As he set foot on the firm white sand, a legion of armed Moors suddenly appeared on the crest of the hill. There were hundreds, perhaps thousands. So Akbar has been warned of my arrival, he mused. He strolled arrogantly toward the soldiers. Show no fear to these womanly heathen—they will scatter like dogs, or so he had always told himself. But Akbar's men stood firm, shoulder to shoulder, their burnished weapons and harnesses gleaming dully in the weak winter sun.

Then Roderick saw Akbar standing in the center of his men, dressed in a brilliant white robe, his hand resting lightly on the jeweled scimitar that hung at his side. Roderick was aware of his own travel-stained clothes, his torn cape and bristly face. He felt hot and uncomfortable, puffing slightly from his climb up the hill. Then he stood face to face with Akbar; he was taller, broader, but the Moor's body held a whipcord strength.

Silently, each assessed the other closely, jealously. Roderick was the first to break the tension.

"I have come for my wife, Akbar al-Kemil."

Akbar had to admire the courage of this man who had crossed a sea, landed on the foreign soil of an enemy, and calmly demanded his wife back. Halconbosque exuded determination, strength, and daring. But he was a fool, Akbar thought; no woman was worth the danger.

"Lady Madrigal is here, under my protection. She does not wish to go with you, I have her word on the matter. I have promised to return her to her father."

"*Lady Madrigal,*" Roderick snarled, "is *my* wife, and I demand that you bring her to me!" His words were slow and deliberate as he fought to control his temper.

"You speak truth, Roderick Halconbosque, but I would prefer to see the lady safely back to her father before you and she are . . . reconciled." The Moor's tone was reasonable and calm, driving Roderick to a higher pitch of rage.

"What *you* wish in this matter is of very small consequence to me!" he hissed through clenched teeth.

"Ah . . . but there you err, sir. As I said, the lady is under my protection and I will not go against her wishes. And since I am in control of the situation here"—he gestured lazily at his men—"I am afraid I cannot satisfy you."

Roderick had to clench his fists to keep from springing at his enemy's throat; he felt a hot pounding in his temples and forced himself to speak civilly. His voice emerged very low.

"Akbar, I know you for an honorable man. Since I cannot convince you to return my wife to me peacefully, I offer you a challenge. We shall fight, man to man, and the winner takes Madrigal with no interference."

"So be it, then," Akbar sighed, acceding to destiny. "I would prefer you to leave in peace and seek your death elsewhere, but if you insist on fighting, I agree."

Roderick drew his heavy sword and stepped backward, but the Moor quickly held up a hand. "Wait. I must give orders to my officers, or they will surely fall upon you." He turned and spoke to his captain, then waved Roderick down the hill. "I do not wish to disturb my wives and children with our quarrel. Let us go down to the beach."

The two figures, one tall and tawny-haired, the other shorter and raven-headed, descended the path side by side. Madrigal, watching nervously from a window, thought they could have been friends out for a stroll. Suddenly she realized what they planned to do, and she knew she could not bear to be the cause of a senseless, violent death. She looked wildly around her; she had to do something—run down to the beach and beg them to stop; grab a sword herself and strike—but strike whom, which one? There was no answer, and in truth, she had no way of stopping them. It was her fate to stand there and watch one bloody man emerge victorious to claim her as if she were a horse or a cow, a possession! She clasped her hands tightly to keep them from shaking and bit her lip to keep from screaming.

The men drew their weapons: the lighter, curved, and deadly scimitar against the lethal, heavy broadsword. Madrigal saw them lunge and parry, feeling each other out, drawing on their battle-trained reflexes to tell them of a weakness in the opponent's guard. Roderick moved like a machine, swinging his sword with great power, but Akbar was quick and light, easily staying out of reach, his blade arcing in a flash of liquid movement. They played with each other for several minutes, then began to use their weapons in earnest. They were a well-matched pair, as different as the hawk and the cat, but each as deadly as the other, as capable of merciless killing.

Their breath came quicker as the duel went on; sweat began to show darkly through their clothes and glistened on their foreheads. Madrigal could not hear the clang of the swords or the grunts of the two men, but their swirling bodies riveted her attention.

Roderick had a small slice of red on one cheek and Akbar's white shirt showed a bloodstain on one arm. The wounds appeared minor, and both men fought on furiously, slashing, sidestepping, parrying. Suddenly

Roderick seemed to falter, stumbling slightly in the sand, leaving his left side unprotected. Madrigal's heart stopped; this was the end, then. Akbar grinned wickedly and lunged for Roderick's heart, but as he stretched forward, Roderick neatly avoided his thrust and the blade. Before Akbar could recover, Roderick slashed his sword across and down. Akbar dropped his scimitar, his right arm hanging uselessly at his side as blood welled from a deep wound near his shoulder. He looked down at his arm in surprise, then looked up at Roderick. A grim smile curved his lips.

"You have bested me, Baron. You are a worthy foe as always. Now, do what you will. I have given my word."

"I have no wish to take a life for the lady. I repeat, I wish only my wife back."

Akbar was not surprised that Roderick did not finish the task; he himself would undoubtedly have spared the Spaniard's life. In reply, he said, "And you shall have her, even though the lady purports to despise you. Allah's will is done." He held a torn piece of his shirt to the bloody wound.

"We have had our differences," Roderick growled.

"Differences! Yes, I can imagine. Come, I must reassure my captain. He will be frothing with worry over my condition, but I fear you will have to lend me a hand. Your expert swordsmanship has left me quite lame."

The two men walked slowly up the hill, Akbar leaning on Roderick's arm, his face pale now from the loss of blood. When they reached the ranks of soldiers, Akbar explained the situation to his captain, assuring him that all was well. Soon afterward, Izak, the physician, appeared, carrying his bag of medicines and bandages. He pushed his way through the men to his master's side and quickly cleaned and dressed Akbar's wound. He then turned to Roderick and did the same

206

to the cut on his face, deftly putting in two sutures of catgut before Roderick could protest.

"Ye gods, man! What have you done to my face?" Roderick shouted, pushing Izak's arm away.

"It is customary in facial wounds, milord, to suture, as it makes for a less evident scar," Izak replied matter-of-factly.

"And what is wrong with a fairly won scar, Physician? 'Tis a mark of honor in my country." He sneered at the doctor.

"My friend, do not berate Izak," Akbar interjected. "He has been taught to care for the human body as if it were a treasure. He only wishes to do his best by you. Now . . . let us go to the harem."

Roderick followed the Moor and two guards down the long, brightly decorated corridors. He felt insignificant, humbled by the magnificence of Akbar's home. The blood lust of battle had ebbed from his brain; he was exhausted. How would she greet him? he wondered nervously. He realized his past cruelty to her and was willing to go half the distance toward reconciliation, but if she insisted on trying to escape him, he would have to punish her. Maybe she liked it here, in this ungodly Moor's house, lolling in luxury and sharing his elegant bed. Maybe he should have killed the damn Moor when he had had the chance, but Akbar was too good a soldier, too honorable a foe, to be slain over a worthless female's wantonness.

They came to an archway closed by carved double doors that were polished to a deep gleam. A huge eunuch stood in front of them, his massive arms folded over his chest, his flesh draped in corpulent folds. Roderick tried to open the doors, but a Herculean hand stopped him.

"This is the harem, Lord Roderick, and no man is allowed inside except me. He is only following orders," Akbar explained.

"Get my wife." Roderick addressed the eunuch coldly. The vast bulk shifted its gaze to Akbar with no change of expression. Akbar nodded, whereupon the eunuch opened the double doors and disappeared inside.

Roderick waited impatiently. The weeks had been long, the voyage tiring, the battle with Akbar almost senseless. He wanted his wife, he wanted peace, and he wanted to be gone from this hellish palace as quickly as possible. The moments stretched out. Then he heard a woman's voice, crying, begging, alternately angry and desperate. The eunuch appeared in the doorway, holding the struggling girl in his arms, his turban tilted crazily to one side. She was still trying to kick at his legs and push his arms away; her efforts were those of a butterfly fighting the wind. When she realized the eunuch had released her, she turned to the two men standing there. She gazed intently at each of them, her tear-filled eyes huge and fearful.

Then she gave a long, quavering sigh of utter defeat. "Why . . . Roderick . . . why?"

"You are my wife, Madrigal, I mean to have you back."

"You do not want me! You only want someone to torment! Leave me here, *please*. I am content, and Akbar has promised to return me to Castilla-verde. Let me go!"

"I shall never let you go—you belong to me! Whether you like it or not has nothing to do with the matter." His voice was as hard as she remembered it.

"I belong to no one but myself, Roderick. Remember that well, for I'll never bow to your will!"

Akbar could see that the situation was worsening. He admired the girl's spunk, having faced the baron himself and lost. He would truly miss her when she was gone. It was fated that he would never taste the delights of her body.

"Madrigal, may I speak with you a moment?" He took her aside, feeling her tremble as he held her arm. "Your husband has won you fairly in battle. I am a man of my word and must keep it, even though I shall weep bitter tears to see you go. You will go with him."

"Am I to be forever bargained for and foisted off on new owners, willingly or unwillingly?" she stormed. "What of *my* desires? *My* feelings? Does no one ask *me?*"

"No, my dear," said Akbar, smiling gently. "Beauty such as yours will always be sold to the highest bidder; it is the way of the world. And he"—he pointed to Roderick—"he is the highest bidder now. Make the best of the situation—it is your fate—and in the end all will be as Allah has ordained."

"Fate!" She spit the word and turned her back, but Akbar could see she had relented and bowed to necessity. He moved toward Roderick, who was still glowering.

"She will go with you now, Halconbosque. Treat her gently; she has been through much. Given a similar situation, I hope you would treat my wives with as much respect as I have shown yours."

"Respect! I can imagine what your notions of respect are!" Roderick remarked coldly. "Come, Madrigal, let us be on our way. We have a long journey."

"You must allow me time to say farewell to my friends here. I ask this one favor of you, Roderick." She avoided his eyes.

"Very well, say your good-byes, but, *por Dios,* quickly! It will be dark soon."

Madrigal turned and entered the harem, feeling her heart about to burst from misery. The women were gathered just beyond the doors, listening while Pitra translated for them. Madrigal embraced each one, giving the youngest wife's baby a kiss on his fat brown cheek. Jemil stood aside, his dark eyes filled with pain, for he had heard every word. She went to him and put a hand on his head.

"Now I shall never be able to repay my debt, Madrigal." He was near tears but tried manfully to hold them back.

"The ways of Allah are infinite in their wisdom, as you have so often reminded me. There will come a time, never fear, Jemil."

The boy clung to her for a moment, then straightened himself. Madrigal felt an immense pride in his show of restraint. She also felt a deep sadness, for there would be no boy of her own to comfort her through the years.

Chapter 27

Madrigal's health had been restored during her stay at Adha al-Allahu, but now she wondered if a relapse were not imminent. Perhaps it was a case of nerves, or simply exhaustion from the quick crossing to Tarifa. And if she had been secretly gratified when Roderick had come for her, now she again felt too empty, to sick inside, to think about it. Roderick had not spoken two civil words to her since the evening they had left Adha al-Allahu; he frequently grabbed her arm roughly, leading her here and there, thinking her incapable of following simple directions. When she pulled away from him and said she could not abide his touch, the familiar, bitter scowl twisted his features and she feared to speak to him again.

They were presently camped some fifteen miles from Castilla-verde, and Roderick planned to arrive there tomorrow. She prayed he would leave her there and return alone to Halconbosque. Why had he bothered to come for her at all? Did he actually enjoy their painful relationship?

Madrigal stared into his golden eyes as they sat across from each other, eating a rabbit stew by the evening fire. She could still feel the bruises under her breasts where he had gripped her in front of him on the saddle. The man was cold, hard, and cruel; even his well-muscled body bespoke his harshness.

She shifted her weight tiredly and said faintly, "Roderick . . . I trust you will behave honorably toward my father . . ."

"What? I cannot hear you—speak up, woman!"

She stiffened her resolve. "I said that I hope you keep your false accusations of my father to yourself."

He flung a stone at the nearby stream. "For all I give a *damn*, milady, your entire family can go straight to the devil!"

"You—you bastard!" she shrieked, hurling her half-eaten food into the dying embers.

He rose quickly and pulled her to her feet, shaking her delicate frame until her teeth chattered. "I will *not* tolerate your cursing! Is that clear?" He tossed her to the dust.

She lay on the ground seething with rage; her dark hair glowed in the patterned firelight. He kept his eyes on her, feeling foolish for allowing himself to be goaded into hurting her. He wondered achingly what happened to his sense of honor and decency whenever *she* was around.

"I am sorry if I harmed you, Madrigal," he said quietly. "Now, here . . . finish my share of the meat." He attempted to hand her his barely touched stew, but she swatted his hand away angrily. "Then go hungry, milady. I really do not care." He sat down across from her, then flung the remaining stew into the fire.

Madrigal gathered her cloak around her body, her eyes purposefully averted from him. Finally she went to her blanket, turned her back, and closed her eyes in an attempt to sleep. Some moments later he came and stood over her, absentmindedly rubbing the bristly growth on his chin. She sensed his presence and rolled over onto her back, her emerald eyes wide open now.

"Move aside, Madrigal," His voice was strangely low. She lay there, terrified, for she knew he would stop at nothing: bitter recriminations, painful bruisings, even rape if he so desired.

He knelt down and pulled her blanket away, his hand coming to rest on her bosom. She remained unmoving, but he could feel her recoil slightly. She looked so tempting, as she had the first time he had tasted of her innocence. His brow drew together as he thought of Akbar's brown hands on her soft, creamy flesh. He wanted to take her then, forcefully, to purge her body of Akbar's touch.

He spoke slowly, his voice edged with pain. "Did you respond to *him?* Tell me."

Her eyes widened in shock. She sat up abruptly and pushed him away. "How dare you accuse me of—of bedding him!"

"Do you deny it?"

"Why, you—you swine! I'll not even deign to answer the insult!" She snatched the woolen blanket over her breasts and challenged him with her eyes.

"No matter, milady"—his tone was sarcastic now—"for I shall not touch you until your monthly time comes again . . . and if his seed has taken, then the truth will be known."

She dropped the blanket and gave his cheek a stinging slap. Her chin was held high, defying him to strike her back. He did not. He merely stood up and glared down into her hate-filled eyes, then turned abruptly and walked away. She watched his retreating back and then lashed out at him with loathing, "I'll never share a bed with you! Never! Do you hear, you—you beast!"

"Think you not? Remember, you are my duly wedded wife. In truth, my sweet, I care little for what use others have put your lovely body to, just so long as you do my bidding when I command you." He forced a laugh at her expression of outrage, but he knew in his heart that his words were lies.

"I hate you!" she hissed. "I'll never submit to you again! You'll need chains to drag me back to Halcon-bosque!"

"Not an unsound thought—the idea intrigues me!" He stretched out beneath his covers and listened for a time to her soft weeping. When sleep came at last, his nightmare returned, a hellish, demonic dream of unattached heads and limbs floating through a dark sea of mist. He awoke, sweating in spite of the chill night air, and sat upright until the images in his mind finally dissipated with the rising of the sun.

They arrived at Castilla-verde that afternoon, and much to Madrigal's amazement, Roderick treated her father and sisters in a very civil manner—more civilly than he deigns to treat me! she stormed inwardly. Well, he is undoubtedly tired from the trip, and as drained as I from last night's verbal battle.

Teresa bubbled over all evening, lavishing love on them both. Lord Jaime had wept unashamedly at Madrigal's safe return, thanking Roderick repeatedly for his bravery in crossing to Morocco to rescue his beloved child. Elena, too, seemed pleased to see her sister alive.

Ignoring Roderick's coolness to her, Madrigal chatted gaily during the evening meal about her adventure. She spoke warmly of Akbar and described the elegance of Adha al-Allahu. Roderick listened intently for any mention of Akbar's use of her, but he found nothing in his wife's tone to betray her. Instead, she sounded completely fascinated by her experiences there. She told them about Jemil's near drowning and his subsequent oath of protection to her, blushing sweetly when she recalled aloud that the boy had mentioned taking her for one of his wives. Roderick sat mutely, trying to envision his wife's reckless swim to save the lad and her happiness when Akbar had promised to return her to Castilla-verde.

Elena replied politely to Madrigal's many questions about the ambush, but for the most part she kept her gaze fixed on Roderick. Finally she asked Madrigal, "Are we to believe that this Akbar, or his men, did not even touch you?"

"Elena!" came her father's shocked voice. " 'Tis not a subject for open discussion!"

"It is all right, Papa," Madrigal replied. "Lord Akbar treated me only as an honored guest." But her brow clouded when she realized that undoubtedly no one would believe her. Her own husband had not, so why should anyone else?

Roderick watched her sitting there, her eyes glistening and her lovely head held high. Mayhap she spoke the truth, he thought suddenly. Akbar was a chivalrous, decent man. And furthermore, what business was it of Elena's to interrogate *his* wife?

"Madrigal," he said softly, "shouldn't you retire? The day has been overly long."

She wondered briefly at his concern, then replied, "Yes, 'tis best." She rose and kissed her father lovingly on the forehead, making Roderick wonder if she could ever bestow a gentle kiss on him. He doubted it, for hadn't she expressed her hatred for him again and again?

When at last the Castilla-verdes had retired for the night, Roderick sat alone in the great hall, drinking thirstily from his wine-filled flagon. His thoughts were dark and brooding. Then he looked around the dim, firelit hall and recalled Madrigal's plea for assistance in restoring the ancient castle to its former majesty. His heart sank when he remembered the harsh argument that had ensued. Was he always to bring pain to her? To enjoy causing her misery and to bend her to his will? Could he pursue his scheme of revenge if it brought him to the depths of despair?

Minutes later, Roderick caught sight of a movement on the stairs. He turned in his chair to see Elena emerge slowly from the shadows, clad scantily. For the briefest moment he had thought it was Madrigal, but even at this distance the mistake was obvious. Madrigal did not have that calculated sway to her hips, nor did she wear her hair hanging loosely over one side of her face. There was always a cold aura surrounding Elena, so different from his wife's unaffected vivaciousness.

She crossed the cold stone flagging. "I thought you were asleep in the guest chamber, milord."

He ran a hand through his tousled hair. "No, I cannot find rest this night." He looked up at her and saw the faint mark on her uncovered cheek left by Stefano's hand; he was not surprised that it was still visible.

"Shall I keep you company?"

"If it pleases you, Elena." His voice was passive and weary, his words slightly slurred. What game was she up to now? he wondered idly.

She stood behind him and gently began to knead his tired neck and shoulders. The heady scent of her perfume filled his nostrils, nearly succeeding in intoxicating him. He recalled how ardently she had pursued him at Halconbosque; her words of love in the bailey at Castilla-verde; the way Stefano had struck her, leaving her lying in the dust. He closed his eyes and tried not to

215

think of his past experiences with this cold, twisted woman. She was there now, her hands were firm and giving on his neck, so why not enjoy her touch?

"How do you feel now about your innocent wife, Roderick?" Her eyes narrowly watched his face from above.

"Elena, 'tis not your concern."

She moved in front of him, her full breasts thrust out tauntingly under the thin linen gown. She stood there for a moment, arms akimbo, then leaned down to kiss him. Her lips parted his while her hands caressed his chest. Then she whispered against his lips, "We need not be wed to share a moment of bliss . . . Come, let us go to your chamber."

Lord, but the thought was tempting! He examined the idea, feeling somewhat fuzzy from the wine. As her lips tasted his again, he inexplicably wished the wench were Madrigal: Why couldn't *she* come to him half-naked, eyes glazed with desire? He allowed himself to dream that this was not Elena's soft, inviting mouth, but Madrigal's. He swore softly against her lips, damning himself for the lie.

Suddenly, almost harshly, he rose and swept Elena into his strong arms, carrying her swiftly up the stairs and into his chamber. He kept telling himself that this willing girl who moaned in his arms was his wife. He saw only Madrigal; yet, in the secret recesses of his tormented mind, he cursed the ugly reality.

Elena undressed hurriedly, afraid that he might sober and turn her away. She was not a fool, and although she both hated and loved him, she could not stop herself from desperately longing to be possessed by him. She told herself that nothing mattered, for this was the moment that had filled her darkest fantasies ever since she had set eyes on him. This time she would not be denied.

Roderick gazed at her lovely nakedness, her full,

high breasts and long, slim legs. Then their eyes met, and what he saw turned his heart to ice: her green eyes were wild with lust and her small tongue licked lips wet with passion. She was truly a witch, a wanton who had cast a spell over him.

He watched her stretch herself provocatively onto the bed and remembered her with Stefano in the meadow at Halconbosque, naked and writhing under him, her flesh white and thrusting. Was *this* what he craved?

"Come, Roderick." She moved sensuously on the bed until he pulled off his tunic and went to her.

"You should have stayed with me on your wedding night," she whispered in his ear when he stretched out next to her. Her hands traveled his body like molten butterflies and finally rested on his hard, flat stomach. She drew in her breath at the complete maleness of him, and then told him of her awe.

Roderick was aroused, certainly, but not to the extent she imagined, for he was accustomed to taking the lead in the art of lovemaking and she had yet to afford him that chance. He was weary, not having slept for two nights now, and he began to hope she would find satisfaction quickly; he longed to sleep and be done with this farce.

Her fingers began to play with him, taking him completely by surprise. "*Dios,* Elena! Where did you learn that?" he moaned.

"I may be an unmarried woman, Roderick, but that does not mean I do not know what pleases a man." Her tongue traced the path of her fingers, and he suddenly, roughly, pulled her head up by her hair.

"In the name of all that's holy, Elena! You act the whore." His tone was harsh.

Her eyes flashed. "I—I love you! Is it so wrong to want you?"

"Do not speak of love to me!" he commanded. "And

yes, 'tis unnatural for a decent woman to caress her brother by marriage that way!" He rolled away from her, cursing the sour taste rising from his stomach.

She tried to turn him back, begging, "Please! I'll do anything, anything you want!"

"No, Elena It was wrong from the beginning. You are my sister-in-law." He rose from the bed and walked to the chaliced window; the first light of dawn lent a dull copper hue to his tawny hair.

"What farce is this? Do you think yourself in love with Madrigal?"

"It does not concern you." He watched a pale streak of gray become milky-white.

"But why, then? She *hates* you! 'Tis plain enough to see—are you a blind man?"

He turned to her, sadness filling his golden eyes. "Go, Elena. There is nothing here for you . . . I am sorry."

She mustered her dignity and donned her discarded gown. Her heart pounded in her chest and she longed to claw his eyes out. But she would wait. He would pay for the insult, she would make certain of that!

She closed the door behind her and leaned against it, breathing deeply. And then, as if she sensed something amiss, she turned her head slowly and saw a dim figure standing motionless in the shadows.

The figure approached. "I trust it was worth it, sister."

Elena laughed; the cold, musty halls echoed the sound that crashed in Madrigal's ears. Then she turned and disappeared into the darkness.

Madrigal went to Roderick's door, her fingers trembling on the knob. She entered silently and saw his gray profile at the window. Standing by the door, she waited for him to turn around, her stomach churning with sickness.

At last he pivoted; his eyes widened on seeing her. "I

told you there was nothing here for you! . . . Elena? Damn, woman, why don't you answer me?"

Madrigal did not speak, but her heavy breathing was audible across the wide chamber.

"Madrigal!"

"*Sí*," she said tonelessly. "I shall go to my sister Rosa's today. I will not return until I receive word that you have left Castilla-verde." She turned to leave but was halted by his firm, gentle touch.

"I know what you are thinking—"

She interrupted him with a strangled cry and attempted to squirm away.

"Hold still! Listen to me for once!"

"No! I won't listen—let me go!"

He held her tightly to him. "*You will listen!* There will be no talk of going to your sister Rosa's! You go with me!"

She ceased her futile struggles against him, and when she did, his hands seemed to scorch her skin through the thin material of her gown. Instantly her hatred for him increased; she was incensed and disturbed that his very touch should affect her. She glared at him—and said coldly, "Your damnable pride won't allow you to leave me in peace. Your arrogance, my husband, will be your downfall, for *if* I am forced to go with you, there will be no kindness in me. I will not tolerate your bed, nor will I obey you." She narrowed her eyes, then added, "Why not take Elena in my stead?"

He tightened his grip on her for a moment, then led her to a chair and forced her into it, kneeling by her side. "Mayhap we have both had our little indiscretions, milady, but rest assured that it is *you* who share my life *and* my bed."

Roderick saw the bitter dismay on her face and wondered why he could not tell her the truth about Elena. Was it because of Akbar? Or because of her ease in believing the worst of him? "Tired as you may

219

be, we still leave for Halconbosque this morn. So go now and make ready."

She felt utterly beaten again in their battle of wills. How casually he behaved after having just bedded her own sister! When they arrived at Halconbosque she decided she would behave exactly as she pleased. Their lives would be separate.

Roderick, Madrigal, and Maria, accompanied by a small group of guards, left Castilla-verde late that morning. Madrigal had said her tearful farewell to her father and Teresa but had purposefully avoided Elena, who had watched their departure from a lofty chaliced window.

As they crossed the drawbridge and headed toward the lower meadow, Madrigal had a painful vision of her family turned hatefully against each other, with Roderick standing smugly aside, smiling cruelly. At that moment she longed for him to die in battle, and soon. Mayhap she herself could see him to an early grave if she kept her wits about her and planned carefully.

The winter wind whipping around her body lent an icy reinforcement to her thoughts, and she wondered why she had never considered killing him before.

Chapter 28

On the morning of the seventh day out from Castilla-verde, Madrigal complained to Maria that she was too tired and too cold to continue another mile. She drew her heavy wool blanket around her chin and rolled over defiantly. No one was going to force her back onto that horse today! She could hear the biting wind tearing at the tent flap, and a chill ran up her spine.

"If you would but eat properly, milady, the cold would not affect you so much," Maria said sternly. "I shall seek out the baron. Mayhap he can talk sense into you!" She was gone before Madrigal's protests could reach her ears.

Several minutes later, Roderick appeared in Madrigal's tent. He frowned when he saw her still abed and looking pale. Was she ill, or was there more to her complaint than a chill? "Maria tells me you are not well. What is the problem?"

The very gall of him, she fumed, to march into my private tent as if nothing were wrong between us! The ruddy color that the wind had put to his cheeks made her aware of her own inadequacy to withstand the elements.

"Well, milady, have you no answer, or do you avoid the issue?"

"Issue? You speak in riddles," she replied coolly, wishing he had closed the tent flap. "I am well enough, milord. If you recall, I have done much traveling these past weeks, and I wish to rest. 'Tis all."

"Maria tells me you are barely eating . . . or is it that you are unable to stomach the sight of food?" His tone was scathing.

"What?"

"Come, now, my sweet. You know of what I speak." He stood over her menacingly, and she wondered why he was so angry with her.

He forced himself to speak more calmly. "Madrigal, I admit that often in the past I have wronged you, but if there is something you should tell me, it is best that you do so now. I promise that the . . . the problem . . . that is, I realize it wasn't entirely your fault . . . ."

The meaning of his words suddenly hit her like a slap in the face. He thinks me with child! Akbar's child! Tears of bitter frustration welled in her eyes and she could no longer hold back her words of loathing. "You

221

nameless cur! You depraved monster!" she spat while rising to face him.

"How dare you call *me* depraved!" He grabbed her by the arms. "I have waited these past days with the patience of the Lord for you to come to me with news of a pregnancy, whether it be yes or no. I am your husband! You owe me that much, wife!" His hands held her so tightly that she thought her bones would break. She cried aloud in pain and tried to kick him with her bare feet, but he ignored her futile attempts. "Give me an honest answer, Madrigal! My patience has worn thin this time!"

Between clenched teeth she managed to say, "Honesty! I shall give you honesty, my beloved husband! I can bear no children to any man! Not to you! Not to Akbar! To no one! And it is all *your* fault!" She saw a bewildered look cross his face as he relaxed his grip on her. She felt utterly defeated; her rage of a moment ago dissolved and she lay on the blanket weeping pitifully, her breath coming in short gasps.

Roderick stood over her, a muscle twitching in his jaw. He was unable to comprehend her sudden shift from anger to tears. What had she meant by saying she could not bear a child? How was this possible, and how could it be *his* fault? As soon as she ceased this ridiculous sobbing, he would clear up these riddles. He walked to the tent opening and looked out over the bleak terrain; the wind whipped the dry dust before him into swirls, but he was unseeing. Would she never stop crying?

When at last her eyes were swollen and dry, and an unhealthy silence filled the tent, Roderick turned away from the opening and asked, "Are you calm enough now to answer a few questions, Madrigal?" His voice was impassive, as if they had never quarreled.

Madrigal searched for her linen handkerchief and sniffled for a few moments, then took a deep breath

and cleared her throat. "Yes, I am. I won't cry again."
Was this weak, uneven voice really hers?

"First, what is this talk of your not being able to
conceive?" He took a few short paces toward her.

She looked up from the blanket into his concerned
gaze. "I was terribly ill when I left Halconbosque.
Akbar's physician treated me . . ." She fell silent for a
moment. Inexplicably, she found herself near tears
again. "He—that is, Izak, the doctor—said there would
be no more children and . . . and . . ." Her eyes filled
and her voice cracked. "And if you had not said those
dreadful lies about my father that morning . . . I would
not have fallen down the stairs . . ."

He watched mutely as she broke her word that she
would not cry again; he did not know what to do to
comfort her. He tried soft words. "Mayhap this so-
called physician is in error. Look what he did to my
face . . . We can always hope." But she sobbed even
more.

Lord! He had never meant for her to come to harm
that morning, but she acted as if *he* had pushed her
down the steps. It was *his* child, too, whom she had
lost—did she think him low enough not to care? He
knelt down by her side. "Come, now, Madrigal, my
mother told me of a similar accident she suffered, and
she was able to conceive again. I feel certain the doctor
is wrong."

In her half-hysterical state she barely heard his
words, yet his tone was soothing, unlike the Roderick
of her experience; and when he began to rub her back
gently, she regained a measure of control. She did not
know how long he remained by her side, nor did she
remember when she fell asleep.

Roderick left her tent feeling dejected and inade-
quate; his marriage was not turning out at all as he had
expected—no, planned. Nevertheless, he had caused
his wife much misery, or so *she* believed, and hadn't

that been the whole idea from the start? So where, then, was his pleasure in seeing her broken? He shrugged his broad shoulders and approached the guards, ordering them to unsaddle the mounts, for they would not travel that day.

During the next week the weather remained bitterly cold, yet Madrigal was feeling better. She had experienced a strange sort of release that morning in her tent, almost a purging, and she had awakened with a lighter heart. Later that day, Maria had explained the importance of unburdening one's soul, and Madrigal had remembered that Akbar had once said the same thing. By that evening she had felt her appetite return and had eaten a hearty meal. During the ensuing days Roderick paid close attention to her, bringing her pieces of dried meats at odd times and coming to her tent each evening to check on her comforts. Never once did he mention Akbar's name or ask her if her monthly time had come; he remained the considerate stranger. Madrigal was grateful for his change of attitude; his exaggerated politeness was far easier to deal with than his ugly, accusing words.

One afternoon Roderick rode up to her and said they were nearing Santiago de Compostela. The sun had at last broken through the clouds and the day was warm, unusually so, he informed her, for winter in Galicia. When he could find no further reason to stay by her side, he appeared reluctant to move away. Was it possible that he wanted to be near her? she wondered. She could feel his eyes on her. What was he thinking while they rode on silently together? She stole a sidelong glance at him. What would marriage be like to a kind and gentle man? How differently she viewed knights of the king now that she had seen their true nature. As a child, she had had fantasies of a tall, shadowy figure, not unlike Roderick, coming to

Castilla-verde and begging her father for her hand. The absurd image had died swiftly after she had met the Baron of Compostela. No, not then, she recalled, but when he had spoken so rudely to her in the forest, thinking her a village maid who would come willingly to his bed. She had begun to loathe him then; *her* knight would have knelt at her feet and begged her for a mere word, a kind token of her affection, or a walk in the fields—he would certainly never compromise her virtue!

She looked over at him again. "Would you kneel at my feet?" As soon as she had spoken so hastily, she wished she had held her tongue.

He threw back his head and laughed, his face guilelessly handsome. "And what, may I ask, put such a notion into your head?"

Her cheeks were scarlet; how *could* she have asked him that? And now he was laughing at her! "I don't know," she replied too quickly.

"Would you like me to kneel at your feet? And to what purpose, milady?" His white teeth showed in a wide grin.

"Oh stop it, Roderick! I haven't the vaguest idea why I said that!"

Suddenly he snatched the reins from her hands and led the horses into the shelter of the trees. She protested fiercely, but to no avail. He dismounted and pulled her down, holding her by the waist as she struggled to free herself. "Come, Madrigal, what was your meaning?" he teased.

"Very well," she conceded. "I . . . I was recalling a childhood dream, nothing more!"

"Of a handsome knight—begging at your feet, no doubt." His eyes crinkled with amusement, and to her surprise she felt herself about to chuckle aloud. He suddenly released her waist, and taking her hand, knelt down on one knee while she attempted to twist out of his grip.

"Oh Roderick! Stop it at once!"

"No, milady," he jested. "First you must tell me what words your knight spoke."

"I won't . . . I can't . . . this is absurd!" She laughed unexpectedly. But her heart was pounding in her chest, and she felt oddly happy to see him kneeling at her feet.

"Did he beg you for a kiss? Lay his sword at your feet?"

"No," she said breathlessly, "nothing like that." Pale rays of sun fell warmly on her cheeks and lit her green eyes. She laughed again nervously, like an innocent child incapable of dealing with a strange situation. To save herself, she said, "All I shall tell you is that he would ask me for a walk in the woods. Now, do not press me further, Roderick."

He began to kiss each of her slim fingers, one by one, savoring their taste. "A stroll in the woods?" His golden stare reached up to touch her eyes. "It sounds as if your knight was not so honorable after all."

"You, sir, are a knave!" But when he stood up, towering above her, she actually wanted to live the dream, to have his mouth cover hers in a warm, tender, endearing kiss. And when he brought his lips down to hers, she responded with an ardor that both shocked and delighted him.

He kissed her gently at first, then with a passion that was timeless and knew no limits. God, how he ached to have her yielding and responsive to his caresses, to recall each of her beautiful curves through his touch! He kept her in an embrace and led her deeper into the secluded woods. The only sounds were those of their breathing and the wind stirring the empty boughs.

At last he stopped and pushed her hood back, loosening her hair until it flowed to her waist in the frosty air. He held one of her hands, afraid that she might still flee him, and spread his cape on the ground.

Please, Roderick, please, she begged silently, do not break this spell! How long had it been since he had last taken her? Yes, she admitted, she wanted him, needed him, to hold and caress her, to make her feel whole and complete again, to drive away the memories of lonely nights and harsh words. But what if he had his way with her now, and then flung her wantonness in her face afterward? She would not think of that now.

He eased her tenderly onto the makeshift bed, the bed made of his cape and hard earth, of dry, dead leaves, and of sun and frost. His mouth covered hers with a fierceness that frightened her, but she knew his desire was equal to her own and she began to return his passionate kiss, her body seeking his.

She felt him raise her woolen skirt; her flesh burned wherever his hands explored her, in every hollow, in every curve. He bent his head to savor the taste of her creamy breasts, until she moaned aloud and thought she would die if he did not take her soon. There were no words of love, no sweet, playful touches, merely an ageless need that could find fulfillment only in the joining of their bodies.

When at last he entered her, she arched her hips to meet his swollen manhood. Her mind reeled with the thrust of his intense, driving desire for her; her senses spiraled upward, higher and higher, until she nearly screamed aloud from the pain and the joy of the moment. As she reached the pinnacle of bliss, he sought her lips thirstily, fiercely, eager to taste her mouth at the peak of their desire. Then he, too, soared over the crest and found release in her soft body.

They lay entwined together for a time, silent in the cool winter air. Finally he forced himself to leave her and rolled over on his side, but still he clasped her tightly. She was a treasure beyond his wildest imagination, and at that moment he refused to think of anything save the extraordinary pleasure she gave him.

Madrigal sighed deeply. "Most likely the guards are wondering what has become of us."

"Hush . . . I was thinking back on your knight. Did he bring you as much pleasure?"

"No, milord. *My* knight always waited until the vows were spoken!"

"But I *am* your knight, and the vows were spoken long ago!" he teased, his mind drifting back to his own childhood fantasies. "Often Sancho and I slew dragons in the forest and saved many a distressed damsel," he chuckled. "Though none of the maids was as capable of draining the very strength from my soul as you, milady!"

She propped herself up on one elbow and absent-mindedly began to trace the line of his sutured wound. His brow knitted together suddenly, and her finger halted its unconscious path.

"I wonder," he said in an odd voice, "if you affect all men this way. Do you respond to their touch as ardently?"

"Please," she cried weakly, "please, Roderick, do not spoil this for me!"

"No, Madrigal, I won't spoil your pleasure . . . at least we share *one* common thing together!"

Hadn't she guessed that he would turn hard and calculating? So why, when she knew he could never change, did she feel tears threatening? Her happiness fled, like the dry, swirling leaves around them, and a knot of indescribable pain formed in the pit of her stomach.

By the time they had nearly reached Halconbosque, Roderick was again coolly polite to her, and she was forced to regard their lovemaking that day in the forest as a bittersweet interlude in a hapless relationship. She realized that she had forgotten her desire to see him dead, especially when his caresses scorched her very core. How could she want to be rid of him one minute and long for his touch the next?

Chapter 29

They entered the hall of Halconbosque late one frosty afternoon, thankful for the inviting warmth. Madrigal and Maria headed directly for the huge open hearth; the girl thought her teeth would never stop chattering, and she thrust her icy fingers toward the life-giving heat of the roaring fire. She felt numb and exhausted, sorely in need of a hot bath and hours of rest. She had turned her back to the flaming timber and begun to remove her cloak when she saw Lady Gwendolyn, Stefano, and an oddly dressed man enter the great hall.

Lady Gwendolyn came straight to Madrigal and embraced her warmly, expressing heartfelt joy at her daughter-in-law's safe return. She did not refer to their last meeting; it would do no good to recall Madrigal's miscarriage.

The two women left the fire to join Stefano, who was introducing the stranger to Roderick. They heard him say, "This is Sir Robert La Valle of Coventry. He comes from King Edward of England, and more recently from King Sancho." The men bowed deeply.

Roderick and Sir Robert conversed for a time in English. Madrigal remained helplessly curious, for she did not speak Sir Robert's language. Lady Gwendolyn explained to her that she and Stefano had entertained their illustrious guest in Roderick's absence, not knowing, of course, when he would return.

Madrigal looked tiredly over the rim of her wine

flagon at the well-groomed knight of Edward I. Although shorter than her husband, he was a very handsome and well-built man, fair-haired, and with a profile that was strong and proud. Lady Gwendolyn explained that he was a Norman, and Madrigal wondered if all Normans had such crystal-blue eyes. Sir Robert, she guessed, was about twenty-three, and obviously of a moneyed family, for his elegant hose and tunic, although of foreign style, bespoke wealth.

Roderick, she took note, was pensive as he listened to the younger man's words. She wondered what possible connection there could be between her husband and this knight from Coventry. Then she surmised that it stemmed from Lady Gwendolyn's side of the family, her English heritage. Whatever it was, was of no small importance, for Stefano had mentioned both King Sancho and the English king. Ordinarily, Madrigal would have gone straight to her chambers for a much-needed bath, but her interest kept her in her seat.

At last Roderick offered Sir Robert wine and nodded in an affirmative manner. He appeared resigned as he turned to Stefano and the ladies. "It seems that I have been ordered by King Sancho to attend the English king and to oversee my inherited lands in Cornwall."

"Penglennyn?" Stefano asked.

"Yes, my mother's childhood home. Her brother passed on some nine months ago, and there is nary a soul there to attend to matters in my stead."

"*Your* stead! I fail to see . . ." said Madrigal, half rising.

"The disposal of the fief has passed to me as the only living male heir. I have a female cousin named Beth living at Penglennyn; undoubtedly she is in need of assistance."

"Cannot someone else be sent to watch over the lands? Mayhap King Edward has a trusted vassal who is landless!" She was just beginning to realize the impact of Sir Robert's visit.

Roderick continued speaking in Spanish, as his next words were not meant to be understood by the Norman. "King Sancho wills me to go. You see, there is talk of a possible French invasion of Spain over the Pyrenees. You must understand that the English and French kings are not exactly on good terms, and King Sancho may seek an alliance with King Edward against the French."

"I do not understand," Madrigal said with a look of frustration.

"Let me just say that Sancho would think highly of my visit to the English court at this time. My real task in England will be to woo Edward the First on Sancho's behalf, for if the French were to think the English and the Spanish have formed a mutual agreement, they might deem it wise to keep to their own soil and leave Spain alone."

"I think I understand now . . . but, Roderick, there is danger. Please reconsider!"

"Do not fret, milady. By the time we return to Spain, you will think of the trip as a grand experience."

"*We!*" Her mouth fell open in astonishment.

"*Sí*, milady. *We* shall leave in a fortnight."

The weight of his words fell heavily on Madrigal's shoulders. She left the hall in a weary depression, although outwardly she appeared resigned. Lady Gwendolyn later reassured her that the journey would be enlightening and most likely pleasant, for the Englishwoman's homeland was not as primitive as one might imagine.

The next days sped by as Madrigal allowed her mother-in-law to manage the task of packing her trunks, tutoring her in English, and lifting her spirits in general with stories of the woman's childhood in England. Madrigal refrained from saying that she really wished to remain in Galicia and dreaded the voyage commissioned by the king. She was afraid for both herself and Roderick.

Roderick's problem, on the other hand, was far greater; someone had to attend to the affairs of Halconbosque during his absence. He knew, of course, that Sancho would provide an overseer if necessary, and an honest one at that, but there remained Stefano to consider for the post. Finally Roderick sent for his banker and merchant friend, David ben Avrahim, and spent much time discussing the urgent matter with him. They decided that Stefano could handle the job, with ben Avrahim keeping the accounts in order.

At last Roderick was ready to depart; he was anxious and oddly pleased to begin a new adventure. During the long days of preparation, however, he had come up against a major stumbling block: Madrigal. She had taken the news of the trip rather well in front of Sir Robert and the family, but it was quite another story when they were in private. She had argued and stamped her feet; once she had thrown a slipper at him, insisting that she had no intention of going to a heathen land and living among those Vikings and foppish Normans. She had raved that ever since their marriage she had been dragged hither and yon, but that *this* was too much. He had had to break their unspoken truce and declare that if she did not accompany him, he would beat her; but it was when he had called her a small-minded, provincial hen that she had finally acquiesced and grudgingly allowed Lady Gwendolyn to assist her in her preparations.

The morning Madrigal walked unsteadily up the gangway, tired from the overland trek to La Coruña, her mind was reeling with the many possibilities of a disaster. She was terrified of the idea of having to sail such a great distance, and on a strange, foreign-built ship. What if they were shipwrecked on the coast of

232

France! Would the French welcome them on their soil? Or would they slay them on the beach?

After Roderick carefully handed her aboard to Sir Robert's outstretched hand, she turned to her husband. "Roderick, I swear that if any harm befalls us and I should live through it, I'll . . . I'll run you through with your own sword!"

Sir Robert caught the gist of her words and, along with Roderick, laughed heartily at the lady's fears. Then the attractive young Norman showed them to their quarters; the cabin was a tiny, cramped cubicle, but the best available on the speedy bark. Madrigal realized immediately that Roderick was correct in leaving Maria behind, for the elderly servant would never have been able to withstand this trip. Only Renaldo accompanied them, but he was accustomed to making do anywhere and remained unfailingly cheerful.

They set sail from La Coruña on the evening tide, on the same vessel that had brought Sir Robert to Spain nearly a month ago. The ship was rigged for swift sailing and not for passenger comforts. Madrigal saw little of the crew, for she spent the majority of her time being tossed about their swaying cabin, practicing her English aloud, and occasionally swearing at the walls.

The ship followed the French coastline north, and for the first few days out, the seas were relatively mild. On the fifth day Roderick secured their belongings with a heavy rope, telling Madrigal that the captain expected a strong blow that night and she was to remain in the crude, wooden bunk for reasons of safety. When he saw the wide-eyed look of fear on her face, he tried to reassure her with words of comfort, but she only babbled on about how her worst fears were coming to fruition.

At midnight, having vomited in a bucket until she was dry, Madrigal attempted to leave the heaving cabin, knowing she would surely die if she did not have

233

fresh air. The bark lurched to port side and caught her off balance, tossing her to the plankings, where she severely bruised her shoulder. She reached up and clutched the latch, flinging it open, then dragged herself onto the deck. She was instantly blinded by the splashing, salty wind and rain, and stood there for some moments crying for help, clinging to the slippery rail. The next thing she was aware of was the crashing of a wave that pulled at her ankles until she lost her footing and was swept along with the flow.

In her near hysteria, she heard Roderick's voice above her and clung to him as he grabbed her arms and made his unsteady way to the mast, holding them both firmly against the pole. She cried aloud when he gripped her arms forcefully; her shoulder ached terribly. Roderick cursed her stupidity over and over again, until she turned her head and vomited weakly. When she was done, she looked up into his face. "We shall die here! Roderick . . . I am so frightened! I am afraid to die!"

He cuddled her against his soaked chest and reassured her. "No, no, it will be all right. The craft is seaworthy and the captain is certain that the worst is over. Hold tightly to me and I'll get you back to the cabin."

His strength braced them both against the driving rain and wind, inching them back to the enclosed safety of their tiny cabin. He helped her onto the bunk and quickly stripped off her clothing, then wrapped her snugly in a warm blanket. Madrigal looked so weak and miserable that he wished he had had the good sense to leave her behind in Spain. This was no place for a woman; his heart sank when he recalled her plea of fright, for she had never admitted to that emotion before. And it was his fault for not trusting her to the care of Stefano.

Roderick stroked her forehead gently, suddenly

realizing the full burden of his marriage to her. Up to now, marriage had seemed merely an irritating condition, such as chafed skin from battle gear. His life had not truly been changed. But now it occurred to him that marriage was a trust, a commitment to care for and protect his wife, and that his life was as duty-bound as hers. While the storm raged, while the ship's timbers creaked and groaned, while the dim lantern swayed erratically in the close cabin, Roderick first understood the significance of his marriage to Madrigal, of man's marriage to woman, and the emotional turmoil that was legal tender of that union.

She retched again, and he held her head while she moaned and cried. Afterward he cradled her in his arms like a child.

"Roderick," she whispered, "when will the storm be over? I can bear no more . . ."

"Soon, very soon now." He could hear the wind still slashing at the rigging, and the violent seas crashing into the hull.

Before she finally slept, he moved a bit and she clung to him, begging, "Please! Do not leave yet—not yet!" So he remained holding her until early dawn, when the storm finally abated. Only then did he close his eyes to rest.

Two days later they dropped anchor in Falmouth Bay. Madrigal was thoroughly tired of hearing about the good fortune of the storm, which had driven them north, on course, and gained a full day's time. She had finally eaten that morning, after Roderick had explained that they would reach the coast of Cornwall that day and she had to be strong enough to debark. Then he had left her with a tray of uninviting food and gone to join the captain and Sir Robert.

After they anchored, he returned to the cabin to ready his belongings, for a small craft waited alongside to carry them ashore. When he strode in, his eyes widened in amazement. Madrigal stood by the side of the bunk, holding his sword shakily in her hands and pointing it directly at him.

"What the devil are you up to?" he half laughed.

"If you recall, my husband, I promised to run you through if harm befell us!"

She must be jesting, he thought, but she looked deadly serious. "Put that down, Madrigal. It's much too heavy for you, and you'll truly harm yourself with this foolishness." He shrugged his broad shoulders when she did not comply, then turned and began packing his belongings in an infuriatingly casual manner.

"How dare you ignore me!" But her arms were too weak to hold the sword another moment, and she let it clatter to the wooden planking. Still he ignored her. "Roderick! Roderick!" He turned an amused eye on her. "Can't you understand that we nearly died out there? And now you expect me to set foot calmly on this heathen soil! Well, I won't! I shall remain here and . . . and pay the captain handsomely to return me to—"

He pulled her into his arms, silencing her with a fierce kiss that left her breathless. After a time he raised his head. "Milady, I can understand your fears, but do you think me so daft as to bring my wife to a land where she might come to danger? Trust me, Madrigal. I think you will be pleasantly surprised."

"But, Roderick . . ."

"And furthermore, milady, you need not wield a sword at me to make your point. I have ears, I am not deaf." Before she could protest, he took her mouth again, only this time in a long, gentle kiss that dissipated her will to argue and left her responding with an equal ardor.

Several minutes later Roderick reluctantly broke

their embrace. He said quietly, "Come, now, it is time we are off . . . and please put your fears aside, for I do not wish to embarrass myself with a wife who trembles before these gracious people."

Madrigal pushed him away with a smothered oath and snatched a leather satchel containing her personal articles. She was out the door before he could explain that he had only meant to say that the English were a hospitable lot and there was nothing to fear here. Yet somehow his words always seemed to come out twisted where *she* was concerned.

He stared at the wooden door for a moment and then gathered up his things, following Madrigal's path down the rough planking to where the rope ladder hung over the ship's side. Ahead, only a hundred yards across the bay, was the coast of Cornwall, the land of wide moors, of boulders and heather, of tin and copper mines; the home of many of his forefathers, a proud, strong people, a noble heritage.

Chapter 30

Madrigal's first impression of Beth Winthrop was that of a soft, plump, brown and white bird, a partridge, perhaps. She wore a plain brown gown of homespun wool and a darker brown wool cloak thrown loosely around her shoulders. As Madrigal and Roderick climbed the steps of Penglennyn to meet her, Madrigal could see that Beth had a flawless complexion, a sprinkle of pale freckles, and beautiful, velvety brown eyes. Her honey-colored hair was braided into two thick plaits that fell to her waist. She had an odd habit of squinting her eyes and wrinkling her nose when she looked at them; Madrigal found out later that Beth was very shortsighted.

Beth was thrilled to see her tall, handsome Galician cousin, but she was not without trepidation, wondering whether he would allow her to stay on in the great house where she had been born. He had, after all, complete power over her fate, for she was without husband, brother, or father to protect her.

Her first words to Roderick, after Sir Robert had introduced them, sprang from her unease at the situation. "Please excuse the poor cart I sent to meet you in Falmouth, Lord Roderick, but the good one is broken and there is no one to fix it . . ." Her voice trailed off as she flushed a furious pink. "I welcome you to Penglennyn, and the lady, your wife, too," she said, turning to Madrigal and smiling shyly.

Roderick noticed her unease and sought to put her mind at rest. "Beth, let me assure you that you are welcome to live here as long as you wish. I am here only temporarily, to help put the fief in order since the death of your father. Then I must return home, for my king has need of me there." He could see the relief flood her gentle face as his words struck home. The poor girl, he thought, alone in the world and with her home threatened by poverty and mismanagement. He would have to arrange things so that she would never again fear her present plight.

"Please enter, Lord Roderick and Lady Madrigal, and you, too, Sir Robert. I have had a meal prepared, for I am sure you are hungry." Beth became the gracious lady of the manor now that her position seemed more secure, and ushered them inside.

Sir Robert said that he would merely have a quick bite and then return to the ship, as King Edward had expected him weeks earlier. The young Norman then proceeded to down a goodly portion of a mutton joint, several thick slices of golden-crusted bread, and numerous flagons of bitter English ale.

"Ah!" he cried, smacking his lips over the last drop of ale. "Good English food has nothing to compare it with, and to be deprived of my ale was a true sacrifice!" Madrigal could hardly believe his appetite; he had not eaten so at Halconbosque or aboard ship, and if the truth be told, she thought the ale bitter and thin, and wished for a good draft of wine. But Beth was obviously pleased with his hearty enthusiasm at her table and beamed at him like a fond parent.

Madrigal attempted to use her poor English, and Beth was polite enough to praise her efforts highly. Madrigal was beginning to understand more of the conversation around her as her ear grew accustomed to the harsh, sibilant sound of English, and she was determined to become more proficient in the tongue, and quickly.

Madrigal wondered why Beth was not married, as she appeared to be about twenty-one and was practically nearing middle age. Perhaps the customs in England were different. Beth treated Madrigal as an equal, as a friend of long standing, rather than as the lady of the house, which Madrigal could be if she so chose. The only time Madrigal noticed a spark in her eyes and a tone of forcefulness in her voice was when Beth spoke of Penglennyn. Apparently she was very attached to her home and would not easily see it taken from her.

Over the meal, Beth told Roderick of the problem. The crops were consistently poor, the tin mine produced no ore, the catch of fish was small, the cows gave no milk, the chickens refused to lay eggs, and the serfs sickened and died. Her castellan, Terence, whom her father had placed in his present position, assured her that he had done everything he could, but the fief continued to decline. The situation had come to a head last autumn, when the grain had been eaten by rats and the last cow had dried up. Beth had no recourse but to ask the king for help. Terence had been violently opposed to her action, as he thought it reflected upon his competence as castellan, but Beth had done it anyway.

"And now it is February, and here you are, dear cousin, to help Penglennyn become a valuable asset to our king again. I cannot tell you how glad I am to be able to relinquish all responsibility to you!" Beth said finally, laying her plump white hand on Roderick's.

"We shall see what can be done to remedy the ills of your home," Roderick replied thoughtfully.

"Oh, no, Roderick, it is *your* home now."

"'Twill never really be mine, Beth, despite the king's order. Penglennyn is yours; that is my wish."

"Oh, Roderick, if only that could be. I could not bear to leave this place, not now . . . I fear 'tis why I've never married." She blushed and looked down at her hands. "I've never met a man who could compare to Penglennyn." She looked up fearfully, as if her confession would elicit disapproval. "'Tis awful to say, and my mother and father scolded me often enough for saying it. But 'tis true!" Her small chin jutted defiantly.

Roderick laughed and assured her that she was probably correct in her estimation of most men; then he translated this exchange for Madrigal, since its humor had quite escaped her.

Sir Robert departed, wishing them all well and reminding Roderick that King Edward awaited his pleasure in London as soon as the most pressing problems of Penglennyn had been solved.

Madrigal could no longer conceal her exhaustion, and yawned hugely behind her hand.

"Oh, Lady Madrigal! I fear we have talked too long of my problems. I know you must be tired, and I shall show you to your room without a moment's delay." Beth rose hastily.

Madrigal smiled politely, not really understanding the rush of words. Roderick, seeing the blank look on her face, translated for her.

"Thank you, Beth," Madrigal ventured, the name "Beth" coming out "Bet."

Beth led them to the east wing, chattering about the history of the estate on the way. The great hall had been the original structure, dating over a hundred years before the Norman Conquest in 1066. The Norman overlord of Penglennyn had built the west wing in the eleventh century, and the east wing had been added a hundred years later. It was a dignified, two-story edifice from the outside, constructed of the omnipresent gray stone of Cornwall. The facade was broken by many narrow windows, with gables and tall chimneys emerging from the slate roof.

The interior was dark and a bit chilly, especially in the February weather. Although Cornwall never became as cold as parts of Spain, because of the warm westerly current, it could be damp and gloomy, with terrible storms off the ocean buffeting the rocky shore.

Beth took them to a vast chamber, where a serving girl was feeding a roaring fire in the hearth. The ruddy-cheeked peasant girl looked up shyly, then curtsied and fled from the strangers. A large, canopied bed filled the room, but the green velvet draperies were shabby and the flagstone floor was bare. It was, nevertheless, an inviting sight to Madrigal; she had expected a more primitive lifestyle. She wanted only to sleep. Tomorrow she would mull over her impressions of this new country.

As the door closed behind Beth, Madrigal lay down for a moment on the bed, but she fell asleep before she could summon the energy to rise and disrobe. She had no recollection of Roderick undressing her tenderly and covering her with a thick woolen quilt.

The next morning Roderick rose early and breakfasted with Beth. He bade her send a servant for Terence, the castellan, with orders to appear immediately in the great hall. After an hour Terence finally arrived, looking peevish and hastily put together. Roderick eyed the man closely, trying to gauge his character. Terence was short and pudgy, with a round pink face pierced at intervals by tiny eyes, a small pug nose, and pouting lips. His ears were small, pink, and fleshy, as were his hands. His fringe of pale hair stood up in disarray on a round head that was sunk into beefy shoulders. When he spoke, his voice was high, thin, and wheezy, as if his throat were fat-encased, too.

Beth interrupted his effusive apologies to introduce Roderick as the new master of Penglennyn. Terence fell silent and turned to face Roderick, surprising the baron with his look of quick intelligence and open hostility. The look was gone in a second, replaced by fawning condescension. His pursed lips curved into a tight smile, and he bowed deeply to Roderick.

"Lord Roderick, welcome to Penglennyn, I am at your disposal, milord, and I hope your long journey has not been in vain. But as I have often said to Lady Beth, I believe there is a curse on the fief, for nothing else explains our misfortunes."

"I intend to find out exactly what is causing the 'misfortunes' of Penglennyn, as you so aptly call them, but I doubt that it will turn out to be a curse."

Terence was taken aback by the large man's steely gaze and grim aspect. Obviously Lord Roderick would not be as easy to deal with as the girl.

Roderick continued. "I wish to cover the fief on horseback today to assess the state of disrepair. You will supply me with a good horse and will accompany me."

"Do I hear you correctly, my lord? The whole fief? Today?" Terence was dumbfounded.

"Yes, of course. How else can I judge the extent of this curse?"

"I—I shall see to it, Lord Roderick." gulped the red-faced little man, declining to admit that he was not certain he could stay on a horse that long. And he was not even positive about the north edge of the fief, which bordered on the moors. He racked his brain for the location of the old sheepskin map of the boundaries.

"I shall need the following information from you." Roderick ticked off the list on his fingers. "The number of serfs, head of stock, type of crops, amount of tin produced, weight of yearly catch of fish, number of buildings, state of repair. That will be all for now."

Terence left in silence, gripped by panic. He would have to fabricate the information, and this man seemed capable of discovering for himself how he had been cheating Beth Winthrop and sabotaging the estate. He was dreadfully afraid his lucrative post would be taken from him by this slippery foreigner with the hard topaz eyes. Somehow he had to protect himself while at the same time putting the Spaniard's obvious suspicions to rest.

For Terence, the day was a nightmare. His fleshy seat was raw from staying in the saddle for long hours, and his stomach grumbled continually from hunger. His mind, too, was exhausted from the myriad questions thrown at him by the damnable Spanish baron. He nearly froze in the slicing wind off the sea, while Roderick seemed made of steel and showed neither hunger nor fatigue. They returned to the great hall after dark, and Terence was heartily glad to hand over the razor-backed nag to a servant and limp to the gatehouse, where he lived. He kicked his spaniel and beat his serving girl for letting the fire go out and his dinner grow cold, and he felt much better after hearing her frantic cries for mercy. At least he still had power over *some* creatures in his small domain!

Roderick entered the hall in a grim mood. It was evident that someone was undermining the resources of the fief. Even from the little he had seen that day, he could tell that much. He suspected Terence: first, because of the way the serfs seemed to hate and fear him, and second, because of his own instinctive reaction to the man. It was not only Terence's unfortunate appearance; he emanated an aura of evil. Roderick was accustomed to trusting his instincts, since his life often depended on his ability to judge a man's fettle in the heat of battle. Terence made his hackles rise. The more he thought about the "curse," the more convinced he became that Terence was its source.

He found Madrigal in front of the huge fireplace, practicing her English with Beth's enthusiastic help. They had already eaten, but had saved him a half-dozen succulent Cornish pasties, a loaf of bread, and a round of tangy cheese. He was withdrawn and quiet as he ate, leaving the two women to make the conversation.

Beth asked him some questions, hoping to hear his opinion of the day's work, but he avoided answering her. Madrigal wondered at his silence but was more accustomed to his moods than Beth and did not pay him much mind.

Roderick and Madrigal retired to their chamber shortly thereafter and left Beth to chain the dogs in the hall before she went to her bed. Roderick had taken off his black surcoat and boots and was sitting in a chair, staring thoughtfully into the fire, when he heard a timid knock on the heavy oak door. He went to the door quickly so as not to disturb Madrigal.

"'Tis Beth, cousin. Forgive my intrusion, but there is someone here who begs audience with you."

"Who is that, Roderick?" came Madrigal's voice from the curtained bed.

"'Tis Beth, milady. Go to sleep. I'll be back shortly." He slipped out into the cold corridor and found Beth there, shining her candle on a man.

"Roderick, this is one of our serfs, Hugo. He wished to speak to you and will not answer my questions. This is highly irregular, but he says 'tis important. Proceed, Hugo."

The man twisted his rough hands and appeared nervous. He finally began to speak, his accent so strong that Roderick had trouble comprehending him.

"Lord, sar, ye've looked like a gude un t'day whan we all seed ye. Th' udder fellas a sent me t' tell ye, sar, that we 'opes ye help us agin thet bad un, Terence. I tell ye, sar, ee bees a bad un . . ." The man twisted his head and looked left and right, as though Terence were hiding around a corner, then squinted up at Roderick and continued. "Ee steals, ee do, sar, an' whips any un thet'd say it. Ee tuk me dotter one time an' thin ee beat 'er till she near died, sar. I tell ye, ee bees a bad un."

"Hugo, why did you never tell me? I never knew . . ." Beth was near tears, shocked at the man's words.

"Ye coodn't do anythin', m'lady. We all knowed thet. What gude ud it've done t' tell ye?"

Roderick was almost glad to hear the man's revelations; it cemented his resolve to get rid of Terence quickly.

"Hugo, my man, you've done us a great service this night. Do not fear. If Terence is guilty, he will be relieved of his duties, and things will improve at Penglennyn. Now, return to your home, and rest assured that I shall take swift action on this matter."

"Tank ye, sar. I do be wishin' ye gude night, an' ye bees a gude man, even if'n ye bees a Spaniard, sar."

At these words Roderick let out a loud guffaw, struck by the man's simple honesty. Beth tittered behind her hand, and Hugo broke into a wide grin, showing great gaps in his yellow teeth. The chamber door opened and Madrigal poked her head out, amazed to see the strangely unmatched threesome laughing in the cold hallway.

"*Ingleses locos!*" she muttered to herself as Roderick's laugh echoed down the dark corridor.

The interview with Terence was sure to be unpleasant, Roderick thought to himself as he dressed the following morning. Nevertheless, it was necessary. The man was dishonest and lazy. Was he potentially dangerous? Roderick considered this point and decided that Terence, although probably vengeful and not unintelligent, was much too fond of his creature comforts to indulge in any foolish attempts to harm anyone. The schemers were often physical cowards, Roderick had found. He dismissed Terence as a threat and thought of what he would say to the man when he faced him.

He breakfasted on left-over pasties with Beth, who always rose promptly with the sun, and told her his decision on the matter of the castellan. She nodded briefly and said she would leave the great hall to him all morning. A servant was sent to fetch Terence, while Beth brought Madrigal her breakfast so that she would not disturb what might become a most distasteful scene. Beth was eternally grateful for the appearance of a savior in the form of her tall, foreign cousin, who was taking matters well in hand. Now, a man like *that* just might be the equal of Penglennyn, she mused.

Terence finally arrived, carrying some of the records of the fief that Roderick had asked to see the day before. He looked freshly scrubbed and studiously cheerful, prepared for another hard day of work. He still limped slightly, and sat down gingerly opposite Roderick, laying the leather-bound ledgers on the heavy plank table.

"Good morn to you, sir. Shall we look at the books now, or did you wish to ride out again?" His small eyes crinkled in rolls of fat.

"No, Terence, we shall not be riding out today," Roderick said. Terence smiled even more broadly at his words. "The fact is that I have decided to relieve you of your duties as castellan of Penglennyn." He paused, and his hard stare fixed on Terence. "You will be off these lands by tomorrow morning. Your belongings will be sent wherever you wish, but you will never set foot on *my* land again."

"My belongings? What?" sputtered Terence. "No longer castellan . . .?" His round head seemed to puff up, turning a deep, ugly shade of red that showed even through his thin hair. "Lord Roderick, I must ask why you have done this. You are making a decision too hastily . . . it may cost you dear in the end."

Roderick's tone was casual but deceptively lazy. "Do you threaten me, Terence?"

"No, no, I threaten no one. I merely try to make my point, that you need an experienced manager here," Terence replied.

"Your point is made, Terence. You may go now." Roderick turned his back on the man.

The castellan was unable to accept the fact that his future had been ruined in this short interview, that this self-important foreigner could come here and tell him to leave. How dare the Spaniard treat him so rudely, so casually, so indifferently? Mayhap it *was* at an end, but he had ways, too. He would go directly to William Poldreth of Trenwell, who certainly owed him something for his years of carefully undermining Penglen-

nyn's resources. He would offer his services directly to
Poldreth, and together they would ruin this high-and-
mighty Spaniard. Perhaps, Terence thought, he would
emerge from the affair better off than ever.

The small, round figure whirled around to leave but
spun back again to shout at Roderick. His voice was
high and shrill. "So be it, then, Baron, but, by God's
teeth, this is not the last you've seen of me!"

Chapter 31

The following day, when Roderick casually mentioned
to Madrigal his final interview with Terence, he immediately wished he had not spoken his thoughts aloud,
for she was quick to worry that the overseer might
make good his threat.

Roderick attempted to reassure her. "The swine is
not worth fretting over, Madrigal."

"But, milord! We are in a strange land, and he may
have friends . . ."

"Enough! The man was angry and spoke in haste.
Allow me to attend to this business." He had obviously
closed the subject.

Madrigal had a nagging, intuitive feeling that
Roderick had not seen the last of Terence, but she told
herself that Renaldo was always there to watch her
husband's back, if he would not watch his own. Then
she remembered that Beth awaited their company for
breakfast, and hastened to dress in a warm, green
woolen gown. As she finished donning her attire she
felt Roderick's eyes on her and turned to catch his gaze.
An unreadable mask covered his features; his golden
eyes looked deeply thoughtful.

"We have seen little of each other these past days,"
he said. He slowly let his gaze travel her form.

She did not like his manner; it was as if she were
nothing more than a caged bird and he the preening
hawk. She wondered if all marriages were like hers, the
woman desirous of a kind word or a gentle touch, while
the husband thought only of a female body to assuage
his urges. It seemed so cruel, so unjust, that she had
been born the weaker sex.

As if he read her mind, Roderick suddenly laughed.
"Have no fear, milady, I do not seek the comfort of
your charms this morn. I was but curious about your
habit of dressing hastily away from my gaze. 'Tis a
pleasure sorely needed by a husband, to watch his wife
dress, and you deny me that."

She whirled on him, her eyes flashing. "Yes! I do
deny you that right. There is nothing in our marriage
vows that commands me to stand here meekly under
your scrutiny."

"Can you say there is no pleasure for you in it?" he
goaded with a slow tilting of his lips, his eyes still
enjoying the view of her hollows and curves.

Madrigal blushed profusely and dared not answer
him with the truth or a lie, so she went wordlessly to the
door and waited for him to finish dressing. She would
have gone down alone to the great hall, but she never
knew what small incident might set off Roderick's
temper.

Eggs, honeyed barley gruel, and raised rye bread
awaited them on the heavy trestle. Beth had already
begun to eat. She seemed cheerful now that Terence
had gone; also she had taken a liking to Roderick,
which was quite evident to Madrigal.

With her long, wheat-colored hair and large, limpid
eyes, Madrigal thought Beth quite lovely, even if
Roderick did not seem to take notice. She was glad that

249

Beth was at ease with him, for it would make their stay at Penglennyn far more pleasant than she had imagined.

"Lady Beth," Madrigal said in her newly acquired English, "would it be convenient for me to open the bright room across from ours for sewing purposes? I should like to put some other furnishings in there, too."

Beth was about to reply that it would be no bother at all, when Roderick surprised her by snapping at Madrigal, "And I suppose you would like a soft bed placed in there, just in case you should fall asleep at night!"

"Roderick!" Madrigal retorted in Spanish. "I am certain that your cousin does not wish to hear of our problems. You are embarrassing her." And in truth, Beth's cheeks were scarlet.

"She may as well know, milady," Roderick scoffed, "for she wishes to remain at Penglennyn, and our differences will come out soon enough."

Madrigal felt so ashamed that she pushed back her chair and tried to leave, but Roderick grabbed her arm and forced her to be seated again. She cursed him silently, flashing green fury at him from under her lashes.

He turned to Beth. "Now, cousin, what is to be done with you? I can stay but a limited time and must spend part of it in London. However, I shall not leave Penglennyn until all is in order and yourself"—he ventured the thought uppermost in his mind—"safely wed."

Beth gave an audible gasp; she had not considered a marriage so soon and had no answer for Roderick's suggestion.

He pressed on. "Is there some man of station who meets your eye? Come, now, cousin, you have much to offer here in tin, crops, even comforts. Surely there is some swain—"

Madrigal interrupted him. "Not all women wish to be married." Then she added with a wicked gleam in her eye, "'Tis often far better to live in seclusion than to marry unhappily."

Roderick shot her a murderous glance and would have made her pay for the insult to himself if Beth had not intervened.

"No, there is no man," she said quickly, "for we are isolated here. But I should like to have a husband . . . that is, if . . . if he were kind and soft-spoken." She lowered her lashes.

Madrigal said in English, "Men of such good quality are truly hard to find."

"Enough, wife! Your tongue is as sharp as a viper's fang, and I command you to hold it!" He turned back to Beth. "I have a man in mind—one who perfectly matches your needs." Her face lit up, and Madrigal looked at him in bewilderment.

He continued. "But let us partake of some cider and consider the matter at hand, for I would not force a strange man on you, cousin, and if I fetch him here, it must be with the understanding that there will be a wedding and, most importantly, children."

Beth rose and went to pour the cider herself, ignoring the servants, for she did not want Roderick to see her embarrassment at his mention of children.

Madrigal took the opportunity to chastise him in Spanish for his open manner. "Roderick! Your cousin is surely a virgin, and you disconcert her when you speak of such things!"

He grinned at Madrigal. "'Tis true enough, but necessary, as you will soon learn. Besides, milady, you can comfort her, having so recently been a virgin yourself!" He laughed aloud when she glared at him, shocked and indignant.

A moment before Beth returned with the tangy brew, Madrigal hissed, "I would have preferred to marry a serpent; at least its disposition would have been sweeter!"

He switched to English. "I know not what has sharpened your wit this day, but rest assured I shall not allow it to continue." He then added, "From now on you will speak in English; mayhap the venomous words will be more difficult to pronounce."

Beth placed the flagons on the heavy oak table and watched Madrigal's face for a sign of humility; when none came she marveled at the young Spanish girl's spunk in the presence of a man as formidable and frightening as Lord Roderick appeared. They sat for a while, each wrapped in private thoughts, sipping on the biting cider.

Excitement besting her, Beth broke the awkward silence first, asking, "Whom had you in mind to husband me, cousin?"

"A woman of business, I see." He looked at her approvingly. "The man is my half brother, Stefano. He is a bastard, however, and I would not force him upon you." Roderick studied her expression and was pleased with what he saw, for she seemed pensive rather than horrified. Madrigal, on the other hand, sat mutely in contemplation of the idea.

Soon Beth said softly, "Tell me of Stefano."

Roderick thought a moment of what he should say about the man's qualities, then shrugged his shoulders, finding the deed too difficult. "It is enough to call him worthy of you. As for his disposition, I'll leave that to my wife—she has the gift of words this day far in excess of my own poor efforts."

Madrigal managed to reply in stilted English. "Lady Beth, Stefano is a fine man of honor. He is soft-spoken and is in great need of a firm and loving hand." She remembered the wine and wenching that Stefano had indulged in, but prayed he had done so in bitterness over his hopeless future. "And he is terribly attractive—dark and distinguished in appearance." Madrigal continued to praise Stefano's best attributes, much to Beth's delight and Roderick's growing resentment.

With one leg slung casually over the arm of the chair, Roderick listened as Madrigal went on almost as if she were describing a lover. He grew thoughtful, recalling the days at Halconbosque, most especially those times when she had been there with only his mother and Stefano.

"Roderick?" Beth broke into his dark musings. "Your half brother sounds well suited to the task here. I realize that if he is sent for, I must marry him, for that would serve my needs." Beth was, of course, relieved to have her position secured at Penglennyn once more, even if Madrigal's glowing account of Stefano's virtues was somewhat exaggerated; she had no choice in any case.

"Then it is settled. This very day I shall draft letters to both Stefano and King Edward, and before the summer, Beth, you shall have your lands secure and a husband in the bargain."

"Will he come, Roderick?" asked Madrigal.

"Stefano has nothing to keep him in Spain. He will come to England to be his own master and to secure a name for a son. Yes, he will come gladly."

They toasted the agreement, and then Roderick left to draft the letters; he would send for a scroll bearer on the morrow. In his letter to Stefano he instructed his half brother to make certain that King Sancho sent a trustworthy man to oversee Halconbosque until he himself could return.

Every facet of Roderick's life appeared in order at this moment, everything but his marriage and the problem of his wife's father. Many months had passed since he had taken her to wife as revenge on the Earl of Tarbella. And, in reality, he had done justice to his plan, for she certainly despised him and called her marriage a curse. Yet this did not give him the feeling of satisfaction he had expected. He wondered if he disliked her as much as she seemed to dislike him. She was most definitely a nuisance, and a rebellious one at that. She fought him at every turn and cut him deeply with her sharp tongue. There was no pleasure in this; he probably should have taken her to bed and made her pregnant without the marriage vows. That would have caused much misery and shame to the earl, and then he could have wed a comely wench who would have stood obediently in the background of his life and laid meekly under him in bed. But when had he ever desired a woman as he did Madrigal? And for all her protests, she responded to his physical body as recklessly as he did to hers. However, he could not spend the entire day wooing her into bed, or raping her when she fought him.

He pressed his heavy ring into the hot wax seal of the two letters, leaving the mark of the black hawk, and sat back, raking his curly hair with his fingers. From where he sat he could see the two women in the hall, their faces flushed and happy. Yet Roderick felt that if he approached them, his wife would turn suspicious and cold. Mayhap if he got her with child . . . but then he remembered that she believed herself barren; this, of course, should fit into his scheme of revenge, as she blamed him for causing her to fall down the steps, those damned steps . . . Still, he doubted that she could not conceive. This idea was no doubt some piece of trickery on her part—but what if it were true? And how would they ever find out, since she allowed him no opportunity to bed her?

He cursed under his breath as he thought of all the

nights they had shared the same bed, naked, but with cold backs turned to each other. Did she know, and probably revel in the fact, that he suffered much physical pain from not being able to crush her lovely body to him? *Perdición!* That woman, that small, slim, girl-woman, his own wife—and yet not his at all. He shook his head, rose, and went to the entrance door, then stood there staring out across the rocks to the moors beyond.

Beth came up behind him. "Cousin, I wish to express my heartfelt gratitude for all you have done here. Whereas my future was dubious at best only a short while ago, now I feel certain all will be well again at Penglennyn." She smiled at him warmly.

"Your aunt, Lady Gwendolyn, will also be delighted to know you are secure. It is partly on my mother's account that I am here, Beth."

"Yes, I remember my father speaking of her often. They were quite close as children, I believe. She will be relieved to know that the family lands are not to be seized by the Crown for lack of management. King Edward will also be relieved to have his tithes paid once again."

Roderick thought a moment. "No, King Edward would never have seized these lands, for they are my inheritance, and, as Edward surely knows, King Sancho would have been sorely vexed by such a serious move before I had been given a chance to claim them."

Beth shook her head. "I had not thought of that. Since my father's death, I only worried about my position here."

"Then 'tis good Stefano will come. You won't have to fear again, little cousin."

Madrigal approached them. "Roderick, Beth has offered to guide me about the fief on horseback. 'Tis mild weather. May we ride today?"

255

"Yes, but Renaldo will go along."

The faithful, one-eyed vassal heard his name and quickly answered his master's call from the place near the hearth that he had filched from the dogs. The women went to fetch their cloaks and Renaldo saw to their mounts, then waited with Roderick by the stable. When the women arrived, Roderick bade them remain within the fief's boundaries. Beth assured him they would ride the well-used trail along the cliffs and would go no farther.

The day was cloudy, but the sun fought its way through the mist to warm their backs and clear the air of dew. Madrigal enjoyed the horse provided for her; he was large-boned and sure-footed, with the massive neck of a late-gelded stallion, which he tossed continually in anticipation of a run while his ears flicked nervously.

They made their way easily around the large, smooth boulders that seemed to dot the land in all directions. Then they came out onto a wide, grassy moor and followed the trail edging the steep cliffs. The ocean glistened and spewed its white foam into the air, then crashed far below on the giant rocks. In many ways her surroundings reminded Madrigal of Galicia. The difference was the lack of trees and undergrowth here; in their place were wide moors and furze and heather among fields of huge boulders.

They rode in silence for several miles, Renaldo keeping up the rear at a safe distance. Finally Beth stopped and dismounted above a particularly lovely cove. Madrigal followed suit, and for a time the ladies walked ahead of their mounts, talking and enjoying the mild February day.

A short time later Madrigal looked up and saw a tall rider approaching them on the trail. Before she could comment to her cousin, Beth said hastily, "'Tis our

256

rude neighbor, Sir William Poldreth. Come, let us turn back before he has a chance to speak to us."

Although Madrigal was confused by Beth's attitude, she attempted to remount her steed, but the horse had sensed the intruder and balked and pranced around her until Sir William was nearly upon them. Beth sat on her horse, warily eyeing the approach of her neighbor.

He dismounted and strode boldly over to Madrigal, taking the reins of her nervous mount and calmly steadying the animal with his hands. When he was satisfied that the steed presented no threat to the beautiful stranger, he looked at her rather keenly and said, "I am Sir William Poldreth, *à votre service*, milady."

Before Madrigal could reply, Beth reproached him, saying sternly, "Be off this land, Sir William. You have no rights here."

He turned his back on Beth, ignoring her protests, and failed to see Renaldo approaching, his bony hand clutching the hilt of his sheathed sword.

Madrigal stole a glance at the tall nobleman; he was dark-complected, sporting a neatly trimmed beard, and bore his large frame well. He could have been called a handsome man, but his narrow-set eyes were cold and fierce despite his flashing smile. She dropped her gaze when she saw that he watched her. "May I have my horse, please?" she asked shyly.

"You are foreign? Spanish or French, I should guess from your dark beauty."

Madrigal blushed at his compliment; he was certainly outspoken beyond his rightful due. He reached for and took her small hand, kissing it before she could pull back. When she did so, he held it tightly and would not let her go.

Beth was indignant now. "Unhand my cousin, Sir William! You have no right to—"

"I'll take whatever pleasures here I wish, Lady Beth." His menacing eyes put a sudden fear into Madrigal.

"Please," she said, trying to save the situation, "I must be gone."

He fixed his gaze on her again, catching the rise and fall of her breasts under the cloak. "Tarry a while, milady. I seek only an introduction."

She would have told him her name and undoubtedly could have put him in his place, except that Renaldo had quickly loosed his sword. The faithful servant, not understanding the language, thought his master's wife in need of succor and came to her rescue, shouting at the stranger in Spanish.

Sir William responded immediately; he drew his blade and pushed Madrigal behind him.

She protested, struggling to be free of Poldreth's broad figure, which stood in her way. "No, Renaldo! I am fine," and then, to Sir William, "Please, he is only a servant trying to protect me!"

But the ill-matched men paid her no heed. Suddenly Madrigal's horse reared and pawed the air, drawing Renaldo's attention. As the horse came down, Sir William lunged at the smaller man, and an instant later the duel was over. Renaldo lay writhing in the dust with a deep wound in his side. The entire incident had taken place in less than a minute.

Madrigal screamed then, and felt her body rooted to the spot. Beth had the presence of mind to dismount and rush to Renaldo, cursing Sir William fiercely to herself.

Sir William turned to Madrigal, ignoring the body on the ground as he wiped the blood from his sword. A slow grin spread across his thin lips. "You are shocked," he said matter-of-factly. "The man was but a lowly serf and got in my way. Come, now . . ." His hand rested on her arm and she pulled away.

"You beast!" Tears of horror spilled down her cheeks. He took her by the shoulders and was drawing her toward him when he suddenly released his grip, causing Madrigal to stumble backward. Beth stood behind him, Renaldo's sword in her hand, pricking his mail.

"Get on your horse, pig, before I run you through." Her tone left little doubt as to her intentions.

The Spanish wench was most definitely not worth the trouble of disarming Beth, Sir William realized, so he remounted and turned in the direction he had come from. Before leaving, he called back to them, "I trust we shall meet again soon," and then laughed deeply as he put spurs to his horse and disappeared down the trail.

Chapter 32

Roderick paced the hall nervously; they had been gone for hours, and he feared something was amiss. At last, he heard horses rounding the bend in the road. His growing alarm fled momentarily and he went to the entrance, standing on the upper step until he saw the third horse bearing Renaldo's body draped over the saddle. He crossed the distance to them in a few quick strides and grabbed the reins from Beth's shaking hand.

He managed to lower Renaldo carefully into his arms and left the women and horses to the care of the frightened stableboy. He carried Renaldo inside and placed him gently near the fire. Beth and Madrigal, following quickly behind him, pulled quilts around Renaldo's crumpled form, and Madrigal propped his head on her lap.

Roderick quickly ripped away the blood-soaked

tunic to assess the damage. The wound was deep and still bled profusely. He looked quickly at his wife's pale face but said nothing to her.

"Fetch me a needle and catgut, Beth," he said gruffly.

"Will he die, Roderick?" Madrigal's lips trembled.

"I cannot say. But it looks bad for my old friend."

Beth returned shortly with a needle and a twist of catgut. Renaldo stirred unconsciously as Roderick worked to seal the wound; he knew Renaldo would not awaken, for he had often seen men in the same condition, and few had lived long enough to see the light of day again.

When he had finished he bade Madrigal and Beth change their riding attire. By the time they had returned, Roderick was seated near the fire holding a tankard of ale, impatiently awaiting the details of the incident. Renaldo, thankfully, was still breathing.

The women recounted what had happened as best as they could, for the details were not clear in their minds. Nevertheless, they left out much of Sir William's boldness toward Madrigal.

On this point Roderick was most confounded. Why had this man attacked poor Renaldo? He questioned again and again, until Madrigal finally cried, "In truth, it was because of the man's manner to me!" She switched to Spanish. "Sir William was overly bold and Renaldo feared for my honor. I tried to stop him—oh, God, it was horrible!"

Roderick rose and went to the hearth. He looked at Renaldo and then at Madrigal's weeping form. His face was hard, a bleak granite mask. He came back and stood over her dangerously.

Madrigal raised her head and went on. "I could have put Sir William at bay myself, but we were speaking English and Renaldo did not understand."

"Undoubtedly," he thundered, "Renaldo saw exactly what was happening! You encouraged the man and—"

"No!" she cried. "'Twas not like that!"

His glare was merciless. "Come, now, my wife, you are cursed with a beauty that drives men to possess you, and you use it to its best advantage!"

Madrigal wept again and would not defend herself against his bitter attack. She had not encouraged Sir William in the least, but in her heart she knew Roderick would never believe her.

Beth helplessly watched the two continue to tear each other apart with cruel words and insinuations. Finally she cleared her throat and timidly tried to calm Roderick by saying, "You have misjudged the situation. I do not mean to imply—"

Roderick silenced her in a harsh voice. "I have never misjudged my wife! Has she told you how we came to wed?" He did not wait for Beth's reply. "Of course not. She bewitched me in the forest with her wiles, and I sought her hand to quench my thirst . . ."

Madrigal was aghast by his twisted words; she leaped to her feet and cried, " 'Tis a lie! I tried to flee from you that day. You forced marriage on me only to satisfy your vengeance against my innocent father!"

He grabbed her by the shoulders. "How very naive you are, milady! Has it not occurred to you that I could have chosen other ways to avenge myself? I need not have wed you at all!" As soon as the words were out, he released her and turned back to the fire, asking himself silently, truthfully, why, indeed, he had married her. Did he feel something for her . . . something that would defeat him? He steeled his mind against that possibility and swore to rid himself of her spell, so that when she fled from the hall, pledging to bar her door against him forever, he only cursed under his breath and gritted his teeth. Earlier that morning he would have followed her and broken in the door, but now he let her go, sensing that perhaps hers was the best way to relieve him of her magic.

Beth waited for him to follow, or to tear the hall apart in rage, but he simply sat down and gazed into the red-hot embers. At last he turned to her and in a quiet manner began to question her as to the roots of Sir William's attitude toward herself and Penglennyn.

Beth told him of the long-standing distrust between the two fiefs and of the small skirmishes over boundaries and mining claims. The feud apparently dated back so far that even Beth did not know how or when it had begun; she knew only that it stretched over several generations and no end was in sight.

"Before I return to Spain, I shall see an end to this quarrel," Roderick promised. "I swear it on Renaldo's life."

"But how . . . ?"

"It is my way to finish a job begun. There will be peace in this land before I depart."

Beth came to believe his words, for in the next weeks Roderick spent long hours with the serfs of Penglennyn, training them in the art of warfare and appointing Hugo as his lieutenant. By the time of the spring planting, the menfolk of the fief were indeed shaping up into a small army. They planted their barley and rye, tended the mine, and sheared the wool-laden sheep, but they also practiced their newly acquired military skills.

Beth was amazed at the improved condition of the fief, for Roderick demanded excellence of his men; in return, he fed them well and took a personal interest in their grievances and their safety.

Mercifully, owing to the special care of Madrigal and his own toughness, Renaldo survived the wound and convalesced rapidly, although it would still be some time before he could move about with his former agility. As the days passed, Madrigal found herself growing fond of him; she had not always been so. She remembered the first time she had seen him at Castilla-verde, on the day Sancho had commanded her marriage; she had felt sickened to look at Renaldo's missing eye and his ferretlike features. Now he would appear unnatural had he two eyes. She had come to feel deeply for this vassal; he was loyal and cheerful, and most endearing of all, he had unquestionably laid down his life for her. And so she watched over his improving health gladly as the spring wore on and the furze and heather of Cornwall turned from winter's brown to a richer shade of verdancy.

Roderick spent his time either in the company of his wounded vassal or out among the serfs and the fields. The weather was warm and sunny, with an occasional rain shower to nurture the crops. Beth confessed that it was not always so; the spring often brought long stretches of cool, damp weather.

With each passing day Beth grew more anxious, for Stefano was certain to arrive any time now. Frequently Madrigal would seek her out for a walk along the moors or down to a sunny cove. Once Beth had ventured to ask about her marriage, but Madrigal had parried the question with one of her own on another subject.

When Roderick was about, which was seldom, Madrigal would find an excuse to seek the seclusion of her sewing room, which she had moved into on the afternoon of Renaldo's accident. Only once during these weeks did Roderick come to her.

It had been a thunderous, stormy night, and Roderick stayed in the great hall, talking and drinking with Renaldo. Madrigal had taken her meal early in her room, as had been her wont of late, and Beth had retired to the other wing. When Renaldo had fallen asleep in the middle of a sentence, Roderick had finished off his last ale and gone up to his room. He had found himself thinking of his empty bed and then of the winsome beauty sleeping only a few steps across the hall.

Although his mind rebelled, he stood before her locked door and finally convinced himself that he sought only to quell the ache in his loins and that the woman lying alone behind the door could be any village maid for all he cared.

He derived a great deal of pleasure in kicking in the heavy door. Madrigal awakened immediately and sat up, terrified, clutching the coverlet around her. But when she saw the tall, shadowy figure that stood menacingly in the opening, she knew instantly who it was.

"Get out . . . before I scream," she whispered.

"No, my wife," he slurred, "I have a great need that will not wait." He approached her unsteadily, then begun to undress while she clenched her teeth in rage, wishing for a lethal weapon.

He drew away her cover and she bit his hand and tried to roll away; but, as always, Roderick was too quick for her, and she found herself pinned to the bed. She twisted and turned to no avail and cried aloud when his mouth covered her breast. Her strength failed her, and he had his way. He spread her legs with his knees and began to force his way into her. She cried out at the pain, his ale-laden breath repulsing her, as he continued his thrusts. He then made slow and rhythmical movements, penetrating her deeply. When she least desired it, and loathing him and herself all the more, she felt a warm tingling spread up her belly until her body moved with his rhythm and her breath come in short gasps.

Roderick had not missed her involuntary change of heart, and he smiled down into her face, taking his time then, pleased that she had been so easily aroused. Such had not necessarily been his intention, but her response had been far more pleasurable to him than if he had raped her. He had brought her to the peak and reached his own at the same time.

"Madrigal . . ."

"No, don't! Leave me!" She had cried, her tone so full of despair that he had rolled away and left her weeping in the darkness.

For the next two days she had stayed in her room, pleading illness. Even after Roderick had repaired her door latch and tried to converse with her, she had ignored his overtures. He had stormed off to the fields, vowing never to seek her company again.

The following afternoon Roderick rode back to Penglennyn and passed Madrigal walking through the gate. They both stared straight ahead, their faces averted, neither willing to look the other in the eye. It was as if they had never met.

Chapter 33

Sam, who normally helped Beth with the kitchen garden, was proving very stubborn, trying to weasel out of planting the vegetables this year. He pleaded the need to train for Lord Roderick's "army" as his excuse, even though he was over seventy and had one withered arm that was nearly useless.

"Sam, the garden must be planted, or none of us shall have any greens to eat this winter! What ails you, man!" Beth's usual complaisance had turned to exasperation in the face of the serf's passive obstinacy.

"Th' lard wisht us'n all t' train with a weepon, mistress," was all she could elicit from his wrinkled, toothless mouth.

"Your wife shall have an extra fat pig this autumn, but please, help me get the seeds in—the season grows late!" Beth wondered whether she could find anyone else to help her, then realized that every man was doing extra duty already.

Finally old Sam agreed to help her "fur un short time," and they began laying out the straight rows of vegetables in the warm, fecund earth behind the great hall, where the two wings sheltered the plot from the wind. Beth wore an old dress of rough gray wool and tucked it up around her dimpled knees to facilitate bending over the rows. Her face was smudged with dirt where she had brushed away an irritating gnat, and her honey-colored hair escaped from its pins, falling in curling tendrils onto her damp neck.

Unlike most titled women, Beth loved this job. It gave her a sense of the continuity of things, repeating the endless cycle of sowing and harvesting each year. She was concentrating on whether to plant more swedes or to put in carrots instead, when a voice hailed her from the corner of the west wing. She straightened up from her kneeling position, shading her eyes with one hand and squinting to see who was calling so loudly, but all she could make out was a blur of color on what was surely a horse. The figure approached at a walk until it emerged from the fog of her shortsightedness into clear focus; it was a man on a jaded horse, his once-elegant clothes muddy and travel-stained. He was dark, and definitely foreign. His black hair was tipped with gray, giving his otherwise jaunty appearance a distinguished air. He was obviously one of the gypsies who often camped for a few days in a nearby cove, and had come to sell a stolen trinket or trade a lame nag for a sound one. Beth was glad that Sam was there, for the gypsies were not to be trusted around horses, gold, or women.

"Good day, sir," she put in quickly before the man could begin his tale of woe. "If you wish some water, the well is under that tree, but as for any other dealings, I am sorry there is nothing here of value."

The man stopped his horse, leaning forward to cross his forearms on the pommel of his saddle, and grinned appreciatively at the girl standing in the middle of the garden plot, her hands muddy and her face smudged, looking a bit defiant, a bit scared, and devastatingly feminine.

"I knocked at the main door, but no one was about, so I took the liberty of coming around here to see what was amiss," said the stranger. "Have you no servant to answer a traveler's knock?" He had a marked accent.

"Of course, but we accept no tradesmen or beggars at the main door. If you wish scraps, the kitchens are there." She pointed a grimy finger at the rear of the east wing.

The man laughed, showing even, white teeth in his swarthy face. "Scraps? No, not scraps, but I do wish to see the lady of Penglennyn, if she is available. I have traveled far this day."

"I do not believe, sir, that the lady of the hall would have any business with you," Beth replied, wondering at this gypsy's gall.

"Who do you take me for, girl?"

"Why, one of the Romany, of course. Don't you come from their camp?"

"A gypsy! How apt!" The man was amused. "I happen to be Stefano, Lord Roderick's brother and Lady Beth Winthrop's intended husband, and I thought I would be expected. Now, would you summon your mistress?"

Beth's mouth fell open, her feet were rooted to the spot, and a hot flush spread up her neck to her cheeks. Dear Lord, she thought, and me groveling in an old dress in a muddy garden and calling him a gypsy! What a way to start a marriage! Would he ever forgive her? Her hands plucked ineffectually at her skirts, trying to pull them down to cover her legs. She tried to gather her scattered wits, nervously brushing back loose strands of damp hair, but succeeded only in leaving more dirt streaks on her face.

"Well? What are you staring at me for, girl? Was I not expected?" Stefano was growing irritated.

"Yes, yes, you were expected, milord. I . . . I am so sorry to have thought you a—" Beth blushed a darker red and swallowed, almost choking. "I am . . . Lady Beth, milord." Her mortification was so acute that she felt giddy and hot and could not meet his eyes when the words were out; she could only stare down at the mud-spattered square-toed clogs she wore. What would he think, meeting her like this in a veritable comedy of errors? What if she disgusted him or left him cold? Would he turn around and ride away, or would he refuse to marry her? She stood there praying silently, unable to move or to look up at him. She heard him dismount and approach her; her heart fluttered like a trapped bird against her ribs. Then she felt his hand under her chin, gently forcing her head up until her eyes met his and could not look away.

His countenance was not young, but he was handsome in a foreign way, with the same hawklike features as Roderick's, yet formed in a darker mold. He looked very serious now, and she was afraid his words would be harsh and disapproving of her mistake. He stared at her until she could not bear another moment of his grave perusal.

"So you are Beth," he breathed, his dark eyes filled with a kind of wonder. "Well! Let us not speak of first impressions now, or we may both regret our hasty words in the future." He smiled at her, taking her dirty

268

hand in his. "I have a thirst worthy of a dragon and am half starved besides. And my poor nag hardly has the energy to walk to the stables, I warrant. Come, my bride-to-be, we shall leave the cabbage patch for now, and you will play the hostess." He led her away from the garden and began talking easily of his journey from London, his port of entry, but they were halted in their steps by Sam's voice.

"Mistress! Ain't ye be finishin' th' garden? Ye've made me help all this hot day an' now ye jist walk off! What in th' name of our dear Lard am I t' do now, mistress?"

"Oh, hang the garden, Sam! I've more important things to concern me now," Beth called back, laughing.

Once inside the main house, Beth quickly excused herself and ran to Madrigal, begging her to entertain Stefano while she bathed and changed her garments. She left Madrigal and Stefano by the hearth, chattering away in Spanish, Madrigal serving him ale and seemingly delighted to see her brother-in-law again.

When Beth reentered the great hall, she saw that Roderick had returned and was slapping Stefano on the back, exclaiming in Spanish. She felt much more in command of the situation now, dressed in her best linen gown of pale blue, its neckline trimmed with creamy braid. Her undertunic was a deep shade of rose.

Roderick went to take her hand. "What do you think of my dashing older brother, Beth? Is he not all that we said?" Roderick was obviously relieved and happy that Stefano had arrived.

Beth did not quite trust her voice on the subject of her betrothed, and changed the topic as soon as she could. Hospitality deemed it necessary for her to offer to help with the guest's bath, but she was uncertain as to whether Spanish customs were the same in this matter.

269

"Milord, no doubt you wish a bath before our meal. I have ordered one for you and will help you bathe myself—that is, if you do not object . . ."

"How thoughtful, Lady Beth. I expect I reek like an old shoe. I have been in these clothes for days, as I was in such haste to arrive . . . and to meet you, milady. I left my belongings in London, to be sent by ship later, and bought the old nag on which you saw me earlier. And now I know why I was in such haste to get here." He smiled charmingly at her while she reddened under his compliments. "Come, let me have my bath quickly, lest I faint from hunger before it is over." He laughed. "The aromas from your kitchens are making me weak!"

The chamber Beth had ordered for Stefano was in the west wing; it had been her parent's room, and it still retained some of its former beauty. The velvet draperies were a deep gold color, and a rose satin coverlet lay across the huge bed. The damask bed hangings had tiny gold threads patterned throughout. A fire had been build in the hearth to heat the water, and the wooden tub stood in front of the flames, steaming gently and invitingly.

Stefano sighed with relief as he slumped into a chair. Beth tugged off his boots and dusty surcoat, carefully unbuckling his sword and laying it aside. She pulled his undertunic over his head and he was left in his hose, his broad shoulders reflecting glints from the fire.

"Ah," he sighed, "this is pleasurable. I have had nothing for days now but cold water from a horse trough and flea-filled hay to sleep on."

"Milord, do you wish to bathe or would you rest awhile?" asked Beth, nervous and shy now that she was alone in the room with Stefano.

"I am Stefano to you, my dear." He took her hands in his and studied her, his head tilted to one side. "You remind me of a pet I once had, a little bird that had fallen from a nest, so tiny and warm and helpless. I carried it home and raised it till it was grown. The bird always remembered me and flew back often to eat crumbs off my finger. It was so . . . soft." Stefano's eyes had a faraway look; then he stared at Beth again. "But I was just a child then and thought people would love me as the little bird did. I have found out differently, much to my regret, but the little bird never knew I was born a bastard." His last words were harsh. "My brother told you, did he not, that I am his half brother, a natural son of our father's?" Stefano's voice was challenging; it frightened Beth.

"Yes, he told me," she whispered, her eyes downcast.

"Look at me," Stefano demanded. "Look at me and tell me truthfully—does it shame you to marry a bastard?"

"Stefano, I can only guess how it feels to be born . . . as you were, but I have been taught to judge a man on his merits and virtues rather than on the false trappings of title with which our community brands us. I assure you I would give you all the loyalty and devotion that you deserve, whatever your birth."

"Indeed, Beth, your words comfort me. You are straight-spoken. I like that. So we both fulfill our needs: you, the whole of Penglennyn, and I, lands and the promise of sons with a name. My brother has solved all our problems neatly, has he not? What think you, my fledgling—can it work?" Stefano's tone was light and jesting, but she could see in his eyes that he was serious.

The firelight played on his hard muscles and drew deep lines in his face. He needed someone, this man who had suddenly entered her life; he needed reassurance and love to fill the tender, wounded thing that was his heart. The sudden realization of his vulnerability made Beth swell with pride and love. He was hers to

271

care for and nurture, as she did her garden or her lambs, or, indeed, Penglennyn.

"Yes, Stefano," she whispered, laying her dimpled white hand on his bare shoulder. "Yes, it *will* work."

Madrigal stood next to Roderick in the ancient gray stone church in Falmouth, torn by mixed emotions; she was glad for Beth and Stefano, but she was also bitterly envious of their happiness. They seemed to have a secret understanding that made each of them burst with pride and contentment. When she thought of her stormy relationship with her own husband, she clenched her teeth in frustration. It wasn't fair that such a miserable fate had befallen her! What had she done to deserve it? No more than many another young girl, certainly. Her mind was drawn back to the present as she realized Roderick was talking to her.

"Do they not make a well-suited pair, Madrigal?" he whispered in Spanish, a bit too loudly in the solemn hush. "I only wish my mother were here; she would be quite pleased to see Stefano become a worthy husband."

The question "Would she not be pleased to see *you* become a worthy husband also?" leaped to Madrigal's lips, but she did not say it aloud. Better to live as a polite stranger than to cause more dissension and turmoil.

She gazed at the couple and had to admit that Beth indeed looked ravishing in her mother's wedding dress of bright blue, the customary marriage color here. Stefano looked most distinguished, attired in a brilliant crimson surcoat with a jeweled belt, and a green velvet cloak lined in white satin. He was certainly the peacock of this marriage, she thought, but guessed shrewdly that Beth was the rock on which their happiness would be built.

The priest finally finished his blessing, the ancient Latin words soothing Madrigal's ear; at least something was familiar in this foreign place. The newly married couple turned to leave the church and lead the procession back to Penglennyn; their faces were so full of joy that Madrigal felt tears come to her eyes. Whether they were tears of happiness for them or tears of bitterness for herself, she could not have said.

The wedding party, seated in several small carts, wound its way through the narrow, cobbled streets as it climbed from the sea toward the moors. The group was merry, chattering and making bawdy jests at the bridegroom's expense. It consisted of a few neighboring lords and their ladies, old friends of Beth's family, and, walking behind, the entire assemblage of Penglennyn's serfs, all of whom loved Beth and were thrilled to see her wed to a good man.

The guests were welcomed at the hall by a lordly feast. There were spitted spring lambs, round loaves of crusty rye bread, several varieties of mouth-watering pasties, fruit tarts, tangy cider, ale, and a cask of French wine. Early berries with thick, sweet, clotted cream, wedges and rounds of cheese, and slabs of roasted chickens filled the trestle tables that had been set up in the great hall. A trio of minstrels played softly from the gallery above.

Beth had exhausted herself in the short week since Stefano's arrival to oversee the preparation of each and every dish, and she had most certainly outdone herself. She thoroughly enjoyed her guests and beamed on everyone. A quiet word to a servant, a suggestion to a serving wench, and all went as smoothly as she could have desired.

After the meal the minstrels strummed old tunes of true love and chivalry until the guests had tears in their eyes, aided, no doubt, by the great quantities of ale and wine they had consumed. The entourage then stood in line to give Beth their gifts of gold coins, wishing her and her new spouse a prosperous and happy future.

From the far corner of the hall, where the serfs had gathered, Hugo struck up a refrain on his homemade flute. The maidens of Penglennyn took up the beat and whirled into one of their ancient Cornish folk dances. Beth clapped merrily to the music, but Roderick and Madrigal were transfixed by the lilting, odd-sounding melody. Stefano merely nodded and smiled continually, eating and drinking but little, watching Beth with adoring eyes.

As the hours grew late, the guests who lived close by began leaving, the others retiring to rooms provided for the night. Stefano and Beth approached the stairs, obviously quite anxious to be alone, and Madrigal took up the duties of hostess.

"Do not fret, Beth. I shall see to the guests. Take yourself off now and please your new husband," she said, forcing herself to sound cheerful. As Beth left, she recalled her own wedding night, the ruse planned by Elena—or had it been a ruse?—the terror she had felt when Roderick had come after her, his arrogant treatment of her. It all came back to her in nauseous waves of remembrance, black around the edges, and she wondered if she had not had too much to drink.

Roderick, along with some of the more sober men, escorted Stefano to the marriage bed. They would have their final jokes and foolish advice for the bridegroom.

When the last guest had been seen to, Madrigal slipped away to her room, glad that the hall was peaceful again. The thought of Beth and Stefano in their marriage bed rose unbidden to her mind, causing her cheeks to flame. She wondered if Beth would enjoy making love, then told herself sternly that it was none of her business. As she drifted off to sleep, she could not help imagining their naked bodies joined together, perhaps this very night creating a new life between them.

She was awakened much later by the insistent rattling of the iron bar placed across the inside of her door. She lay rigid, breaking out in a cold sweat, praying that Roderick would go away and hoping at the same time that he would burst in an consume her in the hot urgency of his passion. But soon the rattling ceased and all was silent again.

Chapter 34

The fact that Beth spent much of her time in the company of Stefano or was ill from her midsummer pregnancy did little to cheer Madrigal; she had become more and more despondent as the summer wore on.

It was August fifteenth, and the morning sun beat down on her shoulders while she strolled idly through the courtyard and past the stable. She was thinking about Beth's pregnancy, and the familiar pain returned as she remembered her own inadequacy as a woman; actually, she mused, even if she could bear a child, there was the matter of her estrangement from Roderick. They had not shared a bed since the time he had come to her, half intoxicated, and all but raped her.

She thought back, her brows knitted together, and could not recall the last time she and Roderick had had a civil conversation. Stefano and Beth artfully avoided the subject of Roderick around her, and so, of late, she had blesssed few reminders of her marriage to the baron.

Suddenly she realized it was market day in Falmouth. She should ride to town and shop for several yards of white silk and trimming, to stitch a christening gown for Beth's baby. Yes, she would do exactly that, and Roderick, should he object, could go to the devil! She would do something, for once, that pleased her!

The notion put an impish smile on her face as she considered the possible adventure; she had been at Penglennyn for half a year's time and had left the fief only to attend Beth's wedding.

She pulled up the hem of her yellow linen gown and ran breathlessly back to the hall. She would not even tell Stefano or Beth of the trip, nor, she thought shamelessly, would she take a servant along. If she were clever enough and dressed the part of a village maid, she could travel unnoticed to Falmouth before midday and return in time for the evening meal. No one would have to know she had gone at all!

After doffing her good gown for an old one, and placing a few silver coins in her shoe, she passed Stefano and Beth on her way out to the stable; she mentioned only her desire to exercise one of the horses.

There were serfs traveling on the trail leading across the Penglennyn moors and into Falmouth. They looked at her briefly, and that only because she rode a horse. She decided to tether her mount in a safe place before actually entering the town, allowing her to walk freely among the throng.

For a fleeting instant she considered the slim possibility of meeting Roderick along the trail, but most likely he was on the opposite side of the moors, where the fields and the tin mine lay, so she dismissed the idea altogether.

When at last she saw the first outlying cottages of Falmouth, she found a secluded spot and tied the horse securely to a tree. There she pulled her thin cape around her shoulders and strode purposefully past the increasing number of houses. The town was small indeed. In the center of the tree-lined square was the old church, flanked by a few shops; narrow, winding alleys led to the bay. The marketplace was set up near the waterfront, and thankfully, there were many other maids bargaining and haggling with the merchants, so that the presence of one more shopper went unnoticed.

She found the proper material and trimming almost immediately and was somewhat disappointed that the journey thus far had proved so uneventful. The only excitement had occurred when she had rounded a corner and bumped into a rather handsome, middle-aged seaman who had at once offered her a coin for her services. She had giggled with embarrassment at his quick offer, then proceeded slowly toward the church, enjoying the various booths and entertainments of Falmouth's market day. She could not resist buying a handful of early gooseberries, and ate them as she meandered contentedly among the fowl and swine that searched the dusty paths for bits of food.

Entering the church, she pulled the hood over her head and knelt in the last row of hard oak benches. She prayed for a long while, then realized that the hour was growing late. She retraced her steps down the cobblestones, her eyes trained on her footing.

Across the square, Roderick, Renaldo, and Hugo were finishing the day's bargaining with the town's wool merchant when Renaldo's ready eye caught sight of a lovely wench just leaving the church. He watched her innocent sway as she walked in their direction, suddenly aware that there was something familiar about her. Then, as she neared, recognition spread across his narrow features. *Madre de Dios!* he cried to himself. If the baron should see her, here and unescorted . . . Before he could finish the thought, two richly dressed

277

men exited a shop, only to bump straight into the girl, causing her to drop her package. Renaldo's brow was damp with perspiration when he realized that one of the men was Sir William Poldreth.

Renaldo was at a total loss as to what he should do. His heart pounded in his chest when he saw Poldreth take Madrigal's arm and appear unwilling to release it. Roderick's faithful servant could not bear to watch a repetition of the ugly scene on the trail above the cliffs, especially when the short, squat man with Poldreth had laughed rudely at Madrigal's futile attempts to depart.

Making a snap decision, he turned to his master, saying, "There is a lass . . . she had just left the church and is being accosted by that low snake, Poldreth! We must—"

Roderick turned quickly, took in the scene before him, and was halfway across the cobblestoned square before Renaldo could catch up. Madrigal's back was turned to them, and Roderick assumed the girl was a simple village wench in distress.

When he came upon the trio, he looked first at Sir William Poldreth and then at the other man, whom he recognized as none other than Penglennyn's former overseer, Terence.

Roderick's look was dangerous, coldly weighing the twosome. Still ignoring the wench's existence, he addressed Poldreth. "We meet at last, Sir William." And then to Terence, "How very interesting to see that you have found a kindred spirit."

Keeping his temper in check, Roderick was actually relieved to at last meet Beth's enemy face to face. If the man chose to delay a wench on her way from prayer, it only showed him to be as boorish as Roderick had expected. There remained, however, the matters of Poldreth's advances toward his wife and the wounding of Renaldo.

William Poldreth answered him haughtily. "Yes, 'tis time we met, Halconbosque. In fact, the girl has just been threatening me with your name."

"The girl . . .?" Roderick spun on his heel to meet his wife's shocked look. He stood speechless for a long moment, and she felt hot and dizzy with fright. But he did not vent his anger on her; instead, amazingly, he turned back to Poldreth. He spoke as if for his own benefit. "You laid hands, *again*, on this lady, and knowing she was my wife, you dared to . . ." His words trailed off in wonder at the man's unmitigated gall. His hand went to his sword's hilt.

"Yes," Sir William challenged now, "and the very feel of her is worth the confrontation, Baron."

Roderick stepped back and began to draw his blade, his face growing stony in his fury, but Renaldo and Hugo were quick to plead the absurdity of dueling in the middle of the square. Poldreth relaxed first and moved away, a snicker escaping his thin lips.

"Mayhap we shall meet again soon, very soon." His stare bored into Roderick's, a small smile still on his lips.

Terence stood close to him, a gleeful spark in his small eyes. Then Poldreth continued. "What say you to a meeting in, shall we say, a fortnight? I wish above all to be fair to your side—to give you time to prepare your ill-equipped peasants." His tone was snide. "And to the winner go the spoils." He bestowed a lewd look on Madrigal.

"Never," she whispered in horrified understanding.

Roderick clenched his teeth, his hand white on the hard steel of his sword. When he spoke, Madrigal realized that she had never heard his voice sound so menacingly cold.

"The spoils shall be mine . . . your lands, your hall, and all the men therein," he said slowly and distinctly.

Poldreth paled slightly at the venom in his voice, then laughed blusteringly and turned to leave, calling over his shoulder, "In a fortnight, milady."

"By all that's holy, I'll run the swine through this minute!" Roderick drew his sword in a curving flash of light. It took the power of both Renaldo and Hugo to hold him back from Poldreth's retreating form. When the man was finally out of range, they released their master, begging his forgiveness. He paid them no mind but took several deep breaths to calm himself. Endless moments passed before he turned to his wife. She cowered away from him, looking like a frightened swallow.

"Milady," he said gently, seeing her about to collapse from fear, "I know not what has brought you here, but you will stay by my side until this business is finished." His tone deepened. "Is that clear?"

She whispered faintly, "Yes, milord."

"And now, if you will kindly explain your presence in Falmouth." He patiently waited for her reply, but in fact, seeing her dismay and her poor, street-urchin gown, he felt more like holding her to him and comforting her.

"I didn't realize . . . I was merely bored and restless and thought to purchase silk for Beth's baby. I know I should have sought permission . . ."

"Permission?" He laughed. "And when did you ever seek my counsel on such matters?"

Her cheeks burned, both from his words and from the shimmering heat reflected from the cobblestones. She lowered her dark lashes to hide her eyes from his mockery. The vision of Sir William's face suddenly came to mind and she shuddered, gasping, "Roderick! What if you lose against Poldreth?"

He instantly saw the direction her thoughts had taken. "Have no fear on that score, milady. You are mine and mine alone, and I have no intention of letting that swine win you, although that would be fit penalty, mayhap, for the villain." He smiled down on her, but seeing her fear, he added, "At any rate, the day will not be lost."

He spoke with such self-assurance that she sighed in relief and put away her fears, glad to have escaped his wrath for her foolish escapade. Renaldo and Hugo began to walk ahead of them, feeling proud that there would at last be a confrontation between the two fiefs. When they reached the corner where their mounts were tethered, Madrigal suddenly turned and ran back to where her package still lay. Roderick was bewildered by her flight until he saw what she was after; he stood with his shoulder to the cornerstone, watching her walk back to him. She was winsome, attired in the manner of a serving maid, her hips swaying gracefully beneath her skirts and her hair disheveled and escaping from her thrown-back hood. A slow grin twisted his lips when he pictured her donning her disguise for the afternoon's adventure. It was just like the minx to do such a thing! He realized then that she would never come to heel meekly and he would forever be chasing after her, fighting her battles. Yet he had already spent a lifetime in active service, and he could think of nothing more tiresome than idly administering a peaceful fief for the rest of his days. He was forced to admit to himself that her quests for independence brought him a relief from boredom, a spark of excitement.

"Roderick," she said, "my horse is tethered outside the town. We must fetch him."

"You thought of everything, I see." He tried to sound harsh but failed.

By the time they reached Penglennyn, Madrigal was exhausted, dusty, and famished. Stefano and Beth were greatly relieved to see the four ride in together, for they had spent long hours searching for Madrigal and had been deeply alarmed by her disappearance. When they chastised her for causing them so much worry, she produced the fine French silk and delicate trimming for the baby's gown, seeking their forgiveness.

Roderick, however, was the one to soothe the awkward conversations, suggesting that they all be seated for the meal. "I fear my wife has always been headstrong and stubborn to a fault. Today, however, her presence in Falmouth has brought to a head an inevitable confrontation." He went on to describe the meeting with Sir William, the outcome of which he anticipated greatly.

Beth was extremely concerned, until Stefano spent the remainder of the meal recounting to her the many battles fought and won by them. Madrigal finished her huge trencher of food and observed her husband while Stefano painted a picture of Roderick Halconbosque that she had never seen before.

She thought about the many scars that his body bore and of the long years in battle necessary to acquire such a noble map of campaigns. She recalled his duel with Akbar. His victory there had obviously not been a fluke. Taking a long drink of her cider, she watched his face for a hint of embarrassment at Stefano's glowing account of his prowess. There was none. A remote look of reminiscence flickered in his topaz eyes, but otherwise he was expressionless.

When Stefano finally sat back in his chair, Beth took up the conversation and declared her inborn hatred and fear of Sir William. By evening's end, it had been mutually decided that the upcoming confrontation between the two fiefs was a practical thing indeed. At the very worst, there would be no less than peace in the land, for Roderick was unable to accept a skirmish with an indecisive outcome; either way, the fiefs would be joined by the result of the battle, no matter who the victor might be.

Long after midnight, when the hall was silent save for the restlessness of the dogs, Madrigal quietly crossed the hall to Roderick's room. She tapped at his door lightly, and receiving no reply, lifted the latch and entered his dim, moon-washed chamber.

His familiar breathing came to her ears and she was certain that he slept, but her mind was in such a turmoil that only he could answer the questions that had plagued her sleep. She went to his bedside and sat down on the edge, placing a warm hand on his shoulder to awaken him.

"'Tis the middle of the night, Madrigal." She was startled to find him awake, but then she remembered that the slightest noise had always brought him to alertness.

"I . . . I could not sleep. I'm afraid for Beth if Poldreth should . . ."

He braced himself on one elbow, very aware of her proximity. "Milady, do you not fear for yourself?" She did not answer, but searched his shadowed face. "Do you actually believe the man has a chance? He could not win the day if, to a man, we fought weaponless. I have my eyes and ears at Trenwell, milady. Sir William does not command the allegiance of his serfs, as we do. They hate and distrust him for his cruelty."

She still felt apprehensive, for Sir William was as large and strong a man as Roderick, and often a battle was won when the leader was felled. She said timidly, "Still, if you should be wounded or . . ."

"Killed?"

"Roderick, I only meant that anything is possible, and Beth, I know, is terribly worried for Stefano, and you, too, of course."

He laughed that she should think him so ill-prepared

283

in the event of his own demise. "Rest assured that I have already seen to your safety. Two of Hugo's men will remain at the hall, and should something go amiss, which I again stress is impossible, then they will see you both safely to London, where you will be under the protection of King Edward himself."

"Thank you, Roderick," she said with relief, and rose to leave.

His soft touch delayed her, and she turned to look down into his eyes, realizing that it had been a mistake to seek him out at this hour. She should have waited until morning.

"Before God, my wife, would you grieve if I should meet my death?"

She did a strange thing then, surprising them both. She took his hand in hers and sat back down on the bed. Finally she whispered, "And what do *you* really believe?"

He said immediately, "If I knew the true answer, I would never have asked."

She answered him as best as she could. "There have been times when I asked myself the same question. And I truthfully admit that in anger I often swore I would feign be rid of you. But when my senses are about me, I should be very . . . saddened if you failed to return." She let her breath out slowly, waiting for his reaction.

"Have you at last made a small commitment, milady?"

"I cannot make a commitment, milord, without equal return," she replied harshly, knowing he spoke of the heart. Then curiosity bested her, and she asked him the same question.

"There is little room in my life for womanly comforts," he replied. "Before you, my wife, I had rarely spent two nights abed with the same wench." Then he smiled. "And certainly I had never bothered with a virgin!"

"Oh," she said faintly, not having known before how little he really cared about the opposite sex. Yet she allowed herself a secret pride in the knowledge that she was his only true maiden.

He continued in measured tones. "But, my little swallow, if I were of a different nature and could succumb to a woman's wiles, you would be the perfect one."

"A mistress, you mean?"

"No. A woman as lovely as yourself . . . Let us just say that a man would be daft if he did not lead you to the altar."

She coaxed him further, with a streak of coyness tinging her voice. "You mean to say that you find me attractive . . . pretty?"

He laughed heartily and reached out to touch her waist-length hair. "*Sí*—mayhap even beautiful, little vixen."

She laughed, too, feeling an uncommon tenderness toward him. At least he had been honest with her, and she knew now that if he were capable of caring, she would be the one he sought.

They talked quietly for a short while longer, and finally Roderick drew her down alongside him, assuring her that he only meant to hold her. She was not certain if she trusted him or, for that matter, if she ever could, after the incident with Elena, but in the end he kept his word in spite of his aching desire for her.

She did not sleep, as he did, but lay awake thinking back on the night of her deepest humiliation, the night he had taken Elena. When the first rays of light stole through the shuttered window, Madrigal had finally, peacefully, put to rest the anger and hurt that Roderick had caused her by that act. Without meaning to, his

285

words tonight had bolstered her self-esteem and erased the painful memories of their last stay at Castilla-verde. As for her father's role in the murder of the elder Halconbosque, she vowed to resolve the matter to her husband's satisfaction as soon as time allowed. Then, and only then, would she feel free of the unreasonable guilt over a brutal incident committed some twenty years past.

Yes, she mused as the light grew stronger, she would make an attempt to bind together the broken pieces of her marriage; she had nothing to lose and much to gain. Her depression of the past months slowly ebbed, until she felt her spirits rise in spite of her drowsiness. She closed her eyes, and the image of her shadowy knight came unbidden into her mind's eye. This time, however, he had a face, and as he knelt at her feet he spoke of her beauty and of his growing devotion.

Chapter 35

The days before the confrontation came and went all too swiftly for Madrigal's liking. Her emotions had flown from one state to another, alternating between nervousness and composure; often she was beset by sudden spells of weeping, for which she had no explanation. She was as perplexed by her odd behavior as Roderick.

Making good his promise to keep her at his side, Roderick often took her to the fields with him to watch the serfs practice their newly acquired skills with the bow and other weapons. She saw them using strange wooden shovels with rocks in them, but Roderick explained that on the battle day the shovels would be filled with molten-hot pitch if a siege were required. Large shields of wood were constructed to cover ten men at a time, and others built for the archers. Trees were felled and trimmed as battering rams, although Roderick hoped these would be unnecessary.

Madrigal asked him many questions about the actual engagement: Would they storm Trenwell? Would Sir William have as many archers? Who would attend the wounded in the field? To each question he gave a patient answer, pleased with her interest.

While he supplied information about the use of weaponry, he refused to answer her questions about the plan of attack, for only he and Stefano would know of the actual strategy. When the plans were fully laid in his mind, he would then share them with Hugo.

The eve of the battle arrived.

Roderick, Stefano, and the ladies were finishing their supper when a tap came at the door. Renaldo answered the knock swiftly, as if he had been awaiting just such an interruption, and called the two men to the door. Hugo stood on the threshold; he gave his message briefly, then departed into the foggy night, pulling his forelock respectfully. When Hugo had left, Roderick sat back comfortably in his chair and relaxed, knowing that the advance guard was safely in position and all was under control. Even the weather seemed to be cooperating with them, promising rain and mist.

Beth and Stefano were deep in quiet conversation, looking very much like lovers, and Roderick seemed to be engaged in thought. Madrigal felt miffed to be so ignored on such an important evening. Finally she summoned a serving girl in an unnecessarily loud voice and bade her heat water for a bath and take it to her room.

The girl returned shortly to inform her that the tub

was filled. Madrigal rose, frowning, and muttered under her breath, "'Tis impossible for the water to be warm so soon . . . Pay no mind, I'll see to it myself!"

Roderick heard her impatient chiding of the servant girl and smiled at his wife. "Would you like me to scrub your back?"

"No, milord. You three may sit here feigning calmness, if it so pleases you. As for myself, I feel quite ill at ease and shall seek my own counsel in private." And with an exasperated sigh, she left the hall.

Roderick chuckled to himself at her anxiety and propped his leg up on the table, leaning back in the chair and sipping his ale. He retraced in his mind the preparations for the battle, and then, satisfied that all that was possible had been done, he let his thoughts wander to more pleasant things, such as his wife's body, probably wet and glistening now, submerged in her tub. It had been months since he had caught even a glimpse of her without her gown or some female regalia, and in imagining her naked body relaxing in the tub, he began to feel a hot surge spread to his loins. Well, he thought as he came to his feet, he'd be damned if he'd sit there conjuring up her body in his mind when the real thing was only a few steps away! And the night before a battle—she owed him that much!

Madrigal had dismissed the useless serving girl and lay back in the large tub, her arms hanging over the sides and her knees drawn up comfortably. Her heavy hair was bound loosely atop her head by green ribbons, with a few fallen strands clinging wetly to her neck and shoulders. Her eyes were closed against the candlelight when she heard her door open, and blinking against the light, she saw him in the portal.

"Roderick! How dare you! Please leave."

He walked to a chair, and ignoring her irritated surprise, dragged it over to the tub and sat down, placing his elbows on his knees, his hands clasped together in front of his chin.

Madrigal sank deeper into the lavender-scented water, easily recognizing the familiar look in his eyes. An unbidden thrill of pleasure quickened her heart. Do I really want him to leave? she asked herself.

"Roderick," she said, "I'll not have you sit here insolently and invade my privacy." But her tone betrayed her.

"Then, milady, I suggest *you* leave," adding, "I myself find it quite comfortable here." His lips quirked wickedly.

"Ooh! You're . . . you're impossible!" she cried. Her furious squirming only exposed more of her soft curves to his heated stare.

He reached out a roughened hand and attempted to re-coil her loose strands of black hair, his fingers lingering on her shoulder, his eyes on the rise and fall of her perfectly rounded breasts.

"Lord, Madrigal, you drive a man—" His words were cut short when he found a soapy cloth flung into his face. He jumped up and uttered a string of oaths, wiping the stinging soap from his eyes while he heard her laughter tinkle maddeningly from across the room. When at last he could see again, Madrigal stood near the window, hiding her body with a long linen towel.

He started toward her.

"Don't you dare touch me! I'll scratch your eyes out, you beast!" she hissed.

He grinned broadly at her brave front, his white teeth flashing. When he swept her into his arms, he was indeed surprised at her attempts to claw him, but he managed to hold her at bay until they fell together on her makeshift bed.

As she rolled and fought against his searching hands, his lips came down and crushed hers in a long kiss. She felt her stiff resolve weaken and began to return his passion in kind. Roderick shifted his weight from her, no longer needing to hold her still. Suddenly they heard a loud, sharp crack, and amazingly, they found themselves on the stone flagging, sprawled among the bedclothes and the shattered wooden frame.

"Perdición!" Roderick growled in annoyance.

Madrigal was half sitting, her legs flung akimbo, and before she cursed his stupidity, she looked down at their undignified positions and began to laugh—slowly at first, then merrily, until her sides ached.

He looked at her in confusion for several seconds; then he, too, began to chuckle along with her and finally threw his head back, laughing deeply.

She managed to say, between fits of glee, "If Sir William could see his formidable opponent now . . ." Her sides hurt so badly that she could not continue.

"Oh, Lord!" Roderick bellowed.

When their mirth had died away into lesser spurts of merriment, Roderick helped her up from the ruined bed. Then he said, "But, milady, there is no place for you to rest this night. May I offer my own bed, which, I might add, is much sturdier than this?" He gestured at the disorder around them and grinned mischievously.

She looked up into his tawny eyes. "And I trust you will be in that sturdy bed, too?"

"But naturally. Come, now, Madrigal, and have no qualms, for in truth, I have need of my rest now."

Yet by the time they lay together in his darkened chamber, Roderick was no longer tired at all, but once again very aware of her soft body curled next to him. Damn, he thought in annoyance, must I always force her? He turned to see if she slept, but she seemed oblivious to all, slumbering peacefully with a small smile on her lips.

She first stirred at daybreak and half opened her eyes

to the sound of distant thunder. Then her hand reached over to find the bed empty on Roderick's side. She sat up with a start, realizing that he had gone without awakening her. Her heart pounded in confusion and fear as she swung her legs off the bed and hurriedly dressed, hoping to catch him. But when she raced down to the hall amid a flash of lightning, only Beth remained to greet her.

As every woman of Penglennyn fief paced the floors of her home and watched the dismal dawn break, Roderick and his small army had already surrounded Poldreth's walled castle.

Stefano, meanwhile, held a reserve of men in the hills that marked the approach to Trenwell. Roderick's plan was to goad Sir William into attacking his men, drawing them away from the castle into the hills, where Stefano's troops would fall on them.

Roderick rode up defiantly to the gates of Trenwell, ignoring the guards atop the battlements, and pounded on the heavy oak with the shaft of his lance. A small door in the gate opened cautiously, and a white-faced guard peeked out.

"Tell your master, William Poldreth, that he may surrender now and avoid bloodshed," Roderick announced. "If he prefers to do battle, I await his pleasure, but tell him to hurry. I do not wish to be late to sup."

The small door slammed shut in his face, and Roderick whirled his horse and cantered back to Hugo, smiling to himself. If that insult does not dislodge the man, I'll climb the wall myself, he thought. He stood in the misting rain with his forces, taut and ready now. Soon they heard the sounds of commotion in the keep, and he felt his plan would undoubtedly work.

The gates of Trenwell flew open, and the ragtag army of Poldreth thundered out with fierce battle cries. The few mounted knights galloped directly toward the center of Roderick's battle line, screaming and slashing with their heavy broadswords; the remainder of the men followed on foot, brought to a fever pitch by Poldreth's promises of easy victory and gold for every man they slew. The lines clashed with sickening thuds, crashes, and screams, and by daylight the fields in front of Trenwell were strewn with the wounded and the dead.

Many of Roderick's men, never having fought before, were unable to bear the sight, nor the cries of horror, but Roderick rode among them, quieting their terror with stern words of assurance. He gathered them around him, and, according to plan, they began a slow, methodical retreat toward the hills behind them. Poldreth's men followed, their cries exultant, as they saw their enemy retreating; they did not notice how many of their own they left lying dead or wounded in the thick mud.

Roderick looked for Sir William in the crowd of men but could not discern his colors. What kind of man, he wondered, sends his vassals out to do battle for him and does not lead them? He shook his head, wiping the rain out of his eyes, then continued the orderly retreat, slashing casually at any serfs who came too close.

When Roderick was a mile from the castle, he gave the order, and his men melted into the cloud-hung hills, leaving the enemy standing foolishly alone, with lowered swords, in the roadway. Then, just as they had begun to think that victory was theirs, Stefano and his troops rose from their hiding places on either side of the road. When Stefano gave his warbling war cry, "Santiago y victoria!" they loosed their arrows.

Poldreth's men had no strength to face this new, fresh army, and seeing the quivering shower of arrows pelt them, they broke rank and ran for their lives, despite the attempts of the knights to stop them. The promise of death at the hands of Penglennyn's men overcame even their fear of Poldreth's cruelties. In moments they were gone, disappearing into the rain, leaving only their wounded lying in the trampled mud, transfixed by arrows. The wails and moans of the maimed echoed hollowly in the gray mist, as if mocking the thunder of the heavens.

Roderick rode back to Stefano's side. The men were soaked to the skin both from the rain and from heavy perspiration. The once-bright gray and purple pennants and the blankets on their huge mounts hung limply and were mud-splashed beyond recognition. Roderick removed his helmet for a moment to wipe his eyes clear; his usually sun-streaked hair was dark from sweat and lay plastered to his head. His purple tunic under the hauberk and mail looked almost black and sorely irritated his damp, chafed skin.

"I fear we shall rust before the day is done," he remarked to Stefano. Then he forced a laugh. "See to the men, and I shall ride to ferret out the elusive Sir William. Mayhap we'll see the warmth of Penglennyn before noon." He pulled hard on the reins and spurred his steed heavily back through the bogs of mud and water until the low fog cloaked him altogether.

Roderick rode fast and impatiently across the now-deserted moor until he spotted Trenwell's battlements. There were no defenses in sight; the gates were open and he did not see even a serf or a dog, only two lone horses tethered in front of the hall.

He flung himself down from his wild-eyed steed and looked around cautiously. The courtyard was empty, and the only movements he saw were the streams of rain running swiftly off the eaves and forming rivers that twisted and splashed through the muddy court.

The door was open. Roderick pushed his way

through the murk and slowly mounted the steps. He stopped suddenly at the entrance when he heard raging voices coming from inside.

Roderick's form filled the portal and he moved forward, unnoticed, seeing two men in a desperately unmatched battle to the death. It was completely logical, Roderick realized, for Sir William and Terence to be dueling. Certainly someone had to take the blame for the rout of Trenwell's forces, and why not Terence? Undoubtedly it had been his job to see their men readied, and he had failed miserably this day.

Roderick watched as Sir William easily backed the small, fat castellan into the wall, then swiftly knocked his sword away. It clanged loudly on the hard stone floor.

"You utter fool!" Sir William shrieked.

Terence slithered down the wall in bleak horror. He moaned softly and begged, "Have mercy, milord! I am defenseless!" Whatever his next words might have been, they were never spoken, for Sir William ran him clear through in one violent thrust.

"Very honorably executed." Roderick watched Poldreth start, then turn around quickly, a twisted smile crossing his lips when he recognized him.

Sir William said, "Thank you. I rather enjoyed watching the imbecile die." Then he walked slowly toward Roderick, his bloodied sword hanging loosely at his side. "Does Lady Madrigal await me?" he goaded.

Roderick did not change his expression, nor did he suddenly raise his sword, as Sir William had expected. Instead, his eyes narrowed slightly, making him appear more dangerously tense than he was.

Sir William continued talking. "Mayhap my serfs have fouled this day, and now you think I shall lay down my sword meekly—"

Roderick interrupted him. "Hardly, Sir William. I

expect no such thing. In truth," he said slowly, "I'll not accept your surrender on any terms."

Sir William laughed forcibly. "And *you* speak of honor? What if I stand here weaponless?"

"'Tis your choice," Roderick replied. "You may lay down your sword and die instantly or hold your weapon steady and seek your death more slowly. In any case, I will greatly enjoy running you through."

William listened to him in disbelief. He had truly misjudged this Spaniard, for not only was the man hard in appearance, but his very soul was forged of steel. He backed away then, and bringing up his sword, said, "So be it—to *your* death." He bowed mockingly.

The two men lunged at each other, their heavy broadswords clanging in the damp hall. Poldreth was a strong man, skilled in the use of the sword, and not tired by the morning's battle. He put Roderick on the defensive immediately and kept his mocking smile, but it was Roderick who drew blood first; he narrowly missed inflicting a mortal wound to Poldreth's left side. Still his opponent was undaunted, and his will remained strong enough to feign a stumble sideways, against an overturned chair on Roderick's momentarily unguarded left side. And in that fateful moment Sir William lunged desperately, his blade plunging deep into Roderick's shoulder. Roderick swayed imperceptibly, grinning wolfishly, his lips pulling back in a snarl.

Sir William straightened, thinking his foe mortally wounded, making precisely the same mistake Roderick had made. In that split second he met his end, for Roderick gathered his strength and felled him with one swift blow to the neck.

Turning and walking unsteadily away from the corpse, Roderick could feel his own blood flowing beneath the drenched tunic and mail, and cursed himself silently for letting down his guard. He left the hall and remounted his tired horse, now barely able to swing over the cantle, wincing with pain at each movement. On through the rain-drenched, muddy moor he rode, until his blurred vision glimpsed Stefano. He headed his horse toward his brother's and mercifully remained in the saddle long enough to reach him. With his last ounce of strength, Roderick asked, "Are the men well?"

"Yes, little brother," said Stefano. "What of Poldreth?"

Roderick grinned painfully. "I fear . . . we have slain each other." He slumped slightly, then fell heavily into the mud and oblivion.

Chapter 36

Madrigal paced the floor of the great hall, starting at every sound, quivering with the dark dread at the rolling thunder. Beth appeared calm, but the pallor of her cheeks belied it. Madrigal tried working on some baby garments, but her hands shook so, she finally put the tiny things away and tried to make conversation with her sister-in-law.

The two men Roderick had promised would spirit them away to safety in case of Penglennyn's loss stood at the entrance portal, their swords at the ready. However, they only succeeded in increasing Madrigal's unease.

When the splashing, sucking noises of hoofbeats finally sounded in the wet courtyard, Madrigal was afraid to glance out the window. What if it were the sneering Poldreth, come to claim her? The thought made her shudder in revulsion. Even the two times he had been near her had taught her too much of his overbearing manner. She crossed the hall to where Beth sat, rigid and white-faced, and knelt by her side, taking one of Beth's cold hands in hers. The two women faced the doors as the hoofbeats and men's voices grew closer. Madrigal kept telling herself that Roderick was invincible in battle, that he had told her he would send word if Penglennyn was lost, but still the panic mounted sickly in her throat as the door was flung open.

Stefano strode in rapidly and threw aside his sword and helmet. He was muddy, blood-spattered, and tense. Beth gave a strangled cry of relief and flew across the hall into his arms. He soothed her, stroking her hair, then looked over her head at Madrigal, still kneeling by the hearth, her green eyes wide with foreboding.

"Is he . . ." Her voice cracked and failed. She tried again, more strongly. "Is he . . . coming?" Her eyes pleaded for reassurance.

"Yes, Madrigal, he is coming," said Stefano quietly, "but he has been wounded . . . quite seriously, I fear. He will need care."

Madrigal sank back onto her heels, her hand pressed against her mouth to stifle a moan of anguish. But why, *why*, should she care what happened to him? He did not love her, nor she him. Nevertheless, her heart pounded dully in her chest and her mouth was dry with fear.

Beth immediately ordered the few servants left in the hall to heat water, tear linen strips, and build a fire in the lord's room.

The great doors opened again, the rain splashing the flagstones, as Hugo and Renaldo carried in Roderick's unconscious body. Beth told them to take him to his chamber at once. Madrigal followed his inert form, drawn as if by a magnet. She had never seen Roderick when he was not furiously alive, in control of the situation; now he lay as if dead, his ashen face washed by the rain that dripped off his sodden hair.

As soon as they laid him in the huge bed, Madrigal began to remove his mail and leather jerkin. It was so difficult to lift and turn him that she had to call on Renaldo to help her. Tucked in the waist of the leather jerkin was an old blue silk ribbon. She held it in her hand a moment, remembering. Could it be that he still carried this foolish token of their first meeting? Putting it out of her mind, she carefully cut away the blood-soaked undertunic and saw the gaping wound. The blade had sliced deep into the left shoulder blade and opened a long gash down his side. He had lost a great deal of blood, but the penetrating hole high on his shoulder was the most serious; she could not tell now deep it was, but she prayed that the blow had not touched a vital area or severed a major artery.

Madrigal took several shaky breaths to calm herself, trying desperately to remember all the healing arts she had learned from her mother. Her gentle fingers began probing the deep hole to see if there were any splinters of bone or foreign matter within, but it seemed clean. Then she bathed the area with moist linen cloths and sopped up the blood that was now welling more slowly. She called for lye and catgut to stitch up the long, open edges of the wound, and while she waited, she wiped her husband's cold, clammy brow and attempted to dry his soaked hair, which was plastered in dark curls around his face and neck. His breathing was shallow, but his heartbeat seemed even. If she could keep the wound from festering, he might yet recover.

When Beth hurried in with the requested items, she was amazed at the cool, competent way Madrigal was handling the situation. The girl was deep in concentration and hardly noticed Beth at all; she took the lye and mixed it with a bit of candle tallow, then spread it on the wound to purify it. She then stitched the gaping edges together, thankful that he remained unconscious, bandaged the shoulder, and stood back, viewing her handiwork. If he lived at all, he would certainly have a memorable scar to show for this battle.

She then called for Renaldo to help roll Roderick onto his right side, cushioning his wounded side with pillows. Now she had nothing to do but wait; it would probably be days before they would know the outcome. She pulled a heavy chair to his bedside and sat down, watching his slow, even breathing, wiping the cold drops of perspiration as they formed on his forehead, *willing* him with her soul to live. Beth looked in occasionally to see if she needed assistance, but Madrigal seemed in a trance, her mind totally absorbed by the still form on the bed. She took no meals, nor did she move from his bedside the whole day, until Beth forced her to come into the great hall to sup. But she left only after Renaldo had promised to sit by Roderick's side while she was gone.

Beth and Madrigal ate alone at one end of the vast table in the cold, echoing hall. Stefano had departed shortly after bringing Roderick home, as he had many details to see to, including the dispensation of power at the newly acquired fief. He had set up an infirmary at Trenwell to care for the wounded, most of whom were Poldreth's serfs. Penglennyn had suffered a minimum of casualties, thanks to Roderick's foresight and planning.

Madrigal heard the news of the day's battle from Beth but paid little attention to the details, beyond asking how Roderick had come to be hurt. She smiled tightly upon learning of Poldreth's demise at the hands of her husband, but all she understood with any clarity was that Roderick lay near death and that she had no right to be away from him. She made her excuses as quickly as she could, leaving her food mostly untouched, and hastened up to his room.

"He rests quietly, milady," said Renaldo. "Do you wish me to remain while you rest?"

"No, I shall stay here. Thank you, Renaldo, but go now; I'm certain you have much to occupy you. Stefano may need help."

She sat down in the hard chair, then rose to search for a warm wool shawl, which she draped around her shoulders. Her mind rebelled time and again against the possibility of his death—but if she were left widowed, wouldn't that be the solution she desired? And why did the thought of his death bother her at all? It does not matter to me, she told herself fiercely, yet her conscience told her she lied. She did not move until Beth entered much later with a candle, lightening Roderick's pitch-black room.

"Madrigal, you must get some sleep," Beth began. "You need your strength. You cannot make him well by sitting here, much as you may wish it. Come, sleep in the sewing room, and I will stay with him. I promise I will wake you if there's any change."

Madrigal looked up, blinded by the candlelight and surprised by Beth's quiet voice. Her eyes showed whitely in the flickering flame.

"Beth, I could not sleep. Could you if it were Stefano? Tell me truthfully."

"No," Beth admitted. "No, I likely could not." She sighed. "Well, then, sit here if you must, but I shall pray for his recovery, too. He has done a great thing for us today. Let us hope that he need not pay for it with his life."

Madrigal winced at Beth's words. "He will *not* die!" she declared. "He will not!"

Early the next morning Stefano knocked quietly at the door of Roderick's chamber. Receiving no reply, he

300

opened it and entered. Madrigal was slumped in the chair, mercifully asleep. Roderick showed no change, although his breathing seemed stronger. He was still very pale.

Madrigal heard Stefano's slight movements and woke, her cold, cramped limbs aching already. Her first gestures were to touch Roderick's head and check his bandages.

"No fever, thank the Holy Virgin," she muttered in Spanish, "and no more bleeding." She managed a weak smile for Stefano.

"You have done well, Madrigal. Now get some rest. Beth and I are worried about you," he said gently.

"Not yet, Stefano. This day will be crucial—I must be here."

They stopped talking on hearing Roderick's voice, weak but perceptible. "Father," he whispered hoarsely. "Father . . ."

"His mind wanders. Is that a bad sign?" Stefano looked concerned.

"I know not," Madrigal sighed. "We can only wait and see."

The next few days crept by slowly for the denizens of the hall. Even the servants were hushed as they went quietly about their duties. Madrigal spent her time putting sulfur powder or rendered fat on the wound to keep it from sticking to the bandages, or merely sitting by his bed. He seemed to be holding his own but was half delirious, recognizing Stefano only once, when he asked him how the fief fared. He fell asleep again before Stefano could answer. As he lay inert, Madrigal began to fear his strength would be so depleted that he would die from lack of sustenance, if not from the wound.

One morning, as Madrigal sat wearily by his side after having bathed him and changed the bandages once more, he opened his eyes. She leaned forward quickly and spoke his name softly. He did not seem to recognize her, but he spoke in a clear voice.

"Oh, that my wife's hands were as gentle and loving as yours." His voice trailed off and his eyes closed again.

Madrigal told herself that he was delirious, that his words meant nothing, but she could not control the tears that filled her eyes and brimmed over, spilling one bitter, hot drop onto his flesh. Just make him well again, she prayed ardently; it matters not that he shuns me even in his delirium.

The next morning Beth and Stefano forced Madrigal to go to her room and sleep, for she was so exhausted that her skin was drawn and gray. She had eaten poorly since the confrontation and was near collapse. She finally consented, making them promise to awaken her in a few hours.

Beth sat in the chair, stitching on the baby's layette and occasionally glancing at Roderick. When she looked over at him again, she was shocked to find his eyes wide open, a slight smile on his lips. For the first time, he appeared completely aware.

"Roderick?" Beth said uncertainly.

"Yes, I think 'tis I . . . How long have I been thus?"

"It has been five days . . . we feared for your life. You took a nasty wound, Roderick, but I think you will recover now. Thanks be to all the saints!" Beth smiled happily at him.

Roderick tried to sit up and groaned, his face breaking out in cold drops of sweat. Beth quickly put a hand on his chest to restrain him, but he fell back on the pillows, grimacing with pain.

"No, you must not move yet. It will be a long time before you'll be up. Do not rush things."

"I feel as weak as a kitten, Beth. That foul Poldreth

has had his revenge on me from the grave!" He panted with the effort of his exertions. "Beth, I thank you for the care you have given me . . . you have no doubt saved my life, although whether that's to anyone's benefit 'tis yet to be seen."

"Oh, Roderick, no, it was not I who cared for you these days, but Madrigal. She did not eat or sleep, nor did she leave your side for a moment. It is truly her skill and care that saved you, if not the intervention of God Himself. She is only now sleeping in her room because Stefano and I forced her to do so. The poor girl is exhausted beyond measure."

Roderick was silent for a time; his eyes closed again and Beth thought he had dozed off, but suddenly they opened and a spark showed in them.

"Beth, help me up. I must go to her."

"Roderick, you cannot. You will reopen the wound, or worse. Be sensible!"

"Beth, help me, or I will crawl there if necessary—and Stefano will blame you for my death! I *will* see her!"

She could see no solution but to help him from the bed. He clenched his teeth in agony, but finally he stood shakily, leaning his great weight on Beth's shoulder. They hobbled across the hall in this manner, the effort causing great beads of sweat to stand out on his brow. Then he was by Madrigal's bed, the one, he remembered tenderly, that had collapsed under them. He certainly hoped it was stronger now.

He watched her white face as she slept; there were shadows under her eyes, and she did not stir while they stood over her. He reached out with his good arm and touched her luxurious black mass of hair. His touch, however, gentle as it was, awakened her. Her eyes flew open, then widened further in surprise. Her lips began to form a word, but his finger silenced her. He sat on the edge of the bed and lifted the quilt, then eased himself next to her and took her hand.

Beth slipped out of the room and closed the door quietly, leaving the two already in blissful sleep, their fingers entwined as if they were small children.

Chapter 37

After weeks of being plied with Renaldo's shrewd advice, Madrigal's knowledge of herbs, and the hearty Cornish dishes supplied by every good wife of Penglennyn, Roderick felt well enough to be embarrassed by all the fuss.

Sitting in the hall early one afternoon in October, he growled at his wife, "If I eat one more potion or bitter nut, or smell any noxious herb near me, I swear there'll be the devil to pay!" Madrigal turned a deaf ear, but he continued his tirade. "In truth, I'm going to ride for a spell this afternoon. I'm quite fit now, you realize."

"Certainly you are, milord. Haven't you told me so often enough this past month?" She forced back a smile, then added, "I think a short ride would do you no harm."

"Truly?"

"Yes, Roderick. I would not have agreed if I thought otherwise. Mayhap I'll join you. I grow bored, too."

"'Tis unmanly to sit here, warming my backside by the hearth with the women," he mumbled, rising stiffly from his place.

"You'd prefer a battle, mayhap, or some local disaster? Would that cheer you, my husband?" She laughed at the scowl on his face, although she sensed that her words had hit home.

"Well, then! Put down that absurd sewing and wrap a cloak about you if you intend to ride with me. And hurry—I grow impatient!"

She narrowed her eyes but did as he bade, for as he mended he grew more difficult to handle, and she had best keep her mouth closed lest he fly into a rage. After donning a warm beige overtunic and a hooded green cloak, she joined Roderick at the stable.

The early-October wind was chill and damp, quickly driving the moisture through clothes and flesh alike; it was, nonetheless, invigorating to the spirit. The horses stepped lively; they had not been ridden recently and were anxious for a run. A short distance along the trail over the moors, Roderick became concerned that Madrigal's mount was too frisky and might bolt and cause her injury. He called over to her, "I think 'tis best we return. Your skills are not equal to your horse's strength."

She had blamed his needling words these past weeks on restlessness, but his insult to her obvious good horsemanship was too much to bear. She gave the frisky mare a hard kick and took off ahead of him through the hills and valleys of gray boulders and across the moors toward Trenwell. Roderick rode behind her, his face dark with anger at her total disregard for his good advice, his shoulder sore from the jarring motion of the horse's gait. Yet she was riding quite skillfully through the jagged countryside, and the adventure of a simple outing was a welcome change from the sickroom. Wishing suddenly that she would turn in a different direction, he came abreast, saying, "Hold, milady!"

She slowed to a trot, her face flushed with delight. "Let us ride to Trenwell. Stefano tells me that not much has been done there, and I have yet to set foot on the new lands of Penglennyn."

"No," he said hastily. "Another day, perhaps."

"But why?" She looked disappointed. "We're nearly there!"

He pulled back on his reins. The horse skittered sideways, eliciting a muffled grunt of pain from him. He thought for a short moment, then said, "I have made it a habit to avoid returning to a place of battle, 'tis all."

"Roderick! Why, how absurd—you're superstitious!"

"Not at all!" he denied heatedly.

"Then we'll go." Madrigal nudged her horse forward in spite of the long string of oaths shouted after her. And then she heard his steed behind her again and wondered why he followed, or, for that matter, why he did not stop her.

At last she had her first glimpse of Trenwell, rising out of the misty moors as if it were part of the earth itself; three turrets of gray stone behind crumbling but still formidable stone walls comprised the whole of the structure. She viewed the lofty castle and found it to be quite different from Penglennyn, which was softer and more suitable as a home, with its separate wings and central hall. Mayhap the Normans had preferred to quarter at Penglennyn on the coast rather than at the inland estate, she mused, for Penglennyn had many modern improvements that only the Normans would have installed.

She led their way across the ditches and mounds of earth and rode through the open gates into the deserted bailey. Turning to speak to Roderick, she saw that he had stopped at the entrance and seemed bent on remaining there.

"Roderick," she called, "come, there is no one about. We can explore Stefano's new holdings."

He walked his horse slowly across the now-hard earthen bailey, which had been a sea of mud when he had last come this way. They dismounted and stood before the massive, closed oak door.

"Milord," she ventured, "if you truly wish to remain out here, I'll go in myself for a few moments and view the hard-won prize."

He did not answer her, and noticing a strange look in his eyes, she timidly opened the squeaking door and entered.

The tables and chairs had been righted again after the violent deaths of Poldreth and Terence, and despite the dusty stone flooring and the cobwebs hanging in the corners, the hall itself looked suitable for living, needing only minor repairs and an inviting fire in the hearth. She recalled that Stefano had mentioned the hall was now deserted and would remain so until he had selected an overseer. The serfs, of course, were still in their own warm huts.

She turned to see Roderick in the opening, absent-mindedly running a hand through his tousled hair. "Why not enter, milord? It can do no harm."

When his feet carried him across the threshold, he felt his brow perspiring, and his hand went involuntarily to his shoulder. Madrigal went to him quickly and led him to a sturdy chair, wishing the sickening smell of mildew had not suddenly assailed her nostrils.

"Roderick? What is it? Please tell me." She did not like his pallor or the way he remained unmoving, distant.

Finally he whispered, "What do you know of it? What *can* you know?" He turned to her in agonized remembrance.

"Do you wish to speak of it, husband?" she asked softly.

He retreated into his shell of echoing pasts, where nightmares and deeds best forgotten dimly awaited their call to consciousness. When he looked back at her, he asked simply, "Do you know how many a young wife I have widowed?"

"Roderick!" She shook his broad shoulder. "Do not torture yourself!"

He shook his head as if to clear the fog from his mind. "When last I was in his hall, I pictured you—in the midst of the horror and death here, I pictured you." She was silent. He went on, trying heedlessly to explain. "You do not see? 'Tis only that you are a woman. Men who often face death try to dwell on pleasant things to drive away their ghosts."

"Ghosts?" she repeated, feeling the damp chill around them.

He forced a laugh, and some of his ruddy color returned. "Yes, milady—the fears and shadows that fill a man's mind."

"Then you have fear?" She almost wished she had not asked this, but persisted. "And the dreams you have had . . . are they of battles fought?"

His brow wrinkled. "Sometimes," he replied. "Only the fool feels no fear. We men are but human after all, and often wonder if we shall see another day, hold another woman in our arms." He took her hand and brought her down onto his knee. "Is this so strange? Are we lessened in the eyes of our women?"

"No, no," she said. "To hear you speak thusly helps me to better understand your strange moods."

He seemed more like himself then, and looked about the hall. " 'Tis not superstition that kept me from this place, but the ghosts in my mind that I see about me here. The room holds the secrets of my fear and my anger . . . Can't you feel them?" He studied her while she perused her surroundings slowly, envisioning the two armor-clad men wielding their deadly blades and clashing heavily together, cutting through the damp air. She could almost smell their sweat and hear the clatter of swords until the blades met flesh and the stones were drenched with blood.

"I have often seen the black face of death looming before me, but never so near as in this very room," he said pensively.

Her hand touched his golden curls. "And so it was difficult to come back here and face all the . . . memories. And I forced you. Why didn't you tell me?"

He laughed and took her off his knee, standing her before him with his hands on her waist. "I could not tell you, milady, for I never voiced my secret fears before, and I did not know them myself." He grinned widely. "And now I am at the mercy of your sharp wit!"

She said quickly, "Never, oh, never would I belittle you, not for that. I only . . . dislike your harsh ways, your cruel treatment of me."

His smile faded; he thought of the many times he had held her forcibly, bruising her arms, and of the pleasure he had derived when his words had cut her deeply. Yet other times, such as when she had brushed by him accidentally or he had passed her door and heard her lilting song as she had enjoyed her bath—those times he had wanted to hold her tenderly against him. In so many ways his life was a conflict of opposing forces. Had he not just admitted his fears when in battle? But at the same time he thirsted for the thrill that brought beads of sweat to his brow and drenched his back. These were the sides of the same golden coin, and he was that coin.

He looked up at her. "I realize, of course, that I have treated you unjustly at times, but you must admit I have also seen well to your comfort and safety." His golden eyes seemed to stare through her and beyond. "I cannot hope to change my disposition toward you, any more than I can cease to rise to the call of battle. 'Tis my way . . . my nature."

Thinking hard on his meaning, she compared his emotions with her own. "Yes, milord. Often I must let my own nature take its course, too, even if it opposes your wishes. Mayhap 'tis not to your liking, but 'tis me."

The afternoon was growing dark so they left the ghost-filled hall and headed back to Penglennyn. Silence hung between them on the ride; they were watching the terrain carefully and thinking of their intimate sharing of words. Yet Roderick realized that several conflicts were still unresolved: for one, her unfaithful behavior with Akbar to which she never alluded; for another, his own innocence where Elena was concerned. His eyes tried to pierce the rolling mists as he thought of her father. It was conceivable that he and Madrigal could overcome their past differences, but his bitter hatred of the earl would not disappear through mere words. No, on that they could never reach a truce, and therefore he saw no solution to their impasse.

Once back at Penglennyn, Madrigal dismounted and winced, rubbing her sore bottom, confessing that the ride was longer than she had expected. He laughed at her gesture, his shoulder aching annoyingly from the unaccustomed activity.

When they entered the hall and sank into chairs before the hearth, she let out a contented sigh while Roderick called for ale to be served. They enjoyed their brew and tasted the savory stew simmering over the fire, waiting for Stefano and Beth to join them for the evening meal.

Beth ate sparingly, tossing much of her portion to the whining dogs chained by the hearth. She had grown rounder with each passing day, and complained that she had no room for food, wishing the new year would arrive quickly. Her husband constantly exclaimed about her condition, as if he had never before gotten a wench with child. Having no knowledge of Madrigal's personal anguish over the subject of pregnancy, he was not being cruel. Both he and Beth assumed that since Roderick and Madrigal kept separate bedchambers, they did not wish to have children.

After the meal had been cleared away, they sat near the hearth conversing. Stefano placed Beth on his lap, hand on her belly, beaming proudly at the babe's movements. Roderick glanced at Madrigal and saw that her green eyes were glassy with threatening tears. He silently cursed the impetuousness he had displayed that morning at Halconbosque when Madrigal had lost their child. He wished he had words of comfort for her, but was unable to voice them in any case.

To take her mind off the subject, he said, "Milady, mayhap we have tarried too long at Penglennyn. It is time we consider our return to Spain."

"But we cannot go until the babe comes! Please, Roderick."

"Yes, yes, of course, But first we shall journey to London and see to my business with King Edward."

She smiled, her face lit up with the innocent joy of a child. "Mayhap there will be time to see the shops!"

His tawny eyes warmed, and he replied, "Yes, Madrigal, that, too. You have not stretched my purse strings, and you must have a gown for court presentation."

"Oh, Roderick! Thank you! I'll take great care not to spend overly much, I promise—but just to see all the sights!"

He grinned, looking young and relaxed. "On that score, I shall personally accompany you to the merchants. Mayhap you will help me select new tunics and hose."

She was completely thrilled at the idea of the trip and did not cease to prattle about it until Roderick chose the day for departure. Then she raced up to her chamber, with a serving girl in tow, and began to pack her trunk at once.

When Roderick left the hearth later to retire, he stopped by her room to view her efforts. Her best gowns and a few woolen ones were strewn everywhere. Each gown had colorful velvet ribbons laid across it for her hair dressing, and slippers in various bright shades sat at their hems. A small pile of jewels lay neatly on her bed; he looked it over and remarked that her collection was sad indeed.

Madrigal stopped dabbling with her perfumes and stiffened her back. "My sister Rosa has most of my mother's jewelry. You seem to forget that Castilla-verde was pillaged by the Moors, while your home remained untouched!"

He had certainly not meant to point out her family's poverty. "Mayhap we shall find some emeralds to match your eyes and some gold to adorn your wrists. Would you like that?"

She was embarrassed by his generosity. She lowered her lashes, saying, " 'Tis not important to spend your coins on silly things. We shall shop only for clothes that are necessary."

"I think not, milady." He turned to leave. "I should like to present my wife at court with the elegance due her station."

"I have perfectly suitable attire to meet King Edward."

Damn her pride! She would adore a new gown, but after his low insults to her family, she would never let him know it.

"Milady," he said over his shoulder, "you would put to shame these fat, blonde English wenches whether you were dressed befitting a queen or wearing nothing at all. Let me assure you of *that!* In truth, I think my time will be spent fending off the young court swains, who will undoubtedly write you poetry and swoon at your feet!"

After Roderick had left her, she sat on the bed for a moment, thinking. Then she laughed aloud at his ridiculous notions, wondering all the same if she would enjoy the notorious frivolity that the court gossip boasted.

Chapter 38

Three days later all was in readiness for their departure to London. Roderick had decided to take ten men-at-arms, with Hugo in command. Renaldo had balked at the idea of spending his spare hours in London seeing to the care of "those beetle-brained English serfs," and was to be Roderick's personal squire. Hugo glowed with pride at his new rank, showing his gap-toothed smile often, excited beyond measure to be visiting London town.

Roderick was waiting impatiently in the hall for Madrigal when Beth approached him shyly. "Cousin, I wish to warn you that London is a town of robbers and of plagues. Even the inns along the way are noted for their dishonest keepers and bad ale. I, thanks to the Lord, have never had to make the journey." She thrust her round chin out, hoping he would change his mind even now.

He smiled indulgently at her. "Beth, am I to understand that you are trying to deter me?" She nodded solemnly. "Milady, I can only assure you that we shall take great care. The visit to King Edward is one of necessity, however. Not only do I bear a message from my own king, but I must make known

Stefano's right of arms where Poldreth's fief is concerned, and also, I might add, the good news that shortly there will be an heir to Penglennyn."

"Oh! But what if the babe is female?" Her brow wrinkled.

"Then you must keep trying," he teased, knowing that King Edward would be greatly pleased to have Beth bear many loyal subjects to his throne, no matter their sex.

She blushed. "Will Madrigal be presented at court? If so, I must also warn you that a lady's virtue is hardly safe there. And your wife is very beautiful."

"Beth," he chided, "I shall keep her in my sight at all times when at court." And then he laughed. "'Tis a pity you have not been to fair London town. In my country the king holds court wherever he may be, while here you are afforded the luxury of a palace for the royal court."

She drew her mouth down into a frown, thinking she would never wish to travel away from Cornwall, and most especially not to London, whatever its attractions.

At last Madrigal appeared in the hall and saved him from more of Beth's dire prophecies. She was dressed in a lavender wool shift and a crimson-red velvet-lined cloak. Her dark hair was coiled atop her head and she carried a fox muff, which matched the fur on the cloak's hood.

They planned to allow six days for the journey, stopping at inns along the way, for Roderick would not see his wife bedded down alongside the road on the cold nights, as so many travelers were forced to do.

At long last, and after many farewells, they were off, all on horseback, since Roderick did not wish to be delayed by men on foot or by carts. They followed the road inland, past Trenwell, traveling northeast across the brown moors until they reached the softer, low-rolling terrain near Tavistock, where they quartered for the night.

The inn, contrary to Beth's warnings, was quite accommodating, and the keeper provided a tub for Madrigal. As for thieves along the road, Roderick's party encountered none, for the weather was coldly uninviting and a highwayman's luck at such a time would be negligible.

By the second night they had made Exeter, and rose at dawn to cross through heavily wooded country, arriving at Taunton by nightfall. When Madrigal awakened the next morning in the Boar's Head Inn, she was chilled and sniffling, apparently coming down with a cold. Roderick decided they would rest there for the full day, as it was pointless to go on until Madrigal felt better.

The following morning did not see an improvement in her health; on the contrary, she seemed to be worsening, but she nevertheless insisted that they proceed east to Salisbury. Against Roderick's better judgment, he acquiesced and they journeyed that cool, damp October day, reaching the Wiltshire town some hours past sundown.

Had there been an inn along the way, Roderick would have stopped immediately, for Madrigal's face had been flushed, her eyes glassy. By late afternoon she had slumped in the saddle. Ignoring her protests that he would hurt his wounded shoulder, he had brought his mount alongside and scooped her into his arms, placing her shivering body in front of him and cursing his foolishness for having let her have her way.

They stayed outside Salisbury, on the west edge of town, at an inn that boasted comfortable, warm rooms. The innkeeper's wife, a pleasantly rounded woman of indeterminate age, took one look at the pretty Spanish lady and rushed straight to the kitchen, emerging with a steaming kettle. She then led Madrigal up to her room and placed the kettle over a blazing fire, adding some powders that soon filled the chamber with an odor of camphor and noxious herbs.

Leaving Madrigal snug in the warm bed, she waddled down the narrow, creaking stairway and called for more water to be brought up. Roderick, quaffing ale with his men in the large dining room, was thankful that the woman seemed to know her business. He ordered food for the party and made further arrangements for the morrow. When at last the men were bedded down in the stables, he climbed the steps to see how his wife was faring.

The innkeeper's wife was clucking over Madrigal like a mother hen as she placed hot linens from the vapor kettle on her bare chest. Finally satisfied that Madrigal's fever would break soon, she chattered orders at Roderick and left them alone. He continued the heat treatment himself, until Madrigal broke out in a healthy sweat and could stand no more of the poultices. He then wrapped her in several blankets and finally sat back to rest. Their food still awaited them: a cast-iron pot of mutton stew and hot bread with jam. Madrigal propped herself on the bedside, confessing that she had no appetite, but Roderick brought her a bowl of stew and insisted that she try it.

She ate a few bites and then lay down again under the heavy bedclothes. Roderick polished off the food and went to the frosted windows, gazing out over the courtyard and the stables. Assured that all was well, he undressed, snuffed the candles, and lay down beside his wife.

She was still awake, and although her breathing was raspy, she was, thankfully, cooler to the touch. On this journey they had shared the same bed out of necessity, but she had always sought the very edge of it, tucking

316

the blanket safely under her so that their naked bodies could not touch. This night, however, she let Roderick bring his arm around her, drawing them snugly together.

When she did not protest, he let himself warm to her nearness, for there was nothing to compare with the feel of her soft, velvety flesh against his skin. Her firm, round breasts burned his side where they nestled into his ribs, and he found his fingers gently stroking their peaks until they stood pert under his touch.

Roderick buried his mouth in her long hair. She turned her face to his and they covered each other's lips in a fiery kiss. Pulling her slim, tantalizing hips under his own, he entered her slowly, until she thrust herself up against him and met his ardor with her own passionate longing. A blissful eternity later they lay locked in an embrace, and Roderick thought he could feel her warm, salty tears against his hard chest.

"Is there something amiss?" he whispered.

Madrigal sniffed her reply. "*Si* . . . 'tis not fair . . . I shame myself." Her bosom heaved in a long sob, and he could think of no answer for her. There was no truth in her thoughts, of course, but it was true that, for the most part, they shared little between them save a rare encounter in bed. She had steeled her heart against him, against any hope for a lasting marriage, and he would be damned if he would try to break through her reserve. And now she lay next to him, racking her heart with guilt for enjoying a small pleasure of her married state. What was he supposed to do, Roderick wondered, when he could hardly stand to be near her without crushing her to him? And when his better judgment fled and he took her, she sobbed and moped about until his conscience tortured him.

Lying on his back, his golden eyes focused on the slanted, beamed ceiling, he thought back to their first meeting in the woods and to when she had shyly given him his bath and he had formed the idea of marrying her. *That,* he thought, had been his own foolish mistake! Why in the name of all that was holy had he not simply taken her on the spot and been done with it? There had been other women of great beauty whose dispositions were far more tempered than that of his wife. Yet he had always tired of them quickly. This chit, with her damned jade eyes, was impossible to purge from his system.

He slowly pulled his arm from under her sleeping form and slammed his fist into the pillow, then cursed the pain shooting through his shoulder. He rolled over and turned his back to her.

When Madrigal rose the next morning, she felt much recovered and went cheerfully about her toilette until Roderick awoke, already muttering and in a most foul mood. She wondered briefly at his dark scowl but assumed that he chafed at the delay she had caused. They ate a hearty breakfast with the men-at-arms and soon were on their way to Guildford, near London.

After a night in that town, the sun broke through the thick mist and heralded their speedy approach to London town, where they took rooms at a reputable inn on the banks of the Thames.

Madrigal was elated with the sights and sounds of London, for, other than Tangier, this was the first real city of her limited experience. Even if Roderick ordered her about harshly, her pleasure at being amid the throb of life in this famous capital could not be diminished.

The innkeeper, a distinguished, middle-aged man named Milsworn, boasted of the hundreds of noblemen who had slept in his beds and had partaken of his excellent cuisine. And indeed, the White Horse Inn was a marvelous, three-story structure of brick and heavy beams, stretching around a busy corner for nearly a full block. Their two rooms were comfortable and richly decorated with dark gold hangings, a thick green carpet, and somber wall tapestries. When Madrigal gasped and exclaimed at such sumptuous quarters, Roderick merely sneered. " 'Tis only befitting my status as a baron. I cannot see why you ogle so over a simple bedroom!"

"Well, Baron of Compostela," she quipped, "I only sought to express my pleasure at being here. If you are so high and mighty that you cannot appreciate the simple pleasures of us lowly folk, I say fie upon you!" And with that she swirled her skirt around, holding it in one hand, went to the misted window, cleared the pane with her handkerchief, and looked out upon the street below.

Roderick's eyes narrowed momentarily at her remark, and then he strode purposefully out of the room and down the stairs, calling loudly for ale.

Several hours later he was engaged in conversation with three knights of King Edward who lodged at the White Horse Inn, and the Duke of Devonshire. Suddenly they all ceased their drinking, lifting their eyes to behold what their alcohol-befuddled brains took to be a vision.

Lady Madrigal stood halfway down the stairs, searching the large room nervously for her husband. She wore a red velvet gown which was tied under her breasts by a silken sash, displaying more of her creamy skin above the low neckline than Roderick considered wise. Her mass of black hair was pulled severely back from her perfect face and was bound into loops with red velvet ribbons.

Roderick's gaze hardened when the Duke of Devonshire found his voice. "Ye gods, men! There be a tasty morsel! Where's the dark beauty from? Another of

Milsworn's dainties? Methinks I'll escort the wench to our table and find out." The duke rose, going directly, if a bit unsteadily, to the stairs and holding out his beringed fingers to Madrigal.

She blushed profusely at his gesture but took his proffered hand and followed him back to his comrades. She looked at him askance, finding him quite attractive, with his light blue eyes, blunt-cut, long blond hair, and tall, slender frame.

"Thank you, milord," she said, taking a seat between him and Roderick.

"Pray tell me, my dear, what is your name?" The Duke of Devonshire took her hand.

Madrigal's eyes widened. "Oh—I thought—that is, I thought my husband would have—oh, my!" She flushed in confusion.

Roderick stood, and holding his flagon in her direction, said, "Gentlemen, this is my wife, Lady Madrigal."

The men around the table laughed heartily at the obvious embarrassment of the duke, who nearly choked on a swallow of his brew. Madrigal wished she could crawl under the table like a child, for her husband's tone was recklessly dangerous; but of all those at the table, only she knew that his deep voice signaled barely controlled anger.

When they were seated again and food was brought for Madrigal, the duke managed to overcome his embarrassment and engaged her in a low conversation, completely unaware of Roderick's dark wrath.

His temper inflamed by ale, Roderick leaned over to her and whispered in Spanish. "Milady, unless you wish to spread your favors among those present, I suggest you cease your flirtations and retire to your room. It grows late."

She turned and looked into his flashing eyes. A

sweet, coy smile curved her rosy lips; and when she spoke, her voice was honeyed. "Why, I am not tired at all. What possible pleasure could I find in *our* chamber? No, milord, begging your pardon, I think I shall tarry here a while."

He clenched his fist around the flagon and slammed it down on the table, sending a spray of foamy ale in every direction. For a brief moment the group was silent, but when he reached out and grasped Madrigal's arm roughly, pulling them both to their feet, the men grinned and chuckled as if conspiring with him.

Roderick led her easily up the stairs in spite of her heated protests. He further humiliated her by calling back to the men, "In Spain, my friends, we often must teach our women a little respect. Hold, and I shall return shortly."

All Madrigal could hear when he banged open their door was a loud, drunken cheer of "Bravo," which still rang in her ears when he dumped her unceremoniously onto the bed.

"You knave! You cad!" She spat fire from her eyes, her hair tumbling down her back.

He laughed and stood there with his hands on his hips, surveying her as if she were a common serving wench. Finally he retraced his steps to the door. "Mayhap this will teach you to take my *suggestions* as orders henceforth."

When the door closed behind him, she screamed, "Never!" But he did not rise to the bait, even though he had heard her.

The rest of that night Roderick spent sharing tales of battles fought and won with his new comrades, who had gained much respect for the iron-fisted baron.

While he sat spewing forth his accounts of the wars against the Moors, Madrigal lay awake in her bed, cursing his very name. She watched the early streaks of dawn light the eastern sky, vowing to flirt outrageously at court with any lord she wished, and to do it directly under her husband's nose. For, she surmised, he wouldn't dare mistreat her in the presence of the English king. He simply wouldn't dare!

Chapter 39

When Roderick finally swung his legs out of bed, his hands holding his aching head, it was well past midday. He draped the linen sheet around his midriff and walked unsteadily to the window, shielding his eyes from the sallow, mid-October light and absentmindedly rubbing the ache in his wounded shoulder. Madrigal sat in a chair by the hearth, choking back her snide laughter at his misery over his long night of carousing.

He turned in time to catch her amused look before she cloaked her face with false compassion. His mouth turned down in a frown and he muttered, "You find amusement here? Or mayhap my pain is a jest!" She gave no reply and lowered her lashes, thinking it served him right for his unspeakable behavior toward her.

She was dressed in a day gown of red and gold velvet with a fur collar and long sleeves. Her matching cloak was hung over the arm of a chair.

"And where do you think *you're* going, milady?" He dropped his sheet and began to pull his tunic over his head.

"I thought that if you did not awaken soon, Renaldo might escort me through the streets."

Grumbling something inaudible, he went to the pewter vase and poured cold water into the washbasin and then splashed his face, emitting a throaty groan.

322

His golden, curly hair clung wetly to his neck and face, and his eyes were red-rimmed and dull. Even his deep tan seemed faded, and the long, puckered scar on his shoulder showed whitely.

"You look to be in misery, Roderick. Mayhap I should postpone my excursion till the morrow."

He did not miss the glint in her eyes. "And now I am supposed to succumb to your womanly wiles and plead to take you shopping!"

She laughed lightly, knowing this small victory was hers.

Roderick finished dressing and they went down the stairs into the dining hall. After eating a hearty meal, he felt he might survive the day after all, and told Madrigal to fetch her cloak.

When at last they left the White Horse Inn and blended into the flow of life on the narrow streets of London, Roderick explained that it would be at least a week before they would have an audience with King Edward. It seemed the king had recently returned from Scotland, where he was forever plagued by the warring clans, and had much business to attend to before he could turn his attention to less urgent matters. If Roderick was annoyed by the delay, Madrigal was quite content to be in London for as long as possible, for she loved the constant excitement denied to her all those months at Penglennyn.

She seemed wont to stop at every shop and view the wares that were imported from lands she had never heard of, and Roderick found his mood improving with her obvious delight. The day, although damp, was mild, and the myriad entertainers who flooded the market streets were happy to display their talents for a few tossed coins; there were jugglers and acrobats and men with one arm or leg who begged Roderick to play a game of chance for a mere copper coin. Women, dressed in rags and barefoot in spite of the cold cobblestones, shoved their handiwork under Madrigal's nose, while the more affluent shop owners beckoned her from their doorways.

At first Roderick was slow to open his purse, but by late afternoon he was spending his coins freely on almost any item that caught his wife's eye. At one vending stand that displayed intricately designed perfume vials of silver from Byzantium, she insisted, "Please, Roderick! I was only viewing the beauty of the work—you need not purchase it for me!"

He smiled down into her eyes. "Mayhap 'tis only my light head from last evening's frivolity, but you best take all I choose to purchase now before my mood changes."

So she allowed him to buy the gift but insisted that he bestow it upon his mother. They began to weave their way back through the crowds toward the inn, when Roderick spied a jewelry shop that, from its facade, appeared to be of higher repute than most. He took Madrigal's arm and led her inside; she immediately marveled at the variety of gems and precious metal, which the owner displayed on red-velvet-lined shelves.

In the rear of the narrow shop an elderly man with skillful, bony fingers sat soldering and forging the beginnings of a gold necklace with a ruby center. The younger shop owner was quick to introduce his father, who did most of their work, and he further explained that the old man had recently been commissioned by Queen Eleanor herself to fashion a ring for the king's birthday.

Madrigal found her eyes fixed in mute fascination upon a three-stranded necklace of emeralds and diamonds with an enormous green stone in the center of the third strand. The workmanship was exquisite, the likes of which she had never seen. When Roderick saw where her eyes rested, he also took an interest in the piece and asked the owner about its history and price. The story that unfolded from the shopkeeper's lips was not difficult to believe, for the jeweled necklace bespoke deft, foreign skill. Originally it had been fashioned in one chain by a Parisian craftsman and purchased by the Duke of Salisbury on his return from the Holy Land in 1162. It had been passed down the line of male offspring until 1284, when the current duke had bestowed the precious necklace upon his London mistress, who had born him several sons. After the duke and his lady had parted ways, she had been forced to sell the necklace to this very shop owner, whose father had changed it from one strand into the present treasure that they now beheld.

The history of the item, although fascinating, was not the deciding factor as far as Roderick was concerned, nor was the extravagant price. His mind was made up when he saw the piece on his wife's lovely neck, the green stone matching precisely the rare color of her eyes.

Madrigal was speechless when her husband announced he would buy it on the spot, and she could only stammer her appreciation and joy at receiving such a fine gift. By the time they had reached the inn, she began to think that perhaps her husband cared for her more than he admitted.

She ran lightly up the inn staircase, childishly anxious to try on her new necklace in front of the looking glass. She threw her cloak carelessly on the bed and clasped the lovely strands around her neck, admiring the sight in the mirror. She had a sudden inspiration and pulled her jewelry box close to search for the item she wanted. She drew the bracelet out and was about to put it on when the door opened and she saw Roderick's reflection in her mirror. A smile lighted his face as he saw the beauty of his wife adorned in the necklace, then flickered out when he noticed the unfamiliar gold filigree bracelet she held. He commented on the piece and reached out for it, taking note of Madrigal's sudden change of expression.

"Where does this come from?" he asked while dangling the bauble on his index finger.

"It was . . . a gift," she whispered.

"From whom, milady?"

"'Tis of no importance—I don't really care for it," she added hastily.

"Answer me, Madrigal." His brows were drawn together threateningly. "I want to know if you are receiving . . . favors from someone."

She could not mistake the emphasis he put on the word "favors" and was silent for a moment, then looked him straight in the eye. "Akbar gave it to me."

His face turned cold and distant as her words sank into his consciousness. A muscle ticked in his cheek. He spun around and strode to the hearth, looked down at the bracelet for a time, then, with a low curse, flung it into the burning embers.

"No, Roderick, you can't!"

He felt her hand on his arm, but it was too late. The damage was done and he pulled away from her.

"But why?" she cried futilely. "It was only a gift!"

"A *payment*, don't you mean?" He threw the words in her face; they felt like scorching coals from the fire.

She sank into a chair, sobbing, "I did nothing . . . nothing . . ."

Roderick placed his hands on the arms of the chair, hovering over her. "How do you think I have felt during these past months, when every time I look at you I envision Akbar taking his pleasures—" Her hand came up and struck him hard across his cheek, but he remained glowering at her, motionless.

326

"He took no pleasures with me! How *dare* you accuse me when *you* flew straight to my sister's arms!" She tried to rise from the chair, but Roderick caught her wrists and held her in place.

"If I were a man," she raged as tears flowed down her cheeks, "I would kill you! I loathe you!"

"Kill me?" He threw his head back and laughed bitterly. "Mayhap you think your father should have done the job after he murdered my father!" He grabbed her chin and twisted her face to his. "Is that what you think, my loving wife?"

"Yes," she whispered, the word sounding more like a hiss. "Yes, I wish my father had killed you, too!"

Roderick pulled her to her feet and held her before him. He looked furious enough to crush her with his bare hands, yet she lifted her chin proudly, defiantly. Had she humbled herself, or even begged, he might have turned and left. But instead, she stood unflinchingly, bearing his brutal grip and saying nothing. He brought his hand up and struck her face with a head-reeling blow that sent her sprawling onto the carpet at his feet. Still her eyes held his and she would not utter a sound; her hand went inadvertently to her cheek to feel the painful welt he had left there.

For endless moments Roderick stood over her, the white-hot fury in his mind obscuring all feeling; she had reopened a deep wound, and in his eyes she was cast from the same mold as her despicable father, the blackguard Earl of Tarbella. The silence in the room was heavy, tomblike, until suddenly a log cracked in the fireplace, breaking the spell. Roderick drew in a ragged breath, trying to gain control of his emotions, then straightened and walked to the chamber door. He turned back, saying grimly, "Renaldo will come for my things—I'll take quarters across the hall." He opened the door and left, slamming it behind him.

A short while later Renaldo came to her room and, with much embarrassment, gathered up his master's belongings. Madrigal sat with her back to him until he approached her silently.

"I do not wish to disturb you, but milord has bade me see to your . . . your welfare," he said, leaning over and looking closely at the ugly red welt on her cheek. He flinched visibly at his master's handiwork, not truly fathoming Roderick's actions but feeling very sorry for the little mistress. Still, his master had shown concern when ordering him to see if Madrigal's cheek needed attention.

"'Twill heal quickly, milady." His fingers gently touched the swollen area. "I am truly sorry . . ." He could find no comforting words for her, so he merely bowed and took his leave.

Renaldo found his master below, a flagon of ale in his hand. The hour had grown late, and although Roderick refused to eat, he sent food up to Madrigal. Despite his conversation with the Duke of Devonshire, his mind was on the young girl he had taken to wife. The rift between them was beyond all hope of repair, nor was he certain he wanted it otherwise. So when the duke suggested that he remain in London through the Christmas season, which promised much merrymaking, Roderick thought the idea a sound one and decided to send Madrigal back to Cornwall as soon as the court presentation was made. He was tired of their endless battling and needed a respite. Mayhap there was a wench at court who could comfort him, he suddenly mused.

The tray of steaming food sat untouched on the table by the hearth as Madrigal stood at the window, watching the passing boats on the river. She, too, had come to an inevitable decision. She would bide her time until they reached Halconbosque again, and then she would leave Roderick once and for all. Perhaps she would even seek the solace of a nunnery; that step was not unheard of. There were other options open to her: she could return to Castilla-verde or she could even beg Akbar to have her back. It mattered little just as long as she was free of Roderick.

Her eyes followed the movement of a town crier, swinging his lantern in the increasing dusk. She laughed to think of the many compliments she and her husband had received as a couple: how elegant and lovely she was and how handsomely Roderick bore himself. What a farce! she thought with tears glistening in her eyes. If people only knew the pain and suffering we bring to each other! But she would end the misery as soon as possible, even if it meant excommunication. Nothing could be worse than to continue this travesty of a marriage.

Chapter 40

The day of the audience with King Edward dawned unusually bright and clear, and there was an invigorating snap to the air. Madrigal could see the plumes of white breath from the early peddlers as they hawked their wares in the street. As she stared out her window, she felt the boredom of the long hours ahead of her weigh heavily. Roderick, of course, would be gone until the late afternoon; he had carefully planned his schedule so that he would be absent most of the time. Yet it suited her mood to see as little of him as possible.

How she wished she were at home in Castilla-verde right now; the weather would be chilly, perhaps, but never like the raw northern cold of this desolate island.

She sighed to think of the orange trees readying their sweet, golden crop and the warm winds from Africa caressing the land. The familiar sound of her own language, the easy, relaxed routine of her home, the golden Mediterranean light—oh, to experience those things again! They seemed a dream of another life, one in which she was an innocent, happy child. Her mind conjured up the details of Castilla-verde while her eyes were forced to watch the London scene beneath her window. A ragged, toothless hag, her feet bound in strips of cloth, hobbled past, her wrinkled mouth mumbling. Thin children scurried by, their faces gray and pinched from hunger. A mangy dog chased a squawking chicken across the street, only to be knocked aside by a woman's broom as she sought to save her hen.

Madrigal sighed, dropping into a chair by the fire and picking up a piece of embroidery for Beth's baby. At least it would pass the time until Roderick came to take her to Westminster Palace. They were to dine with King Edward and Queen Eleanor after Roderick had discussed his business with the king. Once the affair would have thrilled her, but now she dreaded the evening, as her husband had warned her to behave and let the king believe all was well between them. His Majesty doted on his queen and his two-year-old son, and respected a happily married man above all others. *Too bad I cannot produce a child just for the evening!* she thought bitterly. *Roderick would like that!*

When Roderick finally knocked on her door later that afternoon, she was quite ready. She had spent hours on her toilette, as she wished to show the English king and his henchmen that a Spanish lady was every bit as elegant as one of theirs. She wore the gown that had been ordered especially for the occasion, knowing it flattered her unusual coloring. She turned slowly in front of the rippled mirror and was pleased with her reflection; the flowing lines of the shimmery silk velvet gown made her look tall and imperious. The forest-green color accented her creamy skin and green eyes. Her black hair was braided with silk ribbons and wound intricately around her head, leaving her slim neck bare. She had used rouge on her cheeks lest she appear too pale and had applied some black lines to her eyelids, giving her eyes an even more exotic appearance. As a last gesture, she had put on the necklace that Roderick had bought her on that fateful day. Let it remind him of all his cruelties, she had thought, and let it also remind him of Akbar, if he insists on thinking the worst of me. A tight smile tilted her lips, but her eyes remained cold and glinted like the huge emerald that lay on her breast.

Roderick was struck by her appearance. He hesitated for a moment on the threshold, his eyes narrowing. He said nothing, but picked up her fur-lined cloak and placed it on her shoulders, his hand lingering a bit too long on her arm. They were silent as they walked down to the entrance of the White Horse Inn, as they climbed into the separate sedan chairs that had been provided to take them to Westminster Palace, and as they entered the gray stone edifice itself.

Once inside, they were met by Sir Robert of Coventry, and the three of them were led to the audience room by a page. The small chamber was cheerful and cozy compared with the long, gray corridors. A fire roared in the hearth and cast a flickering glow everywhere. A polished table stood at one side, a brightly patterned Oriental rug graced the floor, and gorgeous tapestries covered the walls. The king and queen were seated on plain wooden chairs near the fire. Several ladies stood near the queen, and a lone man hovered in the background.

Madrigal had time to study the royal English couple while Sir Robert made the introductions. King Edward, although seated, was obviously tall and lanky, with long, muscular legs that showed off his white hose handsomely. He had a proud mien and was black-haired and quite attractive, except for a drooping left eyelid, which, Madrigal learned later, he had inherited from his father. His wife, Eleanor, was a nondescript woman, somewhat ill-looking. However, she had lovely skin and expressive, kind eyes, and it was said that the king adored her.

His Highness rose and greeted Roderick in French, the language still spoken by the English court, then turned to Madrigal and switched to English. "Lady Madrigal, I understand you do not speak French but have become quite conversant in English. 'Tis well, for I would have the pleasure of talking to you during the evening. It is rare that one so lovely graces our court." Madrigal curtsied low, thanking him, and noticed that he spoke hesitatingly, as if he stammered and took care to control it. She was then presented to the queen, after which a few moments of polite small talk ensued, with everyone speaking English carefully so that Madrigal could follow the conversation. Then the queen and her ladies-in-waiting, as if on a prearranged signal, turned to leave the room, Eleanor suggesting to Madrigal that they would take some refreshments in her private suite. It was obviously time to leave the men to their affairs, for the other man in the room had come forward with a quill and parchment.

The queen entertained Madrigal quietly for an hour, chatting easily about her life in England and her two-year-old son, Edward. Madrigal found herself confiding her inability to conceive and her sadness at not having children, for she suddenly felt starved of feminine understanding. The queen was sympathetic, as it had taken her many years to bear a living child to inherit the throne of England.

"Do not despair, my dear," said Queen Eleanor. "If God wishes you to have a child, it will be so, and if not, then your duty is to bear His will with dignity and patience."

Madrigal agreed aloud but nonetheless felt resentful at having to bear life's vicissitudes.

They were finally summoned to the hall to rejoin the king and Roderick for the state dinner in their honor. Madrigal was seated on the queen's right, Roderick on the king's left, so they had no need to talk during the long meal. The table stretched far down the hall, accommodating the scores of nobles who obeyed the king's word directly. Their rank corresponded to their nearness to the king, the lowest knights being relegated to the foot of the table.

Madrigal conversed with the queen and with Sir Robert, who sat on her other side and flattered her outrageously, but her real interest was captured by Sir Lawrence DeMaire, a young knight seated next to Robert La Valle. He was a dissolute, darkly handsome man, of an old Norman family; indeed, his father ranked highly in the king's army, he was quick to point out to the charming foreign lady seated near him. He leaned insolently in front of Sir Robert and flirted conspicuously with Madrigal, until La Valle spoke half jokingly to him of the lady's husband.

"What of him, Robert? In this court a husband but frees a lady to do as she will—he's convenient for giving a name to a spare babe or two, but hardly for more." The young man was somewhat drunk by now, and his eyes devoured Madrigal feverishly across Sir Robert's body. She felt the blood rise to her cheeks and glanced quickly in Roderick's direction, catching his wary, golden look. She quickly tossed her head and turned back to her admirers, hoping no one had noticed her husband's ill humor, and vowed to give him good reason for his anger.

"My dear Sir Lawrence, what was that you said about husbands? I cannot believe such things of this court. Why, surely you jest!" She smiled demurely at him.

"Lady Madrigal," said the young man hungrily, "that is a subject I should dearly like to discuss with you soon. Do you have a spare afternoon . . . or evening?"

He was outrageous, but she thoroughly enjoyed his attentions and led him on until the last course was served. By then the young knight was so in his cups that the game had become tiresome, and Madrigal turned back once more to her left. The queen had sat patiently during the dinner, smiling serenely through the long hours and speaking rarely. Madrigal heard King Edward talking earnestly to Roderick, who paid him close attention. They spoke in English, oddly enough, but Madrigal realized that was to avoid being understood by the French knight seated next to Roderick.

"As I said previously, Lord Roderick, I can only promise *not* to interfere in Spain. I cannot in faith promise any support to King Sancho in the way of men, nor can I give advice to King Philip of France. My position is delicate."

Madrigal tried to follow the men's quiet words without seeming to eavesdrop.

"I quite understand, your Highness, as does my liege. He wishes only to have your moral support in this matter, and the promise that you would not side with France in the event of a full-scale invasion of Spain."

"On that you have my word, sir. Philip of France has taken on more than he can handle if he thinks to invade

334

Spain and put Sancho's nephew on the throne in his stead. We learned long ago in England that having a child as king is not expedient for the nation."

"Sire, I shall report our discussion faithfully to Sancho. He will be pleased," said Roderick, and the two men raised their goblets of wine to toast their understanding.

The talk became general thereafter, and Madrigal grew thoughtful. Her husband, despicable as she thought him, was a close and trusted adviser to his king. *His* words and manner might save Spain an invasion or soothe the constant internal strife between Sancho and his dead brother's family. How could Roderick be such a courtier here and such an unfeeling beast at home? He was a puzzle to her, one with no seeming solution.

Chapter 41

Madrigal slept late the next morning and awoke to a loud, insistent knocking at her door.

"Who is it?" she asked groggily.

"It is your husband, madam. Kindly let me in. We have important matters to discuss." He sounded impatient.

"Un momento," she called while she found a robe and wrapped it around her slim body.

Roderick entered and closed the door behind him. She immediately became apprehensive and began to fumble with her robe, drawing the red fabric more tightly around her.

"Humph! I am surprised not to find that young whelp DeMaire bedded down with you after last night, milady. You made yourself a fine fool with him!"

Madrigal sighed in vexation. His insinuations do not merit an answer from me, she decided silently. Let him stew.

"What do you want?" she asked coldly, and was glad to see his face whiten with anger.

"You will be returning to Penglennyn today. Renaldo and the men-at-arms will accompany you."

"So soon? Oh, well, it is all the same to me. This country is dreary from one end to the other. And what will you do? I take it you do not return with us." She yawned widely, putting a hand to her mouth and unconsciously letting the loose sleeve of her robe fall back to show her white arm.

Roderick felt an irresistible urge to reach out and stroke the smooth skin, but he turned his eyes away quickly and continued. "I have further business here, but you need not stay. It is best you return to be with Beth—her time draws near."

"As you wish, Roderick."

He hesitated, as if to speak further, but seemed to change his mind and left her sitting in the chair, a ray of morning light slanting across her body, causing the red robe to glow like fire.

When she was alone again, she rested her chin on her hand, staring mutely into the cold hearth, then shook off the momentary feeling of despondency and began to pack her belongings.

Early that afternoon Renaldo and Hugo carried her bags and trunk down to the extra mules they had bought for the trip. Madrigal was returning with more than she had arrived with, and there were supplies for the fief, bolts of cloth for Beth, and gifts for everyone.

The early November weather was cold and clear when they departed London, following the riverbank and leaving by the old Roman gate to the west. The muddy streets were already frozen into ruts, causing the horses and mules to trip and stumble often.

Madrigal was very glad to leave the city she now considered pestilential. The clean country air refreshed her body and her spirit, and with each passing day she began to look forward to seeing Beth and Stefano again.

A week later she arrived at Penglennyn, tired and longing for a hot bath to relieve her chilled bones. As she dismounted, the heavy oak doors burst open and Beth descended the steps as quickly as her heavy body would allow; she threw herself into Madrigal's arms and burst into tears.

"Beth, what is it? Has anything gone wrong? Is Stefano . . .?"

"No, Madrigal, it is only my own foolishness. We are all fine, although I have been much alone of late—Stefano is so busy these days." Beth wiped her eyes and smiled through her tears.

"Never mind, now. I shall be company for you."

"And where is Roderick?" asked Beth, then flushed as she realized her indiscretion.

"He still has business at court and told me to return. London is a filthy place, and I had no wish to stay overlong. I'm glad to be back." Madrigal spoke casually, hoping that Beth would ask no more embarrassing questions to upset her.

"Did you really meet the king and queen?"

"Yes, and they are worthy folk as far as I can tell. King Edward is a fine, tall man and Eleanor is sweet and retiring. I don't believe the pomp at court is much to her liking."

"I would have died of nervousness to meet the king, Madrigal. Thank heaven I have nothing to do with royalty—'twould be the death of me!" Beth took Madrigal's arm and led her inside while she talked. "Stefano is wonderful. He has solved so many problems here already, but he works hard and is gone all day. I do believe he is happy, though, for he tells me he

337

had no hope of lands of his own before, and now he has two fiefs!''

Madrigal could not help feeling a stab of annoyance at the unabashed worship in Beth's voice when she spoke of Stefano. She was going to say something spiteful about his past behavior, but clamped her mouth shut tightly before the words escaped. After all, it was not Beth's fault that *her* husband was such an ogre! She would have to make the best of it until they returned to Spain; there, he would no longer be able to hold her against her will. There were nunneries where he would never find her, or any number of other escapes from her situation. She would talk to a priest about it; surely someone could help her.

Madrigal's life at Penglennyn settled into a routine during the next month: to rise early for breakfast and see to the baking, the roasting of meats, the making of ale, the sweeping and cleaning of the many rooms, the visiting of and ministering to sick vassals or women in labor. Then came the midday meal, when Stefano might or might not appear, and after lunch there was sewing, mending, or embroidery. Beth was often tired and was grateful to let Madrigal do most of the chores, but they always sat together in the early dusk of winter to stitch and gossip. It was often dark by the time they had their evening meal, when Stefano would usually arrive, or emerge from the room full of ledgers and papers to join them. The relaxed pace calmed Madrigal; without Roderick to chafe her temper she was tranquil and, if not happy, at least content. With Christmas approaching rapidly, she often thought back on the holidays of her childhood at Castilla-verde, filled with joy and prayer; and on the last one at Akbar's home.

But the evenings were always long and lonely. Stefano and Beth retired immediately after the meal because they were both exhausted by then, so Madrigal was left in front of the fire with the dogs and the few servants who cleaned off the trestle. She could hardly understand their thick Cornish accents and found it difficult to talk to them. She, too, often retired early, out of boredom, and lay in her bed feeling very small and alone. Sometimes she would wake at night and reach out a hand automatically, but the place beside her was always cold and empty.

Roderick found himself at a loss. True, his business with the king persisted still, but his leisure time lay heavily on his hands, especially with the approach of the holidays. Renaldo was not even around as company for a quick ale in a tavern. Roderick was drawn more and more into the company of the Duke of Devonshire, who surrounded himself with several rich young idlers who had too much free time on their hands. Their major interests appeared to be women, drink, and gambling, in that order, but Roderick found their company jolly and easygoing. They soothed his ruffled feelings, his loneliness, his conscience; they were the perfect antidote to Madrigal's memory during this festive Christmas season.

It was through Sir John de Grenville that he met Lady Francine. She was very wealthy, young, and voluptuously beautiful, and had been married off at fifteen to a bald man forty years her senior.

When Francine first noticed the tall foreigner at a court function, she had asked her maidservant to find out who he was. The girl came back shortly with the information that he was the Baron of Compostela, a Spanish nobleman on a diplomatic mission to King Edward. His arrogant good looks appealed to Francine; here was a man who might be interesting in bed, and elsewhere. It was not difficult to arrange for an introduction through her old friend and onetime lover, John de Grenville. The baron was a cultured man, she discovered, who spoke English well, having learned it from his English mother, and who was not a wild, fanatic foreigner at all. Their relationship quickly developed into an intimate one, and although many of their mutual acquaintances knew this, no one gave a tuppence what they did. It was most convenient to use Roderick's suite in the White Horse, which he had kept, and their afternoons were often spent there, drinking French wine and rolling in the great bed that Madrigal had once shared with him.

If Roderick felt any guilt, he kept it tightly under control and tried almost desperately to enjoy himself with Francine. Physically, their relationship was satisfying, but on an emotional level the English girl soon began to irritate him. She started to cling, to sigh, to demand assurances. He felt annoyed that her womanly feelings should obscure their pleasant pastime.

"Roderick," she said one gray, rainy afternoon just after the new year had begun, "will you be staying in London much longer?" She tossed her auburn curls back and smiled coyly at him. "You know, don't you, my love, that I am neglecting my other admirers for you?" She traced the ridged line on his scarred shoulder with one ruby-tipped finger.

He ran his hand down the curve of her naked hip and she giggled, pressing her large, rose-tipped breasts against him. His hand found the swelling of her buttock, and he caressed the warm flesh, then suddenly gave her posterior a resounding slap.

"Ouch!" Francine sat up precipitously, pouting and rubbing the sore spot. "Why did you do that, Roderick, my love? Do I not please you?" She attempted to pull him to her again, but he disengaged her hands.

"I detest women who ask too many questions, Francine, and besides, I must be off soon. 'Tis my last meeting with the king before he hurries back to

Scotland. I need to dress and be at Westminster within the hour. So be off with you, sweet. I'll send you a note saying when we can meet again."

He rose and began dressing in his court finery, of which he was growing heartily sick, and ignored the sullen looks Francine directed at his back. He left before she was fully clothed, giving her a quick peck on the cheek in passing as he swung his cloak over his shoulders.

As it happened, Roderick was saved further annoyance by Lady Francine when, several days later, Renaldo appeared with the news that Beth had given birth to a boy the previous week. Roderick was expected at the christening, as he was to be godfather to the child, who had been named Guy, after Roderick's own father, Guillermo.

Renaldo's narrow, one-eyed countenance had greeted Roderick upon his return from an errand, and broad smiles had broken out on the faces of both men.

"How are all at Penglennyn, Renaldo? And especially Lady Beth?" Roderick asked now.

"She is fine, milord, a bit peakedy when I left, but in good health, and the babe's a fine, lusty boy with a head full of black hair. Lord Stefano is right proud, bursting out of his britches, I'd say, sir."

"I can imagine. Think of it—my bastard brother, Stefano, a father!" He hesitated before asking the next question. "And Madrigal?"

"She is fine, sir. Happy for Beth," Renaldo said, daring to defend his mistress, "but maybe a bit sad for herself. She is a great help to everybody."

"I see. Well, we shall have to return to Penglennyn soon, then. Bah! I've had enough of London anyway. I'll send a message to the king, finish up some business, and we'll be off in a day or two. What say you, Renaldo?"

"*Bueno,* sir. I don't like this place—reminds me of a monstrous chamber pot, milord, if you'll excuse my saying so."

"You've got a point there, my friend," laughed Roderick, feeling the last weeks of sordidness slough off him like old skin. "Back to Penglennyn we go. You've saved me, Renaldo, from more than you could ever imagine!"

Chapter 42

The morning had dawned cold and gray; by noon one of the rare snowstorms that occurred in Cornwall was in the offing. At first the flakes were mixed with rain; then, as the air grew colder, they swirled out of the sky like eiderdown flung from a celestial counterpane. Madrigal could almost hear the crashing of the ocean as it heaved at the rocky shores, nearly a mile away. She shivered involuntarily and pulled her wool shawl closer around her as the thick snow slanted against the windows on the west side of the great hall, then slid slowly down the glass, leaving blurry, wet trails behind. Even the dogs were quiet today, as if thankful to be out of the storm. Madrigal stopped to pat the head of a great hound of whom she was especially fond. He turned his limpid brown eyes up to her, and his tail thumped heavily on the stone flagging.

"'Tis good to be inside this day, Tache," she said absentmindedly, then passed on toward the kitchens, hoping to find more warmth there. Suddenly Tache growled, the hackles rising on his neck. Madrigal turned to see what had caused him to act so, and then heard a muffled noise at the front doors.

Who on earth could it be? Madrigal wondered as she hurried to unbar the doors. It was probably a serf with a sick child or a wife in labor, for surely no visitors would venture out on a day like this! She wrestled with the heavy bar until it finally swung down and the door could be pulled open. On the threshold were two figures so muffled against the weather and whitened by the snow that she could not recognize them.

The taller figure strode through the door first, brushing snow off his wool cloak while the second figure entered. She heard a familiar voice emerge from the folds of the hood. "By God, woman! You took long enough to open the blasted doors! A man could freeze just waiting for you to make up your mind!" He turned to the second figure. "Renaldo, see that one of the servants puts the horses in the stable and feeds them. The poor beasts served us well this foul day."

Madrigal tried to appear casual, although her heart thumped wildly in her breast. Her reply to him sounded as if she were breathless. "*Dios!* You frightened me out of my wits!"

Roderick bowed deeply, an infuriating grin on his lips, and went to warm himself by the hearth. He turned back to her shortly. "And where are Stefano and Beth?"

She swept past him and went toward the stairs. Pausing midway, she replied, "Stefano went to Trenwell this morn, and Beth and Guy are napping."

He watched her mount the remaining stairs and disappear from his thoughtful gaze. Renaldo returned and drew his master an ale while Roderick dried himself by the welcome fire. It was good to be back at Penglennyn and away from the useless frivolity at court, he mused, even if his wife preferred to keep herself estranged from him.

Madrigal avoided him neatly, busying herself during

the next few days with the myriad preparations for the baby's christening. Therefore, she was quite taken aback when Roderick announced one night at dinner that he had sent Renaldo to Falmouth to arrange for their passage to Spain.

Madrigal's hand froze in midair, spilling some drops from her goblet as the words sank in. She looked at Roderick a long moment. "We shall leave, then, so soon?"

"Yes, my wife. Matters are well in hand here, and I have need to report to Sancho."

She sat back in her chair and felt saddened about departing from Penglennyn, yet here was her chance, finally, to escape this bitter situation. Was this not what she had wanted ever since coming to England?

The morning of the christening arrived and promised to be fair-skied, much to everyone's delight, for several families had been invited for a feast after the services in Falmouth.

Madrigal spent the late morning in her chamber, putting the finishing stitches on the baby's gown, while the other family members were dressing themselves for the affair. She had donned her own gown earlier as an excuse to return to her room after breakfast. She put aside the needle, and rising, placed the christening gown on the bed, smoothing and ruffling the delicate white silk and admiring her careful handiwork. She had fashioned her own silk dress over the Christmas season to while away the days. It was a rich shade of wheat, with long sleeves and yards of flowing material in the skirt. The neckline was trimmed with white fox, as were the cuffs of the sleeves. Her hair was hidden this day under a wimple, giving her an austere but strikingly elegant appearance.

Satisfied that baby Guy would look beautiful in the traditional gown, she picked it up carefully and was about to leave when her door opened and Roderick appeared in the portal. He had also taken care with his attire for the ceremony. Dressed in a red velvet surcoat trimmed in gold, he looked almost like a rogue of King Edward's court.

"I have not seen your coat before, Roderick. It would seem you had much spare time in London to attend to lesser matters . . . matters, that is, other than your business with King Edward that kept you gone so long." She had tried to sound casual and cutting, but her tone emerged high-pitched and brittle.

"Could it be that milady missed me?"

She showed him her back. "Don't be ridiculous, Roderick." Then she turned around to face him. "What has brought you here?"

" 'Tis only to inform you that I must ride to Hugo's for a moment. Some last-minute problem . . . Then I shall return to escort you to Falmouth. We've plenty of time."

Beth, Guy, and Stefano departed a short while later, and Madrigal waved good-bye from the entrance, assuring them that she and Roderick would follow as soon as possible. She was about to close the door when a solitary rider stopped Stefano's party, and after a short exchange, headed into the courtyard, then dismounted and approached her.

"I've a letter for the Baron of Compostela. Is he about?" asked the red-cheeked youth.

"Why, no, not at the moment. But I am the baron's wife and can see the letter safely into his hands."

The boy hesitated for an instant but then remembered his instructions had been only to ride to Penglennyn and leave the epistle, so he handed Madrigal the document and left her standing in the cold sunshine.

She watched him ride off and then turned her

attention to the tidily rolled parchment. This was surely not a message from the king for the seal was strange to her eyes. Madrigal turned the letter over in her hands and reentered the hall. She placed it on the table and went to the hearth, her back to the leaping flames.

Yet the temptation grew. And when Roderick did not return for some time, she found her curiosity besting her and moved quickly to the table, snatching up the parchment and accidentally breaking the wax seal.

Well, the damage is done, she told herself to excuse her action, and then unrolled the letter fully and went to the window, where she could better decipher the words.

It began with the date and place, London; the body of the letter read: "I have engaged a young squire of letters to write this. I should chastise you severely for leaving without sending word, but I shall save my words till I see you again, my noble Spaniard. However, all is not lost, for I intend to travel to Cornwall to visit my cousin's estates. I plan to arrive there in mid-March and hope to send you a message. London without you has been dull indeed, and I trust your life has been the same . . . Till we may meet again, your obedient admirer, Francine de Voge."

The letter dropped to the floor at Madrigal's feet and she stared blankly out the window.

"I don't care—I don't care!" she cried, her words echoing off the walls, but her cheeks were flushed and her eyes brimmed tearfully.

Some moments later the sound of hooves in the courtyard reached her consciousness, and she gritted her teeth, snatched up the letter, and fled up the stairs. Before she had a chance to dispose of the damning proof of his infidelity, she could hear Roderick calling her name from below.

Suddenly, as quickly as it had come, her panic fled and was replaced by anger. She squared her shoulders and wiped her eyes dry, finally answering his call and returning to the hall. He stood waiting impatiently, her cloak in his hand. Still she said nothing and allowed him to drape her in its folds and escort her out to the horses. The few miles they rode together into Falmouth seemed unending. Both were silent, lost in their separate thoughts.

Only once did Roderick speak. "Pray tell, milady, what has put the glint in your eye today?" he asked.

In reply, she kicked her horse into a canter, leaving Roderick riding behind her in bewilderment.

They reached the church only minutes before the scheduled mass and took their places in the front row with Stefano and Beth. Guy bawled and squealed, but to no avail. The priest had spoken the long mass many a time over an unwilling babe, and he continued the service, undaunted by the piercing cries. Even Roderick seemed not to mind but looked proudly on the infant and felt a sudden grief that he had no child of his own.

It was Madrigal whose nerves jumped with each healthy bellow Guy emitted. In truth, it was more the agonized yearning of her young body that screamed for the fulfillment of motherhood. Her knuckles were clenched whitely, her breath came in snatches, and her head reeled dizzily. Suddenly, surprising even herself, she was running back down the aisle, the cumbersome folds of her skirt nearly causing her to stumble. But at last she was outside, gulping great breaths of air and racing toward her horse.

A wide-eyed livery boy quickly ran out of the stable and tried to help her mount, but she paid him no attention, grabbed the reins, and galloped wildly up the cobblestoned street and toward the moors.

Once safely home at Penglennyn, she could not remember the frenzied ride back. Her cloak was still at the church, she had lost her wimple on the moor, and the horrified looks on the faces peering from the aisles flooded her memory. What in heaven's name had come over her? And what would Roderick do—how would he react?

Racing up the stairs to the safety of her room, she threw herself on the bed and sobbed ceaselessly into the pillow. At long last, her chest heaving, she sat up and reached for the letter she had tossed on the bed table hours before. Her eyes blurrily scanned the words again, as if she almost relished the anguish they brought her. They made the past months of living with Roderick seem less confused, their estranged relationship easier to excuse.

Madrigal was standing by the window when she saw Roderick riding toward Penglennyn at a furious pace. She shivered inwardly to think of the inevitable confrontation, for she knew she could not keep silent on the subject of this other woman.

But Roderick did not come to her room. Even after Beth and Stefano had led their guests back and had been below for some time, he still stayed away. The suspense threatened to drive her mad, and as dusk settled over the grand house she paced the room in dread.

Beth had been fitfully concerned over Madrigal from the moment she had fled the church, but Roderick would not allow her to go up to his wife. Stefano tactfully kept out of the affair and went about the pleasant task of entertaining their guests. When at last the feasting was done and the men returned to drinking the smuggled French wine, Roderick still remained withdrawn. He had skipped the meal entirely and drunk far too much for rational thought, so that when he could no longer contain his anger, he found himself at Madrigal's door, with no recollection as to how he had arrived there. He knocked, but she did not reply, so he banged on the heavy oak frame with his fist until he heard the latch fall aside. When he entered, she was standing with the candlelight behind her, and he could not see her face clearly.

"I'll have an explanation for your misbegotten behavior at the church." He closed the door while keeping his stare fixed on her. "Answer me, woman!" He took a menacing step forward. But still she remained frozen, clutching the parchment tightly in her hand.

"By God, Madrigal!"

"This, I think, belongs to you!" She flung the letter at him, striking his cheek and leaving a small cut that welled slowly. "Now, be gone from me!"

Confusion played on his face for a moment before he reached down to retrieve the paper. He then walked cautiously around her to the lighted candle. After his eyes had quickly scanned the contents, he slowly lowered the damning evidence until it hung limply from one hand. When he turned finally to face her, his expression was not one of guilt, nor was it hard, as she had expected. Surprisingly, he looked saddened.

"What did you expect, my wife?" His voice was a low whisper.

"I expected . . . honor at least, respect toward me, that was all." She clutched her hands before her to still their trembling.

Roderick mulled over her meaning for a time before replying. "I shall make no excuses. However, I wish to give you a full accounting of why I got involved in this . . . affair." He tossed the letter on the bed and folded his arms across his chest. "I tell you this only because the blame rests on *your* shoulders."

Madrigal's mouth opened in disbelief and sharp words flew to her lips, but he quieted her with a gesture, continuing. "A man needs a willing woman to share his bed or mayhap speak a comforting word of endearment in his ear. You give none of these, milady. You choose to fight me at every turn, even though your body may know better. I feel your hatred burn my very soul." He thought a moment. "There is no love between us, not even simple affection."

Madrigal's blood pounded in her ears and tears streamed unheeded down her cheeks, dropping onto her chest. Finally she stammered, "You—you dare to speak of love? You force me into . . . into a despicable marriage of vengeance and expect me to think of love? What of *me?*" She sobbed without control, and in between gasps she moaned, "Am I *so* loathsome that you seek another's bed to humiliate me further?"

Roderick approached her and took her by the shoulders. "If 'tis truth you want, Madrigal, you shall have it. There is no other woman to compare with you—none so lovely or so pleasurable in my bed."

She looked up into his tawny eyes and managed to say, "'Tis a child you want, then! And I can give you none!"

"That, milady, is *your* opinion. I prefer to believe that you have not conceived because you don't wish to."

"'Tis a lie!" she cried, and then covered her eyes with her hands, but he pulled them away and held them in his own.

Her hair had come loose and hung about her shoulders in disarray, and his eyes traveled to her heaving breasts. "Mayhap we should spend more time abed," he murmured.

"No!" She tried to twist her hands away.

Roderick pulled her toward the door while she

struggled in vain to free herself. When he grew tired of her efforts, he reached down and picked her up. "I think my bed shall better bear the weight than yours."

"Please, Roderick—don't!" she protested sharply against his chest.

He crossed the hall, kicking his door ajar, and strode toward the huge bed. He then carefully set her on its edge and bade her undress without a hysterical scene.

"No . . . I cannot . . . I won't. I'm no whore like your Francine!"

He eased himself down alongside her and forced her to look at him by turning her chin to him.

"Believe me," he said, "when I tell you that she was a mere dalliance. I grew tired of her wagging tongue. 'Tis you I burn for, Madrigal . . . even when I was with her."

He was lying, she was certain, but her heart leaped inexplicably, nevertheless. Yet when his fingers began to fumble at her belt, she attempted to pull away once more.

"I should hate to spoil such a lovely gown, but do not doubt that I will," he cautioned.

"So I am to meekly submit, the way I did on our wedding night?" She sighed hopelessly. "For haven't you always proved your strength over me?"

"Yes," he whispered, "and I shall continue to do so as long as you persist in fighting me, little fool."

A low hiss came from her lips. "I'll never submit again—never!"

Roderick stood up, and if he had not consumed so much drink, he might have stomped from the room, for he did not truly relish the idea of hurting his wife. But he wanted her; he ached to feel her soft flesh in his hands, to join their bodies and reexperience her unresisting submission.

Grabbing her arm, he turned her around and took

hold of the fabric, ripping downward until the seams gave way and the gown tore to her waist. He then spun her toward him and pulled the bodice from her chest. Amazingly, Madrigal remained pliable, like a broken doll in his grip. She steeled her mind against his attack, and even as she shivered, repelled by his cruelty, she vowed to remain unfeeling. This was her only defense against his lust—to display no emotion, to remain cold and uncaring.

"Damn you!" he growled when she neither cried nor fought him, and then he threatened, "You'll respond yet, my sweet!"

He ripped away her delicate underclothing and stood haughtily over her, viewing her curves and hollows leisurely. Then he undressed, tossing his clothing to the floor unheedingly. Even when Madrigal lay passively next to him, he was still determined to reap a response from her. His lips came urgently down on hers and he kissed her cold mouth with great passion.

But she remained unresponsive under his heated assault. Cursing under his breath, Roderick lowered his head to her neck, nibbling and teasing, and then moved his lips to her breasts. He reveled in the sweet taste of her, playing with her shrinking flesh until at last the sensitive peaks stood aroused in his mouth while a low moan escaped her lips.

She rolled her head from side to side, humiliated, begging him to stop. He ignored her whispered pleas and continued to caress her arms, breasts, and belly with his searching tongue while she writhed in reaction to his overbearing will, her skin aflame where he touched her.

Still Madrigal fought to control her treasonous body, and when she felt herself losing that control, she stiffened perceptibly and tried desperately to shove him away. Roderick winced when her hand hit his wounded shoulder and caused a sharp pain to shoot through it, but he ignored the ache and took advantage of her momentary weakening, poising himself above her and spreading her thighs with his knees.

Madrigal panicked; she arched her back and twisted frantically, so that in order to enter her he had to hold her arms with one hand and still the twisting of her hips with the other. Inevitably, in spite of the curses she flung at him, he found the opening and forced himself into her. She continued to fight him, only to succeed in arousing his lust further. Finally, when his own artful movements began to overtake her vows to feel nothing, she quieted somewhat, exhausted, perspiring heavily under his oppressive weight.

Sensing that she no longer had the strength to battle him, he slowed his rhythm and held himself in check until she began to move against him in spite of her frustrated pleas. His mouth covered her perfectly formed breast, then he murmured, "There is no other who can torture me thus. You fever my blood."

She cried and moaned and swore at him, but her senses were spiraling skyward and her breath was coming in weak snatches. Still he continued his rhythm, and before she had recovered her lost senses she felt a pulsing, frenzied wave of desire swell in her womb; when it peaked, culminating in a long, blessed release, she cried aloud and clung tightly to his body, still shaking and arching against him.

Then Roderick stiffened and groaned, spilling his seed deep within her. "It can be like this lways," he gasped, "if you'll but allow yourself . . ."

"No, never," she wept. "I cannot."

He felt an aching sadness in his chest, for in spite of her physical response to him, she still remained stubborn and willful.

By the time of their departure a week later, Madrigal

had refused even to speak to Roderick. She had crept silently back to her room the night he had taken her, and had lain awake until the dawn had come, alternating between despair and self-hatred.

She had spent the days in the company of Beth, guarding against meeting Roderick alone. She felt a true affection for the girl and did not know how long it would be until they would meet again.

On the appointed day Roderick and Madrigal rode out toward Falmouth, where the ship awaited them. They carried the blessings of Stefano and his assurances that he would bring Beth and Guy to Spain one year. As they rowed out to the trim vessel in the harbor, Madrigal drew the fresh salt air deep into her lungs and pledged to herself that once she had set foot on Spanish soil, she would remedy her unhappiness by ridding herself of her presumptuous husband forever.

Chapter 43

"Madrigal, my child," said Lady Gwendolyn, "I must see to the baking this morn. Please join me."

"*Gracias, madre,* but truly, I am still tired from traveling. Another day, perhaps?"

"Very well, but do join me for the midday meal, my dear." Gwendolyn sighed resignedly but would press no further. She was worried about her daughter-in-law. Madrigal ate little; she was pale and obviously unhappy, closeting herself in her sewing room constantly. The only person who could rouse a sign of life in her was Maria, her old servant from Castilla-verde, whom she had greeted tearfully on her return from England.

The girl turned her large green eyes on the older

woman, then shook her head mutely, as if not trusting her voice.

"All right, my dear," Gwendolyn said, and quietly closed the door behind her.

Later that morning, as she was overseeing the task of sweeping out the great hall and changing the rushes on the floor, she noticed that Madrigal had finally left her room and was crossing the stone flagging toward her.

"Mother, would you walk with me to the chapel? I must speak to you." Madrigal seemed nervous and ill at ease.

"Why, of course, Madrigal, I would be glad to. Just let me find Patrick to watch over these lazy girls, and I shall be with you." She returned in a moment with the dour *mayordomo,* and then the two women left the hall and silently crossed the courtyard toward the small stone chapel. As they were about to enter, Madrigal put a hand on Gwendolyn's arm to stop her.

"I . . . I do not feel right, after all, to speak my mind in the chapel. Mayhap you should hear me out here."

"My dear child, what is it? What can be troubling you so?" Gwendolyn could see both pain and determination fighting for ascendency in Madrigal's face.

"I am leaving Halconbosque. I am leaving Roderick. I must—it is the only way. We cannot go on." Her eyes begged for understanding.

The older woman was pensive for a moment, then said, "I see . . . Madrigal, do you realize the gravity of such a decision? It is against the Church, against God . . ."

"*Sí,* but there is no other choice for me any longer. I cannot believe that God condones such a loveless marriage as mine." Her voice was firmer now. "Your son cannot bear me. Perhaps if I could conceive . . . but that is not to be, and so there is no reason for me to stay. We . . . we cause each other too much pain."

"Madrigal, have you ever thought that the pain you cause each other may stem from an emotion other than hate?"

Madrigal looked at her quickly but was silent for a time before answering. "Mayhap I wish it were so, but I can answer you truthfully. There is no such hope for us, milady."

Gwendolyn sighed for the two young people, so lost in the maelstrom of their agonies. It would do no good to argue with Madrigal.

"You must do as your heart tells you, Madrigal. Does Roderick know of your decision?"

"No." Her voice was faint again. "But I shall inform him."

"He will not take kindly to your resolve, you realize."

"Yes," she almost whispered, "I know." Her voice rose. "But he cannot stop me, and he will soon come to believe that it is for the best. It is only his pride that will pain him, not my absence."

"Madrigal, let us pray in the chapel. It may be that prayer will help where words cannot." Roderick's mother took the girl's hand, and they entered the stone structure, kneeling at the foot of the small gilt icon that was surrounded by ornate hangings. Madrigal looked up at the calm, dispassionate image of Christ and wished with all her heart that she could bear her suffering with the patience that He showed.

That evening, after a strained meal, Roderick retired to the room that held all the fief's ledgers, accompanied by Vitorio de Rojas, the bailiff sent by King Sancho to oversee Halconbosque until Roderick's return. Vitorio was the youngest son of an old and honorable family but had no lands of his own, so Sancho sent him on many missions such as this one. He was middle-aged and very dignified, as thin and straight as a poker, with narrow features, a jutting nose, and a full head of wavy, gray hair. He got on well with Lady Gwendolyn and had once fought alongside Roderick's father. He was to leave soon, on another mission for his king, as soon as his accountings were satisfactory to Roderick.

"Lord Vitorio," Roderick was saying, "you have done well. The last time I left for an extended time, I'm afraid my brother did not see to his duties, and I had rather a mess to clean up when I returned." Roderick frowned, remembering the former state of the fief. "But now Stefano has his own lands and seems to be much more diligent in his care of them. As I said, I will report to Sancho in Burgos."

Vitorio nodded. "I must also report to the king, as he has a new task for me. May I suggest you visit Santiago de Compostela to see David ben Avrahim. He has written me that he has your yearly tithes collected and locked in his storehouse, and also that the Cortes has raised another tax for the king's war against the Moors. You will be expected to arrive at Burgos with your share of the tax."

"Ah, yes, the Moors." The thought of Akbar's dark, well-favored face teased his mind, then withdrew. "I think our king has more to fear from the French to the north than the Moors to the south. But that I must discuss with him in Burgos. And how is Sancho these days, Vitorio?"

"Hard-set-upon, milord. The pope, Philip of France, Abu Yusuf of Morocco, even his own family—they all seek their dues from him. But he perseveres in spite of all his troubles. He is a staunch man, King Sancho," said Vitorio solemnly.

"And so he is." Roderick smiled in spite of himself at the man's long face. "But mayhap I bring a ray of light to our beleaguered king, Vitorio."

"I do hope so, milord."

There was a faint knock on the door, and Vitorio rose to answer it. Madrigal stood shyly on the threshold, her right hand twisting her gold wedding band.

Roderick looked up, surprised. "Yes, Madrigal?" His tone was brusque, more out of discomfiture than from irritation.

"May I . . . may I have a word with you, Roderick?" She looked agitated.

Vitorio quickly excused himself and left Roderick and Madrigal facing each other over the table that was littered with ledgers and documents.

She looked so young and innocent standing there, her eyes downcast, her black hair streaming over her shoulders, that his heart inexplicably went out to her.

His tone softened. "Is there some problem . . .?"

Her eyes flew up to meet his, and he was shocked to see the intensity of feeling in them, and the fear.

"I am departing Halconbosque," she said. "I am leaving you. I shall not return this time under any circumstances. I shall be done with you." Her last words hissed through her teeth. She swayed, as if she were about to faint, but put her hands on the edge of the table and leaned on them, continuing to stare at him.

Roderick's mind was numbed. The force of the hatred he felt emanating from her delicate body buffeted him like a storm. Vague thoughts flitted through his mind, delicately, like hummingbirds: she cannot do this to me . . . it is shameful . . . she is *mine*. But in the end, he knew that she would leave, and that in his pride he would not reach out a hand, or speak a kind word, or beg her to stay. His heart thumped heavily like a stone in his breast, and his face became hard, withdrawn, remote.

"Do as you will, Madrigal. You are a woman grown. I shall not impede you. Just let me know where you will be . . . in case people . . . inquire. I would not be so shamed as not to know where my own wife is."

Her face blanched perceptibly, but she was silent, and soon she straightened and turned to leave. His voice stopped her as if it were a dagger in her back.

"You will be provided with an escort and enough gold to keep yourself in a state befitting my wife, wherever you wish to live. Do not try my patience by attempting to depart alone. Do you understand?"

She nodded and continued out of the room, closing the door behind her. Roderick sank into his chair, staring blankly at the door, his face as hard as the Galician granite of which the walls of Halconbosque were built.

Chapter 44

Drawing deep breaths, the stallion heaved its well-muscled chest, which was richly lathered from the furious pace that Roderick was maintaining in his haste to reach Burgos. The animal instinctively sensed Roderick's urgency and behaved accordingly on this third morning out from Halconbosque. Roderick had already stopped in Santiago de Compostela to collect the taxes due the king.

Laden with moisture, the spring air was warm and cloying in Roderick's lungs, and his hauberk felt oppressive. In the past Roderick had habitually looked forward to riding to his king, but this particular journey weighed heavily on him. It most certainly would please Sancho to hear of Roderick's words with Kind Edward, but inevitably the Spanish liege would inquire about Madrigal. And what would Roderick reply then? That she had shunned her marriage vows and denied the wisdom of the Church?

Yet he himself had allowed her to flee and was almost content to see her gone. And although Sancho had his own sensitive problems with the Vatican, he would strongly disapprove of this estrangement, for there would be no heirs to serve the monarch and Halconbosque itself might fall to ruin, unable to provide the throne with its due tithes.

In the late morning Roderick stopped at a familiar inn, saw to his horse's needs, and then entered the whitewashed building to refresh himself. He ordered stew and hard bread along with his wine, and while he sated his appetite he began to wonder if Madrigal had yet reached Castilla-verde. His heart lurched for an instant when he wondered if she had encountered danger along the road, but he relaxed again upon realizing that the men-at-arms who had accompanied her were quite capable of giving her full protection in this time of truce.

His mind was drifting farther away as he sipped his wine; he was thinking about the many times his wife had sat alongside him at an inn and of the heads that had invariably turned in her direction. He remembered his angry feelings when she had blushed slightly or kept her eyes coyly fixed on her plate. Was he actually jealous? He watched the young, round-bottomed serving girl approach him to clear the table and noticed that she had dull, muddy-colored eyes, and thought again of Madrigal's sparkling emerald ones.

He reached out suddenly and pulled the grinning wench onto his lap and offered her some of his wine. He'd be damned if he'd waste his time brooding over a wife he disliked intensely! After all, there were many Francines in this world, and he would sample their charms until the image of Madrigal dimmed in the excess of carnal pleasures.

But as the morning turned into early afternoon and he found himself aloft in the inn with the comely girl, he wondered if he had the will to bed her. She lay undressed on the narrow, uncomfortable pallet, her full bosom and fleshy hips curving invitingly under his gaze.

"Come, love," she beckoned with a plump white finger, and Roderick found himself undressing, a bemused look on his face.

The girl ogled and whinnied when he stretched out naked, next to her, for although his coins had persuaded her to oblige him, she thought him a most intoxicating man of great height and breadth and as handsome as any she had bedded.

When he was done and the girl lay entwined in the covers, her white flesh pink now where he had touched her, he felt empty and unsatisfied. He quickly donned his tunic, hose, and hauberk and left her smiling contentedly on the bed while he put a gold *tarín* on the washstand.

Passing the unfinished flagon of wine still sitting on the table below, he almost felt like remaining at the inn and drinking himself into a stupor, but Burgos still lay many miles ahead, and his business there was certainly more pressing than a dalliance. He left the inn and remounted his rested horse, riding eastward at a more leisurely pace toward the city where Sancho held court.

Unfortunately, Roderick had much time to muse as he whiled away the long hours in the saddle. He came to the conclusion that his decision to allow Madrigal to return to Castilla-verde had been a sound one; there was nothing between them but misery and pain. In truth, he allowed, there had been nothing from the beginning, for it was his own prurience, that fateful day they had met in the forest, that had driven his mind beyond reason and compelled him to possess her. What man would feel otherwise? he asked himself. He even recalled Juan de Vegas, her betrothed, who had loved her and had been willing to accept her untamable nature. But Roderick knew his own character was such that he could not live with a temptress possessing a volatile tongue.

Roderick rode into Burgos one splendid April evening and crossed the river to the castle where Sancho was now quartered. He was welcomed by the *mayordomo* and led through the mighty, resounding halls to the room where Sancho held court. That he was tired, dusty, and hungry mattered little to his king. The mere presence of Roderick after his long absence brought a quick, brotherly smile to Sancho's lips.

" 'Tis time enough you have spent away, my friend. I am in sore need of allegiance these days." Sancho rose from his immense, carved chair, and the two men embraced each other warmly.

"Yes, my king. I, too, am pained of late," Roderick found himself confiding to his old friend. "I would that these knights who protect you so well be gone from us."

Sancho waved his elegantly ringed hand and dismissed his men without a word. He and Roderick moved toward the hearth, where a decanter of wine rested on a table, and took seats together in the more intimate setting. With the exception of Sancho's three hounds and his favorite falcon perched nearby, they were quite alone, each with his separate thoughts and concerns.

Roderick filled their cups and began: "Sire, I am well aware of your unholy problems from the north and the south alike, but I have given much thought to their solution and think it one of diplomacy and well-tuned words rather than one of bloodletting."

"*Sí*, my knight. I also weary of the loss of life in battle. What news have you from Edward?" Sancho swung one leg over his chair's arm and sat back comfortably, stroking the head of a hound.

" 'Tis good indeed. The English spend their time fighting to the north, in Scotland. Edward assures me that he has no time to dally in the affairs of the French."

"What of assistance to our own cause?" Sancho asked earnestly.

Roderick ruffled the ears of a spotted hound and replied slowly. " 'Tis said in court that Edward has growing problems with the French and would be heartily pleased to see them squelched rightly. The English king is shrewd and seeks to have his throne secured for his son, young Edward. 'Tis my opinion that the man keeps a wary eye on his neighbors across the Channel, although in words he would not admit such, and will not aid their cause."

"But this is as much as I could expect!" Sancho slapped his knee and grinned handsomely. " 'Tis as I hoped . . . yes, King Edward would do well to keep his eye on Philip of France. Mark my words, Roderick, England and France will come to war yet." He laughed. "And 'tis welcome news you have brought."

"If I have assessed the situation as it so stands, then yes, my liege, I, too, feel our problems are lessened."

"Enough, I say. I shall read your report later." Sancho reached over and gave Roderick a healthy slap on his back, causing him to wince as his old wound twinged.

"What is it, my friend? Have you become so tender in the fullness of your years?" Sancho looked concerned.

"No, my liege, only a small reminder of a . . . a disagreement I had with a certain lord in Cornwall. But he is in worse condition, being quite dead, milord."

" 'Tis typical of your travels, I have no doubt. You must tell me of this 'disagreement' some time. And what of my favorite good dame, your mother—she fares well?"

"*Sí,* as spry as ever, and prettier by the day, I vow."

"And Madrigal?"

Roderick's cheerful mood dimmed. He looked into Sancho's eyes and remembered their many years together as callow youths and unaccomplished lovers. Sancho would be the one man to understand. "She is gone from me," he replied, and then he gritted his teeth. "We bring each other a sorry misery . . . but I shall attend to her future welfare. I'll not have my wife shame me in poverty."

Sancho was speechless for a long time, and when Roderick would have spoken again, he waved his arm in a plea for silence. Finally he said, evenly and with great care, "When we were ten years old, you found a hungry bear cub . . . do you recall?" Roderick nodded. "And the skinny rascal bit your hand, but still you swore to keep him and brought him back to my father's home. When my father bade you to cast away the mangy beast, you argued like no other dared, until my father grew tired and allowed the cub to remain."

Sancho stood up, the huge mug in his hand, and turned toward the fire. "The cub grew and ate until he was the horror of the maids at court, yet still you kept him and still he nipped your hand."

"Yes, I well remember. But he also licked and nuzzled my wounds when his temper was gone."

Sancho turned around and looked hard into his friend's golden eyes. "So what, pray tell, is the difference?"

Roderick slammed his flagon on the unyielding table. He rose and faced Sancho, his eyes flickering dangerously. "Can you compare my love for the motherless cub to my marriage?"

Sancho's temper flared but then simmered, for he knew his oldest friend would not have spoken thus if he were not in great anguish. "You have evidently sought my counsel. And I have given it. Your decision to marry the girl was made as much out of loneliness as from anything else, as was the keeping of the bear when your father was lost to you. Yet there grew a love out of need, even though often your hand was mauled."

"I do not love the girl, Sancho!" Roderick protested, amazed that his friend had so misinterpreted the situation.

Sancho grinned widely. "Then, Baron of Compostela, you are still an arrogant fool!"

"By all that's holy, Sancho! You think me such a simpleton not to know how I feel for my own wife?"

"Yes," Sancho declared warmly against Roderick's wrath, "I most certainly do, for, if you recall, I have seen the girl and appraised her nature, and I know yours."

"Then you have sorely misjudged her temperament! 'Tis much the same as the black-deeded Earl of Tarbella's!"

Sancho's brow furrowed. "So *that* is the reason for her leaving! You are so blinded that you see her in the light of the old earl."

"Yes," Roderick admitted, "I do! She is bred from the same blood!"

Sancho crossed to the far side of the table and thought for long moments on how best to relieve Roderick's pain and confusion. Finally he said, "Go seek her out. I command you to do so, for I would see heirs to Halconbosque, and I also command you to ask for her affection. If she cannot respond, then bring her here to court, for I alone can protect her from the hand of the Church."

Roderick sat down in his chair and slumped tiredly into its hard comforts. At long last he replied, "If you so command, I shall obey. But I warn you, Sancho, the meeting will be tormented indeed, and I fear you will soon have your own bear at court to bite your hand."

"Then so be it. But seek her out within the month

and do as I have ordered. I shall expect you returned here with your wife during the days of June if she needs my protection."

Confusion, anger, and a hint of rebelliousness played in Roderick's voice when he answered his king. "I unwillingly obey your bidding. But when she is returned here, we shall see to matters of state, and I shall not discuss her future or see her again. It will be out of my hands."

Sancho bowed mockingly, which brought an endearing grin to Roderick's lips. "I should hate to prove my king wrong," he said, "but in this instance I fear I shall have to do so."

Roderick left Sancho to seek his rest before he returned to Halconbosque. He had hopes of waylaying Vitorio before the man had departed. Sancho would have to do without the bailiff's services for a while longer, as it was Sancho's order that would now take Roderick away from his fief once again.

He arose the next morning to the sound of rolling thunder and the promise of a muddy return to Halconbosque; this did not lighten his mood at all. He dressed and went to break his fast with Sancho before taking his leave.

They ate a large meal in the company of several knights and Sancho's wife, Maria de Molina. When she heard of Roderick's intent to ride first to Galicia, she chastised him for delaying the inevitable confrontation with his wife and then turned to Sancho.

"Can't you send a messenger to Halconbosque in Roderick's stead? Surely Lady Gwendolyn would be delighted to know that her son is taking his marital problems in hand."

Sancho smiled conspiratorially at his wife. "Sí, 'tis a far better plan. Vitorio will remain at his station until I notify him otherwise." He turned in time to catch the grim look on Roderick's face. "'Tis a sound plan, and you will be off to your wife this very day." Sancho waited patiently for Roderick's reply.

The baron finally said, "I must fetch Renaldo, my vassal, at Halconbosque first, so 'tis best I carry my own message."

"Renaldo," said Sancho in an amused tone, "can well see to himself in this instance. He will await your return. *Verdad*, I think this is a job for you alone, my friend."

There was no arguing with Sancho, and especially not with the iron-willed Maria, who was in staunch agreement with her husband. Roderick realized his plans had gone far astray this day, and he fervently wished he had never sought the king's advice in the first place.

He left Burgos that morning in a dark, angry storm that raged equally in the sky and in his mind. This time he did not race his mount toward their destination; instead, he plodded wearily along the rutted, soft road, splashing through the muddy water and soaking himself to the skin.

By the next morning, when the clouds had parted and the sun warmed his shoulders, he found himself tiredly cursing Sancho and the destiny that had brought him once again to seek out his wife. He actually convinced himself that a hellish plot of unknown origins had been formed to cause him anguish and torment.

Roderick took an exceptionally long time in his southward trek. He often stopped at a roadside inn or in a convenient town for long periods, seeking out the comforts of wine and women. Yet each time he began his journey anew, and usually with a racking headache, he found himself sickened by his own actions; still, he could not control his urges to search out forgetfulness, and often, oblivion. But his nightmare returned to him frequently at night, as if in warning, and he would wake, sweating, by the side of one or another of the wenches he had bedded. Then he would imagine Madrigal's warm hand on his shoulder, waking him from the dream, and he would toss and turn in bitter unrest until morning.

His sun-streaked hair grew longer and hung untidily to his shoulders, his mail and leather were in sore need of polishing, and, in general, he looked like one of the poor, landless soldiers who wandered the countryside, always searching for a patron. By the time he had journeyed through Andalusia and neared Castilla-verde, he found that the services of even the village wenches were hard to come by, and the very smell of wine began to turn his stomach.

A day's ride from Madrigal's home, he stopped and bedded by a spring. The next morning he awoke feeling somewhat better after a night without anything to drink. When he washed the sleep from his eyes, he caught his reflection in the water and sat back on his haunches in disgust.

Well, he thought, he'd be damned if Madrigal was going to see him in this sorry state! No, he would not allow her, or her despicable father, to gloat. He stripped his clothes and took his knife into the spring with him, then he washed himself thoroughly and did a passable job of shearing his hair and scraping the whiskers from his cheeks. Finally, he soaked his filthy clothing and sat on the bank while his clothes dried, polishing his mail, boots, and harness.

When his work was done, he had to admit that he felt much renewed. He stood over the water and viewed himself again in its ripples; he was clean now, and his hair, although still unruly, was shorter and caught the sun's light.

Roderick Halconbosque, messenger and knight of

King Sancho, mounted his steed and rode that brilliantly clear morning in the direction of Castilla-verde. He could almost envision the greeting he would receive from the earl and decided to put the evil old man in his place once and for all. But then he thought of meeting Teresa again and he smiled widely, as he truly felt a deep affection for the young girl. And, of course, Elena would be there, he realized, the grin fading from his lips.

The rich green of the forest that spanned the meadows below Castilla-verde came into view. Roderick stopped his horse for a moment and fought to control the memories flooding his brain at the sight of those woods. How different his life would have been had he taken the other path, the well-traveled one, that spring morning two years past; instead, he had taken a promising shortcut through the forest, and now he stood at the crossroads again.

Inexplicably, Roderick directed his mount toward the verdant seclusion. Perhaps the towering trees held a secret truth that would clear his vision. He hastened toward the peace he hoped to find therein.

Chapter 45

The past months had been idyllic in their own way, thought Madrigal, leaning on the deep stone ledge of her window, except for one nagging complexity. Her father had been immensely happy to welcome her to Castilla-verde, carefully not asking too many awkward questions. Teresa had been innocently happy also. Elena had reacted as Madrigal had expected her to: maliciously triumphant. There had been no outward evidence of this in Elena's behavior, but Madrigal had recognized the gloating behind those cold green eyes, so much like her own. She had tried to ignore the few pointed remarks directed at her by Elena and, so far, had been able to disdain her sister's attempts to elicit a sharp answer.

The one complication, the one snag, was a significant one. Madrigal was pregnant. The thought of her secret, and Maria's—for she could not fool her old servant—sent shivers of fear through her, as well as a deep thrill. She had finally escaped from her husband, only to find herself irrevocably tied to him by this new life growing in her womb. It had taken many days to comprehend this incredible miracle, but when she had finally accepted it, she had reveled in the knowledge. How Roderick would crow if he knew! He would surely force her to live with him then, and the king, the Church, even her father, would have to agree. So Madrigal had sworn Maria to silence and told no one, not even Padre Sebastiano, who beleaguered her with questions as to why she was there without her husband.

Her life was at least peaceful now, no tantrums, no stormy scenes and arguments, no passion. She felt like a nun on retreat: chaste, calm, complacent. But, she realized, smiling wryly, there was one great difference between herself and a nun—she carried a new life within her body. Already her waist had thickened, not noticeable to her father or to Teresa, but Elena eyed her speculatively from time to time. Madrigal felt extraordinarily well in this pregnancy and had a huge appetite; perhaps that would suffice to explain her rounder figure, for a time at least.

She had been glad to see her oldest sister, Rosa, and Rosa's family, which now included an infant son. She had acted gay and carefree with them, saying only that she was visiting for a while, as her husband was on the king's business. She had also seen Juan de Vegas once when she had been riding with her father; he had looked the same, his large, dark eyes sad at the sight of her, but he had smiled and spoken politely, then had excused himself and ridden off. Madrigal had felt soiled, corrupted, under Juan's gaze. *He* would not have tormented her, deceived her, but she also knew he would not have whirled her to the heights of pleasure she had known with Roderick.

This warm June morning she decided to walk to the meadow on the far side of the crumbling wall outside the moat. She had seen wild mint growing there and wanted to collect some to ease a stomach complaint of which old José had complained. The ancient *mayordomo* grew increasingly feeble, but Lord Jaime was too softhearted to relieve him of his duties; it would surely be a death sentence to retire the old man into idleness and obscurity.

Madrigal picked up her old woven basket, remembering another warm June morning when she had gone to collect herbs in the forest. That morning had been fateful, directing her life into a pattern that was both bizarre and unhappy. This morning would merely be the start of a summer's day, one of many. Her yellow gown was bright and cheerful, and she had taken to fastening her sashes higher to hide her waistline. Her hair was tied back carelessly with a red ribbon, the black tresses cascading to her waist. She thought to tell Maria where she was going but decided against it, as she knew the old servant was sleeping late these mornings.

Madrigal descended the familiar worn steps to the great hall and came upon her father eating breakfast. She bent and gave him a quick kiss on his cheek.

"Papa, I am going for a walk, to the field left fallow this year on the edge of the old wall. If I do not let Maria know where I am, I fear she will fret. Do tell her, *por favor.*"

"Yes, child, but do not stray far. *Verdad,* I grow tired of telling you such things, Madrigal."

She smiled indulgently at him. "I will not be gone long, Papa. Send Teresa for me if you worry." She snatched a bun from her father's trencher and laughed, then hurried through the hall and out to the bailey.

The sun dazzled her eyes and she blinked a moment in the glare. Then she set off toward the field where the wild mint grew, humming an old lullaby under her breath.

Later that morning Jaime Castilla-verde was seated at the large table in the great hall, bent over one of his scratched and blotted ledgers, when he heard Teresa's voice shrilling excitedly from the bailey. What was the child up to now? he wondered. She becomes more volatile every day. Then she burst through the front portal, flying to where he sat.

"Papa! Roderick's come back! He's here, Papa, he's right here now!" Her voice piped animatedly, her cheeks flushed with emotion.

"Roderick? What on earth . . .?"

"Should I go fetch Madrigal? She will want—"

"No, *querida,* not yet. I shall speak to him first." He wished his formidable son-in-law were anywhere but here. He squared his shoulders, drew a deep breath, and prepared to do battle.

Roderick entered the hall just then, pausing for a moment to let his eyes adjust to the darkness of the chamber. Jaime took advantage of his slight hesitation to be the aggressor.

"Lord Roderick, welcome to Castilla-verde once

again. May I offer you some refreshment?" The man looks a big haggard, thought Jaime. Has he been ill?

"Not at the moment, Lord Jaime, *gracias.*" Then, without preface, a note of anxiety edging his voice: "Where is Madrigal?"

"She is out in the meadow, searching for some of her herbs, I believe. She said she would not be long, milord." Jaime hesitated, afraid to say what he knew had to be said, but the thought of his daughter's welfare steeled him. "Lord Roderick, I must be frank with you. Madrigal is happy here. Leave her be. You can only cause her more pain. As her father, I must protect my daughter from such misery. I cannot bear to see her so abused."

"She is my wife, old man. No one may stand between those who have wed in the eyes of God," Roderick growled arrogantly.

"True, but she has suffered much from her marriage to you. Surely you realize that, sir. I love my daughter. I have been a good man in that respect—which is more than you have been."

Roderick threw back his head and laughed. He turned his fierce, golden eyes on the earl and spoke slowly and vehemently. "You, a good man? You cruel, murdering fiend! Your evil act of over twenty years past blemished my life when I was but a child—you killed my father in front of my eyes, and for no other reason but to satisfy your own insanity! And you dare to speak of goodness!" Roderick's voice had risen, his face a mask of cold fury, his fists clenched whitely at his sides.

Jaime took a step backward, shocked and confused by Roderick's unreasonable wrath. "Your father? *I* never killed your father."

Roderick drew off his gauntlets and threw them savagely on the table. "You despicable liar!"

"I have killed men in battle, true, but . . ." Castilla-verde slumped into his chair, searching his memory. "Who was your father?" He frowned in deep bewilderment.

"It was on the plains of central Spain . . . he was the man you dismembered and beheaded! Do you deny it?" Roderick raged.

Lord Jaime stared mutely into his lap for an endless moment. When he looked up at Roderick again, he said, "The plains of central Spain? Wait a moment . . ." He rose and approached Roderick, looking deeply into his gold-flecked eyes. He was uncertain how to begin.

"Yes, I remember having heard a sorry tale like this, but it was not I who killed your father—it was my brother, Jorge. He was the earl then. He was known throughout the country for his foul deeds and his madness, riddled as he was by the pox. I am truly sorry you have been so mistaken about me. . . . It explains much."

Roderick's face had gone white, his chest heaving deeply. "No," he whispered. "No, you lie—it was *you* . . ."

Jaime took command of the situation by saying, "If you do not believe me, go now to the chapel crypt and read the epitaph on my brother's tomb. Padre Sebastiano will verify those words, my son." He spoke clearly and distinctly, as if to a child. "Roderick, you know I speak the truth. Your heart has told you so long before now, yet you would not listen. My brother, the blackguard earl, has been dead nearly twenty years, destroyed by the pox."

Roderick sank weakly into a chair. He stared into space without seeing, then suddenly dropped his face into his hands.

Jaime laid a hand on his shoulder. "Go to her," he said softly. "Go to her and pray that it is not too late to make amends."

Chapter 46

It was a long, arduous hour before Roderick could fully comprehend the monumental proportions of the error he had made. He searched his memory futilely in an attempt to recall the faces that had surrounded his father, yet he could remember little. In the end, Jaime coaxed Roderick out of his state of lethargy and convinced him to put aside his past hatred to seek a new beginning.

Madrigal had still not returned to the hall. Roderick began to mull over the words he would say to her but felt in his heart she would never listen. It took all his strength and courage to rise from his chair and go to her.

Madrigal was searching through the crumbled stones and high weeds along the east battlement wall, her herb basket nearly full, when Roderick first saw her. Almost simultaneously, he noticed a puff of crumbled mortar spring from high above her, and his heart pounded as he helplessly watched the loose stones fall, barely missing her. He thanked God that she had heard the disturbance and quickly jumped backward.

Roderick called her name, but she had looked up at the battlements for a moment and was now walking swiftly away from him in the direction of the forest. He hastened his stride through the tall, thick grass to catch up to her. Several long paces in her wake, he stopped and watched as she bent to pluck a few strange-looking weeds.

The air was fragrant with the rich smell of wildflowers and herbs, but Roderick was unaware. He stood frozen, nervously viewing his wife. Small fluffs of insects fluttered around her skirt and sparkled in the sunlight like glittering jewels. When he again called to her, his voice barely rose above the sound of the breeze swirling through the trees. But this time she heard him.

Whirling around quickly, Madrigal also stood frozen for a moment, her bright yellow skirt molded to her frame by the breeze. She shaded her eyes against the sun, and when she saw her husband standing only a few feet away, she swayed perceptibly and dropped her basket.

Roderick crossed the distance between them in a few uncertain steps. He steadied her gently by taking hold of her arms. "I am sorry . . . I did not mean to frighten you," he murmured.

"Oh, God . . . no . . . please," she moaned, tears welling in her jade eyes, her bosom heaving.

His intended speech fled his brain and he led her over to a nearby tree, helping her to sit in its shade. Madrigal lay back then, her eyes open and staring weakly up through the swaying branches. She could not think clearly.

He stood over her for a time and then knelt down by her side, taking her hand in his. Still he said nothing and remained motionless while his eyes painfully drank in her beauty. Slowly, inevitably, his golden gaze rested on the bulge of her abdomen. He looked into her pale, rigid face and then, as if he could not believe his eyes, he looked again at the swell beneath her yellow dress.

"Madrigal," he whispered, "you are with child?"

She did not answer, but rolled her head to the side, away from his disbelieving eyes. Roderick gently, firmly, took her face in his hands and turned her toward him.

" 'Tis true?" he asked.

Finally she moaned, as if in great distress, "Yes," and then, "Why have you come? There is nothing . . . nothing for us . . ."

He placed his finger on her lips. "Hear me out, 'tis all I ask. And if you but say the word, I shall be gone from you."

Madrigal realized that Roderick's face bore an expression she had not seen before. He was still just as handsome, with the sun pouring through the leaves to light his tawny curls, yet he was not the same; there was a difference, a softening. Finally, with her heart pounding against her ribs, she nodded an uncertain assent.

"I do not know exactly how to begin," he said. "Mayhap 'twas the moment I first saw you in this forest. I never before nor since have wanted a woman the way I wanted you, and in my blindness I convinced myself that it was to avenge my father's death that drove me to possess you." He paused a moment and then continued. "But that was a lie, an excuse I told myself when I feared I might want you too much. Mayhap I feared to . . ."

Roderick's face grew thoughtful, and he rose from his sitting position and turned his back to her, his fists clenched in agony. He drew a deep breath, then faced her again. "I had . . . desired you from the first." He laughed bitterly, his head tossed back. "Do you not see the jest, Madrigal? Now, when I can declare the truth, it is too late, for I have destroyed what chance we had."

Madrigal bit her lip and stood up weakly, dizzily, unable to trust her own legs and unable to catch her breath. Was it possible? Had he felt a fondness for her after all? At last she spoke, her hand reaching out toward him. "You cared for me?" Tears of chagrin flowed down her cheeks. "Why . . . why do you tell me this now?"

He took her arm. They began to walk slowly toward the deeper verdancy of the forest, and it was then that he was able to tell her fully of the long years of hatred and promised revenge against her father, and finally, of his grotesque error in mistaking the earl's identity. All the while they walked, Madrigal was silent, not able to trust her own voice. When at last they stopped and sat together on a fallen, mossy log, she knew the time had come for complete truth between them.

She said weakly, "When first I saw you, I sensed that you were to be special in my life. You were all a woman could wish for, and even with your arrogance and harshness, you filled a void in me. But when you spoke of possessing me"—she stared hard into his gold-flecked eyes—"I turned my heart to ice, for that was my only protection. And when I became pregnant that first time, when I most needed a gentle word, you thrust those lies at me, and in my pain I came to despise you."

Her words stung Roderick, but with each prick he felt a lightening of the spirit, a purging of the soul. Never had they been so open with each other, and the new experience, although painful, was intoxicating.

"But, Roderick," she went on, "I could have cared for you even after you accused me of bedding Akbar. There was still a strong desire to be near you."

He interrupted her suddenly, unable to stem his thoughts. "You did not bed him?"

"No, although he was kind and good to me." She almost told Roderick that it was Akbar who had stopped them in time, but it seemed pointless to confess something that had not taken place. In the secret recesses of her mind she knew the ultimate truth would cause Roderick needless torment. To change the subject, she mused aloud, "And do you know, I still miss his son Jemil. That child was so sure he would repay me one day. Do you think it possible?"

Roderick smiled, the words coming easily now that he believed her innocent. "*Si, preciosa*, 'tis certain that Allah has it in mind for you two to meet again."

They talked for some time about the misery and useless anguish they had caused each other, and they spoke sadly of happier moments together, shared so seldom. Finally, and when Roderick knew it had to come, she said, "You wrecked all possible hope for us when you bedded Elena. Why, Roderick? Had you come to loathe me that much?"

He did a strange thing then, she thought; he smiled charmingly at her. "I have never slept with your sister, Madrigal. She used every wile, I vow, but it was you who filled my brain. It was your soft body I wanted, and never hers."

"Truly?" she whispered, her breath coming rapidly.

"Yes, milady." His voice was deep and soothing.

"What of Francine?" she asked suddenly.

"That," he confessed halfheartedly, "was another thing altogether. I have pledged to speak truthfully now, and I admit there have been several women." He saw her bite her lip and went on hurriedly. "But in all honesty, and as God is my witness, it was only you I wanted in my arms. Only your image filled my brain."

Unexpectedly, she giggled. "Your lady friends were sorely cheated, then, I'd say."

"They most assuredly were, but no less than I was when I could have had the genuine article in my arms!" He laughed, too, feeling that Madrigal understood his lapses. And in reality, she did, for only she knew how close she herself had come to falling abed with Akbar when it was Roderick whom she desired.

The afternoon grew late and the sun filtered through the woods in long, slender shafts, caressing and warming the moist earth at their feet. After they had exhausted their words and relaxed in the secluded comfort of the green forest, Madrigal felt content and at peace with her husband. Yet she felt also uncertain and wary of his power over her.

" 'Tis fitting that we have at last cleansed our souls, Roderick, but what good has come of it?" Then she added firmly, "I'll not return with you."

"And I do not expect you to, Madrigal. You are far too good to spend your life shackled to a fool such as I." Roderick stood up and stretched his long, sinewy legs. "I ask only that I might visit the child from time to time."

Her eyes filled with sudden tears and she felt overwhelmingly nauseous. Between deep breaths she said, "Of course, Roderick, whenever you wish." She rose and began to walk slowly back toward the castle, an inexplicable sinking feeling threatening to overcome her.

Roderick followed several paces behind. He, too, fought to control his emotions and longed to crush her to him. If only she could love him a little! But she had not spoken of that, and neither, he realized, had he!

He stopped in utter confusion and disbelief. "Madrigal!" he called in an angry tone. She turned around, a bewildered look on her face. He approached her almost threateningly, and she would have fled, but he took hold of her arms and held her rooted to the spot. "Madrigal," he said, his voice deep and even, "I shall not let you go! I . . . I love you too much . . . beyond measure . . ."

His mouth came down on hers in a hard, searching kiss that snatched her breath away and sent her reason flying. Her heart fluttered in bliss, and she stood on tiptoe to meet the passionate onslaught until he raised her willing body from the ground and held her easily in his embrace. His lips left hers and kissed her throat, cheeks, and ears while he moaned his love and desire for her. "You're mine . . . I'll make you love me, too . . . just never leave me again."

380

She fought to control her happiness. "Roderick! I *do* love you—you—you great fool!"

He almost dropped her for an instant and then crushed her tightly to his chest. "You—love me?"

"Yes. I think I always have, but I feared you would scorn me if I spoke of it."

"Dios! If only I had not been so blind!" Then he chuckled, picking her up and swirling her dizzily around until they fell together in the soft grass, joyously aware of the novelty of their love.

He had softened Madrigal's fall carefully on top of himself, and she looked happily down into his adoring eyes. Then she entwined her fingers in his unruly mass of hair and brought his face to hers. "I have much lost time to make up, milord." Her voice was forceful and playfully low. "And I have a great thirst for you!" Her lips hovered enticingly over his, and then she kissed him until he squirmed under her attack and swore to bed her on the spot if she did not cease.

The final weak rays of the sun receded slowly from the meadow. A solitary bird hovered above the lea for an instant and then flew quickly over the battlement and the woman who stood there motionless, her eyes fixed on the couple at the edge of the woods.

Chapter 47

Elena sat near the head of the long table and could not touch her food. The all-too-obvious happiness of the newly reunited couple sickened her and made her heart pound heavily in her chest. The sight of Madrigal and Roderick making cow's eyes at each other only intensified Elena's loneliness, frustration, and unhealthy lust. She fumed inwardly at having to sit there smiling politely, seemingly joyful, when her body was burning and her mind was reeling furiously. Roderick must be a fool after all, she raged, an unworthy simpleton, to still want that simpering female. Why can't he see that *I* am the one meant for him, the one to match his passion and temper with an equal measure of my own? Elena took another long draft of her wine, put the goblet down, and sat glowering at the cheerful crowd at the table.

Roderick rose and attempted to be heard over the noisy chatter, but several moments passed before everyone quieted enough to hear his words. He looked contented and young tonight, his curls burnished by the candlelight, his eyes blazing gold, his tall form relaxed and graceful.

"*Silencio, por favor!* Madrigal . . . my wife . . . and I have something of importance to tell you this night." He looked at her fondly, and she blushed as she realized what he was going to say. She smiled up at him shyly, her cheeks glowing pinkly in the light from the fire. Roderick continued. "In not too many more months there will be born a new lord and heir of the Halconbosque. Is that not good news, indeed?"

Jaime smiled broadly, patted his daughter's hand, and raised a flagon to Roderick. "*Felicitaciones,* my children! Let us drink to the new heir!"

All drank but Elena, who sat in stunned silence. Her face had gone pale and her hand crept unconsciously to the birthmark on her cheek, covered though it was by her wimple. So it *is* true, she thought. They are to have a child. I *knew*, I felt it! The little she-wolf, the bitch, the sly puss, she knew all along and only waited for him to come to her! It is not fair that she gets all that she wants—the man, the riches, the whelp, everything!

While I am left here in this rotting pile of stones to while away my life taking care of an old man and a silly child! No! No, it shall not be! I'll fix her, I'll ply her with misery enough for us all!

Elena felt that she would suffocate in the hall, heated by the fire and too many bodies, too many red, glistening, laughing faces, all leering at her. She pushed back her chair and stood up dizzily. Teresa was the only one to notice her departure and called to her, asking where she was going.

"To my room," answered Elena, barely able to speak. "I do not feel well." She shook off Teresa's hand and walked unsteadily to the stairs, then faded into the shadows of the upper hall.

The festivities went on in the venerable hall of Castilla-verde until Lord Jaime's head whirled and his ears rang like cymbals. He felt at peace for the first time since the huge golden hawk had appeared two years before to snatch his favorite daughter from him. He thanked God and the saints fervently for the happy ending to the tale.

Teresa was very excited at the thought of her sister's baby. She begged Madrigal to let her visit them at Halconbosque and care for the infant when it arrived. Madrigal and Roderick and Lord Jaime smiled and nodded, causing Teresa to bubble over with joy and kiss the three of them. She suddenly felt a compulsion to tell Elena the exciting news and raced from the hall to the stairs.

The door to Elena's room was ajar, and there was a stripe of light lying across the corridor from the crack, so Teresa knew that Elena was not asleep. She pushed the door open and walked in, her happy words dying on her lips as she saw that Elena was strangely occupied. A black iron arm was swung out from the fireplace, and Elena was dropping pinches of powder into the small pot that hung from it. She seemed totally engrossed in the task, measuring small bits of dried matter from various containers, carefully adding liquid, then mixing the brew over the fire. A pungent odor filled the room, somehow frightening Teresa.

"Elena," the girl began.

Elena whirled around, gasping, then seemed to calm herself upon seeing Teresa. "Have I not told you a thousand times not to creep up upon me like that? It gives me a fright, little fool!"

"Truly, I am sorry, Elena, but you must hear my news! I came to tell you especially. I am to go with Madrigal and help take care of the baby! 'Tis true! And Papa says I may go, and so does Roderick!"

"Ha! The baby! So you, too, are deceived by their fetid joy." Elena's words were spoken quietly, almost to herself. Then she regarded her sister and said, without thinking, "Teresa, do not make great plans for the future, for there will be no child."

"What do you mean? Roderick has said, and Madrigal agreed . . ."

"There will be no child, now or ever, if I can help it, you idiot! Do you see that pot?" She pulled Teresa closer. "In that pot is a substance, devised from the knowledge of long ages of midwifery and a few notions of my own, that will cause any woman to miscarry. Just a few drops every day for a week or so—"

"Elena! You would not do that! Madrigal wants her baby desperately—and this is a sin against God!" Teresa was horrified, unbelieving.

"God! What does He care? He has not done *me* abundant favors!" Her hand stole to her cheek and she stroked the livid birthmark, bared now that she had removed her wimple.

Teresa gasped, shocked by Elena's blasphemy. She could think of nothing to say, but she knew she had to convince Elena to stop behaving like this, or her very soul would be in jeopardy.

"Elena, please." She put her small hand on her sister's arm. "You must destroy that stuff and kneel here with me asking God to forgive your sins."

Elena shook her hand off, irritated. "Let me be, Teresa. Return to the party, but speak not a word to anyone. No one would believe you anyway." She returned to her concoction, adding some new ingredients.

Teresa's mind was filled with horror, but she knew one thing: she had to destroy the poison before Elena could use it. An idea came to her like a bolt from the sky, and she thought it would be easy to accomplish, especially with Elena's back turned.

Teresa took a deep breath, then moved up behind Elena, waiting for the right moment. Then she lunged forward, trying to tip the contents of the pot into the fire. Elena realized too late what Teresa was attempting to do, and as she saw the liquid pour into the hot flames, it was as if her life was also consumed by the fire. She reached forward frantically, trying to save the brew. Some of the substance fell on her hand, scalding it, and she screamed brokenly, a long-drawn-out wail of frustration. Her foot caught on the hearth rug and she tripped, flailing her arms to regain her balance, falling, falling, her head striking the foundation of the hearth with a sickening thud. She lay sprawled on the stones, her long black tresses flung toward the leaping flames, which licked at them and filled the chamber with the acrid odor of scorched hair.

Teresa was unable to move, frozen with terror. Her hands were clenched together in front of her face, her eyes open and staring. Suddenly her paralysis dissolved and she ran wildly out of the room, screaming in fright. She almost fell down the worn stone steps, catching herself frantically at the last moment, and continued screaming breathlessly until she felt her father grasp her firmly by the arms and shake her.

"Teresa, what is it, child?" he asked, still holding her.

She could only gasp and stammer, crying and mumbling incoherently while everyone crowded around her. Finally she managed to get out the word "Elena," and they all looked toward the stairs, anxious expressions creasing their brows.

"Let me go to her," Madrigal said. "Whatever has happened, I can talk to her."

"Madrigal, I insist on going with you," Roderick said. "Whatever this is, my arrival has precipitated it, have no doubt on that score, *querida*."

The two climbed the stairs and approached the door of Elena's room, finding it open wide, light spilling into the corridor. Madrigal entered first, then drew back in horror at the sight of her sister lying in a heap before the fire. The smell of singed hair blended with a strange, underlying pungent odor, filling the room with a dark miasma. Madrigal turned and buried her face in Roderick's broad chest, for he stood in the doorway and had taken in the scene at a glance. He gently disengaged himself from his wife and told her to wait in the hall. Then he knelt by Elena's body, feeling for a pulse, but he knew that she was dead; the broken sprawl of her body had already told him that. He removed her long hair, so like Madrigal's, from the fire and smoothed it back, straightening her limbs until she lay as if in repose. Her face looked peaceful now. Even the birthmark appeared oddly faded in the tranquil grasp of death.

Jaime Castilla-verde appeared in the doorway and gasped. Roderick turned from Elena's body and stood up. "Lord Jaime, call Padre Sebastiano. I fear that

Elena is . . . gone now. She seems to have hit her head on the hearthstones. It must have been an accident . . ."

The earl drew a hand across his eyes, then went to kneel by the body. He stayed there for several moments, then rose and led Roderick from the room, closing the door gently. Roderick took Madrigal in his arms and held her; she sobbed quietly against him.

Her father sighed, then spoke softly, as if to himself. "God forgive me, but mayhap this is best. She was so tortured these last months. Her mind seemed to weaken. She had begun to remind me of my brother in his later years . . ." He looked beseechingly at Roderick. "Will our Lord forgive her sins?"

"*Sí,* milord. She was a young girl, misguided and tortured, but still a young girl. Do not worry yourself. She will be laid to rest in peace and contentment and will surely reach Heaven's door."

"I did not know that she hated me so, Roderick. I can hardly believe Teresa's story. It gives me an eerie feeling to know this only now, when she is . . . dead. Why, why did she hate me?" Madrigal's tearful voice broke the silence of their chamber later that night.

"Because you are good and beautiful and all that she was not. She was jealous, my love," answered Roderick, stroking the smooth skin of her arm.

"Jealous? Jealous enough to kill my baby?" Her hand rested protectively on her abdomen. "To do such a thing?"

"She was crazed, Madrigal. I do not know why, nor shall we ever know the reason, but her mind played her false. Thank God she did not succeed, but still, I would not wish her dead, poor thing."

"And now I begin to recall many small things . . . things that happened even before you appeared. I never knew why such things happened, but now I am forced to believe she did them all. Sometimes . . . the halls were unaccountably dark . . . and do you remember the toad on our door . . . and the snake? And the stones that fell from the battlement just today? They were no accident, Roderick." She shuddered, pressing closer to him. "I shall pray for her soul."

There were not many mourners at Elena's funeral: Lord Jaime, Teresa, Rosa and Enrique, Roderick and Madrigal, and the servants. Padre Sebastiano spoke the prayers over her body, and the coffin was placed in the family crypt, next to her mother's. When the ceremony was over, the family members went their separate ways, not wanting to press their discomfort upon one another.

Roderick and Madrigal walked out of the bailey, crossed the drawbridge, and struck out across the flower-speckled fields toward the woods. They were silent, having no desire to discuss the sad event that had just taken place. They felt, somehow, that the death of Elena was an end to the old era of their discord. Now they would begin anew, their love tempered as strong as a fine steel blade.

A hawk appeared, soaring across the bright sky, its powerful wings thrusting against the air and carrying it to the treetops beyond the meadow. They watched as the splendid bird flew unerringly, a twig held in its hooked beak, to repair its nest in the high branches of some forest patriarch. Somewhere a lamb bleated, and a warm breeze caressed them as they stood together in the high grass, watching the hawk return home.